RAVEN LORD

THE HARDRADA SAGA, VOLUME 2

JC DUNCAN

Boldwood

First published in Great Britain in 2024 by Boldwood Books Ltd.

Cover Design by Colin Thomas

Cover Photography: Colin Thomas

Map Designed by Shaun Stevens

A CIP catalogue record for this book is available from the British Library.

Paperback ISBN 978-1-80549-819-3

Large Print ISBN 978-1-80549-818-6

Hardback ISBN 978-1-80549-817-9

Ebook ISBN 978-1-80549-821-6

Kindle ISBN 978-1-80549-820-9

Audio CD ISBN 978-1-80549-812-4

MP3 CD ISBN 978-1-80549-813-1

Digital audio download ISBN 978-1-80549-815-5

Boldwood Books Ltd
23 Bowerdean Street
London SW6 3TN
www.boldwoodbooks.com

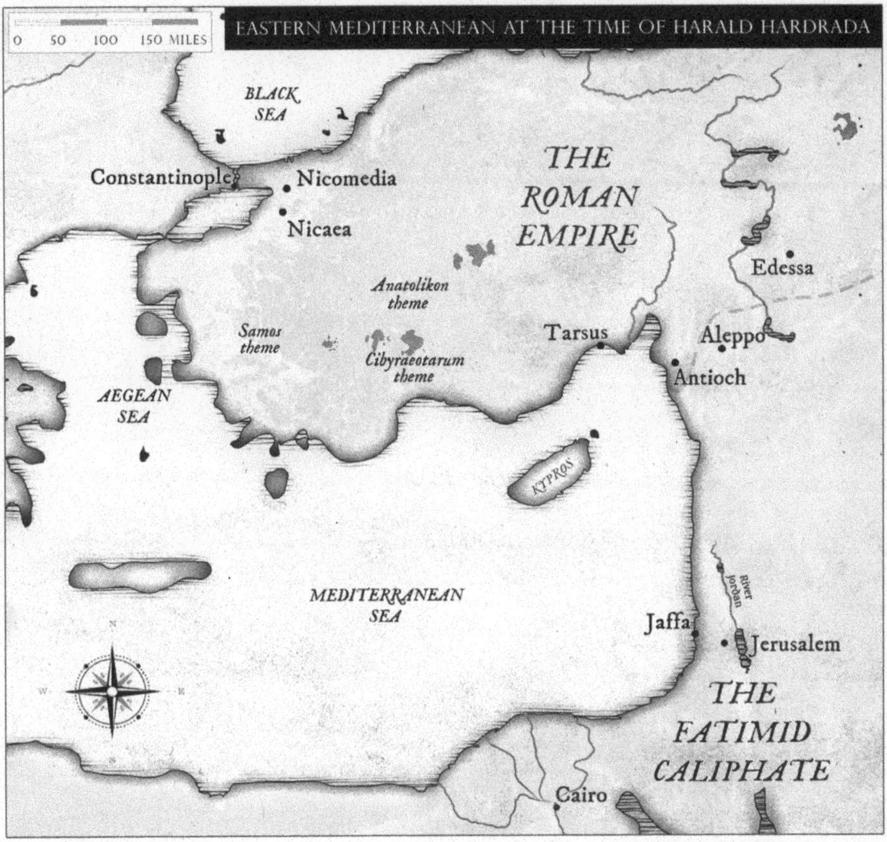
EASTERN MEDITERRANEAN AT THE TIME OF HARALD HARDRADA
0 50 100 150 MILES
BLACK SEA
Constantinople
Nicomedia
Nicaea
THE ROMAN EMPIRE
Edessa
Anatolikon theme
Samos theme
Cibyraeotarum theme
Tarsus
Aleppo
Antioch
AEGEAN SEA
KYPROS
MEDITERRANEAN SEA
River Jordan
Jaffa
Jerusalem
THE FATIMID CALIPHATE
Cairo
N
W
E
S

CAST OF CHARACTERS

The Kingdoms of Norway, Sweden and Denmark

Afra the Constant: Elder of the bandit brothers who follow Harald.
Eric 'Sveitungr' Alvarsson: The narrator, Harald's closest companion and follower.
Harald 'Hardrada' Sigurdsson: King of Norway 1046-1066, half-brother of King Olaf, and claimant to Danish and English thrones.
Halldor Snorrasson: Member of Harald's warband, cousin of Ulf.
Ingvarr Hakonsson: Son of Hakon.
Jarl Hakon: Petty jarl, on his way to join King Magnus barefoot in his campaign to the Southern Isles.
Jarl Halfdan: Lord of Tinghaugen.
Rolf Hammerbeard: Member of Harald's warband.
Rurik: Member of Harald's warband.
Tjodolv Arnórsson: Skald of Harald's court when he was King of Norway, his favourite poet and storyteller.
Thorir the Cuckoo: Younger of the bandit brothers.
Ulfr Ospaksson: Member of Harald's warband. Cousin of Halldor.

The Kyivan Rus

Olga: Kyivan palace serving girl and Eric's wife.
Yaroslav the Wise: Grand Prince of the Kyivan Rus.

The Byzantine Empire

Aki Freysson: The komes of the second bandon of the Varangians the Wolfhounds.
Báulfr the Broad: Commander of the Varangian guard.
Bardas: Greek mercenary commander.
Eyvindr Saemingsson: The komes of the seventh bandon of the Varangians, the Sea Spears.
John the Parakoimomenos: Eunuch and close advisor to Emperor Michael IV.
Maria Arantios: Byzantine noblewoman.
Mercurius: Byzantine nobleman, follower of Theodora.
Michael IV the Paphlagonian: Emperor of The Romans.
Styrbjorn the Goat: Komes of the fourteenth bandon of the Varangians, the Warborn.
Sveinn: A Swedish member of the Varangian guard.
Theodora Porphyrogenita: Sister of Empress Zoe.
Zoe Porphyrogenita: Wife of Michael IV, Empress of the Romans.

The Fatamid Caliphate

Nassir Al-Quasim: Commander of the Jerusalem garrison.

PREFACE

When Harald Sigurdsson sailed south from Kyiv in 1034 he was still just a nineteen-year-old man. But despite his youth he was already a famed mercenary having been promoted, however briefly, to command the personal guard of Grand Prince Yaroslav of the Kyivan Rus. That was a position he achieved not only through his personal connections, as they were related by marriage, but also by success on the battlefield and, presumably, no shortage of the power of personality he would become so famous for.

At the end of my previous book, *Warrior Prince*, Harald had made the difficult decision not to return to his home in Norway to seek the crown. It was clear to him that the child Magnus, the illegitimate son of his beloved half-brother and deposed King of Norway, Olaf, was going to be installed on the throne by a powerful coalition of Norwegian nobles and their Danish overlords.

This was a bitter pill to swallow for Harald, whose single driving ambition was to regain his brother's throne. But with just a couple of hundred men and no allies, he had no chance of winning a conflict with the puppet masters behind the new boy king.

So Harald instead sailed south, headed for the one place that all Norse fighting men knew fame and glory could be earned in unparalleled measure: Constantinople, the city that they called Miklagard, which quite simply meant 'the great city'.

And great it was. It was undoubtedly the greatest and richest city in Europe at the time. The empire was at the apex of a renewal of sorts, driven by one hundred years of military and political reorganisation and success. The empire needed soldiers, and with a relatively small loyal population of Greeks and Romans, it hired mercenaries by the shipload. Of all the mercenaries available, the Norsemen, the ones who the Greeks called 'Varangians', were the most highly sought after, and those that survived imperial service would often return home as very wealthy and famous men.

Varangian means 'sworn companion', and in the empire the reputation of the Norse as both supreme fighters and as men who could be trusted to keep their word was what made them so valuable. In the 10th century, the emperors started preferring the Varangian guard company (tagma) over even the elite Roman cavalry units, and they became the personal guard of the emperors both at home and on the battlefield, earning themselves a fearsome and enduring reputation.

Harald has another reason for heading south too, a reason that drives many powerful and prideful men: revenge. His fall from grace in Kyiv was driven by his conflict with the Greek noblewoman Maria, who he had loved and who had cast him aside when he was no longer useful, and her mercenary captain, Bardas.

Maria and Bardas were part of the great game of power around the imperial throne, trying to manoeuvre themselves into position to choose who ruled the empire. Maria's patron Theodora, her sister Empress Zoe, and the new emperor Michael were part of three great rival factions, each of which were trying to manipulate and murder their way into sole power over the fabulously wealthy but fundamentally unstable empire.

The previous emperor died with the empire precariously balanced and divided, and in the political fallout from his succession the swirl of plots, murders and intrigue that Harald will find himself entwined in will give him both a new swath of opportunities, and a fearsome array of threats. To have any hope of returning home to rule Norway, he must first not only survive his time in the east, but prosper there.

War and political conflict are descending on the empire, even as Harald's ships sail into the Black Sea. Harald is about to enter the great game of Roman imperial power, the real game of thrones. With a little luck and a great deal of bloodshed, he might just become the perfect player.

PART I

GUARDSMAN

1

NIDAROS, NORWAY; SPRING 1098 AD

'I don't want to miss him start,' Ingvarr said, glowering at Jarl Hakon as his father fussed over the remainder of his evening meal.

'It is early, it is not even growing dark yet. The hall will be empty and we will look the fools for rushing to it.'

Ingvarr snorted contemptuously, his plate long since emptied and abandoned, fidgeting with impatience and constantly turning to look at the flap of their shared tent, as if he could see past it and across the fields to the great hall of Tinghaugen, where Eric the follower had promised he would continue his tale of his life with King Harald Sigurdsson, the Hardrada.

Hakon was amused by Ingvarr's roused spirit. The boy had not stopped talking about Harald Hardrada since the previous evening, when they had heard the tale of Harald's adventures and achievements in the Kyivan Rus.

The boy was sixteen years old, and thus like many of his age usually slow to accept counsel, and difficult to engage with. Hakon was taking him to the Frostating and the proposed spring campaign to the southern isles in no small part to try and draw from the boy the spirit and temperament needed to be a leader, to be able to take over their family lands and his position as a jarl when the time came.

King Magnus was expected to arrive in three days, and would spend the time before the Frostating gathering support for his proposals before they were put to a vote. Hakon knew he would support the king already and needed no convincing. He had his own reasons for going, one last campaign before he was too old, but primarily he was going so that he could take his son and let the boy earn his manhood in the old ways.

Ingvarr had aggression and confidence, but in wisdom and understanding he was lacking. Hakon would have paid a fistful of silver to have the boy sit for a few nights and listen intently to older, wiser men and learn from them. It amused him that now he would not have to. Not only that, but he was sure the headstrong boy would have refused if the idea had come from his father.

Finally, still hiding his smile to avoid pricking Ingvarr's pride, he finished off his meal and held up his hands in submission. 'Fine, boy, let us go.'

Ingvarr shot to his feet with a nod and was out of the tent before his father had finished rising. They walked briskly through the fields, past the few tents of the men who had arrived for the Frostating before them, and into the town proper, weaving down the narrow streets and past the low, thatched houses of the year-round residents.

Finally they reached the central ring, and the imposing hall of the lord of Tinghaugen, where King Magnus would hold court in three days' time.

Hakon saw to his surprise that the great door was open, and as they walked towards it, they could see men already gathered within.

'I told you!' said Ingvarr with a spiteful look.

'You say a great many things with confidence, my boy. Occasionally, you will be right,' Hakon said with a relaxed smile, although internally he felt a prick of annoyance, hoping that Eric had not already begun his tale.

As they went through the door his eyebrows rose, and he saw that the tables were already half full, with men sitting on some of the chests and benches that lined the walls. He was stunned.

Everyone in the room was focused on a single table in the centre, where Hakon's old friend Jarl Torvald sat next to the wizened figure of

Eric Sveitungr, the old companion of the long-dead King of Norway, Harald Hardrada.

'We are too late for a seat close by,' hissed Ingvarr in anger, his fists balling, not even looking at his father.

At that moment, as Hakon mumbled an apology, Jarl Torvald pointed at them, and Eric slowly twisted his head around, his bushy white brows rising as he set eyes on Ingvarr and Hakon.

There was a moment's pause and then Eric waved a thin hand, beckoning them to the bench beside him, him and another man shuffling along to make space.

Hakon felt suddenly exposed, with many of the gathered men looking at him as the old man, as if a close acquaintance, invited him to sit from across the hall.

He followed his son through the room, making awkward greetings to men as he passed, before, bewildered, he took the proffered seat at the central table.

Torvald grinned and reached across the table to grasp Hakon's hand, and then Ingvarr's. 'We weren't sure you were coming. I was just telling Eric to start without you.'

Ingvarr looked abashed and mumbled an excuse, while Hakon just looked confused. 'You were waiting for us?'

Eric's lined face cracked into a sly smile, and he looked at Ingvarr with his bright, piercing stare. 'It was you that asked me to tell you the tale of Harald, was it not?'

'Yes, Eric.'

'Well, I said I would do so, and I am a man of my word – famously so.' He gestured around the room and then pointed a skinny finger at the boy. 'These other men are most welcome to listen if they wish, but I am no court skald to entertain them, and I am telling the story to you.'

Ingvarr flushed with pleasure at the honour the old man was paying him and couldn't stop himself from grinning, even as Torvald laughed.

Eric took a languid sip from the horn mug of ale that sat on the table in front of him and sat up, coughing, and cleared his throat. Someone called for silence in the audience near them, and Eric looked around with a nod of thanks as the room fell into an expectant quiet.

Eric stretched his hands out in front of him, fixing Ingvarr with a stern gaze. 'Now, I believe we had just arrived in the Empire of the Greeks, who call themselves the Romans.'

* * *

Well, it was late in summer in the year of our Lord 1034, and we had just sailed down the Dnipr from Kyiv in two ships, Harald as our leader, with 130 men and all the riches that we had earned in the service of Grand Prince Yaroslav. We had nothing else but our weapons and our skill to offer. It was not an exciting journey. The Black Sea is famous for its pirates, but we looked like warships and none dared bother us.

We reached the Bosporus, the great narrows that divide the Black Sea from the Propontis south of Constantinople, and we lowered our sails and rowed until we came into sight of the great city itself.

We had thought Kyiv was magnificent, that white city on its hill above the great Dnipr river, but as the lord is my witness, Constantinople, the heart of the Empire of the Greeks, is the most magnificent sight I have ever seen, or ever will.

It is vast. I have never seen Rome itself, and some say its ruins are larger and more magnificent still, but the city of Constantine is a marvel of the spirit and industry of men, impossible to understand for one who has lived their life in our quiet Northern kingdom.

The whole city is surrounded by magnificent stone walls of layered grey stone and red bricks, studded with towers like a necklace with beads. On the landward side the wall has two rings, and great citadels at each corner, but even the seaward side is enclosed.

The towers and domes of the churches crown the hills and line the sky above the city, looming over the great palaces and the houses of the people alike.

They say five hundred thousand people live in the city, half within its great walls alone. That is more people than live in all of Norway, perhaps more than live in the lands of our brethren the Swedes. In one city! And it is a city of the water, surrounded by it on three sides, the hub of an empire that rules by trade and by might, all transferred across the sea.

There are so many ships coming to and fro that the city has three great harbours, each of which would be the pride of any of our biggest towns, and several smaller ones besides.

And this is the sight that greeted us, our band of Northern mercenaries and exiles, as we sailed into the narrow waters of the Golden Horn, the inlet that ran along one side of the city, mouths agape and eyes wide like the full moon. This was the empire we had come to fight for, so immeasurably richer than wealthy Kyiv which we had just left.

Because that is what we were thinking about when we saw all of that. We were not men looking for a home, we were not here to admire beauty or gaze upon fine wonders of building. No, we were men in search of silver in exchange for our service, and this city exuded wealth in every aspect. We could only imagine what its people and rulers would pay to protect what they had built.

We were seeking to join the service of the new emperor, Michael IV, who had risen to the throne a few months before, to join the famed mercenary guard, the Varangians, who only accepted battle-tested men of Northern blood. Legendary in battle, and for the wealth and fame they could earn, Harald believed that through service in their ranks he could earn enough fame and fortune to return to Norway and claim the throne.

'Rolf, come to me,' said Harald, as he stood in the bow of the ship where we were standing, drinking in the sight of the city. For while I was still spellbound at the sight of it, Harald was already thinking ahead, to what we must do.

Rolf, who we called Hammerbeard for his long grey beard – thick on his cheeks but dangling low from his chin looking like the old pagan symbol of Thor's hammer – had joined us in Kyiv before the battle with the Pechenegs. He was already an old man by our standards. A lifelong mercenary and as tough a soldier who ever lived, he had been in the service of Emperor Basil in southern Italy, Bulgaria and Greece, and had left with a small fortune in 1025 when the emperor died.

In less than five years Rolf had spent the riches he'd earned in the service of the empire, frittered it away on women and wine and good living, until he had been forced to seek service once again, this time with Yaroslav, and after that, with Harald.

We mocked him for his profligacy, his age and his ridiculous beard, but Harald valued him highly for his experience, his fearsome skill in battle, and in particular, his knowledge of the empire we sought to serve.

He was also, critically, the only man in our party who could properly speak the language of the Greeks. He had spent much of the journey from Kyiv telling Harald everything he could about the city and the empire.

Rolf came up to stand next to Harald, who pointed at the shore before us, where a series of grand terraced buildings rose up to the crown of the promontory overlooking the narrows. 'That is the palace?'

'Yes. And the great cathedral called the Hagia Sophia, which means the Church of the Holy Wisdom, beside it.'

'And how do we get there?'

'When we enter the Golden Horn there will be two harbours on the palace shore. The first is for royal use only, the second for trade and visitors from the North. We will go to the second, and announce ourselves.'

'Good, you will do that.'

'Of course.'

'Will there be trouble, arriving with so many armed men?' asked Harald.

'No. The harbour is walled, manned day and night by the Vigla or the Noumeroi. We will only be allowed in if they choose so, and we pose no threat if they choose not to allow it.'

Ah, yes, who are the Vigla, you wonder? Well, they are one of the many units of guards, like a hird, but more organised, professional soldiers. Look, for us simple Northmen, this is all very confusing and complicated. Here, the king has his hird, and they protect him and fight with him on campaign. But the Greek Emperor then had five main companies of guards, which they call tagmata. Each tagma had different duties, each guarded against a different threat or treachery. It is complex, but you will learn more as I speak of our time there.

'But they will allow us in?' Harald asked.

Rolf shrugged. 'I cannot be sure, but they have no reason not to. The emperors are always seeking new Varangians, especially after ascension to the throne when they need to secure their position with strength.'

Harald nodded and fell silent, but I could see that he was still nervous.

We turned into the inlet of the Golden Horn, a dozen or so other ships of various sizes coming and going from its broad mouth. Rolf nodded his head at the great stone bastion on the southern bank where the inlet narrowed, and then at another in the fortified town on the northern shore. 'That is where the chain is raised during times of war, or to protect the harbour from raiders.'

'A chain that stretches across this whole river? How is that possible?' I said, like the ignorant that I was.

'You will see,' said Rolf with a knowing smile.

Well, as we drew closer, I could indeed see with my own eyes what would have defied any attempt to explain. A long chain of iron, slender enough at a distance to look like rope, but close up visibly a string of long iron loops, hung from the towers on each side. The chain draped over a series of anchored log rafts, holding its weight above the surface. Between the two central rafts, covering the greatest span of perhaps fifty paces, the chain sank beneath the waters.

Rolf saw me staring at it in wonder. 'In the towers the ends are connected to great windlasses that can be manned by fifty men. When they turn, the chain shortens, and the span in the centre rises, high enough to prevent passage by ships.'

'That is extraordinary,' I said, for it was. Even to this day I find it remarkable that man is capable of such feats as forging a chain of such length. It must have weighed as much as a thousand men, using more iron than an army would carry into battle.

Well, we passed over the gap in that monstrous chain, watched silently by two guardships, small dromons in the Greek style. They are completely unlike our ships. Tall, thick, heavy ships with two layers of oars and a small sail. Ponderous under sail, but lethal under oars, almost as quick as a good longship despite their weight. The guardships were small and nimble, but the big ships of the imperial navy docked on the southern side of the city could be twice as large as our ships, and carry two hundred men apiece.

Rolf directed us into the harbour, bustling with activity on that late summer day, and a well-dressed man in a small boat shouted at us and directed us to an empty berth near the shipbuilding sheds on the southern side.

There, waiting for us when we pulled alongside and shipped our oars were a dozen bored-looking guards eyeing us Norsemen blankly.

'Men of the city watch, the Noumeroi,' murmured Rolf. 'Not Vigla.'

'Is that good or bad?' asked Harald quietly.

'Good. They can probably be bribed if we have problems.'

'And the Vigla?'

'Never try and bribe a Vigla guardsman. They are the palace guards, they are paid too much to accept bribes, and rewarded handsomely for handing over those who try and corrupt them.'

Harald nodded at that slowly. 'I will remember that. For now, don't tell them who I am. Just say I am Harald Nordbrikt, a Norwegian mercenary here with my men to join the Varangians.'

Rolf nodded and waved to the man standing at the head of the guards, and shouted cheerily to him in Greek, pointing at us and our men and presumably explaining who we were.

There was a short exchange and the guard waved Rolf onto the quay.

'We can go, four of us. The rest stay here with the ships until we get permission to go into the city.'

'Four?' asked Harald, taken aback.

'They aren't going to let a hundred unknown armed men into the city. They don't have the authority. We need sealed orders from one of the guard commanders.'

'How do we get those?' asked Harald in annoyance.

'He will take us to the Varangian barracks – for a price. The commander will decide if he wants to take us on.'

Harald sighed, clearly annoyed with the process. He would have to get used to it; the empire of the Romans ran on a never-ending web of officials and permissions and seals. No, I tell a lie – he never got used to it. Harald spent his entire time there trying to break the system rather than bow down to it, and in some cases, succeeded.

Harald looked around at us, and nodded at me and Afra the bandit before disembarking onto the stone quay.

I rolled my eyes at Afra who smirked in reply. It was always our lot to be with Harald for any problems like this. We were the ones he trusted and used to take care of things he could not, or would rather not, take care of himself.

'Halldor, Ulfr. You are in charge until I return. Leave half the men in the ships, rest the others on the dock. Don't let anyone aboard or interfere with our cargo.'

Ulfr looked at the clutch of guards who still lingered on the shore. 'And if they insist?'

'Don't use violence, but make it clear they are not welcome. Push off and wait out in the narrows if you have to. Eric, Afra, come.'

I did not envy Ulfr and Halldor their task. They did not speak Greek, and they would have no idea when we were returning. But they were capable men, cousins from Iceland who had been with us since the campaign to the Cherven towns in Poland two years before.

We followed the guard along the beaten earth track behind the docks towards the city wall. It was imposing, even on the waterside where it was just a single wall. The Romans had built it tall and thick and I had seen nothing like it before. It was already old, hundreds of years old, and plants grew in the cracks between stones, and some of the bricks were starting to crumble. But it still looked strong.

We were taken through a broad, brick-lined gate. Its thick wooden doors were propped open, men and carts queueing to pass through in both directions carrying all manner of goods. This was the main gate from the northern harbours, and a great deal of the city's vast commerce flowed through it.

On the other side the space opened up to reveal a line of large, low buildings. Storehouses for goods and wares that were coming in and out of the harbour. While I gazed in awe at their scale, the guard ignored them and set off directly along the stone-surfaced street up the gentle hill into the city.

'This is where all the foreigners and Northern merchants live,' said Rolf, as we passed blocks of strange houses, two or three or even four floors high, crowded together like stone haybales in a way I had never seen before.

I assumed we were on the main street of the city, so well was it paved and adorned, but soon we turned off it onto another, greater street, wide enough for two carts to pass. In moments we had passed two churches that would have been the pride of any Norwegian town and I could not believe what I was seeing.

Then, we crested the hill, and came out from behind a large building, a palace maybe, and that is when I saw the Church of the Holy Wisdom for the first time.

How can I describe it to you, you who have not seen it with your own eyes? It is a mountain of man-made stone, vast in its every detail. It is magnificent beyond description. My mouth is incapable of relating to you the sheer size and splendour my eyes beheld. And it is five hundred years old, so they told us. And it was no lie, because you could see its age in the stones and the discolouration and the crumbling of its details. But yet, despite its age, being older than any Norse nation, older than any building in all the North, it was still beautiful and breathtaking.

By the lord, how we think ourselves superior, and how wrong we are. The Romans were building marvels like this before our kin were placing one stone upon another up to the height of a man and covering it with branches to shelter from the snows. And all that work in building it is dedicated to the glory of God and his wisdom. It took the breath from my throat, friends. And I looked to my left and was surprised to see Harald staring, mouth agape like a child. Harald, who never showed a care.

He looked at me with wide eyes. 'I could never imagine such a wonder.'

'How can men build such things,' said Afra with a devout whisper. 'I had no idea such a place even existed.'

'Come,' said Rolf with a soft smile. 'There are many more wonders to see, and our escort does not appear to want to wait while we look upon them.'

I tore my eyes from the gargantuan building and its myriad domes, and saw the guardsman standing impatiently at the edge of a long, broad square that lay alongside the great church, waving at us like we were wayward children.

I cannot tell you everything that I saw that day, it was overwhelming.

It changed my life forever, to see such things that men were capable of in the rest of the world. I love our country, the land of my kin. I love our little fjords and towns and even this fine wooden hall. But let me tell you with no insult, we are big people in such small houses compared to the Greeks. They might be small and strange to our eyes, but they build with the hands of giants and the vision of heaven.

2

'The Chalke Gate,' said Rolf, as we reached the end of the great square outside the church and were met with an enormous gatehouse, fronted with shining bronze gates three times the height of a man. A wonder, all to themselves, standing almost unnoticed in a city of wonders.

On our right, above the roof of a series of low domed buildings, a huge construction loomed. A wall of stone arches and niches, richly decorated with statues and banners. I did not know it then but it was the hippodrome, an arena for the racing of chariots with space inside for tens of thousands of citizens to watch and be entertained, although all I could see at the time was the vast outer wall of one end.

The guard stopped to talk to the men standing watch there. These guards were different, I could tell from their uniform and equipment.

They were not Greek, for one thing. I could see immediately there was a pair of Northerners there, and perhaps some Rus or Bulgars. They were taller, fairer skinned, and magnificently equipped.

'Vigla guardsmen,' said Rolf. 'This is the boundary of the palace grounds. The Vigla are the emperor's watchmen and guard the perimeter of the palace, or his camp when he is outside the city, and control at all times who gets within sight of the emperor.'

'I thought the Varangians were the emperor's guards?' I said.

'The Varangians are his bodyguard in battle, and his might when he is absent. Combat troops, mainly,' replied Rolf.

'Good,' muttered Harald. 'I did not come here to guard a palace again.' The contempt in his voice was clear.

'They are not mere city watch, Harald. They are mercenaries also, many with years of battle experience. They are underestimated at their enemies' peril, good at what they do. No match for the Varangians, of course, but for almost anyone else.'

Harald grunted at that, clearly not impressed. Neither was I. In my experience watchmen made poor soldiers, more used to bullying tradesmen and chasing thieves than fighting real warriors. Well, our arrogance was misplaced. We would spend years guarding the palace, more time than we spent at war. That is the Varangian life.

The guard we had followed finished his conversation with the Vigla, and spoke quickly to Rolf.

'We are allowed through to the Varangian barracks,' he said to us with a satisfied smile.

'How many more men will we have to pass through?' asked Harald in annoyance.

'Oh, a few I expect. It has gone unusually well so far,' replied Rolf brightly.

The guard passed us off to four Vigla guardsmen, who stared us down with something bordering on hostility, and formed up around us to march us, almost like prisoners, through the massive and ornate gateway that led into the palace compound.

We passed immediately from the crowded city streets into a lush garden. A tree-lined path led off to our right along the hilltop, with great red-tiled halls, churches and cloistered porticos scattered along both sides.

We walked a short distance past the gate until we reached a squat stone building, two storeys high, and broad, with a tiled hall at one corner. The Vigla guardsmen went to the large double gate and spoke to two mailled warriors standing there.

'Varangians,' said Rolf with almost a sigh of pleasure.

I looked at the warriors with interest, because uniquely among the men we had seen so far in the city, they looked much like us, except dressed more finely. Their maille armour was trimmed with woven patterns, their cloaks dyed bright colours and the rims of their helmets lined with riveted bronze. They both carried long axes, unadorned, battlefield weapons, with swords sheathed at their sides. I could see the glint of gold and silver on their wrists and at their necks and they both had full, well-kept beards.

The Vigla marched us over and exchanged some sharp words with Rolf, who nodded, and then the Vigla left while one of the Varangians slipped inside the door.

'We are lucky – the commander is in the hall today. If he was not, we might have waited for days. Word has been sent to seek an audience,' Rolf said with a smile.

'Well, ask the guard if we can wait inside at least,' said Harald, because he, like the rest of us, was sweltering in the southern heat.

'I speak your language, boy. And you can wait outside with me,' growled the guardsman, his words familiar, but his accent strange.

Harald stiffened, and I felt my heart hammer in my chest, praying he would control himself at the insult. But my fears were short-lived as he managed to bite his tongue and merely nod politely.

Well, we stood around outside for quite some time, making what use of the shade of a large, broad-leafed tree we could.

Eventually, the doors opened and a small party of finely dressed men appeared. The man at their head, a Greek in gold-trimmed clothes, clean shaven and beautifully manicured, looked at us with interest, eyeing us as they passed. Harald and I stared right back at them in confusion. These were not warriors, clearly, but nobles of some kind. The first we had seen of the ruling class of the Greeks.

Behind them, one of the Varangian guards motioned to us to come to the now open gate, and allowed us through.

An old warrior met us inside the gate, strongly built and plainly dressed. His hair was grey like a stormy sky but his eyes were still sharp and his exposed arms muscular and tanned.

'I am here to meet the commander,' said Harald in a clipped tone.

'So I hear. Follow me.' The warrior motioned.

Harald looked aside at Afra and Rolf. 'Wait for us here. I will not be long.' Afra sighed and Rolf nodded nonchalantly; he was much more used to the heat.

We walked out of the gateway and passed a door on each side, before exiting into a shaded colonnade surrounding a large, dirt-surfaced training yard.

'What is this place?' Harald asked, looking around.

'This is the barracks of the Excubitors,' the old warrior replied. 'The old cavalry guard of the emperors.'

'And where are the Excubitors?' Harald asked.

The guardsman's shoulders rose and fell in a contemptuous shrug. 'They fell from favour, and we replaced them. Their remnants were sent to Italy. Now we call their barracks and hall our home.'

'Fell from favour?' I asked, curious.

'Yes. We proved better at their job than they were – more ferocious, more trustworthy. They were rotten to the core, centuries of favouritism and nepotism hollowing them out until they were just bright clothes on slow horses, beautiful in ceremonies, but quite useless as guards and as likely to sell the emperor as to protect him.'

We were reaching the other end of the long training ground now, and the guardsman headed for a door, opening it and leading us inside to a small entrance hall and a stairway, which he climbed.

On the balcony at the top he opened a final door and walked through into what looked like the quarters of a clerk or officer. He walked around to the far side of a table spread with parchments and letters, and sat down.

'Well, my name is Báulfr. Tell me, why do you wish to join the guard?'

Harald stumbled momentarily as he suddenly realised the old warrior was the commander. I almost laughed, but restrained myself to a sly smile as Harald took the only chair opposite the older man.

'I have heard men say it is the greatest fighting company in the world, and I wish to learn, prove myself as worthy,' Harald finally replied.

Báulfr smiled softly. 'And why should I take you? This may indeed be the greatest fighting company in the world, but I keep it that way by only taking the best. Why would I take you and your men?'

'We are battle-tested, all of us. I fought for years in the service of Prince Yaroslav, these men with me. I…' Harald struggled to continue, trying to find a way to describe what we had done, without telling the commander who we were.

'You fought Poles in the Red Cities, and then the Pechenegs. Quite the victory that was, or so I hear,' said Báulfr with a stern gaze, as Harald grimaced.

'You know who I am,' he said with a disappointed air.

'Of course.'

'How did you know?'

Báulfr snorted. 'It is my job to know any potential enemies of the empire, and who serves them. Yaroslav certainly is a potential enemy, and I know of only one company of Northmen recently in his service who might be looking for silver elsewhere.'

'Well, then you know my reputation, and my worth,' said Harald proudly.

'And I know you disobeyed your prince and murdered a guest on the docks, in front of a royal party,' said Báulfr with an accusing stare. Harald slumped in his chair slightly. 'How can I trust a man like that?'

Harald did not immediately answer, and the commander stood and tapped his hand on the table. 'Let me tell you why the Varangians are trusted to be the emperor's inner guardians. It is because we hold to our oaths with the utmost ferocity. We cannot be bought, we cannot be swayed, we cannot be seduced or distracted. We are the emperor's personal warriors, resolute as iron, and every man in this company would die before he would be shamed with breaking faith. It is all we have, that faith. The moment one of us breaks it, we will be cast out and replaced like the Excubitors before us.' He stared harshly at Harald. 'So why would I risk a reckless young prince who just sees this as a step on the path to his crown, and might break that faith for a petty blood feud?'

Harald slammed to his feet. 'It was not some petty blood feud!' he spat. 'That was my brother's murderer, my king's murderer! Wouldn't you want your men to have that dedication to justice? If the emperor was slain, would you not rest easy knowing I would avenge him on his enemies no matter the cost?'

Báulfr met Harald's anger without flinching. 'No,' he replied calmly.

Harald was taken aback. 'No?'

'No. Harald, our oath is to the throne, and whoever sits on it. We preserve the empire and its current ruler, at all costs. We do not embark on crusades of revenge that would only weaken the palace. We guard the institution and the embodiment of royalty who leads it. We do not engage in blood feuds and vengeance.'

Harald deflated slightly and sat down again. 'Then why bring me in here just to refuse me?'

Báulfr was silent for a moment. 'Because I am not refusing you; it is not my decision. The akolouthos has also been told you are here, who you are, and has decided you will be admitted.'

Harald looked up again, his hope reignited. 'The akolouthos? Who is that?'

'The commander of the Varangians.'

'But... I thought you were the commander?'

'No, not entirely. I am the leader. I train the men, discipline them and lead them in battle. But it is the akolouthos who gives me my commands – it is a position only a citizen hand-picked by the emperor can occupy. He was here meeting with me when you arrived; you saw him leave. He has commanded me to take you into our service. So I shall, even if I do not like it. That is the meaning of service.' Báulfr looked at Harald without a trace of empathy, and his presence and command were intimidating, even to me.

'I fear you may be too arrogant, too self-involved and too ambitious to be a good member of this guard. We *serve*. The guard *obeys*.' He tapped the table for emphasis. 'We may grow rich, we may even become powerful, but in return we *serve*, and we willingly give our blood and our lives for something greater than ourselves. Tell me, Prince Harald of Norway. Do you believe in anything greater than yourself?'

Harald sat through the admonishment grating his teeth, but he nodded. 'Two things: my brother's legacy, and the lord.'

Báulfr tilted his head. 'It is a start. But you will earn respect for this unit and the empire before I give you authority. The guard will not be your plaything or your vessel for self-aggrandisement.'

Harald looked away, barely able to contain his anger at being spoken to this way.

'You will learn to take criticism first of all, and show discipline. Stand up!' he barked.

Harald pushed himself to his feet, just quickly enough to avoid being insolent, and I squirmed in discomfort behind him, knowing just how badly he would take all of this, but struggling to disagree with the commander. Who really would want Harald as a subordinate? He knew no limit, accepted no ultimate authority. Well, he wouldn't have been a great man if he did.

Harald was an imposing presence, even at nineteen years as he was then. But standing there, face to face, Báulfr dominated him. His power, authority and righteous anger filled the room, and I could see easily how he had risen to be the commander of the famed Varangians. Any lesser man than Harald would have crumbled in the intensity and power of that disapproval. For Harald, it was merely fuel for his fire of resentment.

Báulfr took a moment staring into Harald's taut face, and then he returned to his chair. 'You and your men will be split up, spread among two or three of the weaker banda, and you will not command them.'

Harald huffed and looked down to protest, but the look the commander gave him showed none would be heard. 'You said you wished to learn, so first you will learn humility and service. I will not put your men into a single bandon and command them as a petty fiefdom, undermining the company I have spent my entire life building. When you prove yourself, I may give you a flag.'

'A flag?' asked Harald in a husky, pained tone.

Báulfr sighed. 'There are thirty banda in the guard, in theory, each of two hundred men. Each bandon has a commander, the komes, and a flag-bearer to accompany him and be his second. The flag is the standard of each bandon, and must be protected at the cost of everything except the emperor's own safety. Being given a flag is the mark of a new komes, usually after years of good and faithful service to the throne.'

Harald's eyes opened. 'There are six thousand men in the guard? This barracks is far too small for that.'

'No. There have not been six thousand men in the guard since before

I joined, in the time of Emperor Basil. I have seventeen banda, and many are understrength. We can put two thousand men in the field, at most, leaving the bare minimum to guard the palace.' Báulfr looked at Harald with a conciliatory softening of his features. 'Your men are most welcome, Prince Harald, even if your ambition is not. These are difficult times, and you will face many difficult fights.'

'We live for difficult fights,' said Harald proudly.

'Then I hope you will prove my doubts were wrong.'

Harald said nothing, and Báulfr pulled out a sheet of parchment and pushed it across the table. 'I will need the names of every single one of your men. We will accept only those who were born in the Northern lands, are well-equipped, have battle experience, and are in full health.'

'Every man who follows me is worthy; I do not allow those who are not.'

Báulfr was unmoved and tapped the blank sheet. 'I still need their names. And each will need his joining fee.'

Harald started. 'His what?'

Báulfr looked up, confused. 'Nobody told you?'

'That there is a fee to join? We join to be paid!'

'And you will be, handsomely. Forty gold solidi per year.'

'And the joining fee?'

'Ten pounds of gold per man.'

'Ten!' Harald exclaimed in outrage. 'I have a hundred and thirty men! That's thirteen hundred pounds of gold,' he said in shock. 'We don't have that.'

'We accept the equivalent in silver,' said Báulfr with a shrug. 'So... eighteen thousand pounds of silver.'

Harald looked at me in horror. 'We don't have that much, either.'

I shook my head. 'Ten thousand, maybe.'

Harald looked back at Báulfr, who was nonplussed with our reaction. 'What madness is this? I thought you were warriors, but you *buy* your place in the guard?'

'And I thought you were famous mercenaries, who would be rich in silver and gold. We only want the best, and the best mercenaries are rich men. But you do not have to pay the whole sum upfront. You can pay some, and then owe the treasury the rest, to be deducted from your earnings and share of any loot until the debt is settled.'

'That would take...' Harald paused and looked at me for help. I was always better with numbers.

'About a decade of pay,' I said, and my voice fell.

'It is nothing like a decade in practice,' said Báulfr. 'On your pay alone, yes. But you are going into the combat units, not the palace guard, and you will have the opportunity for plunder and bonuses, as well as imperial gifts for service. Most men pay back the fee within three to five years, depending on how much we campaign.'

'So, you make men into slaves with this debt,' Harald said with barely concealed contempt.

'No, we make them into loyal soldiers. It means no one joins the guard on a whim, or only intending to serve a few seasons,' said Báulfr firmly. 'Now, do you wish to join or not, because it will cause me no pain if you decide to leave. Regardless, my time is short.'

Harald swore under his breath and nodded sharply. 'We wish to join.'

'Good. Then go and get a list of your men and...' The commander looked at me earnestly. 'And what was it you can gather, ten thousand pounds of silver?'

'About that,' I said with a sigh.

'Good. I would sell your ships too, you will get good money for them and the docking fees will eat their value within months. There are always merchants looking for good ships; you will get a fair price.' The commander smiled at me hungrily. 'You can add it to your payment.'

3

'An empire of thieves!' Harald raged as we walked back across the large square outside the Hagia Sophia. I said nothing. Harald had to let out his pent-up anger or he would likely kill someone.

'And the things he said to me, the way he—' Harald bit his lip. Afra and Rolf had not been there and he did not need to relate to them his humiliation.

'Ten thousand pounds of silver,' he muttered. 'All we ever earned from Yaroslav, gone.'

'It is a... shocking amount.'

'And we will still be in debt for years. Years! I came here to be paid, not to provide money to the empire.'

'It is a clever system, you have to admit,' I replied, trying to be soothing but not achieving any part of it.

Harald continued to simmer and rage as we made our way back down to the harbour, getting lost only once in the well-laid-out streets. Eventually, we reached the harbour and handed the sealed token Báulfr had given us to the guard on the gate, who barely looked at it before waving us through.

We went to the shipyard and found the supervisor, a middle-aged Greek official with a sharp eye and a sharper mind. You can say many things about the Greeks, and I will, but many of them are ruthless in both their intelligence and their competence.

'I wish to sell one of my ships, and keep the other here for my own use, if I require it later,' said Harald through Rolf.

The Greek looked at our ships, which were fine Norse longships, but of less use in the waters of the empire. 'I will give you no silver for it, but for the giving of one, I will store the other in the yard for three years, free of charge, and consider it a fair bargain.'

Harald grimaced. 'It costs a third of the value of a ship every year just to dock it?'

The Greek smiled and shrugged, casting a gaze and a sweep of his hand around the compact harbour. 'There are many ships wishing for space, and little space itself. Space is worth more than ships, especially ships such as these. If it was a pair of good dromon I would give you silver, or five years in the sheds for one of them.'

'And if it is in the yard, how long between me asking for it, and it being ready to sail away?'

'A day, no more,' said the man with a curious smile. 'Perhaps you are thinking of a situation where you need it more immediately.'

Harald looked at me and then nodded curtly. 'I am.'

'Only one year on a launching slipway.'

'One year?'

The man shrugged again. 'Launching space is very valuable.'

Harald shook his head and looked around the harbour again. 'Draw it up on the shore over there, facing the water, where those racks are. We are experienced with launching the ship, we will do it ourselves when needed.'

The shipyard master scrunched his eyebrows and looked at the sliver of empty space outside the yard where racks of drying equipment and sails were sitting. 'It will not be under cover; it will swell and warp in the rain and sun.'

'We will come and tend to it occasionally, and launch it to wet it. It will survive three winters.'

The man grunted to make it clear he did not agree but nodded his head in acceptance. 'As you say. Three years on the shore, but if it sinks when you launch I take no responsibility.'

Harald stuck out his arm to seal the agreement, but the Greek looked perplexed until Rolf explained. It turns out the Greeks do not grasp arms to seal their words the way we do. Instead, the official wrote the promise down on parchment and stamped a wax disc with his large gold ring.

Bah, the perfidious Greeks require such things to hold to their words, while we require only the memory of them being spoken. It is one of the many ways I believed we were superior, although as I said and you will hear, there are many others where I learned that we are not.

Well, we gathered our accumulated wealth from the ships, all our bounty from Yaroslav's service. It was a sad proceeding. The men added what they could spare, pulling pouches from belts and rings from arms, until we had gathered together the full ten thousand pounds of silver, or near enough. It left us a little for whatever else we needed, because I did not know if the palace would provide for everything.

When we had all made our way back up to the barracks we were allowed through with escorts from the Vigla and the Varangians, a hundred men in full armour, with axes and shields in hand. I suspect it was a typical precaution. They could not allow the chance that we were part of some plot against the emperor. They looked far better than us I admit, in their superb armour and glorious cloaks, helmets shining in the sun. But they were not just ceremonial seat warmers either, you could tell. Their weapons bore the marks and repairs of battle, their faces and hands too. They regarded us with disdain, but not a hint of fear. They had total confidence in their ability to slaughter us, if we turned out to be false.

We were taken through into the training square of the barracks, told to leave our weapons and equipment along one side, and then the Varangians lined the columned portico while we stood in a loose huddle and waited. Harald looked at the perfectly arrayed Varangians around the square, and then at us, and he sneered in distaste, barking at men to array themselves in ranks and stand up like soldiers.

Well, we had done some ceremonial duties in Kyiv, and we did not array ourselves perfectly, but we managed to look less slovenly at least.

Shortly after Harald had finished his embarrassed fussing over our formation, Báulfr arrived with half a dozen more men in tow – three armed and armoured, three in normal clothes, one clutching a small writing tablet.

He stepped out onto the dirt and gazed over our ranks with displeasure. 'The list,' he said, holding out his hand, and I went forwards at a trot to hand it to him. He squinted at my barely legible scrawlings in annoyance and handed the list to the man with the writing tablet.

'I hope your men can fight better than they can stand still or write,' he said to Harald.

'As well as any man,' Harald replied proudly.

'Any man? I have no room for boasting here. Let's find out.' He turned to the closest of the Varangians. 'Sveinn, practice swords.'

'What will be proven with wooden swords?' asked Harald.

Báulfr smiled. 'This isn't an army barracks; we don't practice with wood.'

The man called Sveinn came back from a side room with a pair of old swords.

'We just take a little of the edge off old steel,' said Báulfr.

Sveinn walked along our ranks assessing us, and then tossed one of the swords to a man in the front rank, a warrior called Rurik. Harald smiled softly. Rurik was one of the blood-marked, those had been with us since Stiklestad. He was one of our best.

Rurik looked at the weapon emotionlessly, weighing it and shifting his grip until he was comfortable. Sveinn beckoned him out into the open space beside our men, who backed away and formed a loose semi-circle around the two combatants. Sveinn stood, sword resting on his shoulder, watching Rurik, looking completely at ease.

Rurik was perhaps unnerved by his supposed opponent's lack of action, or even preparation to fight. He got into a fighting stance, but then looked around at Harald for reassurance before he attacked a member of the palace guard.

Harald gestured at him angrily to begin, and Rurik shrugged and turned again to face his motionless opponent, before starting forwards to make a half-hearted attack.

That was a terrible mistake. I felt for him. It was extremely hard for him to commit fully to attacking this man, who did not even look ready to fight, in such strange circumstances with no preparation. Rurik might have been a terrible foe in battle, but there was no spirit of war in him as he lunged forwards and threw a flat cut at Sveinn's stomach, and it was too slow, too easy to see coming.

Sveinn brought his sword down off his shoulder in a flash, retreating his left leg and slamming Rurik's blade down into the dirt. Then he snapped his sword-hand back up to strike Rurik in the forehead with a crunching blow with the pommel.

Rurik grunted and fell back, going down like a felled tree.

There was a sharp intake of breath and muttered complaints among our men. It felt dishonourable, and I wondered if the blow might have been fatal.

Sveinn returned his sword to his shoulder and looked across at Báulfr, as expressionless as before.

'It is a shame your man is finished so easily. Is that what I can expect from all of you?' said the commander, looking at Harald. But Harald was not looking back at him, and the corner of his mouth curled.

'I don't think Rurik agrees with you.'

We all followed the commander's gaze around, and I saw Rurik levering himself unsteadily to his feet, shaking his head, one hand held to the side of it, blood appearing in a thin trail down his temple.

He squeezed his eyes open and shut a few times and then fixed his gaze on Sveinn, and there was death in his eyes. He bent down to pick up his sword, and without any words being spoken or permission being given, he attacked again.

This time he was striking to kill, and Sveinn parried a vicious lunge at his groin, before barely ducking a cut that would have separated his head from his shoulders, blunt edge or not.

Sveinn countered with a swing to buy himself space and their blades met and rang like a hammer on anvil. No warrior would ever use a battle-ready sword like that, it would ruin it in an instant. But with no shields and blunt weapons, the two men hacked and stabbed at each other in an extraordinary whirl of violence, both taking thumping blows to their maille, and Sveinn a nasty cut to his chin from a slash he could not quite avoid.

But for everything Rurik threw at him, Sveinn was a match. As the Norwegian tired, Sveinn stepped into a cut rather than stepping back, and with his mailled arm deflected the blade like he would with a shield, wearing the painful blow to surprise his enemy and get close enough to deliver a vicious stab to the belly that folded Rurik in half.

With a properly tipped sword, the blow might have gone through the armour. It was quite beautifully done. Despite his maille and the tipless sword, Rurik had the wind knocked out of him and he went down again, wheezing and croaking.

Sveinn, panting and sweating, stepped back and nodded to Báulfr, who nodded thoughtfully. 'Well, a fine performance, even if ultimately futile.'

'He isn't finished,' grated Harald with a dark expression, staring at Rurik, loud enough for the humbled, kneeling warrior to hear. Rurik raised his face, pain creasing his features, breath coming in short gasps and blood running down the left side of his face.

'He. Isn't. Finished!' said Harald more loudly, hands falling to his side and stepping forwards, eyes blazing as he ignored the commander and stared at his fallen warrior. 'Stand up, Rurik, and show them who we are! We are the ones who survived the black marsh, who broke the Pechenegs. We are strongest when our enemies think us defeated. Stand!'

Rurik's face tensed and he nodded. His cheeks went red with the effort of standing, still gasping for air into his tortured lungs, but he got to one knee and then levered himself to his feet with his sword, back uncurling as he finally stretched out to his full height and Sveinn looked on in surprise, emotion finally cracking his stoic features.

'Harald, you have made your point,' Báulfr said with an edge of anger in his voice.

'I have not even begun,' replied Harald. 'You wanted to find out who we are, and this is it. Your man will yield, or one of them will die.' Harald looked at Rurik with a predatory snarl, and motioned with his head for his warrior to resume.

Rurik, finally getting some air back into his lungs, brought his sword up again and gestured to Sveinn, who was now the one looking uncertain.

'I didn't command a fight to the death,' said Báulfr.

'It is the only type we know,' said Harald, never taking his eyes off the two combatants. 'If you don't wish it to end in death, you can command your man to yield, for mine will not.'

Rurik made the most of the time he had to recover, and then, when Sveinn was looking uncertain, jumped into the attack. He made Sveinn parry a single unavoidable cut and then rushed him, jamming a knee into his thigh and wrestling for his sword arm, trying to gain leverage to throw him to the ground.

Sveinn shouted loudly at the pain from the strike, but managed to stagger out of the throw and wrestled for control of his sword, losing his own grip on Rurik's, who punished him for it by pummelling the cross-guard into his ribs in a series of short, sharp jabs that hurt the bigger man visibly.

Sveinn leaned into the embrace, trying to get his bruised ribs away from the painful assault, and Rurik snapped his head up, catching Sveinn under the chin and stunning him, but also losing his grip so that the two fighters separated, Rurik huffing and Sveinn's eyes wide and stumbling from the blow.

Rurik swung again, exhausted, all anger and no control, and Sveinn barely blocked it, both swords ringing and Rurik's being knocked from his shaking grip. He didn't try and retrieve the weapon, he just roared and grabbed Sveinn's mailed tunic with both hands and headbutted him viciously, the blood from his temple and Sveinn's chin spattering and mixing as the two floundering men, who had been so calm and skilled earlier, desperately wrestled and gasped for air. Sveinn's wide eyes and shocked face showed real fear now, and it gave me joy. Everyone around the training ground was watching in stunned silence, Báulfr included.

Rurik landed another headbutt and got a knee in the groin in response, temporarily subduing him. Sveinn backed off a step and cut at Rurik, but the Norwegian lunged desperately forwards, trying to grapple the bigger man around the waist to tip him over. Sveinn resorted to hammering on Rurik's back and ribs with the pommel of his sword, but each strike was more and more lethargic, reaching the end of his power.

As he tried to back up he stumbled, and went down into the dirt with a thud, Rurik on top, howling like a madman and climbing up him, dragging himself up the Varangian's body with his hands, clawing and punching and elbowing as Sveinn used his sword in both hands like a staff, putting it between his body and his half-crazed attacker, but he could not resist the weight and fury of the assault.

Just as Rurik got in reach of Sveinn's face, and Báulfr started to shout at the men to stop, Sveinn managed to twist his hips with an almighty heave and threw Rurik off. Sveinn elbowed the downed man in the side of the head with a crunch of maille and then hauled himself to one knee. As Rurik weakly pawed at his sword-hand the guardsman raised his sword to strike down on the defenceless Norwegian's face, eyes wild and panicked.

'Enough!' screamed Báulfr, in a voice that must have cut across a dozen battlefields.

Sveinn, as if realising what he had been about to do, blinked in confusion, chest heaving, and looked down at Rurik, whose arms had fallen to the ground, mouth open, the fight finally gone from him.

Sveinn got control of himself and nodded. Blood covered his face and his maille, his cloak was torn and filthy. He dragged himself a few steps away and then drunkenly rose to his feet.

Báulfr looked at Harald with a thunderous expression as Harald looked at his defeated man emotionlessly.

'I would have let your man kill him, just to make sure you understood,' Harald said, finally looking at the commander. 'And that was just one of us. Imagine what we are like a hundred wide in a battleline.'

'I imagine that you are just as insolent and stubborn as you were here today,' snapped Báulfr. But then his gaze softened and he nodded wryly. 'But yes, I expect if I can teach your wild thugs to fight like us, and take commands, you will be the terror of our enemies, and worthy to stand beside us.'

There was a rumble of stone and maille as the Varangians around the training ground stamped their feet in agreement, and Harald finally smiled.

'You two, take that man away and get him treated.' Báulfr pointed at the still-prone Rurik. 'And Sveinn, go clean yourself up. Your duties are finished for today.'

Sveinn nodded and hobbled away, his injured leg almost locked with cramp.

Báulfr turned to gesture to the three armed men who had arrived with him. 'This is Aki Freysson, my deputy and the komes of the second bandon, whose men you see lining the training yard. They are the prime of our combat units, the leading bandon of the guard, and you will watch them and learn from them, or not live to regret it.

'Aki is who you will deal with on most matters, as I have more important duties to attend to than dealing with you.' Then he pointed at the other two men. 'This is Styrbjorn the Goat of the fourteenth and Eyvindr Saemingsson of the seventh, whose banda are both severely understrength; they will divide up your men to fill their ranks as they see fit.'

Báulfr summoned Harald with a finger as the three komes stepped forward and in low tones started discussing how to divide us up. Our ranks seethed with disquiet at that, but no one was foolish enough to protest.

I didn't hear what Báulfr said to Harald, but when Harald came back his face was tense and strained. I looked at him inquiringly and he just shook his head. Whatever it was, it cannot have been good.

'You provoke him too much,' I muttered. Harald did not respond, but his eyes narrowed further and he stalked off towards the right of the ranks, perhaps to be away from my admonishment.

The three komes had finished their discussion, and decided on a method. Aki stepped forwards to address us. 'You will be divided in half. Those on the left will join the seventh bandon, the Sea Spears, with Eyvindr. Those on the right, the fourteenth bandon, the Warborn, with Styrbjorn.'

The other two komes stepped forwards to mark the divides and barked orders for us to separate. Afra and I, at that moment, were standing in the left section, and Eyvindr, a hard-looking bastard if I ever saw one, with a badly healed nose and a sunken top lip, unceremoniously pushed us back into the ranks.

That was the moment it really hit home. Harald was in charge no longer. I looked right and saw Harald also being put into line with the men designated for the fourteenth, separated from me by a moment of chance, now a soldier in a different unit. I saw him look over at me with a flicker of concern, quickly wiped away. He could not afford to show weakness.

I looked around to see who was in the seventh bandon with me. Afra and Thorir, Rolf Hammerbeard, a few Norwegians from Stiklestad and a big clutch of more recent recruits, not all of whom I knew well at all. The Icelandic cousins Halldor and Ulfr were with Harald in the fourteenth with most of the Norwegians from Stiklestad.

Aki stepped forwards and put his hands behind his back, staring at us. 'I see you all looking around for friends and comrades, wondering if you should ask to exchange. Don't waste your breath. You are not joined to them any more. You are going to be Varangians, and each man in the guard will be your brother equally. You will train as a bandon, live as a bandon, fight and bleed as a bandon.

'Faithfulness will be rewarded with respect; disobedience will be rewarded with shame and suffering. We do not beat, whip or chain men in the guard. We do not foster men who would be cowed by such things. Those who disobey will be stripped of their weapons, armour, position and honour, cursed to clean and carry and live in the servants' quarters until they correct their ways or give in to the humiliation and leave.'

He stopped and walked down our ranks, looking at us intently as if for the first time. 'I have seen brave men who would fight all the beasts of hell weeping like children after being forced for a year to wear a servant's clothes and bear the shame of missing a campaign, of losing brothers in battle without having been there to fight alongside them. You will obey, or you will be humbled and then obey, nonetheless. If any of you comes into this yard thinking you cannot accept that, leave! No one is forcing you to remain. Sell your worthless service somewhere else, for we will not tolerate anything but utter discipline and dedication.' He stopped and stared around us in challenge, and, to my relief, not a man moved.

'Good. You are all now men of the guard, but months of training and learning awaits you before you will set foot on a battlefield alongside the other banda. You will learn to fight like us, learn to love your brothers like they are your own, and the emperor as if he is your lord and father. Then, and only then, will you take your oaths and be allowed to go on duty, being the fist and fury of the emperor wherever he so chooses, the infallible and fearless vanguard of the empire. We have a reputation to uphold, both here and among our enemies, and you *will not* tarnish it. If you only live by one thing, let it be this: The guard obeys.'

He paused, stepped back and pointed at the wall where we had left our kit. 'Now you will collect your equipment and go to your quarters with your komes. Seventh bandon, south hall – first floor. Fourteenth bandon, north hall – second floor.'

I cast a last look at Harald, seeing his uncertainty about what we had committed to, and then set off after Eyvindr.

4

Eric stretched in his seat, looking up at Ingvarr and then around at the audience. 'So, that is how we started our eight years of service in the guard.' He laughed gruffly. 'I know you cannot all sit here and listen to me speak of eight years of service, so, I will not tell you of all of it. In fact, I will not tell you of most of it, or this boy will be as old and fat as the rest of you before I am finished.'

He looked around the room. 'There are many more of you today. Have any of you served in the guard?'

'Aye,' said a single voice in the background, and Eric's eyes lit up with joy as he turned his head to look. In the shadows at the back of the hall, he saw a dark figure step forward – a middle-aged warrior, silver and gold on his arms.

'Ah, wonderful! There are so few of us. What bandon?'

'Tenth, the Spear Breakers.'

Eric smiled in pleasure. 'The tenth had a different name in my time. I am pleased to meet you. What is your name?'

'Hafthor Ericsson.'

Eric laughed. 'My, what a great name. I am not your father, am I? You are too young to be a son I left in Miklagard.'

'No, my father was a farmer of no name. But I heard of you, Eric the follower, while I was in the guard.'

'Ah. I suspect not good things.'

Hafthor laughed wryly. 'No, not particularly.'

Eric shrugged. 'Well, we didn't end on good terms. But don't ruin my story! Come, sit at my table, Varangian, and share a horn with me.'

Hafthor pushed his way through the growing crowd and took the last space at the table, putting his mug on the wooden boards.

'Try not to correct me when I get things wrong, eh? It has been an entire lifetime, and some things fade.' Eric gave Hafthor a wink and looked around the table again, clearing his voice to resume.

* * *

So, what is worth telling? Well, we spent all that autumn and winter training. I say winter, but truly there is no winter in Constantinople, not as we understand it. It gets cool and it rains, but it almost never snows. The winter there is like our autumn, except the days are longer.

Anyway, I did not see Harald often, and it is Harald's story you came to hear. We trained and ate and lived in our bandon, and mine was a fine group of men. I didn't like them all, but they were superb soldiers to a man. Afra spent the months trying to decipher the political workings of the palace, with only some success, and on the occasion where Harald and I had no duties at the same time, Harald would spend it studying. Studying what? Well, everything.

Let me explain briefly. On one of our winter evenings in the guard, we were given instruction on the formation and tactics of the imperial army. This was done by the commander, and he gathered all of us new men together, sitting us around like children while he explained it all. Not the kind of thing us warriors were used to. For some of it, he had a translator read from a great tome of a book.

We were all quite bored, but Harald was spellbound.

At the end of this training I tried to talk to him, because I had not spoken to him for a while, but he went straight to the translator, who was quite an important man. The Varangians had a whole flock of translators who worked with us, because very few of the men learned to speak

Greek. We were encouraged not to, in fact, to make us more immune to politics and bribery and to keep us separate.

But we had to integrate with the army and the other guard tagmatas, so we had translators everywhere. The grand translator was a very senior man in the palace hierarchy, responsible for translating directly to the emperor himself.

Anyway, I forget this unfortunate man's name, but he was assigned to Harald's bandon.

'The book, what is it?' he asked the translator.

The Greek scribe looked at him with a raised brow. 'It is the Tactica of Leo and Constantine. It lays out the tactics and operations of the imperial army.'

'Can I read it?'

'Do you read Greek?'

'No.'

'Then no.'

'You will translate it for me,' Harald said.

'Which passage?'

'All of it, and you can teach me Greek at the same time.'

The translator laughed, naively assuming Harald was joking. When Harald just stared at him in annoyance, his laughter faded. 'You cannot be serious. This is hundreds of pages, of extraordinary detail. Only the most senior commanders actually read this.'

'Perfect, then that is exactly what I wish to know.'

The translator looked at me for support and I just shook my head.

'That would take months, and you will be training.'

'We will use the evenings,' Harald said firmly.

The translator looked aghast, seeing his spare time dissolving in front of his eyes, but his duty was to translate for the guardsman of the banda, and I suppose he could not refuse, or simply did not dare to.

He gulped and held the great book a little closer to his chest. 'Not now. I can start tomorrow.'

'Excellent,' said Harald, and he smiled and turned to walk away with me.

'You will learn Greek? And that entire book?' I asked.

'Yes. How am I to rise in this world if I cannot communicate in it? How am I to rise in the army if I do not know its ways?'

They were good points, but I had never thought about it that way. This is why he led and I followed, you understand?

I laughed at how ridiculous it was.

'Don't laugh so easily, Eric. You will find a translator and do the same. I don't care if you study the books, but you will learn the language, and quickly.' He looked at my horrified expression. 'What? What use are you to me if you cannot even speak to anyone without help?' And then he left me standing there cursing him in both Norse and Greek. You see, that part of the language I had picked up very quickly, as all soldiers do.

* * *

Well, nothing of importance happened until the spring of 1035, and that is when we took our vows. A tiny handful of our men had left. The life of the guard was not for everyone. But most of us lined up on a fine spring morning in our full battle gear, standing in the view of all the rest of our banda, to take the oath with our komes and the commander.

I cannot tell you the details of that ceremony or our oaths, because the first of them was to keep them secret. But it is enough to tell you that we were bound to the throne of the empire, blood and soul, until we died or were formally released from service. And those oaths were taken with the utmost seriousness, even by Harald, as you will later see.

Now that we were full guardsmen, and our training was complete, we had a lot more freedom and time on our hands. Our men went out into the city to drink and whore and let off stress from six months of near confinement, and Harald, Afra, Thorir and I went to find somewhere quiet to drink and talk, as if it was the old days again.

The rich Greeks did not drink ale like we do. Mostly they drank watered wine, and some local drinks that I never took a liking to. And they did not drink in halls, mostly in half-open buildings and shaded gardens in the lower city near the public squares, where they would sip their wine and eat morsels of delicate foods and pastries, sometimes with music or readings of famous works.

I try and sound derisive, but truly I enjoyed it. So the four of us sat around a table in a nice taverna, and Harald ordered our refreshments in his newly acquired Greek, which earned a few raised eyebrows. Everyone knew that we were Varangians, of course. We went out into the city without our armour, but our bright tunics and belted seaxes and pale skin, not to mention our beards, gave us away to all the locals.

Thorir had learned to speak Greek too, of course, although we did not find that out until later.

Anyway, Harald was not there to be social; Harald was there to interrogate Afra and Thorir away from prying ears in the palace.

'So tell me, what have you learned that I should know? Where are Bardas and Maria?' I stiffened at the mention of the pair, who Harald had not mentioned since we left Kyiv. The betrayal by Maria, who had been Harald's lover, and the treachery of Bardas, who had left us to be slaughtered by the Pechenegs, had hurt him deeply. To later learn they were secretly co-conspirators had been too much for him to either forgive or forget.

Maria and Bardas had left Kyiv to return to Constantinople when the previous emperor died, with the intent of trying to once again manoeuvre their mistress Theodora, the sister of the empress Zoe, into power. Three times they had tried and failed in rebellions and plots to overthrow Zoe and replace her with Theodora. Three times they had failed, yet Zoe could not, or would not, have her sister executed, instead confining her to a monastic life of seclusion.

I had known that one of Harald's motivations for seeking service in the empire was probably to hunt his enemies down and get vengeance, but in the months without mention of them, I had hoped he had let the matter go. Clearly, that was not the case; he had merely been biding his time as Afra and Thorir gathered information.

Thorir looked up at his brother and inclined his head, letting Afra start.

'I do not think they are in the city. As far as I can tell, Theodora's faction is still brewing trouble, this time in Anatolikon Theme, to the east. There are rumours of sedition. I assume Bardas is behind it, and Maria will be there, or with her mistress Theodora in her monastery.'

'The monastery is in the city?'

'No, in Nicaea, across the water.'

'And can we get to it?'

Afra shook his head. 'No. It is well-guarded, and only women are allowed within its walls.'

Harald nodded his acceptance. 'And what of the new emperor?'

Afra laughed quietly. 'Well, that is quite a story.'

'Give me the important details.'

'Emperor Michael was a minor court official and Zoe's lover. They probably murdered her previous husband, Emperor Romanos, and Zoe had Michael put on the throne.'

My eyes widened considerably. I had heard rumours about the imperial couple, but nothing quite so scandalous.

'Are you sure?'

'I am certain,' said Thorir quietly, and we all turned to him, including Afra.

'Really?'

'Yes, I have it from an excellent source.'

Then Thorir fell silent again, giving no clue as to who his source might be. But we had all learned to trust him at that point. Thorir could worm his way into a nest of snakes and be invisible. And mark my words, the palace was a nest of snakes and we were only just starting to learn the extent.

'As I hear it,' I said, wanting to feel important, 'Michael and Zoe were married the same day that Romanos died, and Michael was crowned that afternoon.'

'You are correct,' said Afra with a wink.

'But Michael was a nobody, and he was crowned within a day? How?' asked Harald in shock.

'A great deal of gold changed hands, or so I hear. The patriarch of the Church is a much wealthier man now than he was last winter.'

'And the people accept this man as emperor?'

'Well, I think it is Zoe who they accept. She is immensely popular. As, in fact, is her sister Theodora,' replied Afra.

'So Zoe is the real power, Michael just her puppet?'

Afra and Thorir looked at each other and Thorir made a little shrug of uncertainty.

'It is unclear,' Afra finally said uncomfortably. 'I think that was certainly her intent, to control the empire through him, but although it is heavily shrouded, from what I can gather they are now at odds. My understanding is that Michael quickly started to compete for power with her.'

Harald sat back in amazement. 'So this Michael, a man of no standing, murdered the emperor, stole his wife, and then usurped the whole empire... and nothing was done? You must be mistaken. Something else is at play here.'

Thorir swirled the wine around in his cup. 'There is another power at play, but I am unsure who it is. Whoever it may be, they play a very careful game and I have yet to decipher it.'

Harald's brows furrowed. 'And how did they murder Romanos without the guard stopping them? Were they complicit?'

'He was drowned in his bath by his own servants,' said Afra. 'Or so they say. No Varangian could have intervened.'

'It is true, almost certainly,' said Thorir. 'How the plotters came to corrupt the inner circle of his attendants is something I am yet to understand. They are among the most protected and cloistered people in the city, for exactly this reason.'

'Well, until we decipher the centre of power, I cannot align myself with it. If the emperor and empress are in conflict, we must be very careful not to appear to be on the wrong side.'

'Not least because of our oaths,' I said in a serious tone, for I took the commitments we had made very seriously.

Harald nodded curtly. 'I know, and I don't intend to violate them. If the two rulers are in conflict our duty is very confused. We are here to protect their lives, and the throne.'

'And I wonder which of them, if either, supports Theodora and her rebels,' said Afra.

Harald's eyes widened. 'I had not considered that. Yes, it is possible one faction has made common cause with Theodora's.'

'Perhaps we should stay out of this?' I said, pleading. But I knew it was futile. Harald was drawn to these games of power like a moth to a flame. 'It does not matter to us who controls the empire, only that we protect them and remain in service, to earn our wealth and reputation. That is what we are here for, is it not?'

'I will be careful, Eric. Don't worry,' said my leader, in a way that did nothing to calm my worries at all. Then he sipped his wine and looked at Afra again. 'And what of home?'

Afra looked uncomfortable. 'Magnus is king.'

'Magnus is a child. Who rules?'

'His mother and Kálfr Árnason actually rule in his name, so I hear.'

'And the people accept this?' said Harald with a snarl.

'Yes, there is little resistance to his rule.'

Harald's face clouded over with anger. 'Our people disgrace themselves. Have they forgotten my brother Olaf so easily?'

'No, he has become something of a hero amongst the people, as you predicted. His canonisation was very popular.'

'Then why do they disgrace his memory by following the very men that murdered him?' said Harald, his face reddening and veins standing out on his neck.

Afra looked sympathetic. 'Magnus has been declared as the heir to his legacy, and Kálfr Árnason's role is very... understated.' Then Afra looked downright uncomfortable. 'I believe Rognvald has been instrumental in smoothing over Magnus's ascension to power.'

Harald looked aghast. Rognvald had been his closest advisor and ally while we were in the Rus, but had left to return to Norway with Magnus, having made a deal with the child and his mother to secure his own disputed lands in return for support. Harald had forgiven him for what felt like a betrayal, because he recognised Rognvald was merely doing what he had to. But to hear our old friend had helped Kálfr Árnason, the man who had killed Olaf, was rage-inducing.

Harald slumped back into his chair, picking up his wine and draining what was left of it. 'So there is no path back for us, not yet.'

'No,' said Afra, shaking his head sadly.

'Then we must make the most of our situation here, and make sure we understand the shifting of power within the palace.' He nodded to

Afra and Thorir. 'I want you keep learning as much as you can, it is essential I understand.'

Afra nodded. 'As you request.'

Thorir just smiled slightly, which was all the acknowledgement he needed to give.

* * *

Well, we did not have long to wonder at the machinations of the palace – as was always the way with Harald, they caught up with him.

Harald and I were relaxing in the spring sunshine in the palace grounds after morning training when a nondescript figure approached us, a slim middle-aged woman, a palace servant of some sort.

'My lords, I beg a moment of your time,' the servant said in halting Norse.

'We are not lords,' I said in amusement, wondering who the servant thought we were. We were finely dressed, and could have been one of the endless flow of dignitaries and ambassadors that came and went from the palace, awaiting receptions in the great hall just to the north of our barracks, or even a personal audience with the emperor in the Hall of Nine, just to the south of where we sat.

'And we speak Greek, lady. Or at least, I do,' said Harald with a smile, and the servant nodded in relief.

'I apologise for the secrecy, Prince Harald, but my mistress would like to meet you, and discretion is essential.'

That got Harald's attention. It was a widely known secret in the guard – who he really was – but he still went by the name Nordbrikt and pretended to be merely a noble's son. He looked up at the servant intently. 'And who is your mistress?'

'I cannot say.'

'Then I cannot go. It is against my oaths to even risk corruption with secret meetings.'

The servant looked around uncertainly, with some annoyance, and finally leaned in. 'The meeting would be in the garden behind the women's quarters of the palace, if that helps you decide. The guards on duty have orders to admit you. Please be there quickly or not at all.'

And with that, the servant walked off again in the direction of the palace.

Harald looked at me with a glint of mischief in his eye. 'That can only be one person.'

'The empress Zoe,' I said.

'Indeed.'

'You should not go,' I said, with a firm shake of my head.

'It is tantamount to an order from the empress. I have no choice.'

'Nonsense. If it were a proper meeting, it would be arranged in a proper way,' I said angrily.

'Well, I'm going to go anyway,' Harald said, jumping easily to his feet. 'Come with me, to ensure nothing untoward happens.'

'I was not invited,' I replied with a sigh.

'No, but you were also not explicitly *not* invited.'

'You think in circles,' I muttered, but I could not refuse. He would get into far more trouble without me.

'Come, this is the most interesting thing that has happened since we arrived.'

* * *

We walked down the back path to the east side of the palace, where the high wall surrounded the private garden of the women's quarters. There was only a single gate, and two Varangians from the first bandon, the Emperor's Shields, the primary guards of the palace, were standing on guard in all their finery.

They looked at us suspiciously, recognising that we were also Varangians, but looking uncertain.

'We were told you were expecting us,' Harald said pleasantly.

'And you are?'

Harald paused while he contemplated how to answer, but decided the truth was the safest path. 'Harald Nordbrikt of the fourteenth, and Eric Alvarsson of the seventh.'

'We were expecting only you, Harald.'

'I'll wait here,' I said, stepping aside.

Harald shook his head. 'This reeks of plotting, brothers, and I can see you feel it too. Eric is here to witness the meeting, to ensure everything is correct. Tell whoever summoned us that we both come in, or neither, and that we may report this to the commander.'

The guards looked at each other with discomfort and had a whispered conversation. Then one opened the door and went inside while we stood in silence and waited. Finally, he returned and spoke to the other. 'They may both enter.'

Harald nodded his thanks and made to step past them, but one of the guards caught his arm. 'But whatever you see and discuss in there, is best kept private. If it does not break our vows, the affairs of the palace remain in the palace, understood?'

'Completely,' said Harald, and the grip on his arm relented.

We walked through the gate and into a wonderland of flowering bushes and shaded, delicately trimmed trees. The same servant was there waiting for us, wearing a distinctly venomous glance for me, and then turned and inclined her head for us to follow.

We went with her into a maze of every kind of plant, many of which I had never seen before, passing fountains and stone benches until we reached a secluded semi-circle of deep green bushes, shaded by a broad plane tree, with an elaborate fountain in its centre that cooled the air pleasantly with a fine spray of droplets.

Sitting on bright cushions on a marble bench against the backdrop of the bushes, looking out over the garden in front as if we were not there, was a woman in a fine silk dress, patterned with gold and purple, belted at the waist with a flowing skirt. It was modest, bright, and obviously fabulously expensive.

The servant put a hand on my chest and, with surprising strength, pushed me to the side to stand next to a bush. She raised her hand to her lip to indicate for me to be silent. I understood. I had been in the presence of great people before, and I was not one of them.

Then she prostrated herself before the sitting woman, and, rising to her knees, addressed her quietly. 'Basilissa, I have brought for you Araltes the Exile, Prince of Norway, brother of Saint Olaf.' Then she dipped her head to the floor again and awaited instruction.

The woman finally moved her gaze and set it on the servant woman. 'You may introduce me, Hypatia.'

'Thank you, Basilissa.' The servant rose to her knees and then her feet, keeping her head bowed as she retreated three steps and then turned to Harald.

'Araltes, Prince of Norway, you are in the presence of Empress Zoe Porphyrogenita, daughter of Constantine, protector of the empire of the Romans. You may prostrate yourself and be acknowledged.' She gestured to the marble floor in front of the empress, who still did not look at us. Every part of this process, even in private, was clearly a rigid ceremony. Until Harald presented himself correctly, he simply did not exist in the empress's awareness.

'A simple bow, for a prince, will suffice in this case,' said Zoe in her silky voice, without looking.

Harald, who had clearly been uncomfortable with the idea of lying full flat on the marble in the eastern way, even for the empress of the greatest empire in all the world, stepped forwards and executed a perfect bow. You see, he had been brought up correctly as a young prince.

'Basilissa, it is my great honour to be received.'

Zoe finally turned to look at him and smiled graciously and nodded, gesturing him to the cushions across from her. The servant Hypatia came back to stand near me, and then went as still as a statue. Zoe never even glanced at me, I had been enforced on her, I had not been introduced, and it was beneath her dignity to even accept my existence.

Harald sat at a respectful distance and smiled shyly. Even he was affected by Zoe's presence. She was already beyond her fiftieth year, but she was beautiful, nonetheless. Skin fair and unblemished from a lifetime of careful attention and the finest lotions and cosmetics. She was properly dressed, covered from neck to toe, but I caught myself admiring the fine figure her dress subtly revealed. I had heard stories of Zoe, of course, of her legendary beauty and vanity. She was not beautiful in the way a bright young woman might be, but in a regal way; serene, a fine nose and chin and soft cheekbones, powerful, confident eyes. She looked every part the empress. It was quite captivating.

'How can I serve you, my lady?' said Harald finally.

'I merely wished to meet you, young prince. Should I not meet a foreign prince who comes into my lands?' Her smile broadened a little. 'Even one who does not announce himself, and comes in disguise.'

Harald dipped his head. 'I apologise for the deception. It is not meant out of disrespect, just to avoid controversy. I am not here as a prince, I am here as a soldier.'

'So I see. A member of my guard of vicious Northmen. But with some manners – so rare among your breed.'

'I... thank you, my lady.'

Well, I was struggling to keep up. My Greek wasn't nearly as good as Harald's by that point, but the rest of the conversation was all politeness and niceties. No conspiracy at all. As swiftly as it had begun, it was over, and we were politely and firmly dismissed.

***

As we walked back towards the barracks, Harald was smiling while my brows were furrowed.

'What was the point of that?' I asked. 'She said nothing of importance.'

'Hmm?' muttered Harald, snapping out of his thoughts. 'Oh, she was just taking the measure of me. Remarkable woman, isn't she.'

'I... suppose so.'

'Such grace, such poise, such power.'

I murmured something non-committal, but Harald was too enthused to notice.

We walked a while longer, and then I stopped, causing Harald to stop and look at me. 'What?'

'Why the secrecy? Why not have a formal audience?'

Harald shrugged. 'She could not have a proper audience with a lowly guardsman, not without publicly declaring who I am.'

'And why doesn't she want to do that?' I asked.

Harald bit his lip for a moment and stared at the ground. 'It's a good question; I'll have to think about it. Let's not concern ourselves for now. We have duties to perform.'

Well, I didn't like it. I didn't like it at all.

5

Our duties as guardsmen who had finished our training were monotonous. We were, as Harald had once derided, merely palace guardsmen. We mostly guarded inner buildings of the palace, where there was no real threat, or the big public buildings in the city during events or ceremonies. We were there for show, to remind visitors of the power of the emperor and his fearsome mercenaries. We might as well have been statues.

But as Harald and I were on duty one day outside the senate chamber in the great public forum of Constantinople, where a number of dignitaries and representatives were being received, a woman walked past us without giving us a second glance, and Harald almost sputtered in surprise, 'Maria?'

The woman stopped, eyes widening at being called to by a guardsman, and then saw the source of the outburst. She laughed, and her face lit up with a smile. By God she was still a beauty. Alluring and intelligent.

'Harald? By the saints, it *is* you. I had heard rumours of the mysterious Northern warrior who some say is a prince, and I knew it must be you. Did you come to find me? How sweet.' She walked over and held out her hand for Harald to kiss, and he had no choice but to take it and kiss it because we were in public, although he cursed under his breath while he did so.

'So, now you are a palace guard here instead of in Kyiv?' She turned to look at me. 'Ah, young Eric. Delightful. What a pretty boy you still are.'

'And are you still a traitor?' growled Harald, fingering the hilt of his sword.

Maria's eyes sparkled. 'No, not at all. My mistress and the emperor are quite reconciled.' She leaned in conspiratorially. 'It was really the previous emperor who we had the trouble with.'

'And with Empress Zoe, who you tried to replace,' added Harald with a sneer.

Maria's eyebrow rose suggestively. 'Is she still the empress?'

'Watch your words; you toy with treason,' said Harald, his anger rising uncontrollably at the woman who had so deeply betrayed him.

'No my love, I toy with *you*. And such fun it is! But I must go, I have an appointment with someone rather important. It was delightful to see you again.' And with a charming wave, she set off again with her companion, leaving Harald fuming and unable to move in her wake.

I have to admit, I would have laughed if Harald wasn't so angry he might have struck me down for it. Maria was a consummate wielder of words, and she could lift up a man to the heavens or reduce him to rubble just with their use. What can I say? I was impressed. Excellence deserves respect in all cases.

I don't think Harald spoke again for the rest of the day.

* * *

Our komes, Eyvindr Saemingsson, came into the part of the barracks where we of the seventh bandon lived, first thing on a fine late summer morning. 'Pack up your gear, we are going east tonight. We are likely to be on campaign until next year.' And then he left.

Eyvindr was a man of few words at the best of times, but this was particularly abrupt. That is the life of a guardsman. You might sit in the palace for a year, bored, waiting for assignment, and then a crisis rears its head and you are assigned to a distant land, potentially for years. A man who lives like that cannot easily have a wife or family; you cannot know where you will be the next day, let alone the next week.

Maybe some of you remember I had a wife, left behind in Kyiv. Olga, a wonderful woman. Well, I had chosen, out of cowardice, not to bring her to Constantinople. I could claim that decision was wise, for it would have been a miserable existence for her there with me living in the barracks and then her left alone when I was away on campaign, but the wisdom in it was incidental and unknown to me at the time. While in Constantinople I am ashamed to admit I put her from my mind for many months.

I once found a Rus merchant heading to Kyiv during that first winter and gave him a letter and a gold solidus to take it to her personally, but I never received a reply. Why did I marry her? Who knows. I had nothing to offer her, but I had been in love and love is the enemy of logic and good reasoning as arrows are the enemy of flesh.

Well, we were all ready, and we packed our equipment and gathered in the training yard. There were six banda garrisoned in the city, not including the permanently stationed first bandon, who were apart from the rest of us and never left the palace except when the emperor himself went on campaign.

Five of them were being gathered outside the barracks along the broad central avenue of the palace. The second, seventh, fourteenth and two others. As soon as we saw that, we knew that it was serious.

We gathered silently in well-ordered ranks and waited, and soon enough Báulfr came down from his small office, armed and armoured for war. That might not sound special to you, because he was a warrior despite being an old man, but I had never seen him armed before. This could mean only one thing: he was coming with us. For the first time in a decade, the Varangian guard was taking the field in force, and I was in breathless anticipation to find out where and why.

'Varangians, blessings are upon us this fine day, for the emperor has commanded that we are to go on campaign.'

There was a heartfelt, guttural acclimation at this news. Everyone in the combat banda of the guards joined at least in part to go on campaign and get the chance for loot and combat bonuses. For us newcomers, still heavily indebted to the treasury, it was welcome news indeed.

'In the east, the Egyptian caliph's forces move north to threaten Edessa and even Antioch, and have captured many other towns and forts around them. The dukes of Antioch and Edessa have asked for aid, and the emperor sends that help in full force.

'However, the enemy has spurred trouble in our path. A fleet of pirates infests the waters of the Anatolian shore, aided by rebels and bandits in the coastal hills. We cannot safely transport the army to Antioch, and supply it, until these pirates are destroyed. For this, the emperor commands the Admiral of the Samos theme to send his fleet to support the Cibyraeotarum theme's ships.'

Báulfr stopped and looked around. 'The fleet lacks the fighting men and the skills to clear the coastal strongholds of these pirates, so we, his best tagmata, are ordered to set sail with the fleet, and scour the Anatolian shore in advance of the army's arrival.'

The men in the courtyard shouted in elation and agreement as the commander looked on with pride.

'The five banda here will join the three from outside the city, and four from Nicomedia and Nicaea.'

There was a ripple of shock through the ranks; that was twelve of the seventeen active Varangian banda. Two would remain in Constantinople to protect the palace, two were in Italy on campaign against rebels and too far to summon, and another was already in Kypros guarding against invasion. The Varangians had not gone to war in such numbers since the time of Emperor Basil. That is how we knew the threat from the east must have been extreme.

'The other units have already been sent their orders, and will meet us at Samos. Your komes will give you your instructions, and take you to your ships.' Báulfr drew himself upright and glared at us all. 'Remember, Varangians, you represent and protect the very body and reputation of the emperor, even when he is not present. You will conduct yourselves on this campaign in such a way that his enemies fear to ever challenge him again. You will be bold, you will be merciless, and you will die or be victorious. For God and emperor!'

'God and emperor!' we roared in our massed ranks. Oh it sends chills down my spine just to think of it. What men we were.

* * *

We were ordered to make our way to the ships for midday, giving us no longer than required to fetch missing equipment, or attend to debts or messages.

Harald and I, having no roots in the city, and with all our equipment in perfect order, had nothing to do but wait in the shade of one of the trees outside the yard. Other guardsmen were around, standing in groups and talking excitedly, or snatching a short sleep in the shade like the seasoned soldiers they were.

As Harald and I stood there, in comfortable silence, one of the many anonymous palace servants who walked to and fro almost unnoticed approached us and I recognised her as Empress Zoe's attendant.

She walked past us and did not even pause or look at us as she said in a low voice, 'You are required,' and then headed off towards the back of the senate house in the lower palace grounds.

Harald heard her too, and looked at me with a raised eyebrow. We could have ignored her, of course. We were about to set sail and this clandestine invitation was hardly a royal order, but Harald was instantly intrigued, and he would never pass up such a request.

We nonchalantly picked up our kit and followed. Guardsmen were everywhere, and no one spared us a second glance as we strolled after the servant, going behind the barracks and then into the quiet gardens behind the senate house.

The empress's attendant stopped under an overhanging bush to talk to another grey-robed servant, and we went over to see what she wanted.

'Where is your mistress?' asked Harald, looking around in confusion, a prickle of fear that this was some sort of trap clearly spreading to him as it was also infecting me.

The second servant turned to face us, and it was a few moments before I recognised her. Harald saw her too, and he blushed in embarrassment and bowed his head. 'Basilissa, my apologies.' He looked at her in alarm.

'Do not do that, not here,' snapped Zoe's attendant, looking around.

Harald straightened. 'Of course, as you wish.'

My mind was racing. The empress of the Romans, meeting two guardsmen in a corner of the palace, dressed as a servant. None of the implications were good.

Harald stood awkwardly, not knowing what to do or make of the situation, looking from one woman to the other.

It was Zoe who spoke first, and her voice was halting, diminished. Nothing like the supremely confident woman we had met before. 'Prince Araltes, I have a favour to ask you, and let us speak as two people. I do not meet you here as the empress, but as Zoe, a servant of the empire like you.'

Harald shifted uncomfortably. 'My lady, I am leaving for the east, this very day.'

'I am aware.'

'Then I do not know how I can help you, nor the reason for meeting me like this. But anything you want me to do and is within my power and my oaths, you can merely order me as empress and I am your servant.'

'I cannot order you in this,' she said with a fraught expression, her eyes locked with Harald and pleading. By God, she looked nervous. Suddenly I saw the woman, where before I had seen only the empress.

'Then it is something outside of my oaths?' asked Harald, straightening slightly.

You may be interested to know it surprised me at the time, because he later became famous for it, but I did not expect Harald to take his oaths to the empire that seriously. Yes, I see you there, horrified that I impugn his honour, but hold your outrage. Harald was an honourable man and his oaths were important to him, desperately so. But he always found a way to twist their meaning to his needs, looking for opportunity to gain advantage from them without breaking them, merely straining them to their limits.

But something in Báulfr's words to him, and in those secret oaths we took, had deeply affected Harald. I think, for the first time since he was with his brother Olaf, he had seen something greater than himself, worthy of his life and his sacrifice. Yaroslav and the Rus had merely been a way of earning status and riches. He had risked his life, of course, but he had held no intent of dying for the Rus prince out of mere duty.

But in the empire... Something about the history and grandeur of that wondrous place had shifted him on his foundations, the majesty of the city, and above all the deep, deep brotherhood of the Varangians. So, I could see that he revolted at the very idea of corruption. It was quite the change, I assure you.

Well, Zoe shook her head rapidly, almost pleading. 'No, it is not outside them... It is complicated, the situation...'

'It is simple,' replied Harald. 'You know my oaths. If you have a request of me, order it, and it shall be done if I can do it. If not, this is unseemly.'

'Your oaths are to the throne, and those who sit upon it.'

'Yes.'

'And what if those who sit upon it are separated?' Zoe asked, and Harald paused, his brows darkening.

'My lady... Zoe, you truly wish me to speak honestly, not to the empress?'

The attendant shot him a filthy look promising pain and suffering for the disrespect, but Zoe calmed her with a small gesture of her hand. 'Yes.'

'I hear that the emperor is only seated on the throne by your hand, that he was a low official and your lover. Was it not your intent to control him?'

The attendant hissed in anger and Zoe turned to her, putting a hand on her cheek and whispering to her. The attendant's face sank, and she nodded, taking a step back, but giving Harald one last withering look of disgust.

'I apologise. Hypatia is my most loyal follower.'

'You have nothing to apologise for, my lady. I am fortunate enough to have such supporters too.' He turned to give me a warm smile, and my heart sang. I stretched to my full height and suppressed my desire to grin like a child.

Zoe looked at me then, the first time she had ever met my eyes. 'I am glad of it, Eric, for there is high honour in being a loyal follower to a great man.' I was breathtaken. Even with her fearful, narrowed eyes, far less elaborate make-up, and her simple servant's clothes I was overcome. I have told you of this before, of the power of certain people over us normal men. Yaroslav had it, Harald had it, but Zoe was the mistress of them all. If she had demanded me to sink to my knees, renounce Harald and swear to her, I would have done it. That she even knew my name! Ah, how can I explain it to you? I was a simple farm boy and spear warrior, and the empress of the Romans knew my name, without me ever being introduced to her. And she spoke so highly of me?

Oh, it brings a tear to my eye, even now. But of course she had inquired who I was. She wanted Harald's loyalty, so she made sure she knew everything about him, and everything around him.

You see, control and loyalty. These are not achieved through magic or force of personality alone; it requires talent and preparation. But I was very naive then, and I was overwhelmed by it.

Anyway, I am being distracted. In that moment Zoe had won my heart, and then she turned back to the man that actually mattered to her. 'It is true, everything you said. Michael was such a soft man, so kind and gentle. And I knew that I could rule with him at my side, for the empire would still not allow me to sit the throne alone.'

'And he turned out not to be so soft?' said Harald with a rude laugh.

'No, he is. But it turns out there were other hands on him, subtler and more forceful than mine.'

Harald looked at me briefly, and I thought back to what Afra and Thorir had said and I nodded. 'We have heard rumours,' I said, unbidden, but no one objected.

Zoe's face fell, her dark-lined eyes falling to the ground in shame. 'I was so sure of myself that I ignored the signs. As I believed I was controlling him, another was using that against me.'

'Who, my lady? Who is the traitor? Speak his name and he will die for it.'

Zoe coughed, a single ironic heave as she waved a hand away in amusement. 'If he was a traitor I would order his death.'

'Then the emperor and you surely can act together to throw off these chains?'

'Why? Michael does not chafe against this control, he welcomes it. He knows he has no legitimacy without me, and he knows he cannot control me alone. He is not a captive to those who oppose me, he is a willing ally. A conspirator against me, against the throne, against the empire.'

The words poured from her like a torrent, anger and frustration and powerlessness from a woman who must be used to absolute power. I felt for her, so deeply. It was all so unfair.

Harald thought this over and then nodded slowly. 'So you are set against him, and he against you.'

'Yes.'

'My lady, I cannot intervene.' He looked at her sadly, and I looked at him like he had just kicked a kitten. How could he not want to help this wondrous woman?

'My oath is to the throne, and whoever sits upon it. Both you and Michael do, and thus I must protect both your interests and desires. If your desires collide? I cannot take a side.'

Zoe nodded sadly. 'I know, Araltes. I know you cannot intervene directly between us. This disaster is a mistake of my own making and it is not what I ask of you.' She took a step towards him and took one of his hands gently in hers. 'Whatever you have heard of me, whatever you think, know this: I care for nothing but my family's legacy. I fight, I have fought my whole life, to stop weak, ambitious men from taking the empire, my father and grandfather's legacy, and ruining it for their own enrichment.'

Ah, that was brilliant. She struck to Harald's heart with that, for what else was he than a man trying to protect and grow his family legacy and recover his kingdom from the men who had stolen it?

'If I had been born a man I would be the emperor and the empire would be flourishing. Instead, I have been forced to try and rule through the voice of others, and I have nearly failed. All I ask is this: Do not let them destroy me. I cannot ask you to tear my enemy down, but I can ask you to make sure I am not forever silenced. Dark plans are afoot, my own family are used against me, my poor, innocent sister

Theodora is used as a weapon against me by those who seek my power. The throne itself is used against me, and you are sworn to protect it above all else. The throne, and everything it stands for. If I am destroyed, the legacy of my family will be destroyed, and the empire with it.'

'Theodora is used against you?' said Harald carefully. 'It is not her doing, these rebellions?'

Zoe shook her head miserably. 'No, it is merely another hidden faction using her for their own ends.'

Harald nodded carefully, saying nothing, and I froze. We knew who that hidden faction was, or at least, we thought we knew. It was Maria and her dog Bardas. But Harald had loved Maria. Was he willing to give her up? If Zoe knew Maria was part of the faction manipulating Theodora, she would surely be executed, or worse.

She looked around nervously and then let go of Harald's hand. 'I must go. Please, remember my words, and protect me if you can.'

'Name them,' said Harald, taking a step forwards and grasping Zoe's arm, making her look down at it in shock. I doubt a man had ever handled her like that, not one who had lived to speak of it. 'Name the man who controls Michael.'

'He is not a man,' she said with a shake of her head, which confused me.

'What? Why will you not name them?'

'Because once you know, one of you will die. I see you and it is your nature, and I cannot allow that. It is too soon, you are not ready.' She tore her arm away and retreated a few steps.

'How can I protect you from a threat I do not recognise?' said Harald in desperation as the two women turned to walk away.

'You will recognise it when the time comes. Just be watchful and be ready,' she said, looking back over her shoulder, and then the empress was gone.

Harald snorted in frustration and looked at me, and then back at the corner of the senate house where the women had disappeared.

'We should go to the ship,' I said finally, with nothing to say that would help assuage the feeling of helplessness that afflicted us both.

'I will not let her be destroyed,' said Harald with clenched teeth. 'If she cannot risk telling us who threatens her, we will find out ourselves.'

'And what of our oaths?'

Harald pursed his lips. 'We will not act against Emperor Michael, but nothing says we cannot block any plans he has against the empress. As for Maria and Bardas...' He paused, conflicted. 'They have no such protection, there are merely traitors.'

'This is an extraordinarily dangerous game,' I said, knowing that would not change anything. 'How does getting involved help us gain what we need?'

'Eric, we are playing the most dangerous game there is, for that is the *only* way to gain what I seek.'

6

We set out from the grand naval harbour on the south side of Constantinople that afternoon, Harald and I still chewing over the strange conversation with Zoe, and wondering how on earth it could matter, away on campaign. If the emperor came to kill her while we were away, what could we do?

But Harald was sure that would not happen. The empress was far too popular and important to dispose of so openly. Even Theodora, twice a failed usurper, had been too beloved to execute. The sisters were the very image of the ruling dynasty that had raised the Greek Empire up from a denuded rump to the great power it was in that day. They had been born in the purple as the Greeks called it, raised in the palace nursery reserved for the children of emperors with its purple marbled walls. They were untouchable.

Well, that is what he was so sure of. I had my doubts. But what could we do? Nothing, not then. So all we could do was focus on our task, the war against the caliph and his pirates.

It was our first time on one of the Greek ships, a dromon. A dromon is a very hard thing to describe to someone who has only seen our longships and the fat trading vessels of the Franks and Saxons. It is long and not very broad, but its sides are nearly straight, not curved. It is tall too, because unlike our ships, it has two decks of rowers, sitting one above the other like a large hall, but with less space between levels. The upper level sat in the main deck, like in our longships, but the boat was so deep that beneath them the others sat, still above the water.

This meant the ships were heavy and lay very deep in the water. They were not river ships, they were made for the open sea. They were powered by one or two triangular sails, depending on the size of the ship, and just like us, took the sails down for battle or to go into harbour.

On the stern is a large steering area, and in the bow a fighting platform. Now, the way of making war at sea in the empire is far removed to our own. Our ancestors for generations past fought in ships the same way: you bring your ships together in great rafts, move them towards the enemy who do likewise, and then fight a battle as if on land.

The Greeks use the ships themselves as weapons. There is a great iron reinforced spike on the front of the ship like a spear, low at the bow and then rising. This spike is used to ride over the oars of an opposing ship and fold or snap them with the weight of the onrushing ship, immobilising the opponent and causing carnage inside their hull, with men crushed by the chaos of broken and twisting oars.

But in that regards the empire have one advantage that none other on that sea has: their ships breathe fire.

Hah! Yes, you can laugh all you want. You think I am an old man telling stories, an addled mind embellishing the tales of his youth. Well, it is true, although a man has to see it happen to understand it fully. Later I will tell you of the first time I saw it.

So, we boarded our ships and to my surprise we were not assigned to oars. We were well-used to rowing, and expected to be used as such. But the rowers were all Greek professionals, men of the navy who had served for twenty years. They would no more have allowed us to join them at the oars than we would have invited them to don our cloaks and stand in the shield wall with us. Each bandon was split onto two ships. I was with the first half of seventh bandon.

We were given space on the deck to put our things, and old sails were rigged up to shade us. So we were cargo, like sheep or goats. In battle our duty was to repel boarders or to board enemy ships that were not burned with the fire. In this campaign we would also be landed to root out the nests of the pirates.

Well, I would like to tell you where we sailed, but no one saw fit to tell us. We passed a great many arid islands and a rugged coastline dotted with fortified towns and fishing villages as we sailed south. At every port where we stopped for the night other ships would join us, until our fleet was half a hundred ships. A vast and impressive sight at sail on the sea each morning.

It was at least five days like that, gathering the fleet, before we arrived on the south side of the Anatolian region where the pirates were supposed to be preying.

Look, I say they were pirates, but this was not a few opportunistic thieves. It was a great mass organised with a single purpose in mind: to cut off the empire from its easternmost ports to help in their capture.

There were reported to be more than a hundred ships of all types and sizes involved. They would outnumber us three to one, but that did not concern our leaders. We were a trained and organised fleet of large warships, and they were not.

What day at sea was it when we first sighted a group of them? I don't know. Perhaps it was the seventh or eighth day. No matter. The point was we were so bored and sun sore and restless that merely seeing a half dozen sails on the horizon was a huge excitement for us.

The enemy turned and fled as soon as they saw us, of course. We followed for a good time, but eventually we had to turn back to our safe harbour; we could not risk chasing them into the night, or putting ashore in enemy territory and losing the fleet to a burning in the darkness. Or so the commanders thought. I felt differently, and I knew Harald would be chafing at whoever would listen to press the chase regardless.

Well, this pattern continued for weeks. We sailed in force, sometimes all together, sometimes in groups of ten or fifteen ships. We sailed up and down the coast between safe harbours, chased pirates away, escorted supply ships that were stranded in port, and achieved very little.

One evening, in a walled harbour on the great island fortress of Kypros, Harald came and found me on the dock, and his mood was dark.

'I don't need to hear your thoughts, Harald. I can read them on your face,' I said with a grin, beckoning him to a seat on the stone wall where we were resting.

'Our leaders are cowards,' he spat.

'Our leaders are not in charge,' said one of the other men. 'The admiral is, and he is careful.'

'We should pursue the enemy more aggressively.'

'Maybe, but then we would be scattered, and vulnerable at night. We might lose ships to raids and ambushes, and ships are very hard to replace – much harder than us.'

'Well then they should put us ashore and let us clear the land, remove the enemy's places of hiding.'

'And then, if the whole pirate fleet turns on the navy? Without us on board they might lose a battle. Ships are hard to replace, and losing a fleet would cost us half the empire,' said the Varangian veteran, unconcerned.

Harald sighed. 'Then what is the point of this? We were not sent here to avoid defeat, we were sent here to win.'

'I agree, but this is merely the opening phase, Harald. You are new to this, but the empire has been fighting on the sea for a thousand years. It can be slow, and frustrating, but eventually sustained pressure will wear them down and we will corner them.'

Harald bristled at the mild insult. 'And how long will that take? How many more towns and fortresses will be lost while we wait?'

The Varangian dipped his head in acknowledgement. 'It is a risk. Our enemy is not idle.'

'Yet we are,' spat Harald. Then he stood. 'I'm going to speak with Báulfr.'

The Varangian laughed. 'And why would he speak to you?'

Harald grinned. 'Everyone does.' He waved at me. 'Come, Eric. It always looks better to have men at your shoulder.'

I groaned in annoyance, more interested in sitting with my back to the cool stone after a hot day at sea than listening to Harald arguing with our leaders, but I hauled myself to my feet and followed him down the harbourside in the warm, humid evening air.

It is a very strange place, the far south. The heat in summer can be unbearable, although it is often better at sea than inland. Inland there is often nothing but dirt and sand. But even in the evening it can be hotter than a summer day here in Norway. All manner of strange insects come out in the evening on the coastal areas, and they chatter and chirp and rattle and make noises that you cannot understand, from hidden places that you never see.

Well, we walked along the dock in the evening light with the gentle chatter of the strange creatures and we found Báulfr and other leaders gathered around a table as they did every evening. My komes Eyvindr was there, and Aki, and I put a hand on Harald's arm, worried he would barge into the meeting and achieve nothing. Remember, he had no authority there officially – he was just a junior guardsman, although in practice who he was was well-known, and the fact he had arrived with a hundred men and a reputation for great victories gave him influence and respect.

'Wait, don't rush in, not this time,' I whispered in his ear.

'Eric, you know me too well,' he replied, and I let go of his arm.

And then ignored me. By the gods, the balls on that man. He strode into the meeting like he belonged there, and all eyes were upon him, and not many of them friendly.

'What do you want, Nordbrikt?' said Aki. 'Styrbjorn is not here, if you seek commands.'

'I do not.'

'Then wait.'

'I would prefer not to. We have done enough waiting for a lifetime.'

Well, that darkened the mood as much as you would expect.

'You are out of place, guardsman,' growled Báulfr.

'I am. Perhaps send me away. I suggest to wherever the enemy is, for surely they are not here,' he said, meeting Báulfr's gaze and not wavering.

'This is an overzealous new recruit, drunk on dreams of glory, with no knowledge of how we make war,' said Aki with a sneer. 'I will deal with him.' Aki walked over and put his hand on Harald's shoulder to push him away, but Harald was immovable.

'Give me my men and three other ships and let us take this war to the enemy where they are, not where they are not.' He looked at Báulfr. 'It is true I do not understand your way of war, but you do not know mine. Give me four hundred men and the freedom to cause trouble and I will find a way to victory. I always do.'

'You imagine we have not considered these things, guardsman?' said Báulfr in annoyance. 'Your arrogance is astounding. We are meeting on this very subject. It has always been part of our plans, but we must be cautious with the admiral and his ships, neither of which belong to us.'

'Then what can we do?'

'If we land all of our men to chase bandits, the fleet will be vulnerable without us to fight with them. We must choose our moment carefully, and the last few weeks we have been testing their reactions, gathering information – this is the way of war done by professionals, not children.'

'So begone, child,' said Aki with blazing eyes. 'You will be disciplined later.'

'Just give me the men and I *will* be gone. We can stand here all day arguing about rank and authority and rules and ways of war. But how many enemy ships will that sink? How many soldiers will that clash of words kill? For weeks we have achieved nothing because we risk nothing.' I was shocked at the arrogance and insolence of the words, even from Harald.

Báulfr did not react immediately, and, looking around the group, I could see that Harald's words were being received far more sympathetically than I expected. It was apparent that perhaps many of the leaders wanted to be more aggressive, but none dared challenge the emperor's authority. Well, sometimes you need a man like Harald to do the stupid thing that no one else will do.

'And whose bandon do you think we will strip to give to you?' said Aki derisively.

'He can have mine.'

We all looked around the circle in surprise and our eyes landed on Eyvindr. The Varangian looked around and nodded to Báulfr. 'With your permission, I would agree with Harald's plan. I have voiced it before. We need to strike at their nests, not chase them around the sea.'

'And you would put your bandon under his command?'

'By the saints, no,' said Eyvindr with a laugh. 'But I would go with him and control his anger. Let this pup prove his bite matches his bark.' He looked at Báulfr. 'It would get his yapping away from you, and not weaken our forces significantly.'

Báulfr nodded his head slowly. 'A small force to detach and raid their nests, chase their ships to ground. It might shift the balance, force them out into the open where we can do the real work.'

Báulfr thought about it for a while before he spoke again. 'So be it. Eyvindr, take the seventh and Styrbjorn with his twelfth, and your four ships. We sail tomorrow for the Anatolian shore and the day after set out hunting again. If the enemy is sighted in suitable numbers you will be detached to pursue, and run them to ground wherever they may go. Your orders are to destroy them and then return to the fleet. Are your orders clear?'

Eyvindr put his hands on his belt and nodded. 'Yes, Commander.'

'Now get out of my sight,' said Báulfr to Harald. 'And we will speak when you return, at length.' And his look promised what manner of meeting that would be.

Harald had the good sense to look humbled and he bowed before turning to leave without a word.

'That went well,' he said with a joyous smile as we left.

'Did it? You have made some powerful enemies, and undermined our commander. You are insane. I asked you not to force your way in like that.'

'You did, Eric, you did. But while I value your advice I do not always agree with it. And of course it went well. We are going to war, for real now.' He looked at me with a big smile and slapped me on the shoulder. 'And what could be better than that?'

7

'Sails!' came the shout from the watcher in the bow. I sprang to my feet and looked to the horizon where the man was pointing. I could barely make out what he was looking at, but I saw a smudge against the haze of the midday sea and soon that smudge grew into more of a defined shape.

We had sailed north and then east along the Anatolian shore, following the coastline towards the distant bay of Antioch, some hundred miles to our east.

We were at the front of the great crescent sweep of the imperial fleet, the seventh and twelfth banda in the four fastest ships. Away to our left and right the rest of the ships spread out for several miles like a great net, with the intention of sweeping along the shore and driving all enemy before us.

Soon the scene before us became clear. A large single ship was being chased towards us by half a dozen or so others. The pursuers looked close to their prey and the gap was closing. It had to be pirates chasing some sort of trader.

'Who will reach them first?' I asked one of the crew standing in the bow, readying the ship for battle.

He looked up and squinted. 'If they are brave, the Moslems will. But they are not brave, they will turn away. They would have no time to escape with their prize anyway.'

Well, he was right. The pirates had almost caught their quarry when they finally turned and started running back the way they had come. We passed the pursued ship, a big Italian trader, and continued, waving back as they shouted their thanks and relief across the water. We had just saved them from a lifetime of slavery.

Eyvindr was on the same ship as me, and he came into the bow, looking at the scene ahead and then across at the admiral's ship. A man in the bow of that ship raised a red banner on a pole and waved it side to side, twice, and then dipped it before putting it down completely.

Eyvindr smiled wolfishly and looked at me.

'We are released?'

'The signal is to give chase.' He turned to look at the steering deck at the aft of the ship, but I could see the captain was already reacting, shouting orders to his men to trim the huge triangular sail. It had been let out loosely, spilling wind to let the slower ships of the fleet keep up. Now the crew hauled in on the ropes controlling it and brought it tighter to the wind that was coming across the side of the ship, cutting across our path.

I could feel the ship react immediately, with a low groan and a rumble as it tilted slightly more to the left and started picking up speed, and the rigging protested and strained.

'Will we catch them?' I asked.

'Too early to tell. They probably don't expect us to chase, I think they let us get a little too close. Perhaps we will reach their heels before nightfall.'

As the sun raced across the sky, and the four ships of our little hunting party raced away across the open sea in pursuit, it become clear we were as fast as the bulk of the enemy ships, if not slightly faster.

The captain coaxed everything he could from the sail, fussing over it, berating the helmsman for being too heavy on his steering oars, and shouting at men to sit on the windward side, to balance the ship perfectly in the water.

His efforts paid off, and we drew ahead even of our companions, the sleek bow cutting through the warm waters and white, turbulent currents being left in our wake.

One of the enemy ships was struggling, slower and left behind by its fellows. I do not know what was wrong. Perhaps they had been at sea for too long between cleanings and their hull was fouled with weed and barnacles. Perhaps they had a damaged sail, or their hull was old and crooked. We will never know. But either way, we were reeling them in faster than the sun was falling from the sky.

The captain came up to the bow for a better view, and spoke to Eyvindr. 'We will catch them well before evening. We must not let them slow us.'

'No boarding?'

'No boarding,' agreed the captain.

'We give them the fire?' asked Eyvindr, with nervousness in his eyes. He had the right to be nervous. Fire on any ship is dangerous, and sometimes the mysterious system below our feet would fail when heated ready for battle, setting fire to the ship, or even exploding.

The captain nodded. 'We give them the fire.' And a cruel grin spread across his face.

He climbed down to the guarded door to the forward compartment, and spoke to the two men standing watch there. Even the captain was not allowed inside that room, and we had all been warned that to try and enter meant death. I knew nothing of what lay inside, except that it was where the fire weapon was stored, and the men who served it.

I looked at Eyvindr, his neatly trimmed and tied beard fluttering around his neck in the stout wind, his narrowed eyes glaring at the enemy in front, the unmistakable hunter's smile of satisfaction on his face. 'How do we use the fire?' I was nervous, for fire in a wooden ship was a terrifying thing.

Eyvindr beckoned me, and we walked over to the prow, stepping right up onto the step archers used, and he leaned over and pointed down. I joined him, and there, just below the prow of the ship, was the bronze lion figurehead, mouth open, snarling and gleaming in the sun.

Even as we watched, a long bronze tube extended out from it, dark and blackened, the thickness of a man's thigh at its base and of an eye socket at its soot-covered tip.

'What manner of device is that? How does that send fire into an enemy ship?'

'How it works? I do not know. None except the emperor's engineers and the men who serve the contraption know. It is the empire's most closely guarded secret.'

'You really don't know?'

'No. If the enemy learn of its methods, the empire loses its advantage at sea. And we need the advantage, for our enemy is far more numerous than us.'

I looked down at the bronze tube again, even as a gout of foul-smelling vapour belched from its tip and I jerked my head back in fear, much to Eyvindr's amusement.

'Come, the best way to understand it is to see it work. It should not be too long.' We stepped back down into the shelter of the hull and soon after that we smelt smoke. Curls of it came up through the gaps between the planks at the edges of the deck we stood on. It was nerve-wracking. It was the first time I had experienced that, knowing a fire was building in a wooden ship somewhere below me.

Crewmembers dropped wooden buckets on ropes over the sides of the ship and hauled them up, starting to soak the timbers around the bow, repeatedly dousing them in water until it no longer drank the moisture through its surface. A wise precaution to my mind. I was tempted to douse myself.

I looked forwards again and saw that we were nearing the enemy, close enough to see their crew panicking and the captain shouting at his men. Around us, the sailors were preparing for battle, archers setting up their positions, rowers getting into their benches in case they were needed.

Ahead of us, the pirate captain made a last desperate move to avoid us by putting all his oars in the water, dumping his sail onto the deck, and trying to turn into the wind. If he could row up into the wind, where we could not follow without also dropping our sails, he might force us to give up the chase.

Well, our captain was well ahead of his thoughts, and he leaned into the rudders, taking us up, closer to the wind, soaring as if to pass across his enemy's bows. Our ship groaned and leaned, the sail brought right in close, taught and straining. The pirate saw us going up over him and he ordered his rowers to turn him hard to the left, trying to make us overshoot and skip past under our more cumbersome sail.

But whatever he tried, our captain was ready, and he screamed at the crew to slacken the sail, and, choosing his moment, leaned hard into the rudders again, bringing our bow down in line with the rapidly approaching enemy stern, dead ahead of us.

'Oars out and high!' screamed the captain, and the rowers all stuck their oars out through the oarlocks, holding them above the water, ready for immediate use.

'Loose the sail,' he shouted, and three crew unhitched the rope holding the sail against the wind, letting it fly freely, instantly taking the power out of our ship, even as we cruised up behind our prey, almost to touching distance. I stood on the archers' step, transfixed by the skill of it all, as the archers around me poured shafts into the enemy hull, sowing chaos on their deck and in their rowers, preventing them from manoeuvring any further.

There was a moment of balance, where we stopped catching up to the enemy ship, a mere dozen steps behind it, and our speeds matched. With the timing and precision of a court composer, the captain had brought the point of that blackened bronze tube into place above and behind the enemy steering deck. The pirates, looking back and seeing what was about to happen, fell into complete panic. The steersman, too afraid or too stubborn to abandon his post, simply looked up at us with wide eyes and a slack-jawed mouth.

'Release!' shouted the crew leader in the bow, and the gates of hell opened below me.

I had expected flames like from a stoked forge, or something of the kind. I could not have been more wrong. There was a whistling sound, like storm wind through an open window, and then a boiling mass of fumes and intense-smelling oil spat from the tube, blasting forwards and reaching out towards the enemy vessel. As the foul concoction arced through the air, it ignited.

The wave of heat blew me backwards, hands instinctively covering my face as I felt my eyebrows burn and my skin sear. I stepped back in horror and looked up again, just in time to see the burning stream of foulness hit the enemy deck and splash and flow, waves of fire and smoke spilling across the deck, the rear benches, and the steersman.

He lit like a human candle, every part of his exposed body doused in flames. The man batted at his face and chest for a moment, and then staggered to the side, rolling over and splashing into the sea. The flames spread as even more of the evil liquid rushed from the tube, spluttering to a climax and then ending with a whimper, curls of burning oil drooling from the hellish tube, burning and smoking, drops hissing and sizzling against the wetted hull.

I leaned forwards again, looking down, to find that the sea itself between the two ships was on fire where the oil clung to the surface in swirling patches.

'Left oars, drag!' shouted the captain, and the left bank of rowers dumped their oar-blades into the sea in unison, jamming them into the water to slow our progress. The bow swung around to the left, sliding past the burning water and the slowing, careening Arab ship.

The oil was washing through their hull, still burning. I watched with horrible fascination as the fire found its way down into the lower deck, moving wherever it could, fire and smoke rippling and bursting through the oar holes of the lower deck from the stern halfway towards the bow. Burning men climbed out of the lower decks or jumped into the sea, and the screams of the anguished filled the air to the point where I wanted to put my hands over my hears.

'Sweet Mary protect us,' I muttered, appalled and horrified, exhilarated and amazed. I had never seen anything like it in my life, a weapon of such appalling power and hate.

The enemy ship was dead in the water now, the wave of oil burning exhausted, but leaving the flaming timbers behind, the whole aft of the ship engulfed in flames that ate the sail even as I watched, and charred the timbers.

'Oars in, sail up!' shouted the captain, and we swept past the doomed, burning ship, the flames and the cries and the misery receding behind us as we powered up again and set off after the others.

I stood there, amazed at what I had witnessed. Eyvindr chuckled beside me, pointing at the bronze tube, still smoking and air shimmering around it from the heat.

'That is where the true power of the empire comes from. Not from our money, for the Moslems are as rich or richer. Not from our soldiers, for our enemies have more men. Not even from us Varangians, for we are too few.

'The fire of the Greeks – that is the thing that keeps the empire's domination of the seas, and with it, our grip on the empire in the face of so many enemies. And now you understand how.' He slapped me on the back and left me standing there, staring into the rushing water.

* * *

We did not catch the other pirates before evening. I suppose they had not expected us to chase them so far, for we never had before. They had expected to sail out into the open sea, wait for us to give up the chase and continue along the coast, and then head back. When we did not, they were forced to turn north and run for the land, sitting just over the horizon.

Our fleet would have swept along the coast of the wide bay. We were chasing the pirates across its neck and would arrive on the looming shore far ahead of them, isolated. As the sun dipped down towards the sea behind us, the land grew and grew in front, and we saw that we would be arriving at the shore almost at nightfall. A night landing is a dangerous thing, but if the pirates stayed at sea we would have to abandon the pursuit, it was too dangerous to continue.

The pirates chose to spend the night at sea. It was a desperate move, but the only way they could avoid us.

As the darkness started to close we broke off the pursuit and headed for the beach, running the ships up the gentle slope and then anchoring them in place as best we could with anchor stones, their sterns still in the water. They were far too heavy to completely haul out, as we would have done with our own ships.

We set out a strong camp between two of our ships. We had no wine or ale to celebrate our small victory, but spirits were high and Harald came and found me, Afra and Thorir too, and he shook his head in amazement. 'The Greek fire, it was wondrous to behold.'

'It was terrifying,' I said, 'even standing behind it, not in front.'

'Let us never make enemies with the empire then,' replied Harald with a joking smile, teeth pale in the moonlight.

'What do we do tomorrow?' I asked.

'We will sweep the coast again in the morning,' said the ship's captain. 'Perhaps we will catch more of them this time.'

Harald shook his head. 'It will never work unless we find and destroy the inland villages and hideaways where these rats are supported. They will sail out to sea, avoid our fleet, and come back in behind us. We cannot destroy them one by one at sea.'

The captain shrugged. 'That is not our concern. We were ordered to return within three days and we shall.' He gave Harald a harsh look in the firelight.

Harald grunted in frustration. 'An empire full of men just trying to do their duty and no more. No wonder so little is achieved with so little vision of how things could be.'

The captain bristled and turned towards the taller man, but Eyvindr stepped between them. 'No, leave it,' he said, looking at the captain, who nodded gruffly and turned away, muttering. 'Nordbrikt, contain yourself. You cannot understand your fortune that you were allowed even this after your behaviour. Only your name protects you, and that defence is wearing thin. I share your frustration, but you have so much to learn of the way the empire works. You must adapt to the empire's ways, if you are to prosper.'

Harald listened and then shook his head. 'No, it is the ways of the empire that must adapt if it is to prosper. I will break them myself and reform them, if I have to.' Then he simply walked away.

Eyvindr sighed and looked at me with a mocking expression. 'I sometimes cannot tell if your prince there is an idiot or if he is joking.'

I laughed. 'Well, he isn't joking, and every man so far who has thought him an idiot has been made to look like one by his actions.'

Eyvindr screwed up his face in disbelief as he stared at me in the firelight. 'He is so dangerously close to speaking mutiny and treason, Eric.'

I gave my commander my best haughty stare. 'Dangerously close is where we live, komes.' It was unfair, truly. Eyvindr had offered to lead this expedition, saved Harald from himself. But all I saw was another of Harald's victories we were certain to come by if we pressed the pirates more aggressively, another brick of evidence in the wall of his greatness. I believed it; I believed in his infallibility, in the impossibility of his defeat or death. We were the blood-marked, the kin of kings, men of destiny in an army of slavish functionaries.

Ah, the arrogance of the young. Eyvindr glared at me in fury, his jaw and fist tensing and shifting in anger, and then he shook it off and stalked away towards our camp, on the beach in front of our ship.

8

We were woken as dawn broke over the beach. We had left a strong guard watching the camp all night, in case the surviving pirates made an attempt to attack us. But there was no sign of them and the morning was cold and rain was in the air. Waves were already building on the sea beyond the cove where we were beached, and our ships were rocking and grinding languidly in the slight surf.

The captains gave the orders to pack everything into the ships and prepare to make way. There was an urgency to it. No shipmaster would want to watch his ship rock in the waves like that, and, if we waited too long, the weather might pin us in place on the shore.

I packed up my simple sleeping gear and the broad linen sheet that had covered a dozen of us, strung between two posts in the sand. I was trudging back down to the ship when the cry came out.

'Sails!' I looked up, more curious than concerned, and saw a man in the stern of the ship next to us pointing out to sea.

My concern melted into fear as I looked at the headland to our east and saw a pair of ships coming around it, then another, and then three more, all within moments. They were not coming from the east, where the imperial fleet was at harbour some forty miles away. These were pirates.

The captain of our ship went up the bow like a cat up a staircase and looked out towards the oncoming ships. He paused for a fraction of a moment, then turned to us and roared at the top of his voice, 'Launch!'

The navy crew was already running; they needed no further instruction. I was frozen, unsure what to do, unsure even how to launch one of these ships. Up and down the beach orders were being shouted; the crews of all four ships were abandoning everything they were carrying, rushing to cut mooring lines and swarm into the ships to run out the oars. They were seasoned professionals and it showed.

I didn't understand at first; why were they running out the oars? I stood there like a simpleton and watched as barely controlled chaos took hold around me. Finally all the oars were in place on the lower deck, halfway out of their holes, and the crew swarmed out of the hull again, the captain shouting more orders from his perch.

'Get on an oar!' shouted one of the Varangians in my ear, and I snapped into action, dumping my kit and following him down into the crowd, finally understanding. A half dozen men got onto each oar and started heaving against them, using them to push the ship down the beach.

I could see now how it worked – the lower oars were run halfway out and wedged under the seats of the deck above, fixing them in place so that you could use them as levers.

The ship started grinding down the beach under the pressure of two hundred men, and then, with a sickening crunch, it stopped dead.

'Push!' shouted the captain again, and we all threw our weight into the oars, but the ship only bobbed a little and in front of me an oar snapped, throwing a half dozen men to the ground in a heap.

The captain shouted frantically at some men near the stern where the ship was now in waist-deep water, and a handful of rowers splashed into the waves, trying to investigate what was wrong. One of them dove down into the water and then reappeared, shouting to the captain as he wiped the water from his eyes.

'There is a rock ledge, just under the stern! We must have passed over it when the water was higher.'

The captain kept his cool, looking around to survey the scene.

I looked up too and saw the half dozen ships rounding the headland were now over a dozen. On my right the other three ships of our fleet were launching, men climbing the oars and knotted ropes dropped over the bows to get into the hulls as they were returned fully to the water.

The beach was strewn with abandoned equipment, bedding, sails, poles and still-burning fires.

'Turn the stern!' shouted the captain. 'That way! Get me around that rock!'

Someone nearby was relaying the orders and fifty or so men gathered near the stern and started shoving it sideways, pushing with all their might, trying to get it past the hidden obstruction.

'Come on, come on,' I whispered to myself nervously, standing by my oar as men around me shouted encouragement. One Varangian was praying, another, a seasoned veteran with a beard of silver, was carefully strapping his helmet on.

The ship started moving, a little at a time, each bounce from a small wave under the stern stepping it to the right by a half stride.

All the other ships were in the water now, lower oars being run out to full length, upper ones joining them in the water.

Half of the small enemy fleet were now angling across the bay, trying to cut off the three of our ships that were rapidly turning on the spot, one bank of oars reversing, the other going forwards, so that they could make a break for open water.

I could see four enemy ships headed straight for us, sails dropping and oars hitting the water, charging in for the kill.

The stern was still bumping along, bit by bit, and the captain roared at us to keep going. We all threw ourselves at the oars, thrashing and churning the sand and water that was washing over my feet, but the ship refused to move out into the waves, instead slewing sideways, broadside on to the surf.

I looked up and saw the enemy, terrifyingly close, and I realised it was too late.

Eyvindr had already had that understanding. 'Varangians to arms! Get your weapons, now! Prepare for boarders!'

The captain, face wild with fear and anger, turned to shout at us to stay on our oars, for without us to help, it was hopeless. But we ignored him. The fight was coming, and we were going to face it with steel in our hands, not wood.

I ran back onto the beach, looking for my kit where I had dumped it. I had no time to put on my maille. I jammed my helmet on my head and lashed my sword-belt around my waist. My spear and shield were on the ship. I left the rest of my equipment and rushed down the beach to where the ship was lying, crooked and beached sideways in the surf, lolling drunkenly with each wave, oars askew and men both rushing into the ship and out of it.

Unarmed men were climbing into the hull and others, with a wild assortment of weapons and armour, were readying themselves to defend it.

Arrows started to flit over the ship as the approaching enemy got into close range. I ran down into the water, avoiding the tangle of oars and the confused men split between trying to push the ship out to sea, and trying to climb into it. It was chaos. Orders were being shouted but so many men were shouting that none of them were being heard. I looked around for Eyvindr and did not see him.

A voice bellowed out at me from above and I saw a guardsman beckoning. I grabbed an oar and lifted myself up, using it as a foothold as I reached up and took his dangling hand, letting him help lift me up to the side.

A sailor went down beside me, howling with an arrow in his guts. I checked my left and saw that one of the enemy vessels had landed a hundred paces down the beach, and dozens of archers were now able to shoot down the side of our ship. In a few moments they were turning the space under our oars into a charnel house as unarmoured, unshielded men were caught bunched together in the chaos.

Suddenly the hand that was hauling on my wrist slackened, and I looked up to see the guardsman's face twist in confusion. His vacant eyes met mine even as his grip relaxed and I fell, catching myself on an oar by my armpit and dangling like a newborn kitten in a bush, scrabbling and panicking, not wanting to fall down between the ship and the seabed as it rolled and ground on the sand and stones.

I finally got my other hand into one of the oar holes in the side of the ship and steadied myself. I looked up to see the Varangian draped over the side, an arrow in the back of his head, sightless eyes staring listlessly at me as he swayed with the motion of the ship.

I hung there, dumbly, not knowing what to do. Arrows were hissing past me, men were falling everywhere, in the surf, off the sides. I could hear them screaming and crying.

The guardsman with the silver beard knelt in the surf, hands shaking like a leaf as he fumbled at an arrow that had gone through his face from one side to the other, bloodied point protruding from under his left eye.

I felt the utter, soul emptying panic drain me as I watched that veteran gasp and whimper, his eyes full of fear and confusion, all my belief in our invulnerability being stripped away.

'Varangians, on me!' came a voice, cutting through my despair, and I heard Eyvindr bellowing from the deck of the ship. Finally I gathered my wits and climbed the last few planks and grasped the rail, hauling myself up and over and sprawling on the deck.

Getting to my feet I saw that my komes was gathering a number of our men near the stern in the partial shelter of the high sides that protected the station of the captain and steersman. A good number of them had shields, and I grabbed a few spears from the deck and slogged over to join them, handing the spares to men who did not have them.

I pressed into the group, taking comfort from how calm and composed many of the guardsmen looked. There were dead and wounded strewn on the deck, but the imperial sailors were no cowards either, and many of the survivors were firing arrows at the oncoming enemy, or preparing to meet boarders with weapons in hand.

Afra and Thorir were there, and Afra's face was grim. I nodded to him sadly, and I could not think what to say. Those brothers had followed us from the disaster at Stiklestad, through all that had followed. Was it just to die on that beach at the far end of the world?

The captain came down the deck towards us, and his face was drawn.

'Can we get off the beach?' asked Eyvindr.

The captain shook his head. 'It is too late to escape.'

'That is not what I asked. Would it not be better to fight them on the water?'

'Komes!' shouted one of the guardsmen, and I turned and saw what he was alerting the commander to. A pair of enemy ships were coming straight at us, only moments away from ramming into our beached hulk.

Beyond them I saw the other three of our ships racing for the open water, leaving us. I felt anger and resentment, but I knew there was nothing they could do. If they turned around to join us they would be lost, and they were too few in number to defeat the ships that were bearing down on them, nor were the fire weapons ready for use.

Eyvindr's face tightened as he saw the enemy coming for us. He knew what I knew – we were not going to win this fight.

'It is too late for that too,' said the captain with resignation.

'Then we defend the ship here,' said Eyvindr solemnly.

'Yes, you need to win me some time.' The captain gave Eyvindr a firm look. 'We cannot let them capture the ship intact.'

Eyvindr looked shocked, and then nodded curtly.

The captain turned and ran away down the deck. He went down to the door leading to the compartment under the bow, where the two guards stood even then, looking calm and determined in the chaos. The captain spoke to them briefly and then they let him through the door and closed it behind him.

'What is he going to do?' I asked dully, as arrows started to rain down on us now that all the easier targets on the beach were gone.

'He will destroy the fire weapon,' replied Eyvindr. 'They cannot be allowed to capture it. Its secrets must be kept. Now, ready yourselves, brothers. We must defend the ship. Let none of them get aboard!'

The guardsmen shouted their acknowledgement and we all put up our shields and moved out from the shelter of the stern, pushing out to meet the enemy who were arriving, the great wooden prow of their ship rushing on with alarming speed, the deck behind lined with men waiting to get aboard and kill us.

There was a great crash and a screeching of tortured wood as the first of the ships rammed into our stricken vessel near the bow, and the sound of cheers and war cries as the enemy crew prepared to board. The sailors and guardsmen aboard shouted back, archers popping out of cover to fire arrows, Varangians screaming obscenities and challenges in Norwegian and Swedish and half a dozen other languages.

'Come, brothers, it is time,' said the komes, pointing at the enemy on the opposing ship, who were preparing to jump across onto our deck.

Then the first and bravest of them made the leap, and he was cut down, and five or six more followed into death without getting a foothold. But a flurry of arrows knocked down a couple of our men and a half dozen more of the enemy jumped into the space that created, and a dozen more followed.

Then the second enemy ship hit us, alongside the first, and with a great rush there were suddenly half a hundred enemy on our deck, hacking and screaming and trying to force us back, with more pouring on all the time.

We fought. Oh, my long-dead brothers, how they fought. We fought like the cornered lions we were. I put my spear into man after man and we turned the deck slick red with blood. These sea raiders had no art for fighting real soldiers. If we had had a hundred armoured guardsmen we would have run them off, I am sure of it.

But there were barely sixty of us left, and we did not have our armour on. Some did not even have helmets and shields.

Enemy fell beneath my spear and my sword, and the swords and axes and fists of my brothers. But one by one, in pairs and clumps, my comrades fell to the deck, or into the rowing benches below, and we shrank back from the rail and we killed and died.

Then there was a scream of warning from behind us, where some sailors with bows were guarding the shoreside rail, and I risked a glance back to see that the enemy were trying to board us from the shore, and our few men defending the rail were getting cut down in a hail of arrows from archers on the beach as they exposed themselves to hack at the pirates climbing the oars.

Eyvindr screamed at a group of guardsmen to go and defend the rail, or we would be attacked from behind and slaughtered. But that weakened our line, and nearer the bow, where the enemy was thickest, the mix of sailors and guardsmen collapsed under an enemy rush, men being cut down or crushed, and the survivors fell back to join us in the middle, stranding a dozen or so men who were left cornered in the bow.

The fighting against us slackened for a moment as the enemy spread out on the deck and caught their breath and their courage. Afra was at my side, and Thorir too, clutching his left arm, his face pale. I could smell acrid smoke.

Finally, the enemy let out a great shout, urged on by their commanders, and they came for us again, charging down the deck in a wave, ten men across, and we met them with shield and spears and slaughter.

It was not enough. Guardsmen in mere tunics went down with wounds maille would have turned aside with ease. Arrows hacked into our flank even as we tried to hold the attack from the bow, and we stepped back again, ceding blood-stained wood and the bodies of our friends.

Back we went, back and further, and as Eyvindr turned to shout an order some fucking pirate put a spear through his neck and he staggered backwards and pitched over the side.

The last vestiges of order went with him. There were only two dozen or so of us Varangians left fighting, and twice that number in sailors. Over the heads of our enemy I saw smoke rising from the decking over the compartment where the fire weapon was hidden. I saw the last of the men defending the bow being cut down and the two guards defending the door with their lives. I saw them finally taken down in a flurry of blows, and I saw a puff of smoke and flames pulse from the small gap around the doorframe.

I looked around as our defence started to collapse, men fighting in clumps and groups and on their own, falling back closer and closer towards the stern even as enemy climbed into the ship from the shore side and cut defenders down from behind.

The whole disaster was towered over menacingly by a rising pall of smoke and flames from the bow. The attack only slackened then because some of the enemy were starting to panic, more intent on getting away from the flames than finishing us off.

Someone grabbed my arm, and Afra's voice shouted in my ear, urging me to go with him. To where? A dozen guardsmen and sailors fought together on my right near the steering oars, where Afra was dragging me. The rest of our crew were lying strewn around and upon the ship, dead or dying or cowering. The pride of the empire, the greatest soldiers in Christendom. Failed, defeated.

Where could we go?

I stumbled after Afra, shoving over an enemy that rushed at me, taking a cut from his spear as I did. I hacked at him with my sword, oddly annoyed to find I still had it. It meant I could still fight, and I had lost interest in fighting. I just wanted it to be over.

'Over the side!' shouted Afra, shoving Thorir towards the rail on the seaward side of the stern. The smaller man went over, clinging on with his good arm. Afra started shoving other men that way, screaming at them to get off the ship. Some complied, some ignored him, some were beyond caring.

I joined the trickle of those who chose to go over the side instead of dying on the deck. Was it cowardice? I don't know. Dying in the stern seemed as good as dying in the shallows. The result would be the same. I just did it because Afra was shouting at me to, and I trusted him.

I tried to climb down, but my hands were tired and slick with blood and I was still clutching my sword, so I slipped, bouncing off an oar and plunging into the shallow water, hard enough to hit the bottom as the water closed over me. Thank the lord I was not in my maille, or I might have drowned in waist-high water when another body dropped onto my chest.

But I had just enough strength and desperation to roll out and rise. I lost my sword, but I got my arms underneath myself and got to my feet. Being above the water was no better than being below. A knot of Varangians and scattered survivors were fighting their way out of the water, and I staggered through the surf to join them as sailors and guardsmen mixed with Arabs, all butchering each other in the sand and the water and the jumble of oars and the hiss and thud of arrows.

There was a hissing, wailing sound from behind me, unlike anything I had heard before. I turned to look towards the bow, and as I did, the whole front of the ship seemed to twist and expand, and then, with a blinding ball of fire, it burst.

It was like someone had stamped on a rotten fruit, except all the rancid juices that sprayed out were flames, and all the chunks of fruity flesh were hunks of torn and splintered wood.

I was knocked off my feet and dazed by the force of it, dumped into the water once more, as was everyone around me. I levered myself up on my elbows, staying in the water because it protected me from the searing heat, putting my arm over my face as the waves of furnace air washed over us.

Then the worst of it passed, and I unshielded my eyes to see the hellish scene that was left behind. The front of the ship was gone, the middle section twisted and burning. A couple of dozen men, ours or theirs it was impossible to tell which, were staggering or flopping around on the sand near where the bow had been, burning, screaming, rolling. Some threw themselves into the water, others simply dropped to the ground and lay there ablaze. It was horrifying.

The fight, such as was left, had completely ended.

'Eric! Let's go!' shouted Afra urgently, and I saw what he saw, that in the chaos, with terrified, burning or dazed men everywhere, we had a slim chance to escape.

'Come, up and go!' Afra hissed at everyone around us, and a few guardsmen who still had their wits about them got to their feet and gathered whoever they could find.

'We run for the trees or we die here!' shouted Afra. 'Go, now!'

I got to my feet and shoved men towards the land, propelling whoever was still too shocked to react. We staggered out of the shallows and the thick, drifting smoke from the burning wreckage, passing burned, stunned or wounded enemy. Then we were on the beach and running through the remains of our camp. I don't know if the enemy even recognised who we were. We were not a formation of Varangians, we were a loose mob of blackened, bloodied, fleeing men, indistinguishable from the dozens of other such men spread out over the sands. Many, like me, didn't even have a weapon or shield left.

We made it to the scrubland behind the beach without much trouble, although shouts were raised behind us and I turned to see men pointing at us.

I ignored them. We went over the brim of the first dusty rise behind the beach and into the scattering of low bushes. Beyond that, up the gentle slope, was a thicker wood that dropped away into a hidden valley, probably leading to the next cove.

'Go, quickly!' I looked around and recognised one of the battered, blackened men as Thorir, and Afra was helping him along. There were less than twenty others, and it was hard to tell who was a guardsman and who was a sailor with the state we were in.

We quickly got out of sight of the beach and into the next valley, and there was no sign of pursuit. Perhaps, after the chaos and the devastation of the fire the enemy simply didn't see the value in chasing a dozen or so wounded survivors.

We flopped down in the shade of some trees to pause and catch our breath, and I watched back along the way we had come, seeing nothing.

'Eric,' Afra whispered in my ear, the big man crouching down beside me. 'We must run, they are here,' he said, with the urgency clear even through his hissing voice.

'Here?' I said in confusion, pointing at the trail we had come down, where we could see for several hundred paces. 'There is no one.'

'No, behind us.'

I turned to look at him and then the dense bushes. It was impossible, they could not have gone around us so quickly.

'Now!' he said, more loudly.

But it was too late. A dozen men erupted from the undergrowth, and then two dozen more, and they were not Greeks. Before we could react they had penned us in in a half-circle, spears and swords and bows pointed at us as we huddled together, not more than a handful of weapons between us and not a single shield.

'We charge them, perhaps some of us will get through. Good luck, my brothers,' said one of the guardsman in a low voice, readying himself to move.

'There is no need for such stupidity,' replied one of the Arabs in heavily accented Greek, stepping forwards and motioning to us to hold. 'You are defeated. All you have left are your lives; I propose to let you keep them.'

'Why?' growled the guardsman, pointing his sword at the pirate and stepping forwards.

'Because you are valuable,' the pirate said with a laugh.

'You mean as slaves?' replied the guardsman. 'I'd rather die.' And without any more posturing, he rushed at the pirate leader. Three of the pirate's men advanced to intercept him and he batted one spear aside but was impaled on another, sinking to his knees with a cry as the iron and wood twisted in his guts, before the pirate leader stepped forwards and half decapitated him with a precise cut from his narrow, curved sword. I am ashamed to say, none of us had the heart left to go to our friend's defence. Not one of us had moved with him.

'Enough of you have died. Life is better than death my friends, and no one doubts your bravery. Come, it is finished.'

The pirate wiped his sword distastefully on the dying Varangian's wet tunic and then glared at us as we looked at each other in despair. The last few weapons dropped to the ground.

We surrendered.

9

Eric looked around the hall, taking in the expressions of the men listening, and then he nodded sadly to himself.

'I see it, the disgust some of you hold for me. Why am I alive, here now, when my comrade died bravely, with his weapon in his hand, and I did not try and help him?' Eric held up his hands in supplication. 'I could give you excuses. I had no weapon, and it is true, but it is not enough. I was wounded, which is also true, but not so badly I could not rise. I was exhausted and dispirited, and that is also true, but not such that my spirit had left me entirely.' He put his hands down on the table in front of him and looked at them. 'No, none of those are the reason that I chose to remain still while my fellow Varangian chose death.'

'Cowardice,' said another man with a sneer, and a muttering of outrage went around the room.

'Do not call him a coward. You have heard what he has done, beyond what any of us have done!' said Jarl Torvald angrily, pointing at the accuser.

'Yet I have never laid down my weapon while my brothers still fight,' said the accuser, pointing back with much greater anger.

'You have never faced such a choice!'

'Enough!' said Eric's old voice with surprising volume, and he waved

Torvald down. 'Let this not be another time where another fights for me when I would not fight for myself.' He gave Torvald a look that brooked no dissent, and waved him down to his seat that he had half risen from. Then he turned to the man in the crowd. 'Cowardice? Yes, it was cowardice. And let me tell you, I was as outraged to find it within myself then as you are now to hear of it,' Eric said with deep bitterness.

The admission took some of the heat out of the angry warrior, and he blinked and then put his hands in his belt. 'So why did you do it?'

Eric nodded, meeting his eye and smiling softly. 'Because I wanted to live. By God, in that moment I realised how much I wanted to live.'

'It is a disgrace.' The warrior shook his head and turned to look around the room, finding some support for his attack, but more sympathy for the old man. 'No one should stay here and listen to this, it will weaken you to even hear of it.' And then he turned and left the room, and a dozen or more others followed him, and Eric nodded sadly.

There was an uncomfortable silence as the rest of the room waited and the old man stared at his hands. Finally he spoke. 'I have had my whole life to be ashamed of it, and forgave myself long ago. If I had died that day, I would never have done all the other worthy deeds that I have done, would never have saved Harald, my king.' Then he smiled and looked around. 'I would never have raised three good children. That washes away all my failings. Let me tell you, I would have sacrificed all my fame, all my wealth, all my skill and life of experience just to have a good family, to be a good father. That is the true glory, that is the true victory.' He met the eyes of a few men who were still looking at him with uncertainty or distaste. 'So go, if you cannot bear to hear of it, or stay and hear of how I lived a life worthy of preserving, and perhaps one day, you will face such a choice, and understand its true meaning.'

* * *

We were stripped of everything except our tunics and shoes. Weapons, belts, armour, helmets, jewellery, arm rings... Everything we owned. Then they tied us together front to back, hands bound at our waists so there was no possibility of escape. I was tied at the front, by chance of fate, and their leader saw my anger and shame and smiled at me. 'You are no Greek, are you?'

I shook my head stiffly, unable to contain my pride. 'I am a Northman,' I replied, for there was no word for our nation in the Greek tongue.

'So are half of your fellows here, I see. That is good. You Varangians always fetch a good price. Rare and strong. Someone will make a mineworker of you, or perhaps a guard.'

'A guard? If any man is fool enough to put a weapon in my hand, I will kill him with it,' I said, with what scrap of foolish pride I had left to me.

The pirate leader took his knife from his belt without pause and handed it to me, so quickly that it was in my bound hands before I could even think. 'Really?' he said with a smile, stepping close, so close that I could have plunged the blade into his stomach easily, even with my bindings.

But I did not, I just looked down in fresh shame.

'That is why you can be trusted with a weapon, if you know using it against your masters will lead to your own death, and those of you who would choose death have already done so.' He stepped closer, so that our noses almost touched. He gazed into my eyes with utter confidence and whispered to me, almost like a lover. 'You see, once a man has decided he would rather live than fight, he rarely changes his mind – not unless he is driven to it by terrible treatment or insanity of the mind.' The pirate leader took the knife back from my unresisting hands.

'The southern caliphates always want fearsome guards, and who could be more fearsome than you Northmen, as my countrymen on the beach found to their cost,' he added with a flash of anger, before looking away to check the rest of the line was ready to leave. 'No, they will treat you well, and you will serve them. Everyone does, for escape is impossible and a terrible death the only result of rebellion. Now start walking, we have many miles to go.'

'Many miles? You are not taking us down to join your comrades?' I said, confused.

The pirate looked at me like I was stupid. 'Those men on the beach? You burned two of their ships, killed hundreds of their men. If I take you down to them they will take you and I will get nothing. They are no friends of mine.'

'Then where?'

'You ask many questions, Northman. You will need to learn better.'

'Just tell me where we are going, if you expect me to walk there.' The pirate glared at me angrily, and then backhanded me across the face with the butt of his dagger. It was a nasty blow, and it cut my cheek and made my jaw ache so badly I was worried it was broken.

I pulled my head up and tried to grimace against the pain, because I could not reach my face with my hands.

'We cannot take you to the Egyptian slave markets until your fleet leaves, so, for now, we will seek shelter among the people of these hills. Many of them are our people, and they will welcome us in exchange for the work you will do for them and the protection we will grant them. These are hard times in these hills. Now, do not ask any more questions.'

* * *

Well, I did not. There was little else to ask. We carried on walking down the coastal path westwards, away from the plume of smoke on the beach, my mind switching off as the horror of our situation fully sunk in.

So, in my state, I did not even notice when our captors started looking nervous, and only knew something was wrong when there was a cry of alarm.

A group of armed men rushed at us from the front from the cover of some scrub, and there was a brief, chaotic fight. I scrambled desperately to the side of the path, trying to get away, but a shouted order in Norse stopped, me, and I turned to see the ambushers finishing off the last of our captors.

Then a man in full maille who I recognised so well stepped forwards, wiping his sword on the hem of his tunic.

'Eric?' he said, his face creasing into a smile of pure joy as I stared into those familiar eyes. He grabbed me by both shoulders and shook me and I just stared at him. 'Eric, I'm so glad you are alive. God, I'm glad. I'm so sorry we left you, Eric. Forgive me, we had no choice.'

'How? How are you here?' I said, ignoring his plea, and then I was buried in a crushing embrace as Harald laughed and shook me, lifting me off my feet.

'How am I here? I came to find you.' He looked around and his eyes lit up when he saw Afra, and he let go of me to give the old bandit no less of an enthusiastic embrace, then Thorir, and then he was slapping backs and shaking arms with all our bedraggled group. He came back to me. 'Eyvindr?'

I met his look dully. 'He died on the ship, along with most of the men. But you came for us?' And I could hardly hold back my tears.

'Of course.'

'But...' I shook my head in disbelief. 'But how?'

'We sailed clear of the bay and saw you surrounded, so we landed down there and came to help.'

'But... you would not have reached us in time.'

'We knew that,' said another voice, and I saw Styrbjorn walking over with a grin. 'But this fool refused to leave without trying.'

'Well, you have my thanks. We were...' I could not bear to say that we were being taken as slaves, the shame of it was galling. 'We can return to your ships and sail back to the fleet?'

Harald looked at me guiltily. 'We had to abandon the ships to the enemy. They landed behind us. We grabbed what we could and left before they arrived.'

My spirit sank again. 'So what do we do? We are trapped. How do we return to the fleet?'

Harald looked at Styrbjorn. 'We had not discussed that yet.'

Styrbjorn nodded ruefully. 'There is an imperial port not too far to the west, perhaps five days' march. We can get a message to the fleet from there. I don't know how we will explain losing four ships and a hundred men; Báulfr will flay us. Perhaps it is better you two don't return.'

'What about you?' I asked.

Styrbjorn laughed. 'It wasn't me who pressured the commander into allowing this foolish mission.'

Harald looked around angrily, thinking. 'No, it is not that we cannot return, it is that we cannot return defeated. We must turn this into a victory.'

'How can you possibly do that?' Styrbjorn said, but I could see he was interested.

'We go east, not west. That is where all the villages and forts and ratholes that support this pirate fleet are, in the hills to the east. We do what we came here to do – we go and clear them. Our ships were just weighing us down. Without them, and with three hundred guardsmen and perhaps some of the sailors, we have a powerful force. Let's use it.'

Styrbjorn rubbed his chin for a moment and looked at Harald. 'That is a remarkably poor plan... But I would rather not go back to our brothers in defeat. Yes, perhaps death or victory is better.'

'I do not intend to die,' said Harald flatly.

'Everything you have done since you first arrived in the city suggests to me that you intend to die stupidly, Harald,' said Styrbjorn, sheathing his sword. 'But I'm willing to try and avoid the disgrace. Come, let us talk to the captains. I suspect they will want nothing to do with it.'

He turned to look at me. 'Take what equipment you can from the dead pirates. We have nothing to spare you, then let's be gone before the enemy find us.'

We did as he suggested, arming ourselves as best we could, which was not well at all. The pirates were mostly smaller men, and little of their armour fitted us. But we at least managed to take weapons.

Rolf Hammerbeard came to greet me, and Rurik. The cousins Ulfr and Halldor came too, as did almost all of the blood-marked, as far as I could tell, and perhaps all but a few of those who had come with us from Kyiv. We were all gathered again, Harald's blood-marked warband. It was perplexing and joyful, despite the pain of those we had just lost.

The captains of the ships we had abandoned were not so enthused by Harald's plan. They had nearly four hundred armed men, but they were sailors not soldiers, and refused to join us, choosing instead to make the five-day march to the nearest port.

We had no choice but to let them go, so we split from them and headed inland, following Harald's ambitions.

***

'Ten armed men on guard,' said one of the scouts, coming back from the ridge where he had been carefully observing the fort. 'Twenty more in and around the fort, four times that number outside the walls, mostly unarmed.'

We had marched inland up a valley all day, searching for somewhere safe to spend the night. We had stumbled across a small, fortified village at the head of the valley, and had carefully approached it to plan our attack.

'Thirty ready to fight? Well, that is hardly worth arming for,' said Styrbjorn with a wicked smile, and some of the men around us laughed.

Then he looked to the scout. 'How high are the walls?'

'Six feet? Mud and brick.'

'We can climb them easily, then.'

I stood up and started strapping my stolen, unfamiliar sword-belt back on.

'Not you, Eric,' said Harald, stepping over towards me and putting a hand on my scabbard. 'You and your men have fought already today, and do not even have armour. Leave this to us.'

I was furious. I was desperate to wipe the shame of our defeat and capture, but he was right. Our few survivors were in no condition to fight again.

So Styrbjorn and Harald took the fourteenth bandon and set out in the cover of a gully and an olive orchard towards the village, while we few survivors of Eyvindr's crew sat with the rest of the seventh in sullen silence.

It was an odd atmosphere. They were our comrades, but some divide had permanently been made by those shamed to have been defeated, and those shamed by the association with us. Or perhaps it was their guilt at not fighting at our side, I don't know. I didn't blame them for leaving, but perhaps they blamed themselves. They had fled while our komes and our banner were lost. Until we had a new banner, we were not real guardsman. That's how I thought of it, anyway.

We sat there for a while as the sun sank and the shadows lengthened and then the two men who had been watching from the ridgeline wandered down. 'It's done,' one of them said, and everyone stood up, stretching and picking up their bags and shields.

'They better have a good well,' grumbled one man.

* * *

When we arrived at the fort we found men clearing a clutch of bodies from around the large wooden gate. Almost all Arabs, dumped into a pile, but a single Varangian was laid out to one side alone, hands on his chest, blood soaking his stolen tunic.

'They fought bravely, I suppose,' said Harald, walking over to me, his right side sheeted in blood. I looked at it in alarm.

Harald followed my gaze and looked at his arm. 'Oh, it's not mine,' he said, then he looked at me with narrowed eyes. 'What is wrong, Eric?'

I tried to shrug it away, but I felt hollow and nervous, fear balling in the pit of my stomach. Harald saw through my feigned nonchalance and put a hand on my shoulder, leaning in. 'Eric, there is no shame in what happened. You fought like lions, and no man holds your capture against you.'

For all my concern that was what the other men must have thought, just hearing Harald trying clumsily to reassure me it was not true made me suddenly realise it certainly was. To my comrades I was a disgrace. A man who had been defeated and captured, who had run when so many others stood and died. The shame of it nearly broke me, right there, among the bodies. What if my brothers never trusted me again? What if I could never trust myself again?

I looked at him with fresh hurt and he frowned, embarrassed by my weakness and letting go, standing there stiffly and looking at me in discomfort. Oh, that nearly killed me, to see his suppressed disgust.

'Go and find somewhere to rest, Eric. I am sure you need food and water and sleep, and the buildings inside will have all of that.'

I nodded, unable to keep eye contact, and went through the gate. Men made way for me, not out of respect, but surely out of fear, fear of being near such failure and shame. Or so it seemed to me. Maybe it was simply the smell of a man who had not washed for weeks.

Well, I did find water and food, although both were terrible. Cloudy well water, day-old bread and older meat. I washed with a bucket of the same stale water and then I found a quiet corner in a dusty, dilapidated mudbrick house and I lay down and tried to muffle the sound of my tears.

Ah, you came to hear the glorious story of Eric Sveitungr, huskarl of King Harald the hard ruler! Hah! You did not expect to hear of me scared and defeated and weeping in corners, did you? Well that is because you have never seen war, not real war. It breaks men, and the strongest, biggest, loudest and most proud it breaks first of all, for their pride cannot survive the depredations and horror of defeat or humiliation, or of watching your friends die as their wounds rot and eat at them. It cannot stand the constant fear of the enemy or of battle chipping away at your courage.

Bah, I see those of you who don't understand, who think I must be ashamed to say such things, to admit such weakness! But I am not. There are many things I am ashamed of in my life, but fear is not one of them, showing weakness is not one of them. A man who has found no weakness inside himself is a man who has never been fully tested, never taken to the edge of what he is willing to do, never watched as his strong, brave friends die and scream for their mothers or clutch at their insides flowing from ragged wounds in their once glorious bodies.

No, I am not ashamed, because I survived these things with my mind intact. I cried in those corners and yet I overcame it and I won, despite my lowest days.

Above all, I cannot be shamed because I walked the breadth and length of the world with Harald Hardrada, and you all know what that means.

10

Eric banged his empty horn mug on the table in annoyance. 'Where is the ale? A man cannot speak all night without ale. Fetch me some, I must go for a short time.'

'Where?' asked Hakon, looking alarmed.

'Outside! I do not need to answer you, small jarl,' Eric said, with a snap of anger that took everyone by surprise.

Ingvarr, mouth agape, scrambled up and out from the bench to let the furious old man out, standing aside as Eric pushed past with surprising strength, men making way and muttering as he walked through the crowded hall and went outside into the growing darkness.

'What happened?' said Ingvarr to his father with concern.

Hakon looked grimly at the door where Eric had disappeared. 'I think recounting the story is difficult for him. I find the more loudly a man protests he is not ashamed, the more likely it is that it burns inside his chest.'

Ingvarr's face fell and he looked at the empty doorway again, then back at his father. 'Well, maybe he should be,' he said haughtily. 'What he told us, of his capture and his cowardice. Maybe he should be ashamed!'

Hakon scowled at him and motioned him to sit down and be quiet.

Too many men had heard the boy's voice, loud with contempt against the background of the low conversation in the hall.

'What do you know of war, boy?' said a booming voice from the back of the hall, near the dais.

Ingvarr turned to retort, but Hakon lunged over the table and grabbed him by the shoulder, thumping him down in his seat, inciting a cry of protest. 'Silence, boy, you sheathe your tongue,' Hakon hissed. Then he looked up at the speaker, a middle-aged man in a fine, gold-edged tunic and wearing a belted sword. Hakon recognised the man – they had met several times – but even if he had not, the fine clothes and the sword identified him to anyone watching. The lord of the hall, Jarl Halfdan.

'I apologise, Lord Halfdan, he knows nothing of war,' Hakon said demurely, and then he too sat. Halfdan gave him a half nod and his eyes moved on.

The jarl walked up the steps to the dais and went to his seat there, looking around the hall as it fell to silence. 'Welcome, all of you, to Tinghaugen and my hall. I hope the ale was acceptable and be assured, now that I am here, we will open the best barrels.'

There was a ripple of polite amusement around the room and Halfdan smiled. 'And I hear the entertainment has been good? We are honoured to welcome Eric Alvarsson, friend of King Harald Sigurdsson. To hear his story in this place is a great privilege, one I suggest you all suitably respect.' And with that, his eyes set on Ingvarr once more.

'You, young lad. You are brave and full of vigour. You are ready to judge more experienced men?'

Ingvarr had the sense not to respond to the mocking provocation. There was some uncomfortable laughter around the room. Jarl Halfdan could destroy the boy's reputation with his words, if he chose to humiliate him.

'Well, are you brave enough to go and find our esteemed guest and guide him back to the hall? For I wish to hear the rest of his story, although I have heard much of it already in the past. I hear rumour this is a legendary recounting, unlike any he has given before.'

Ingvarr looked around nervously, not knowing if the request was genuine.

'Well, are you too afraid to stand up and answer me, boy?' Halfdan's voice was light, but the words cut like the keenest blade.

Ingvarr stood, face blushing bright red. 'I am not, my lord.'

'Ah! Excellent, a brave warrior indeed, to take on such a dangerous quest. While you are out there, consider carefully the wisdom of accusing one of our nation's most famous warriors of cowardice, and perhaps take the opportunity to apologise to him?' Halfdan smiled, but the smile was edged in iron.

Ingvarr, seeing the depth of the mistake he had made, clenched his fist and bowed his head. 'I will, my lord.' And then he scurried from the room.

Halfdan took a magnificent silver-rimmed and handled horn that was brought to him and looked around the room. 'A young boy's pride can be forgiven, but if I hear of any other man disrespecting my guest, I will have words of a very different nature for them. We will listen to Eric's wisdom and experience, not disrespect it.' He nodded with stern finality. 'Now, welcome to my hall, friends. In five days we hold the Frostating to decide the future course of our nation, but for now, we are here to enjoy ourselves! Drink of my ale and eat of my food as brothers. Skol!'

The warriors around the room stood and raised their drinks and shouted enthusiastically back.

Ingvarr went out of the hall, muttering furiously under his breath, putting his fist to his mouth and breathing hard. The indignity and fury he felt at what he had just experienced in the hall clawed at the edges of his vision with red, seeping rage. He wanted to scream in frustration, but there were still men around the entrance, and he stalked away, around the side of the hall, ignoring his quest to find Eric as his thoughts alternated between trying to calm down, and trying to find a way to vent his anger.

He put his hands on the top bar of the rough fence of the next building over and tensed his fingers on it until his knuckles went white in the gloom. He wanted to smash something, to tear it with his bare hands, to destroy it and scream in primal rage at the unfairness of it and of—

'It hurts, doesn't it?' said a voice of gravel, and Ingvarr froze, his hands slackening on the rough wood.

He looked up and saw Eric sitting on a log, his back to the very same fence, almost invisible in the shadow.

'Hearing men speak of you like that, knowing they think of you like that. It hurts more deeply than any weapon's blow.'

Ingvarr's arms and temple pulsed with the heartbeat of his embarrassment, but he could think of nothing to say.

Eric levered himself to his feet and shuffled over, one hand on the rail for support. 'That is what I felt, that a hundred times over, knowing what men thought of me after I was rescued. Its sting hurts me now, seventy years later; that is how deep the wound went.'

Ingvarr gulped and put his aching hands in his belt, staring at the dark ground. 'You said you were not ashamed,' he mumbled.

Eric laughed softly. 'A lie so obvious even you knew it, my boy.'

Ingvarr looked at him, mouth pinched into a thin line. 'Why do you stand it? You could just not have told that part of the story.'

Eric nodded in agreement. 'Yes, I could. I could keep out all the parts of the story that embarrass me to relate, or pain me to recall. But that would be the rankest cowardice and dishonesty, and I would hate myself for it.'

'But now you are shamed, how is that better?' Ingvarr asked, with a tremble in his voice.

'Shame passes, my boy. It feels like it never will, that men will never forget. But the truth is shame is a dog that you can only silence by facing it down, lest it bark and bite at you all your life.'

'Well, I can't go back in there. I was sent to find you, at least tell the jarl I did. But I can't return to that room.'

Eric gave Ingvarr a warm smile. 'Do you want my advice, boy?'

Ingvarr picked at a splinter in his palm and then nodded curtly.

'Good. Well, come back into that hall with me, side by side, foolish smiles on our faces. Face down that fear and banish it.'

'I will be humiliated again.'

'No, no. You will be respected for going back in with good humour. If you go home alone with that dog of shame it will nip and worry at you all night, and in the morning men will see it on your face. Come, walk with me, as Harald once did, and we will face our demons together.'

Ingvarr was taken aback by the comparison, delighted with it, and he managed a nervous smile, but then his face fell, crestfallen. 'I... uh.' He lapsed into silence.

'What is it?'

Ingvarr met the kind old eyes with shame anew and blabbered, 'I was told to apologise to you.'

'For what?'

'I... I am sorry, I was not thinking.' He wrung his hands, not willing to speak it.

Eric laughed gently. 'Come, how bad can it be?'

'I said that maybe you were... maybe you were a coward and that you were rightly ashamed.' Then Ingvarr's head fell, and he stared at his feet.

'Ah, well. Tell me, why do you think that was wrong?' replied Eric, with no trace of anger.

'Because I have never lived what you have lived, I do not know what it was like.'

'Good. A wise man is not one who never makes a mistake, but one for whom a mistake understood is a mistake never repeated.' Eric put his hand on Ingvarr's shoulder for support. 'Now, I forgive you. I have been called much worse things by much worse men. Let us go inside, for the longer we wait, the harder it will be.'

Ingvarr nodded firmly, a smile back on his face, and the two of them walked towards the door, the young man stopping to let the elder go through first.

When they went inside there was a bubble of conversation through the room, which slowly subsided to a hum as they moved through to the central table, Ingvarr trying to keep a calm expression.

'Eric, it is good to see you again, old friend,' called Jarl Halfdan from his seat. 'I was worried you would not be returning to finish your tale.'

Eric smiled and acknowledged the jarl with his hand. 'Well, the boy youngster here came and persuaded me I should return. Me and my foolish pride, eh?'

Ingvarr blushed again, smiled sheepishly at the generous lie and hurried back to his seat, meeting his father's concerned look and trying to reassure him with a nod.

Eric levered himself into his space on the bench and sighed as the weight came off his feet. He raised his refilled mug of ale to the lord of the hall on his dais. 'With your permission, lord?'

'Continue, Eric. I am pleased to hear your words spoken in my hall again; may we all learn from them.'

Eric bowed his head in obvious pleasure at the compliment and smiled broadly. 'Well, then I shall continue.'

* * *

Let us move on from that sad time, for I do not wish to think of it any longer. We took another several dozen strongholds and hideouts of the pirates and their supporters, and we suffered few casualties in return.

For weeks and weeks we moved through those hills, and for every small victory, and at every meeting of our leaders, Harald's ideas and suggestions became more and more like orders, and Styrbjorn more and more gave up the pretence of being in command.

I was largely ignored. The mark of my defeat was still heavy on me, and Harald, Styrbjorn and their closest followers kept their own council. I was forced to wear the armour of dead, better men, and no one willingly came to sit by the fire Afra, Thorir and I shared with some of our fellow survivors.

But the stain faded with time, and with victory. I was allowed to participate in some of the attacks, and once again coated my spear and sword with the blood of our enemies. By then, we were all Harald's warband, and one day I found myself with Styrbjorn on the wall of a small fort we had captured, and my curiosity got the better of me.

Styrbjorn was an odd warrior. He was not born in the North like us. He was, so the story was told, the bastard son of a Varangian guardsman. His Greek mother had died when he was very young and, with no other choice than being abandoned on the streets, he had been raised in the barracks, paying for his keep by sweeping and cleaning. He had lived there his whole life, long after his father had died in battle, become a child of the guard itself until he was old enough to join their ranks.

It had been a rough life, being the only child in a barracks of hard men, and his name, the Goat, was earned because he would eat anything, even fighting dogs for scraps as a child. That was the story I had heard, anyway.

So he was nothing like any of the other guardsmen, but, in many ways, he was more of the guard than anyone else.

'How long have you been komes of the fourteenth?'

Styrbjorn looked at me with an inquisitive eyebrow. 'Why?'

I thought about the wisdom of saying what I was about to say, but I had to know. 'You are the only komes here, but now you openly follow Harald?'

Styrbjorn guffawed and jerked his head in the direction of Harald. 'As he tells it you have been following this man for five years, yes?'

I nodded.

'Then you know trying to lead him is fucking pointless. I would rather comb my beard with an angry porcupine. Anyway, the Greeks like their ranks and their rules, but we Norsemen like leaders who win, and your prince here gets up each morning and shits victory. So yes, for now – as long as he is loyal to the empire and fights the emperor's enemies – I am happy to follow him.' He winked at me. 'It doesn't hurt that if this fails, the blame will fall more on him than on me.'

I chewed that over, not detecting any obvious deception in Styrbjorn's words. 'And when we get back to the army?'

Styrbjorn laughed. 'Aki will gut him, if Báulfr does not do it first, and I will do what I am ordered to do, as always.'

'Won't you be punished for allowing him to do all this?'

'Oh, certainly.' He looked out over the darkness beyond the wall. 'But I have been punished before, I will survive it. I believe in what he is doing. This is our mission, to clear out these pirates on the coast, and he is very good at it. He has ideas that I don't have, an ability to inspire that I was not given. Don't mistake me; in a battle line, commanding my men, I am as aggressive and as dangerous as any man in the guard. But this? An expedition in enemy territory? I have no experience commanding like this, and your prince does. So, I am content to let him command, for now, despite his arrogance and his impudence.'

I finally smiled back at him. 'I think we have much in common, Styrbjorn. It is like listening to another man tell of my own experiences with him. He respects nothing and no one of authority, and rejects most advice I give. But somehow, he keeps surviving and winning, and I keep following him, though it will surely kill me one day soon.'

'But not this day,' said Styrbjorn with a grin.

'No, not this day,' I replied softly.

* * *

Eventually, we made our way all along the coast until we arrived, with little ceremony, at the imperial city of Tarsus. Now, Antioch was still dozens of miles to our south-east, around a very large bay and over another high ridge of hills, but this was the first major imperial-held town we had been near for at least a month, one of the main cities in the province – which the Romans call a theme – of Cibyrrhaeot. It was once a very important theme, but centuries of war and the depredation of the Arabs' raids and conquests had rendered it to a dangerous backwater.

The first thing we learned from the garrison commander was that there had been a great battle at sea the week before. The pirates, having been driven back both at sea and losing their support on land, had gathered together in force to face the imperial fleet and had been destroyed. Well over a hundred ships had been captured, sunk or burned, and the imperial forces were triumphant.

The city was in a state of celebration over it, for they had been cut off and strangled by the pirate hold on the seas and the dangerous bandits that roamed the coastal and inland roads.

There were no ships there to take us to the fleet, which we did not even know the location of, and Styrbjorn sent messages both to Constantinople and Antioch to request orders.

While we waited for a response we had nothing to do but wait. By that time we could not have been gladder of a place to rest, and we were given accommodation by the grateful commander and settled in to wait for a response.

11

Well, it was three weeks before we received a reply. We had been very comfortable in that city, and very few of the men did not feel we had earned the right to some respite. But eventually ships arrived with orders to pick us up and take us to join the army gathering at Antioch, where Báulfr and the rest of the guard were encamped.

It was approaching winter in the year 1035, and here in the North that would mean campaigning season was coming to an end. In the east of the empire, that held no similar meaning. Autumn and even winter merely meant that the sea would be more storm-wracked, but the heat of the day would be far more bearable.

We set sail in the morning and only a day later arrived at the port of St Symeon. St Symeon is the main port of Antioch, being in the same valley and connected to it by an easy road. It is both a military port and a trade port, and the town was small but prosperous. It is named for Saint Symeon, who lived most of his life in prayer atop a pillar in a ruined pagan temple near Antioch. I laughed when I heard that story, for I considered it a ridiculous life. But no city will ever be named after me. My name will die when the last of you stops remembering my story, and his will last until the stones crumble into dust, so who is ridiculous?

Anyway, we landed there and were told that the army was camped just north of Antioch and that the Arab army had broken off its attempted siege at the arrival of the full imperial forces, and was retreating north-east.

We marched the next day, for it was most of a day's travel to reach the great city, and the evening was already upon us.

The road ran along farmland that covered the valley floor, and the valley was so broad that the hills on each side were in the haze on the horizon.

As we approached Antioch we could see from miles away the castle on the steep hillside above the city, and the imposing walls that surrounded it, wall towers and church domes projecting above like a rank of spears and shields, many shimmering with gilt or bronze in the sunlight.

'Antioch,' said Harald. 'Can you believe we see it with our own eyes?'

'It is a marvel,' I replied in complete agreement, for inside I was still the simple farm boy from a Norwegian fjord, who could not believe how vast and wondrous the world truly was. Can I faithfully describe to you what it is like to travel to Antioch, the city from which St Paul set out on his journeys? When I speak to you of these places, I am sure that you cannot imagine them, for my words are insufficient to explain their true nature.

As we approached the city our wonder dimmed. From a distance it had not been obvious how much of the city was ruined, how degraded the walls were, how some of the domed churches we saw were overgrown and abandoned. Antioch had been on the border of the empire and the Arabs for four hundred years, changed hands several times, and was a shadow of its former glory. It was haunting, half abandoned and dismaying.

In fact, the empire lost it again about twenty years ago. Not to the Arabs this time, but to a new tribe of wild horsemen from the steppes, perhaps relatives of the Pechenegs. I was deeply sad when I heard of it, but the empire is disintegrating and it is only one of many tragedies. We fought so hard, and so many of our comrades died for those lands, but most of them are lost now. I hear the crusaders have Antioch under siege, at this very moment, and I pray they retake it and return it to the empire.

Perhaps the empire has the strength to rise again and rule Anatolia. I hope so. So many good men died for that future.

Not that the disintegration of the empire surprises me. As you have heard, and will continue to hear, the rot was already sinking deep into the empire's bones even as we fought there. A rot that seems doomed to end it all together.

Regardless, we marched into that sad city and its faded glories and we were met by Greek soldiers and given directions to the camp of the Varangians. There was a great deal of nervousness in our group. Only Styrbjorn seemed at ease, but he always was. Harald was silent and we followed behind him in a little gaggle, each deep in our thoughts. It was entirely possible we would all be imprisoned, or worse.

Finally we reached the camp of the guard and were stopped at the entrance. The camp had been there long enough that there was a small fieldstone wall and ditch around it. The stones only piled waist high, but combined with the ditch they made a significant obstacle to any surprise attack.

After messages were passed into the centre of the camp, we were allowed through. Komes Aki was waiting for us, his face a mask of anger, and he snapped at the men to establish their quarters, and then pointed at the group of us standing around Styrbjorn. 'Come. The commander is waiting, has been waiting for weeks, and will not wait any longer.'

We followed him towards the centre of the camp, which was laid out in neat rows of tents in a fashion similar to the way the Rus made their camps. We were ushered into the command tent in the centre, where Báulfr was waiting, hands in his belt, face like a stone mask.

Once we had all shuffled in under his gaze, the commander nodded to Aki. 'Thank you, Komes, you may leave us and see to their men.'

Aki looked furious. 'But I—'

'Leave us,' snapped Báulfr. 'I have enough disobedience from these without hearing yours too.'

Aki's mouth slammed shut and he tensed, saluting briefly and leaving the tent.

Báulfr's eyes then swept across us, resting on Styrbjorn. 'Explain yourself, Styrbjorn. From these foreign newcomers I can expect disobedience, but from you?'

Styrbjorn met the commander's gaze and stood his ground. 'I believed what we were doing was serving the empire, and completing our mission. To retreat and return for confirmation would have been to lose our opportunity.'

Báulfr snorted in derision. 'You had orders, not suggestions. You burned three of the navy's precious ships. Three! And for what? Did you even rescue any survivors?'

'Yes, a dozen or so.'

'A dozen men, for three ships?'

'A dozen of our brothers, for three ships.' Styrbjorn shuffled a little but refused to be cowed. I was starting to understand that his name, the Goat, was as much about stubbornness as it was about his willingness to eat almost anything.

'And how many did you lose? How many good guardsmen did you lose to save thirteen defeated cowards?'

I flashed red at that comment, and my fists balled into rocks. Báulfr saw the movement out of the corner of his eye and stamped the three paces over to me. He was shorter than me, not by much, but by enough that I looked down into his eyes as he glared at me. 'Are you one of them? Are you one of the men who shamed our name with your surrender?'

I was caught like a fish on a spear, wriggling and furious. It was true, and I could not deny it without sounding weak, but to accept his words was the ultimate disgrace. I always counselled Harald not to argue with his superiors and commanders, but sometimes it is hard to follow your own advice.

'Cowards?' I managed to hiss through my gritted teeth. 'We destroyed three ships, fought four times our number as our ship burned around us. We survived a month in enemy lands and a dozen battles and yet we still returned here, swords in hand, to meet your judgement, and you call us cowards?'

Báulfr sneered. 'Go on, boy, prove your bravery. Strike me, take up your sword and test yourself against me. I can see you want to.'

And I did, so desperately I wished to spill his blood and wash away my shame with the flow of it. But I resisted and my nails drove gouges into my palms as I strained against the temptation and stared back at him until he nodded. 'I didn't think so.' And then he turned to Harald.

'And it was you. It was you that led these men astray. I knew when you arrived, I knew you would reject our discipline and our traditions, and use your men for your own desires.'

'So you told me,' said Harald. 'And yet here I am.'

'Yes, a decision forced upon me. I had no conception of the scale that mutiny would take.'

'Mutiny? What mutiny? Our fleet was ordered to chase the pirates from the sea, and destroy their support on the land. We did that, ruthlessly. We scoured them from two hundred miles of coastline, drove them back into the sea, where I hear you and the fleet crushed them.'

Báulfr laughed and turned away, walking to the table that was along one side of the tent. 'Yes, so very clever. I hear what you did. And, you cunning little shit, so did the empress.' He picked up a scroll of parchment, looking at it and shaking his head. Then he held it out for Harald, beckoning him to come and collect it.

Harald hesitated for a moment and then took the proffered scroll, reading it, eyes slowly scanning the text, and a small smile grew in the corner of his mouth.

'The empress commends me on my sending you and your men to so aggressively and devoutly clear the pirates and bandits of the Cibyrrhaeot theme's coast. I have her thanks, and...' He waved in amazement at the letter. 'And instruction to reward me,' said Harald with a childish grin, looking up from the parchment.

Báulfr nodded, and he looked at Harald despairingly. 'Once again, my desired way to deal with you is overruled.'

Harald handed back the parchment, which Báulfr discarded on the table. 'I apologise, Commander. I did not do these things to defy you, but out of loyalty to the empire, and to my men and my mission. I would abandon neither.'

'*My* lost men,' Báulfr said softly.

Harald dipped his chin. 'As you say, Commander.'

Báulfr sighed in defeat, all his anger expended. 'You are too ambitious and clever to be a guardsman, Prince Harald. Maybe you were right this time, and indeed, quietly I might agree with you that the course of action was right. But this guard, this army, this *empire*, is built on obedience and organisation. For every man who disobeys orders and is correct, there are ten who would lead us to disaster.'

Harald looked a little guilty, averting his eyes to the side, but Báulfr had no more admonishing left to give.

'And so, to the reward I am ordered to give you,' he said with a pained expression. 'With Eyvindr dead and the banner of the Sea Spears lost...' Báulfr tailed off as Harald's head rose and he started to smile.

'I can't fucking believe I am saying this, because you do not deserve it even if you have earned it, but Harald Nordbrikt, in my position as commander of the Varangian Tagma, I am raising you to the rank of komes and giving you a flag. You will form a new seventh bandon, name it, lead it and carry its banner into battle in the emperor's name.' He reached behind the table and brought out a plain banner, undyed and blank, and proffered it to Harald, who stepped forwards in surprise and glee to receive it.

As he put his hands on the flag, Báulfr didn't let go, clamping his grip down on the fresh fabric. He forced Harald to meet his eye. 'With this flag comes deep responsibility. You commit to treating it as the emperor's honour, to die beneath it if need be, as Eyvindr did. If you disgrace this position, empress's favour or not, I will have you executed. Do you hear me?'

Harald stiffened but nodded confidently. 'It will be my honour. You doubt my priorities, Commander, and I have given you reason, but have no doubt in my loyalty, for when I choose to give it, I give it fully.'

Báulfr stared at Harald for a moment longer and then released his hands, stepping back, leaving the flag in Harald's grasp. 'I am glad to hear it. Now, you will need a name for your bandon, an icon on the flag and a man to bear the banner and be your second.'

Harald stared at the blank cloth for a moment and then smiled, nodding. He turned to look at us: Halldor, Ulfr, Afra and me. And then he stepped over and offered me the flag, smiling broadly as I held my breath and my chin threatened to betray me by falling open in surprise and delight.

'Eric, will you find someone to paint a raven on this?' he said, and my heart fluttered as I was unsure if that was all he meant. He leaned in and then put a hand on my shoulder. 'And then carry it for us.'

I nodded, laughing in relief. 'You want me to be your second?' I asked, the joy of it washing over me.

'As always, as my brother advised me. Will you stand by my side again?'

'Of course,' I said, the pride blooming in my chest. 'As your brother, my king, commanded.'

Harald embraced me and then stood back, thumping me on the back.

'A raven, eh?' said Báulfr with a raised eyebrow. 'I thought you were a Christian, but you take Odin's sigil as your own? The balls on you, boy.' The commander laughed.

'I am a follower of Christ, it is true, but I respect the old ways and I know many guardsmen still hold them close to their hearts. So my bandon will be the Storm Ravens.'

Báulfr nodded thoughtfully. 'It is a good name. Men will like it.' Then he reached out his arm for Harald to take, and the two men shook like friends. Báulfr returned his stern expression to his face. 'Now, get out of my sight. You have work to do.'

Harald thumped his fist on his chest. 'As you say, Commander.' And then he led us back out into the light.

PART II

BANNERMAN

12

The army spent the winter of 1035 around Antioch. The stratopedarches, a Greek nobleman called George Maniakes, would have claimed we were building our forces, scouting, securing our supply and any manner of other activities of war. But we believed he was simply indecisive and afraid.

The caliph's army was large and far more mobile, far better suited to the landscape than ours. They had a secure base at the city of Aleppo, fifty miles to the east, and were able to take towns and fortresses near that before we could react, mocking our leaden efforts to chase them away.

And Maniakes never took his full force from the safety of the valley of Antioch to force the Arabs into the decisive battle that we would need to defeat them, but which would risk so much.

Harald was more sanguine. 'He is following the empire's manuals of war,' he said, as we sat around one evening in early 1036 and moaned about the boredom.

'He is allowing the enemy to take fort after fort, town after town, almost unopposed.'

'None of those are important to the final victory, they are distractions, provocations designed to lure us out.'

'Then what are we doing?'

Harald shrugged. 'That is a good question, but we are preserving our forces, and our chance for victory.'

'Why do you defend this? It is not what you would do.'

'No, it is not what I would do, but then I have never led an army this size or read the empire's military manuals. It seems like cowardice to us, but there is wisdom in those pages. The purpose of the imperial army is victory, victory not in battle but in war, for through victory in war the empire is preserved. The army does not exist to risk its strength for irrelevant little forts and towns of people barely loyal to the empire.'

I was shocked to hear Harald, of all people, defend these things.

'So they are abandoned for the safety of the empire?'

'Yes.'

'And what is the point of the empire if it will not defend its own people?' I said, in outrage.

Harald nodded. 'I consider that myself. I think that the empire is not like a kingdom. In a kingdom, the duty of the king is to his people first. But the emperor is not a king by another name. His duty is only to the empire itself. Honour and duty to the people is not his purpose, only victory and the expansion or maintenance of the empire's power.'

I snorted in disgust. 'That is a disgraceful system.'

'Be careful,' Harald snapped at me, and I saw real anger in his eyes. 'Your words are close to disloyalty, and you would be wise not to speak them, especially where other men can hear.'

I shut my mouth resentfully, and looked around to see if anyone else was, indeed, listening, but it was only Harald, Afra and me around the fire. The rest of our men were spread around our corner of the camp, talking, eating or standing guard.

I looked back at Harald and grunted my assent. 'I still think this strategy of waiting is pointless.'

'I think it is reaching the end of its usefulness, certainly. The enemy has secured so much ground that they can march on Edessa soon.'

'So what? Will that not be sacrificed in turn?'

Harald shook his head. 'No, Edessa is too important to sacrifice. We will surely fight for it.'

'Unless this Maniakes is too craven to march out and face the enemy.'

'No, I do not think he is craven,' said Harald thoughtfully. 'And he cannot lose Edessa even if he is. It was Maniakes who recaptured Edessa five years ago for the empire. I hear it's the accomplishment that elevated him into the standing he currently enjoys. Failing to defend it would end his career, or worse.'

'And what do you think?' I said, looking at Afra, who was propped up on an elbow, staring at the fire without a care on his face.

He looked up at me and shrugged. 'I try not to think about things that do not interest me.'

'How can it not interest you? You make a point of knowing everything.'

He wagged a finger gently. 'No, you are mistaken. I make a point of knowing everything that could benefit me or threaten me. And guessing the intentions of the strategos does not do either. I will lose no sleep over it, and nor should you.'

'He is right,' said Harald.

'That is what I do. I am right about things and I sleep well without concerns,' said Afra with a smug expression. And then he rose to his feet. 'And now is the time for sleep.'

I cursed at him half-heartedly as he laughed and walked away, and then I resumed my grumbling into the fire.

* * *

Being with the army may not have taught me patience, but we learned many other things. It was the first time we had seen the empire's best units arrayed for war in their full equipment. We had seen Bardas's mercenaries in their scale armour, but we had never really examined it, nor seen the truly exceptional sets available to the richest units in the army like the tagma or the imperial cavalry.

Harald was keen to learn everything, as always. The army of the empire had a dazzling array of units and equipment, from all corners and peoples of the vast lands they ruled.

The Varangian guard mostly still went to war in the Northern style that you are used to here. We wore our traditional tunic and maille, with the addition of fine coloured cloaks around the palace and in the regular parades and processions. But the other elite units wore far more complex and heavier armour and some of the banda of the Varangian guard had adopted that equipment in all or in part for going on campaign.

One day in the early part of the year Harald and I walked past the guard armourers' tents and saw one of them repairing lamellar chest armour, which they called a klivanion, for one of the other banda.

'Look at those plates,' said Harald.

'What of it?'

'I bet they stop an arrow,' he said in Norse to me, walking over to inspect them.

The armourer looked up in annoyance at being disturbed, but saw who it was and contented himself with merely grumbling in Greek, not knowing we understood his insults.

'Will this stop an arrow, from close up?' said Harald in Greek, without addressing the fact the armourer had just voiced a theory about our fathers possibly being stinking boars. The man's eyes went wide with fear.

Then he recovered his wits and nodded like we were idiots. 'Of course.'

Harald nodded and looked around the makeshift workshop. 'Show me the rest of it.'

'What?'

'The rest of the armour, show it to me,' Harald said calmly.

The armourer collected a number of different pieces from around the workshop and piled them on the table, one after the other. I was amazed at the sheer number of them.

Now, here in the North, armour is simple and familiar to all of you. If a man can afford it he wears a hauberk of maille and an iron helmet, with a tunic underneath. In the empire, that would be considered fairly light for the elite soldiers, and as the armourer laid it all out it was the first time I had ever seen it all like that.

'We are unfamiliar with this armour. Show me what it all is,' said Harald.

The man sighed and nodded, picking up a thick, padded tunic and handing it over. 'Kavadion,' he said. The tunic was wool and silk, and I felt it and could tell it was many layers thick, thicker around the chest than on the shortened arms, which were a single layer of tough wool.

Then he picked up a hauberk, similar to the ones we wore but shorter, more a shirt than a full tunic, and with lighter, finer maille. 'Lorikion sideron, goes over the kavadion.' He dropped the maille on top of the padded tunic. Then he pointed at the lamellar chest-piece, but did not move it from the rank he was retying it on. 'Klivanion, over the lorikion.'

Then he laid out a pair of smaller pieces of lamellar. 'For the shoulders and arms.' Next he moved over a pair of leather leg armours with metal strips tied to them. 'Podopsella, for the legs.' And then swept it all aside and held up another piece, this time small metal scales woven onto a woollen skirt. He was holding it up by straps that were clearly fitted to go over the shoulders. 'Kremesmata, for the thighs and arse.'

He laid that aside and picked up a larger, sleeveless tunic. 'Over the armour.' He pointed up at the sun. 'For the heat.' He was talking to us like we were children, in simple terms. Presumably he thought we could barely speak the language, and I was starting to get annoyed.

He dropped that and pointed at the helmet, which was similar to ours but peaked with a tuft of feathers. It had a curtain of maille attached to it much like ours sometimes do, except thicker, in two layers.

'For your head,' he said sarcastically, giving Harald an annoyed look. 'Enough?'

Harald looked at it all thoughtfully and nodded. 'I want a set.'

The armourer looked confused. 'You want a set?'

'Yes, I want to try it.'

'Komes, please, we do not make armour here, we only repair it. You could have it made in Constantinople.'

'Only in Constantinople?'

'Well, no, each theme's city has its own workshops.'

'So Antioch has armourers?'

The man paused, seeing where this was going. 'Well, yes, but...'

'Good, then use them.'

'Komes, you can go and treat with them directly yourself.'

Harald shook his head. 'I would not know what to ask for, and you do. I want a complete set, and that is an order not a request.'

The man's protest died in his throat and he looked furious.

'And I will give you this, for whatever you need to purchase.' Harald held up three gold solidi that he had taken from his pouch.

The armourer's expression lightened considerably. 'As you command, Komes. Please, it will take some days. I will send you a boy to get you when it is done.'

'Good.'

The armourer came around the table and inspected Harald, muttering to himself and then toying with the hem of one of Harald's maille sleeves. 'I will not find a lorikion big enough for you, and it will take far too long to make one new. You will have to wear this under the klivanion even though it is too heavy and thick. You are a large man, you should manage. Maybe we will forgo the kremesmata as your maille already covers you there.'

Harald looked at him blankly and the armourer paused nervously, then realised he had forgotten what the word meant. 'The metal skirt,' he added, gesturing to his hips and thighs with his hands.

'Ah, yes. Fine. Whatever you suggest.'

Then the man went back into the makeshift tent workshop and we heard him shouting for one of his assistants.

'It will be far too heavy,' I said dismissively, looking at the enormous pile of armour the man had shown us as an example. 'You won't be able to move properly.'

'Maybe, but I want to try it.'

'Why?'

Harald beckoned me to walk away with him and we headed back towards the camp. 'What is the main weapon that killed our men during all those sieges and stormings last year?'

I thought about it for a while, and could not remember having noted it. Our casualties had been light since we had mostly been fighting unarmoured and unprepared enemies in makeshift forts.

'Arrows,' said Harald, and I nodded because that made sense. Our maille would turn a sword or axe blow easily, and often a spear thrust, but arrows from a powerful bow would go through maille with ease, and when you are storming a wall, it is hard to use your shield to defend yourself against them.

'We are used to fighting on foot in the North, in a wall, against men carrying spears and swords and axes. But our enemy here is mostly mounted, and uses spears and superb bows, both of which can go through our maille, especially from horseback. If that Greek armour can stop an arrow or a spear to the chest, then maybe we should be wearing it. The Greeks themselves do not wear all that extra metal without reason, and they have been fighting this enemy for four hundred years.'

'I suppose so. But I don't know if we can fight in all that. How can you move properly with so much metal on your arms, and clinging to your legs?'

'I suspect that in this type of warfare, moving properly is less important than staying alive and holding formation. It is the cavalry that force the enemy to fight, and only then can we close with them and finish them off.'

That depressed me. I had no interest in merely being a target for arrows. 'How can you be so sure?' I said without thinking, then I held up my hand to forestall his answer. 'No, I know – you read it in the manuals.'

Harald's only answer was a smile.

* * *

Something like a week later and we were at the armourer's tent again and Harald was standing there like a tree, arms outstretched, while two men fitted his new armour, fussing and adjusting. It was not a hot day, but I withered seeing all those layers going on, especially the padded tunic.

'How does it feel?' I asked, when the chest armour had been fitted and Harald was rolling his shoulders and bouncing on his toes to feel the heft.

'Not as bad as I thought. It is carried well across my shoulder and chest.'

'Can you raise your arm?'

He put one arm up and then the other, the lamella shoulder pieces lifting with them and rattling against the maille that hung from his helmet. 'Mostly, it is a bit more limited, but I could hold a shield over my head.' Then he lowered his arms. 'Not for long though.'

'Your hauberk is too heavy, and too long on the arms,' chided the armourer. 'You should have a much lighter one, then you could hold your arms up more easily.'

'And if the maille was lighter, my arms would be vulnerable.'

The man shrugged dismissively. 'That is what your shield is for.'

Harald laughed at being told how to fight by an armourer.

Finally the last leg armour was in place, and he was free to move around. He walked around in a circle, and then ran back and forth. He looked more sluggish, but he was not trudging like I expected.

He drew his sword and did some cuts and swings and overhead defences. 'I like it,' he said, turning to me. 'I could fight in this.' Then he turned to the armourer. 'It's good.'

The man beamed in relief and pride. 'Excellent.'

'Now, I will send you ten more men, and I want armour for them too.'

The man's smile dropped and he gaped. 'Ten?'

'Yes.'

'But Komes, I told you, we don't make armour here, only repairs.'

'You made one set, so you can make ten. I don't care if you have to get every armourer in the city to help. I will give you the gold, you will make me ten.'

The armourer looked defeated and lowered his chin and nodded. 'As you say, Komes.'

'Good. And be quick, I hear rumours that we might be marching soon.'

I didn't give those rumours much weight. There were always rumours that the army would be marching soon, and it never happened. That was life on campaign, sitting around, waiting for the first rumour to come true.

13

FEBRUARY 1036

'The enemy is marching on Edessa. The stratopedarches has given the order that we will go out and face them.'

I looked up at Afra from my meal to see him grinning at me through the flap in my tent. I leapt to my feet. 'We are breaking camp now?'

'What? No, tomorrow at dawn. Sit down, of course not now. When does anything in this army happen immediately?'

I looked back at him with a foolish grin. 'Never. Where is Harald?'

'Meeting with the commander, he told me to tell you.'

'Hmm, well, I should go and get the men to prepare.'

'Yes, that is why I am telling you. It's not one of my duties,' said Afra with a wink, and then he left.

'Fucking bandit,' I muttered under my breath, and then sat down to finish my meal.

* * *

The next morning we marched out, the entire army, over twenty thousand men. It was twice the size of any army we had marched with in the Rus, four times the size of any force I had ever seen in Norway. To add to that we had a baggage train of another ten thousand servants, workers, wagon drivers, horse handlers and every other type of man that the Roman army requires to sustain itself. It was an entire city on the move.

We marched swiftly out of the valley of Antioch, making camp for the night every fifteen or twenty miles. The camping system was fabulously well-organised, and it had to be to allow the army to cover so much ground. The vanguard would set off before camp was even broken, the baggage train would have the camp cleared down before the rearguard had left, and the scouts would have chosen the next site in advance, in familiar lands, often days before. When the vanguard arrived it would push past and set up a defensive cordon, and the baggage train and the main body would set up the camp behind, finishing it in time for the rearguard to arrive and the vanguard to return. It was remarkable.

We passed the great Arab fortress of Aleppo, that had been a Roman city for over five hundred years and was then the northern bastion of the Arab conquest for four hundred more. But we faced no danger there, for the Arab army was ahead of us, marching on Edessa, the easternmost outpost of the empire.

And then we passed from the green hills of Aleppo into the arid plains of Syria. It is almost a dead place, a land made of dirt and rocks and sand, where almost nothing grows without men to water it from deep wells or isolated springs. But villages survive there, scattered in the wilderness, growing olives and raising goats and sheep who feed on the sparse, tough grasses. The whole land is cursed, and I hated it, despite its beauty.

We were in hostile land now, and the army marched in a great moving fortress, all a well-prescribed and practised organisation that took little time to assemble in the morning. The baggage train with the camp equipment, supplies and non-fighting men moved in the centre, following the smoothest terrain, or road if there was one. Ahead of it marched the men of a theme, four thousand or so, in a broad column. To each side of the baggage train marched another theme unit, in a long thin column covering the entire flank, and behind, another column.

We were the vanguard, and marched a half mile ahead of the moving fortress of the main army, ready to be the first to counter any threats. It was the best place to be, for we didn't march in the dust and horse shit of men in front.

Around the whole army, for two or three miles in every direction, banda of light cavalry screened the advance, with parties of scouts beyond that, up to ten or even twenty miles away. No enemy force could get within ten miles of the army without the general being informed.

Behind it all, behind the last of the infantry, the great heavy cavalry tagmata rode as rearguard. When the emperor was going to war it might have been eight thousand or more heavy horseman in full multi-layered armour, the shock force of the empire. On this campaign there were two heavy cavalry tagmata with us, around five thousand men.

As we approached Edessa, we came upon a town that spanned a crossing in the mighty Euphrates, that famous river that turns the arid plains into fertile farmlands for a thousand miles downstream. The Arab garrison fled at our approach, for it had no wall to defend itself, and then we were across the river and nothing stood between us and Edessa.

The commander left a unit of a thousand men to guard the crossing and secure our water supply and the army camped beyond the next ridge, five miles or so from the crossing. With three days' march left to reach Edessa, and the whole country before it now open to us and the army's mounted scouts, we expected to find the enemy and then offer battle within just a few days.

Now, the scouts of the Roman army are the best I have ever encountered. In fact, they do things we Northerners would never even consider. There is a whole manual just about scouting. I know, for Harald read it exhaustively despite it not being one of our duties. As you know, he wanted to learn everything.

Well, part of their unique talents is that the mounted scouts do not wait for morning. In fact, they often prefer to work at night, as do those of the enemy. So while we slept, the scouts went out in the early morning before the sunrise to start exploring this area on the eastern bank of the river that had previously been barred to us by the river.

When we arose with the sun, they had already located the enemy scouts, skirmished with them, and, in places, driven them back and discovered the enemy camp at dawn.

The enemy were not besieging Edessa, they were waiting for us just beyond the next ridge. We had marched straight into their trap.

Was there panic? No. This was an army built on a thousand years of discipline. The army broke camp as fast as possible and formed up into battle formation with the ease and precision of years of practice. We Varangians were the reserve, formed up in our banda behind the main line of the provincial infantry.

I do not know what the general and his officers discussed then – I was not exactly invited to their meeting – but I saw them gathered on horseback in front of us, debating, and then George Maniakes made his decision, and a cloud of officers and messengers dispersed, galloping to the units of the army to deliver his orders. In the centre, the flags and trumpets of the signallers waited for the orders to be disseminated, and then the trumpets were raised to signal the moment to march.

The entire army started forwards as one. Fifteen thousand infantry arrayed across over a mile of ground, with light and heavy cavalry formations on the flanks. A thousand scouts were guarding the baggage train, where every man who could carry a weapon was forming the carts and wagons into a box, a fortress of its own.

We advanced up the shallow ridge in step, a truly magnificent sight; so many armoured men in perfect order. I was carrying our banner, the black raven on a red background, marching at the head of our banda with Harald, my chest bursting with pride.

Up the slope we went, trumpets calling, feet stamping the arid plain into dust. And over the crest to our front came the first wave of the enemy horse, weapons gleaming in the sun, pennons trailing, the cloth wraps on their heads flowing in the breeze as they ran down to meet us.

The trumpets in the centre blared and the whole army came to a halt, officers shouting orders and men shuffling as the ranks were realigned to present a solid front, the only gaps being corridors between units, left to allow movement and prevent one formation fouling another as it turned or changed its angle, but too small and lined with spears for an enemy to risk forcing through.

The enemy horsemen flowed down the slope, thousands of them, but the army did not panic, did not retreat, did not charge. The front ranks put up their shields and their spears and the ranks behind raised theirs, forming a solid barrier to the storm of arrows that was unleashed upon us.

The Arab horse were not in formation to charge, and a frontal charge against the heavy Roman infantry would have been futile in any case. This was all anticipated, it was all in Harald's manuals. In fighting in the Far East, the horseman is king. The infantry exists to be a fortress, a shelter from which your cavalry and archers can operate. The cavalry could not smash that fortress, and we could not chase them; the movement would expose gaps and weaknesses they would exploit with arrows and spears.

It is not to say that we could not fight back. After suffering the first storm of arrows, mostly unharmed in our heavy armour and broad shields, our own skirmishers stepped out of cover to reply. One in every three soldiers of the themes carried a bow or a bag of javelins instead of a spear. The bowmen took up position behind the infantry blocks and started pouring arrows back at the Arab horsemen, who were forced to withdraw under the hail of arrows.

Under that protection, the javelin throwers filed forwards through the gaps between units and into the open ground, spreading out and covering themselves with their light shields to resist the next stage of the fight.

It was all a dance between partners who had been dancing together for four hundred years. The Arabs knew our tactics, and the Romans knew theirs. The first attack had merely been made to fix us in place in the position of the Arab generals' choosing, drawing us into our static defensive formation, so that he could commit the next step.

'They will come for our flanks now,' said Harald, looking to the left and right, where our cavalry waited in its blocks. 'That will be the real battle.'

And he was right, as the manuals had taught him. With a great flurry of action, more thousands of enemy horsemen poured over the ridge on our extreme right and left, beyond even the positions of our own horsemen, and I thought at once that we must be surrounded and attacked from the rear.

But our own light horsemen, mounted archers and javelin throwers wheeled out in perfect order and spread across the whole open ground, counter-charging to drive the new threat away. The cavalry skirmishers' fight turned into a dust storm on each flank from which we could see little of who was winning, or even if much fighting was going on at all.

'What now?'

'They have drawn our light cavalry out, so now they can commit their own infantry to challenge our centre,' said Harald.

I looked at him. 'Why do we allow them to do these things if we know what they will be?'

'Because each move has a counter, and Maniakes wants them to engage fully. He believes we will prevail, so he allows them to conduct their plan. If we drove them away, we would have to deal with them again. He offers them the opportunity to commit, instead of merely harassing us.'

Well, it was against my instincts, to allow the enemy to decide what should be done, but I was not a general and Harald seemed confident. Maniakes may not have been a brave man, but he was competent and well-trained in the Roman way of war.

Sure enough, as Harald had said, the ridgeline above us soon filled with a great mass of enemy infantry, not in such defined blocks as ours, and in greater numbers. The enemy poured down the slope above us to the sound of their own war horns, and our skirmishers ran out to meet theirs, javelins and arrows flashing in the sun as each side tried to force the other's light infantry back, to expose the main formation to direct missile fire.

The enemy, coming down the hill, slowly managed to push our light forces back. Eventually horns sounded from the centre and our javelin-men, their bags emptied and their shields full of arrows, retreated back between the gaps in our main line, leaving perhaps a hundred of their comrades dead on the ground.

'What now?' I asked, watching in rapt attention.

'I don't know. There are several different moves Maniakes could make. He could push the centre forwards to try and break the enemy attack before it develops, or the flanks, to try and envelop them. Or he could...'

Harald paused as the trumpets blew again. 'Ah, he chooses the third option.'

The central unit, each soldier as one, turned around in place, leaving only the back rank facing the enemy with their shields, and started marching backwards, towards us.

'What? We are retreating?'

'No, we are refusing the centre.'

'We are doing the what?' I said, at a loss.

Harald looked at me, annoyed. 'I told you you should read the manuals. Now is not the best time for me to teach you,' he said acidly.

I looked away, chastened, and stopped asking questions. I was just a warrior, I had cared nothing for the tactics and strategies of armies... until one was bearing down on me. Then I suddenly found myself very interested to know what was about to happen.

Harald relented with a sigh as the next unit in line each side of the centre likewise began to march back, staggering their ranks with the one before. 'The central units will pull back in staggered order, the central one going furthest, and then each one alongside less and less, turning the line into a crescent.'

As he said this, the next units started moving, and I saw the new formation starting to develop.

'Why?'

'It forces the enemy, if they choose to commit to the attack, to push into a potential envelopment in the centre, where they could be attacked on all sides. A very dangerous position. If we had won the skirmishing fight, we might have attacked. This change of formation makes it harder for the enemy to attack us.'

'Does it not expose our flanks?'

Harald smiled. 'You are not completely ignorant. Yes, it does.' He pointed at the flanking units of the line, who were holding their positions unmoved. 'But that is what the heavy cavalry are for. If any enemy unit tries to flank our main line, they turn their backs to the cataphractoi, and that will be the last mistake they ever make.'

'So the enemy will try and occupy the heavy cavalry?' I said.

Harald laughed. 'Finally, you understand the dance. Yes, the enemy will now engage our heavy cavalry units so that they can try and turn our exposed infantry flanks.'

'And then what?'

Harald smiled his wolfish smile. 'And then the dance is over.'

Trumpets blared in front of us again, and on the flanks, half of each formation of tagma heavy cavalry started forwards, banners flying, spears in the air. There was a great roar of excitement from the ranks of the infantry, settling into the crescent line, as they saw the heavy cavalry moving forwards into the attack.

'Maniakes attacks first?' I said, feeling the excitement.

'Yes. A bold move, to disrupt the enemy plans. You know, I am beginning to like Maniakes. Maybe I misjudged his abilities.'

The heavy cavalry thundered forwards into a charge, diving into the flanks of the enemy infantry, taking them by surprise and shattering the edges of the Arab line. Even as they did so, we saw the enemy cavalry reserve pouring over the ridge, angling down to counter the charge of the cataphractoi.

'So the dance is over,' I said, watching the heavy horse formations wheeling to face this new threat, pulling back from the attack on the Arab infantry before they could exploit the initial shock.

'So now someone gets fucked,' said Afra from behind us, with a snort of laughter.

I turned to look at him and he shrugged. 'Where I come from, that's what happens after a dance – someone gets fucked. Hope it's not us.'

Harald laughed heartily and kept watching the battle unfold in front of us. 'I just hope we get to fight at all.'

14

We stood there, fretting and wishing we were fighting instead of watching. The tagmata of heavy cavalry soon got the upper hand on the flanks over their less well-armed and trained opponents, and only another counter-charge by additional enemy units forced them to break off their attack and return to our lines before they were overwhelmed. Some of our reserve mounted archers covered their retreat, duelling with the enemy who tried to pursue them.

The two armies paused to draw breath, the enemy infantry finally re-formed and poised to attack, and our cavalry flanks shaking back out into formation.

Then I heard horses behind us and turned to see half a dozen of our scouts riding hard, dashing through the gap between our bandon and the next, dust and earth flying and hooves missing guardsmen by a handspan.

'What the fuck?' the guardsman opposite me said, flinching from the sudden passage of galloping horses.

'No idea,' I replied, leaning out to see where they were going. The six men galloped straight to the command group and started talking in urgent tones to Maniakes. I could see the shock ripple through the officers around him, and they all turned to stare at us. No, not us; they were looking behind us.

I turned too, but could see nothing.

'An uninvited dance partner,' said Harald grimly.

'Shit. Enemy to our rear? Where?' I could see the baggage train half a mile behind us, but they were not under attack, although there was a lot of activity there.

Then we looked back and Báulfr was running down the slope towards us, Aki and another couple of komes in tow. He ran straight to the centre of the formation, where we were standing with the rest of the seventh.

'Guardsmen! A second enemy force has taken the river crossing behind us. The army is going to withdraw to the crossing and we have to get there first and secure it for them. Prepare to move out by bandon, column of twenty, second bandon to lead! Move!'

'This was a trap,' muttered Harald, suddenly looking nervous. He never looked nervous. 'This whole battle was a trap. They wanted us here, where our scouts had not been able to see.' He turned to me. 'That is what happens when two enemies know each other so well. They knew they had to neutralise our scouts, and the river did that. We did not know what was on the other side. Edessa wasn't the objective of the Arabs; this army was.'

'We are the ones getting fucked then,' said Afra.

'Be quiet,' snapped Harald, looking back up the slope to where the Arab infantry were moving down the hill again to engage the main line. 'The infantry won't be able to retreat yet to support us, not until they win here. We will be on our own.'

Behind us, the second, third and fourth banda had reversed their ranks and marched off in a column twenty men wide, a battle-ready formation, for we might get ambushed on the way. On the flanks, the cavalry reserve, five hundred cataphractoi and the same again in light horsemen, was moving out with us. That much at least I was grateful for. We would be helpless if caught by enemy cavalry in the open alone.

But this was leaving the main army stretched thin, and fully committed. I wondered if they could actually be defeated without their reserves. It didn't matter, it was our turn to move out. Harald and I jogged down to the rear of our formation, me holding the banner high so that our men could see where we were. 'Column of twenty, on me!' shouted Harald, and the depleted banda jostled into position, twenty ranks wide and only six deep, as the sixth bandon filed past, their Gorgon-head banner flying in the wind.

'March!' shouted Harald, and we set off in the dust of those before us.

* * *

We passed the baggage train as they were finishing packing up to move. I didn't know where; maybe to follow us, or just to be prepared to retreat. Then we passed the ridge that led down to the river and the battle disappeared from view behind us. I turned to look at the maelstrom of dust and fighting one last time, seeing the whole army was hard-pressed, the Arab infantry forcing their way into the centre of the crescent, which, without us in reserve to support, was looking precariously thin. On the flanks I saw another wave of the magnificent cataphractoi cavalry making a charge, their ranks still crisp and shining, and then they were all gone from view.

Ahead of us, the crossing came into sight, and I cursed as I saw thick ranks of enemy infantry arrayed on our side, with a forest of archers and skirmishers on the far side of the shallow ford. Enemy cavalry were pecking at our flanks now, trying to stop our march, but our own were combating them, trying to keep them away. Regardless, we ignored them, kept our shields up and our heads down, and pressed on.

When we were half a mile from the crossing, Báulfr roared orders for the rear bandon to run to the flanks and for the whole column to shake out into line to prepare for a full assault. There was no time for clever moves – we would attack with everything at once, and we would break through or we would die there, now or later in the day.

The Varangian guard formed up into a battle line four hundred men across and five men deep, like our Norse ancestors before us, and we advanced into the enemy with our banners flying, our shields up and death in our war cries.

We were the seventh banda, so we were in the centre of the line. I was in the second rank, shield on my back, banner flying from the pole in my left hand and sword in my right. Arrows started raining on us, and our broad shields and thick armour turned them away mockingly. I felt one that had passed over the head of the man in front thump into my chest. I looked down, expecting to see the shaft protruding from my body, expecting to feel the burn and the weakness and see my lifeblood flowing. But the arrow had snapped and fallen to the ground, the only evidence it had ever hit me a single dented plate in my new lamellar.

I roared my triumph to the sky and kept pressing forwards, so close to the enemy line now that I could see the fear in their eyes and the uncertainty in their imperfect line. They knew who we were. They knew what was about to happen to them. But they were brave men also, warriors of a long tradition, and they held their ground as the Storm Ravens fell upon them.

Our shield wall crunched into the enemy with a clatter of steel and wood, and the deafening roar of five thousand scared and angry voices. I stepped over a body, driving the banner forwards, held aloft above me, and the men of the bandon shouted and jostled to keep pace with me as I advanced, pouring into the enemy to protect the flag and to break the enemy line.

A young Arab boy set his eyes on me, full of fear, as I cut the man next to him from this life. But my sword stuck in my victim and, shieldless, he saw his chance and screamed, thrusting forwards with all his strength and driving his spear into me. The spearhead hammered into my side, sliding across iron and tearing through leather straps, scattering a handful of iron plates to flap uselessly from the damaged klivanion. The spear rammed into the maille beneath, and I felt the impact like a punch, and I felt the warmth of blood, and I knew that he had gone through my armour.

I cried in pain and anger and ripped the sword from the previous foe with the strength of desperation. The boy's spear was tangled in my armour even as he tried to pull it back to strike again. I brought the banner pole down and trapped his spear against my side, ignoring the pain, and then I cut his front hand from his body, stepping forwards as he wailed in fear and agony and his fellows pushed in from either side to shield him and to cut at me.

I survived half a dozen blows, I don't know how, and then Harald was there, and another pair of our men, driving the enemy back and pouring into the gap. Harald managed to give me one concerned glance as he passed, and then he was pushing forwards and I let the line move past me as I dropped my sword to the ground and reached down to pull the spear from my side.

I wrenched it from the leather straps and maille that snagged it and tossed it aside. There was no gout of blood, no shivering wave of agony. I carefully prodded at the ragged hole in my armour and felt a flash of pain, but it was not so bad. The spearhead must barely have got through my padded tunic. I drew a great sigh of relief and laughed, picking up my sword and raising the banner high once again. I had been saved by Harald's insistence I try the heavy lamellar armour, and I could not let my men think that we were retreating. The banner had to fly from the forefront, and I pushed my way back into the battle.

I don't know exactly when the enemy broke. It was a vicious fight, but suddenly my foes were fleeing and my legs were in the water up to my knees.

But that was not victory. As the enemy splashed away across the ford, the Arab archers on the bank were able to do their work again, and we were suddenly met with a tempest of arrows.

Our force was not in ranks, our shields were not up and ready in a wall, and guardsmen toppled into the shallows like saplings in a storm.

Arrows and javelins were coming from our front and our left and our right and there was no hiding from it. For a few insane, heroic moments the men of the guard kept pushing forwards into the massacre, trying to force their way across, but no one made it more than halfway before Báulfr's voice roared at us to fall back and re-form the line.

I staggered back, an arrow nearly knocking my helmet from my head and several more thumping into my chest and thigh armour. Men were going down all around me, even as we retreated. Somehow I made it to the re-forming line. But the ground was littered with those of my brothers who did not.

It still makes me shudder to think of it. All those fabulous warriors, among the best men ever to take the field, lying around like sheaves of cut barley.

'Seventh, to me!' I shouted, as some shields were put up around me. I held the banner high, for that was my main duty in battle – to give the men a place to rally to when the chaos of battle was on us.

'Eric!' I heard Harald's voice from somewhere in the shield wall, over the sounds of the wounded and the hammering of arrows.

'Fall back!' the voice shouted, and I shouted my assent and started walking backwards, the wall of our bandon going with me, shuffling over the lines of the dead.

Báulfr was there, blood running down the side of his face, urging us to move, even as horns blew behind us and the sound of horses came clear through the storm of war. I turned and saw that a narrow rank of the cataphractoi were coming down the hill behind us, angling towards the ford.

The commander turned to us with a shout. 'Make way for the scholai and prepare to charge. We take the far bank or we die trying. Fight like the emperor is watching you useless turds!'

We hurried to clear out of the way as the gleaming ranks of the emperor's heavy cavalry came down the slope behind us, spears up, pennants flying in the breeze, small shields held up in their other hands.

They kicked into a trot and then a run, and then they rushed past us in a thundering clatter of metal and hooves, a golden-armoured officer leading in the centre of the front rank, towering and magnificent, the rage and power of the empire in full flow.

A wall of arrows rose up to meet them. The shafts clattered off metal and thudded into maille, riders shuddered and horses shied and whinnied and were wrestled back into line. But none went down.

In front of us, one of the lead horses splayed its legs, staggering drunkenly, careering over and crashing into the one next to it. Both went down in a chaos of hooves and breaking bone, riders crushed like hazelnuts in the mess. The rider behind rose in his stirrups and his mount jumped, clearing the flailing, dying horse in front of it as others sawed at their reins and went right and left, and the formation opened up and closed again the other side.

The riders had to slow as they reached the steeper riverbank, and the enemy archers, who had struggled to adjust to the speed of the charge, had time to perfect their aim. Riders fell limp from saddles with half a dozen arrows in them. Horses went down over injured legs or stumbled on the bodies that littered the way.

For a moment it looked like the whole charge would halt as riders tried to get control of their injured, panicking animals or thread their way through the bodies, but then the golden form of the officer in the lead forced his horse to jump straight into the river, spear raised. The steed half stumbled when it landed, but the officer managed to keep his saddle in the spray and he spurred towards the far bank.

Every archer on the enemy bank turned their attention to the golden figure as it charged across the shallows.

I saw arrows bouncing and skittering off his magnificent armour, I saw some stick. I saw his head rock back as a shaft disappeared under the rim of his helmet and his spear dropped limply from his hand.

But the horse kept going, running in sheer panic as its dying rider leaned back and shook. Behind him, given a moment's respite and desperate to help their leader, a dozen of his men forced their horses into the water, and then more. The golden officer finally fell from his saddle, splashing into the river in a welter of rose-coloured water right on the far bank. His horse, struck by a dozen arrows but running too hard to stop, collapsed onto its neck in the front of the enemy line.

The enemy line shuddered as the dying horse flailed into their ranks and, before they could recover, a half dozen more horsemen were charging across the shallows, spears levelled, armoured forms hunched over their horses' heads.

Two went down, almost at once, whether to arrows or to holes in the riverbed I cannot say. Riders were shot from their saddles by the sheer number of arrows, with some finding gaps in their magnificent armour.

But one rider, red pennant flapping in the wind, made it through the storm. His horse mounted the bank and he stood up in his stirrups to thrust his spear into an enemy, the wooden shaft sinking so deep into the enemy's body that the rider abandoned it, crossing his body to draw his sword and dying with it in his hand as a javelin tore through his neck.

Two riders shoved their way in to replace him, and smashed a hole into the line, and then a handful more joined them. Suddenly we saw the fight shift as dozens of riders were crossing, almost unopposed now that the enemy were focused on the ones who had reached the far bank.

As the last wave of horsemen went past and the focus of the enemy archers went with them, Báulfr turned to everyone within range of his voice.

'God and emperor!' he shouted, pointing his sword at the enemy ranks.

'God and emperor!' we roared back, and then we charged down the slope after the cavalry. We were off to one side now, so other banda headed down to the river before us and we waited our turn impatiently, eager to get into the fight again.

Finally it was our turn. We ran down to the river and we surged across with howls of anger and a desperate thirst for vengeance.

15

We slogged our way through the river, and by the time we reached the far bank the leading bandon had smashed the wavering enemy line, driving them back into the buildings where we could see the fight rapidly moving deeper into the town. Báulfr grabbed Harald, the nearest komes. 'Hold here while I clear the town!'

'Yes, Commander,' said Harald with a disappointed nod. And then Báulfr was running off, shouting orders at two more of the banda that were waiting on the bank.

I heard shouts to our right and I looked, seeing a broad band of dust above the town and more behind us on the other bank, where our screening cavalry were engaging an unseen foe. My heart sank. 'Harald,' I said.

Harald didn't hear me, or ignored me; he was still watching as most of the rest of the guard streamed into town, towards the fighting.

'Harald!' I shouted at him, punching his shoulder with my sword-hand.

'What?' he said indignantly, turning to glare at me. I pointed my sword at the dust over the town, and even as I did, we saw horsemen and flashes of sun on metal appear on the other bank as a large enemy force charged the thin line of our cavalry screen. The enemy was coming for the crossing from both sides.

'Shit.'

Styrbjorn arrived at the head of his bandon and Harald waved him down.

'Styrbjorn, to me!'

He turned as the remains of the heavy cavalry came trotting back down to the river, and the man at their head looked at our banner. 'Who commands?' he shouted.

Harald stepped forwards. 'I do.'

The officer looked at the advancing enemy on the far bank. 'We will hold off whatever is coming down that bank. It looks like a large force, perhaps too large. I will send word to the strategos to make all haste. Good luck, Varangian. God be with you.'

The officer saluted and then turned his horse and guided it down into the river, his men following him as they went to rejoin the rest of their unit across the water.

Harald looked back into town. The sound of fighting had intensified, and enemy were starting to funnel through the buildings on either side and hack into the flanks of the formation of guardsmen around Báulfr, which was starting to flinch and shudder under the threat.

'The flanks, the flanks!' shouted Harald at the komes of the tenth, and he nodded briskly and set off with his bandon, going to shore up the edges of Báulfr's men. Then the nineteenth went to the right and the fifth went to the far left, trying to expand the perimeter around the crossing. Most of the guard was committed in the town now.

Harald looked up across the river glumly as the size of the enemy force became apparent. 'They are going to reach the ford, our cavalry won't be able to stop them.'

He turned to Styrbjorn. 'Take the left flank, I will take the centre and the sixth can take the right.' We were the last three banda on the riverbank, everyone else was committed in the main fight in the town, and our banda was at half its normal size.

Across the river a horde of enemy horsemen was pouring across the ridge and riding along the bank, chasing a much smaller cloud of our own light cavalry away. We could see the cataphractoi forming a line to counter them, stretching from the river's edge to the ridge behind, only two ranks deep and several hundred wide. We were too far away to make out individuals or hear commands, but suddenly the centre surged forwards, the rest of the formation following in order to form a great arrowhead that coursed across the terrain.

The enemy cavalry did not stop, rushing on to meet ours. The imperial arrowhead formation buried itself into the mass of enemy horsemen, the clatter and shouts and cries reaching out to us even half a mile away. There was a swirl of dust and horses that enveloped the tagma as the far more numerous enemy gave way in the centre to the fury of the armoured assault, but curled around the wings unopposed.

At first, the scholai cavalry crushed through the enemy, but they slowed and slowed, and the shining, serried ranks tore and fragmented, until all that was left was a flashing, whirling ball of a melee in the dust.

That dust started to obscure the details, but we heard a trumpet, and saw the mass of the heavy cavalry, their charge expended, pushing their way up the hill, fighting their way clear of the enemy horde that was trying to engulf them.

Styrbjorn came over to join us and he watched in silence as the fighting receded up the hill, horsemen running and whirling and dashing in and out, leaving a trail of broken bodies behind. Finally, the imperial cavalry reached the top of the ridge and disappeared from view.

'Well,' said Harald in a resigned tone. 'We are on our own.'

'Isn't that the way we like it?' I said, trying to be calm.

Harald nodded slowly. 'Not like this. We should have stayed with the army, not separated.'

'It does not matter,' said Styrbjorn with a reassuring grin. 'This is what we were ordered to do, and until death or victory, the guard obeys.' He thumped Harald on the shoulder. 'I will send word to the commander of what is happening. Good luck, Harald,' he added, before walking back to his banner.

Harald nodded curtly and tore his eyes from the enemy on the far bank. 'Get ready,' he said loudly. 'They will be coming for us next.'

* * *

He was not wrong. The enemy headed for the ford in large numbers. We had very few bows, only what we could scrounge from the bodies of the enemy, so we could do nothing as they massed opposite the crossing.

There was little discussion in the front of their ranks, and then orders were shouted and most of the mass dismounted, infantry forming up around a core of horsemen into what I would generously call a block, but was more of a blob. These were not imperial infantry, and marching on foot in formation was not their way of war.

They were not as disciplined as us, they were not as heavily armoured as us, but they outnumbered us ten to one. And numbers count. If we didn't have a narrow ford to defend, they would have washed us away like dust in the rain.

They opened with a hail of arrows.

'Shields!' shouted Harald, which was excessive, since the men all had their shields up already. We ducked and crouched behind our tightly packed shield wall and the arrows did very little except cover it in protruding shafts.

After a while in which no more than a half dozen men were wounded, the arrowfire slackened, and I peeked over the rim of the shield in front of me and saw that the enemy horsemen were almost upon us, splashing through the last of the water to reach the bank.

'Up!' roared Harald, and the ranks stood tall and prepared their weapons just in time for the enemy to reach us.

Fighting in a shield wall is difficult enough at the best of times. It is effective, but it is a fearful chaos of blind stabbing and hacking with your view reduced to the back of a shield and maybe the helmet of the enemy opposite you.

But standing on a sloped, wet riverbank, with hundreds of arrows jutting from our shields, and many of our tired men having lost their spears and just using axes and swords, with cavalry trying to smash through your ranks, was a nightmare.

The only thing that saved us was the slope strewn with the bodies of horses and men, which completely blunted their charge. But even as their horses flailed, their infantry streamed across behind them and threw themselves at our ranks.

The enemy fought with outrageous courage, forcing themselves up into our line, being hammered with our long axes and slashed and stabbed with swords and spears. They clawed and hacked and wrenched at our shields, using the protruding arrows to literally tear at the wall with their bare hands. Horses reared and kicked, knocking holes into the wall that were increasingly slowly filled.

Guardsmen started to go down and, falling on a slippery hill with the enemy downslope of us and the pounding of hooves and feet, few had the opportunity to rise again even if they could.

But we held. We had nothing to do but hold, nowhere to retreat to. The rest of the guard were only a hundred paces to our rear, immersed in their own desperate fight in the streets. So we held.

I jammed the banner in the wet earth behind our line and picked up a shield from a wounded man who had dragged himself back from the ranks. I had no need to carry the banner any more, we all knew where we stood. I was more use with shield in hand, holding it to cover a comrade's flank.

I don't know where Harald was, I just pushed into the ranks and started fighting. My legs were slipping on earth made into mud with river water and blood, my wounded side was throbbing, but my sword-hand was still taking the lives of those who came to crush us.

A horse slammed into me, side on, as it tried to turn in its panic. It didn't even have a rider, so I just stumbled back and stabbed it in the haunch, trying to drive it back into its own ranks. It kicked off with an equine scream of outrage and knocked several of my opponents down.

It didn't matter. There were too many and more simply stepped up to face me, too many to fight. We started to be pushed back, uphill. I can't tell you how hard it is to push a well-formed line *up* a muddy hill. But we were exhausted, and the enemy were overwhelming. It didn't matter how many we killed, it made no difference to their attack.

I took a turn in the rear rank to rest my burning lungs, and looking to my right, saw a flurry of movement and shouts of desperation and fear. The line was cracking. The banner of the sixth, a snake wrapped around a sword, went forwards into the fray; the komes and his banner bearer trying to rally their men.

The fighting grew desperate, each side pulling more and more men to the weak point, and then the banner fell.

I shouted in alarm and ran to the right, calling anyone who could be spared to come with me, and then threw myself into the chaotic brawl that had developed as the line had broken. I punched a man in the face with my shield and ripped someone's jaw off with a swipe of my sword. I shoved forwards and saw the komes of the sixth on his knees, his shield covering the flag-bearer who was trying to fight his way to his feet, the banner still clutched in his hand.

Guardsmen of the sixth were tearing at their opponents in their desperation to reach their fallen commander and their banner. There was slaughter all about as the fighting raged around the downed men, and then the bannerman finally staggered to his feet, the komes trying to drag them both back to safety as I howled and hacked and kicked my way to meet them.

The banner of the serpent-wrapped sword dropped again, the carrier going down into the mire with a spear in his spine. The komes reached down to grab the banner and an Arab warrior stepped forwards with a look of pure rage, and with both hands on the sword raised above his head he brought the blade down, neatly decapitating the komes as he scrabbled for the flag.

The shock of it made me cry out in pain, and the enemy roared and surged forwards, scrambling up the slope and over the slaughterhouse where the men of the sixth had died around their banner, and the men around me started looking over their shoulders, wide-eyed, the true sign of men about to break.

There was no one left to help. Every guardsman still holding a weapon was in the fight. I could feel the line crumbling around me and, with no choice other than to die, I backed away with it. We were pushed back off the riverbank and into the flat, dry ground of the town.

Some more guardsmen came running through the buildings behind me and threw themselves into the fight to try and stop the rot, but it was all unravelling. I took several blows I was too tired and slow to block, saved only by my armour, and I heard cries of alarm and panic and I knew the end was near.

There was a roar from my left, and I saw a small mass of Varangians spear into the side of the enemy breakthrough, Harald at their head, leading the men of the Storm Ravens in a last-ditch counter-charge. It was an absurd thing to do, reckless even. If they failed, the entire centre would have crumbled, and we would have been annihilated.

But I saw him hack into the flank of the Arab attack under the flag of the Raven and none could stand against him. The core of our men went with him, Afra carrying the banner and Halldor and Ulf and others in their heavy lamellar armour widening the carnage he sowed.

The enemy facing me, who had moments ago been howling their victory cries, looked back uncertainly and saw that they were about to be cut off, and the guardsmen around me seized on the moment of indecision and we launched ourselves back into the wavering enemy ranks.

I stumbled forwards, hacking at an Arab, confused to find he was facing away from me. But I didn't care. I just wrenched my blade once more from flesh and sought my next opponent, hacking and stabbing and losing all track of what was happening other than that I needed to kill and move and... rest. By God, I needed to rest.

I kicked a dying Arab off my blade and then looked for another enemy and... And there was none.

I looked up, like a drunk man who has misplaced his cup, and I saw the enemy streaming back down the riverbank and into the river, guardsmen all around me too tired to pursue. I assumed they would re-form to attack again, because they still had the numbers. But their retreat turned into a panic, and my eyes followed their flight and tracked up the slope, where hundreds of men were scrambling to remount, and I saw the most glorious sight.

I opened my parched throat and feebly cheered. I think I hugged the man next to me.

There, coming over the ridge, was the army of the empire, ragged and uneven, bloodied and tired, in a line that stretched from one end of the ridge to the other. They had won their fight on the other side of the hill and returned for us. And, as I watched, the glorious cataphractoi on the flanks put their spears down one last time, and charged.

* * *

I watched as the last attack washed over the enemy forces on the far side. I heard the fighting behind us in the town die down as the remaining Arab forces realised the battle was lost. I sat on a step outside someone's blood-spattered house as the battered but defiant imperial infantry formed a wide protective square around the crossing, a few hundred enemy horsemen harrying them stubbornly but pointlessly.

'I thought you weren't supposed to lose this,' said a voice, and I looked up to see Afra holding the raven banner, offering it to me.

I sighed in relief and levered myself to my feet. 'I shouldn't have left it.'

'It looks like you did enough, Eric.' He looked around thoughtfully. 'We all did.'

'Where is Harald?'

'He is alive, down there soaking up the plaudits for his victory,' said Afra with a wry smile. I peered into the crowd of warriors and saw Harald clasping arms with several bearded veterans. Everyone would have seen his final charge under his raven banner. I almost hated him for it. He managed to make every battle about his personal glory. But I did not hate him for it, of course. I loved him for it, because I was young, foolish... and loyal.

As we stood there in the street, victorious and exhausted guardsmen all around us, there was a commotion from up the street. 'Make way,' called an anguished voice.

We turned to look, and saw a group of bloodied guardsmen making their way down the path, a bier of shields on their shoulders, and a body with a meaty, scarred arm hanging down over the side of it.

'Báulfr!' someone cried out in agonised recognition.

'Oh, lord,' I whispered.

The commander's body was borne down the street by ten men, while guardsmen cleared a path and lined the way. Someone reached out to touch his limp, outstretched hand as he passed, muttering a blessing, and then another did so in turn. Soon every man the bier passed was reaching out to do so, touching the hand or arm of their fallen leader.

The sad procession made its way down as far as us, slowly negotiating the hundreds of men who gathered to see their commander and to touch his hand. They reached the riverbank and carefully laid his body out on the terrace of a building under the shade of a torn awning. I saw a bearded guardsman kneel beside the commander and openly weep, and no one turned away from him in shame.

'He died in the moment of his glory,' someone said, and I turned to see Harald, bloodied but alive, standing next to me staring intensely at the scene. 'A shame he did not live to see it. A great man.'

'You mourn his death?' I asked in surprise.

'I do.'

'I thought you didn't like him.'

'I respected him. And that is what mattered. Look around you. Any leader whose men mourn him like this is worthy of respect.'

His intense gaze turned on me. 'And you fought well, Eric. Any concern that your defeat broke you is vanquished.'

It was an odd thing to say, even for Harald, who was prone to saying odd things. It was a compliment, thinly draped around what felt like an insult. I could not find any reply in my throat to give him.

'Make sure the men get water. The town must have some wells, or send men to the river far upstream of the battle.'

The thought of it exhausted me, having to do things, but after a battle is sadly when there is the most to do. We had wounded to see to, water to gather, a camp to build... and bodies to collect.

As I was standing there, more men came to shake Harald's arm and a small crowd gathered. The guard was leaderless, and some of the men were clearly thinking about who should now be in charge.

Then Aki and the banner of the second came from behind us, where they had been fighting deep on the flank, and he surveyed the crowd of bloodied, battered guardsmen in confusion.

'Where is Báulfr?' he asked, and then his eyes settled on Harald, standing underneath our banner. Harald said nothing, merely pointing to the terrace off to the side where the commander's still form lay on the shields.

Aki looked, and his face fell in sadness before he pressed his mouth into a line and turned to Harald. I could see him trying to assess the situation and make a decision, his eyes flicking back and forth. I assume he was worried Harald would challenge his authority to take over leadership of the guard. The men of the three banda who had held the crossing were gathering behind Harald as he stood there in the street, almost with an air of hostility at Aki's approach. Hah, we Norsemen, our entire history we have been squabbling among ourselves.

Aki saw all this and approached, keeping his expression calm. He leaned in so only we could hear. 'Báulfr's body will need returning to Constantinople, and the general will need his messengers carrying the news of the victory to be escorted. I charge you with this duty. Leave tomorrow with three banda and the messengers, take ship at St Symeon, and sail directly to the palace.'

'You wish to be rid of me, Aki?' said Harald evenly.

'I wish you had died and he had lived,' replied the komes bluntly. 'But yes, I don't need you here undermining me. Do you challenge my authority to command here?'

Harald stared at him, uncowed, for longer than necessary, and then shook his head calmly. 'No.'

Aki grunted, giving Harald one last look of distaste, then he walked off and started calling to all the komes who had survived, giving orders.

Aki had been Báulfr's closest man. The akolouthos would have to select a new commander, but for now, Aki's lead would be accepted. It had not been the time for Harald to press his own ambitions.

Harald turned away seeming remarkably at peace with it, and he pursed his lips. 'We will take what is left of the sixth and the fourteenth. Styrbjorn is still alive somewhere.'

'You have seen him?'

Harald shook he head and started to walk away. 'No, but he is too stubborn to have died.'

16

The cleansing of the pirates and Maniakes' victory near Edessa earned the empire peace. With their army so degraded, the Egyptian Caliphate accepted favourable terms and paid a huge tithe to the emperor in the summer of 1036.

We escorted Báulfr's body, confined in a simple cypress coffin, back to Constantinople as ordered. It was a sombre trip. The men were exhausted and some of the wounded had refused to be left behind, not wanting to forgo the honour of escorting our commander back to the palace. Wounds festered, and the battle claimed a few more lives before we made it back to the barracks.

When we reached the palace we did our best to make a good parade of the coffin up to the palace from the royal harbour, but news of the victory was already spreading and the city was in celebration. Our dignified procession was ignored, even by the palace denizens. We laid Báulfr in the small chapel in the barracks and then came the worst part of every return from war, the not knowing what to do next except sit with your thoughts and the memories of those who had died.

Well, it was not long before Harald was whipping us up from our darkness, setting us to mending equipment and a dozen minor tasks. All to keep the men occupied.

The day after we arrived, one of the emperor's attendants came to our barracks and presented us with a message.

'What does it say?' I asked, peering over Harald's shoulder as he unrolled the very fine, gilded parchment.

Harald whistled quietly and his eyes rose. 'A formal invitation to an audience with the emperor.'

My brows also rose and I looked at the paper, although I could not read it. 'Are you sure it's an audience, not a reception?'

'No, a personal audience.'

You see, the significance of that was considerable. Meeting the emperor of the Romans came in three stages. First, a visitor would be presented at the senate hall, along with dozens of others. The emperor rarely attended those events. Usually palace functionaries of various kinds who acted as the emperor's representatives would conduct the ceremony and hear petitions and embassies and then report back to the head of the emperor's household, who would decide who was worthy of a reception with the emperor himself.

Those lucky or important enough to be so selected might be invited to the Chrysotriklinos, the great throne room in the main palace where the emperor would hold court or greet delegations, clients or allies. The Chrysotriklinos was a large, octagonal building, the hub of the main palace, and attached to its various sides were the emperor's personal chambers, the quarters of his closest advisors and officers, and a passage leading to the women's part of the palace nearer the sea wall.

The audiences at the palace were events of rigid and tedious formality and ceremony, enormously complicated and incredibly dull. Fortunately, standing guard at those events was the strict reserve of the first bandon, who were paid more than us for their endurance of the tedium.

Well, when the emperor held these receptions he would grant certain guests and dignitaries the honour of a personal audience at a later time. This would usually take place in the hall of nineteen couches, so called because it was the imperial dining hall, where nineteen elaborate couches and tables were arranged in eighteen enclaves along both sides of a long hall, with the emperor's on a raised platform at the head. There, the emperor would entertain and converse with his guests, perhaps eat with them, and be able to have important discussions in private.

So, you see, for a man who had never even been formally received to be invited immediately to the hall of nineteen to meet the most powerful man in the Christian world was an unparalleled honour. One Harald, of course, took cleanly in his stride.

'He must be desperate for something,' he said after a moment.

'What?' I was still drowning in the glory of being invited to such a place, not as a guard, but as a guest. Harald, of course, was beyond that, considering the implications and the advantages to be gained.

'To invite a guardsman, even a komes, to a personal audience. He must be desperate.'

'Perhaps he wishes merely to reward us?'

Harald chewed his lip and then shook his head. 'No, a messenger with a bag of gold would suffice. This is something else.'

'What?'

'I don't know. But I want to find out. Get me Afra.'

* * *

Afra came and read the invitation, giving no hint of being impressed or surprised. 'An audience, in five days? What do you need?' he said, looking up at Harald.

'I need to know why.'

Even Afra was taken aback. 'You want to know what the emperor himself is thinking? Harald, even our sources are not that good. And we have been away for months, I am out of the gossip.'

'Well, go and talk to your brother, do what you can. I need every piece of information you can give me before I meet with the emperor; the future course of our lives may depend on it.' Then he shrugged. 'Or it may not. Perhaps he is just bored.'

Afra laughed. 'We both know that is not the reason. Fine, my friend, I will discover what I can.'

'Good. You have three days.'

Afra gave me a knowing look on the way out and I smiled at him sympathetically. Harald had already moved on, and casting the gilded parchment aside he looked at me again. 'Tell me the number of men we have fit and ready for service.'

* * *

In the three days it took for Afra to come back to us, we reorganised the tattered bandon, absorbed the denuded remains of the sixth into our own greatly reduced ranks, had equipment repaired and replaced, and made the guards ready to do their palace duties again and to look the part. Harald was insistent no fault be found with our commitment if anyone came to inspect us, which no one did. We were simply sent a roster of expected duties, relieving the men of the Vigla, who had taken over our posts while we were on campaign.

Afra and Thorir sat down with us in an empty section of the barracks, where another bandon who had not yet returned would normally sleep. It seemed a foolish precaution at the time, the secrecy and solitude, but as I learned later, such things were important in the palace.

Afra looked grim. Even Thorir looked downcast, and he never displayed any kind of emotion.

'So, what can you tell me?' Harald asked.

Afra hunched and spread his hands in apology. 'Almost nothing, Komes.'

'Nothing?' said Harald, looking at Thorir for a second voice.

Thorir shook his head once.

'Why?' said Harald with a tinge of anger, looking back at Afra.

'There is turmoil in the palace and the court. Most of our sources are gone, and everyone else is too terrified to speak. It is practically a war, a war of silence and threats. We could not get anywhere close to anyone who knows the emperor's mind.'

Harald's eyes narrowed. 'A war?'

It was not completely shocking. We knew that the empress and the emperor were in a struggle for power, but when we had left, nothing like that had been happening – not that we had seen or sensed.

'Where have your sources gone to?'

Afra swallowed. 'Servants and staff are beaten and abused, even court officials have been extorted or blackmailed. Some of them have been moved to other jobs, others have disappeared.'

'Fled?'

Thorir shook his head and his look said it all.

Harald sat back in shock. 'Members of the palace staff have been murdered?' He was outraged. 'Has anyone acted? Have the first bandon done anything to stop this madness?'

'No one does anything.'

'Why?'

'Because this is a purge, and it is organised by those in power, who the guard cannot touch.'

'The emperor?' Harald asked, brows narrowing.

Afra pursed his lips. 'I don't think so, not directly. He would not need to resort to such crude methods. This is beneath him.'

'Then who? Zoe?'

'Men belonging to both,' said Thorir softly. 'They are at war in the shadows, the emperor and empress. Everyone caught in between is a potential target, and terrified.'

Harald grunted in frustration. 'I need more than this.'

'I am sorry, Komes. The palace is a closed circle even in normal times, but now? It is impenetrable from the outside. Even finding what little we did caused trouble, questions are being asked. I have been noted,' Afra said, and he looked ashamed. 'This place is beyond me. Nothing like this existed in Norway or Kyiv.'

Harald's eyes narrowed. 'What kind of trouble?'

Afra shrugged. 'Nothing we can't handle. Threats, subtle, but clear. I am watched. I'm sorry.'

Harald turned to Thorir. 'You too?'

Thorir smiled very slightly.

'No, of course you are not noted,' Harald said with a small laugh.

'My brother will keep trying,' said Afra, 'but he must be extremely careful.'

Harald thought about it for a moment and shook his head. 'No, do nothing, risk nothing. I will have to try a different way, more direct.'

'Before you meet the emperor? Only one day remains.'

'Yes, but I have a source of my own,' he said with a wink, standing and looking at me. 'Come, let's see if we can pay the gardens a visit.'

* * *

Harald sent word via a servant and, to my surprise, a reply was immediately returned. We could meet with Zoe, but only if we went to her quarters. It was a surprise, since our previous meetings had been in secret. By going to her quarters, we would be noted. Being the day before meeting the emperor, it seemed a deliberate provocation.

Not that Harald minded a provocation. We dressed in our simple uniform tunics and cloaks, without our weapons except our seaxes, and went to the women's quarters of the palace. I had not been inside before; only the first bandon guarded the imperial family's inner buildings and gardens, and our duties never took us there. The separation was deliberate; it kept the chances of corrupting the guards low by limiting their number and controlling carefully who could hold the position.

We were stopped at the entrance, and again in the ante-hall, this time for longer as a guardsman went to seek instruction if we were to be allowed in. As we stood there patiently waiting, I noticed a strange, lean, beardless man walking down the long hallway that led from the main palace, a string of servants and other attendants following him. It was bizarre, for he was dressed quite simply, but those following him had an air of utter subservience. He was whispering instructions to one of them in a rapid tongue.

As I stared at him, Harald noticed my confused expression and turned to follow my gaze. As he did, the thin man saw us and his brows knotted and his stride faltered for a moment, and then he stopped to issue some final instructions to his gaggle of attendants before clasping his hands together at his waist and walking confidently over towards us.

To my utter surprise, the four guardsmen on duty dipped their heads to him and parted to allow him access to us.

'You are not first bandon. What are you doing here?' he asked.

My confusion only deepened, for he had the voice of a teenage boy, not a grown man. Its weakness matched the weakness of his frame – slender and narrow, almost feminine.

Harald looked the strange man up and down and gave no impression that he felt the need to answer, but eventually relented. 'We are invited.'

'Invited? You are mistaken, Varangian. Return to your duties. No one in the palace would invite you to...' The slender man paused and a flicker of understanding flashed in his eyes, and the corner of his mouth curled up in a little smile. 'You are Harald Nordbrikt?'

Harald couldn't suppress a little pride at being recognised, but he said nothing. The man's eyes flicked across to the corridor leading to the empress's quarters. 'Has he asked for admittance to the empress's residence?' he asked the guardsmen.

'Yes, he has. He says he was invited.'

'I have heard nothing of the sort,' said the man, clearly intrigued.

'Why would you have heard, it is not your concern,' said Harald with irritation. 'Go about your own duties,' he commanded, in the voice that would send lesser men scattering in fear.

The man was not in the least intimidated. In fact, he laughed – the joyous, carefree laugh of a child. 'Oh, Harald, prince of the North, how little you know.'

As Harald stumbled, taken aback by the laughter, two guardsmen returned from the corridor and both acknowledged the thin man respectfully. He snapped his fingers at one. 'These men are invited?'

'Yes. Should we allow them?' the guard asked nervously.

Harald bridled. 'If we are invited, we obey. Stand aside, guardsman.' He stepped forwards, but the two guards closed in front of him, shaking their heads firmly. Harald was outraged, but the two men were resolute, their eyes flicking to the thin man.

He watched Harald in fascination, toying with him. Then he waved a hand casually at the two guards. 'As the empress wishes. Go with them, ensure they leave immediately afterwards.'

Harald's mouth opened and closed, incensed that the guards were taking orders from this plain man, when Harald was a komes of the guard and they should be deferring to him. But he knew better than to make a red-faced protest, for nothing erodes authority like blustering and claiming to have it, and then being shown you do not. He slammed his mouth shut and satisfied himself with giving the stone-faced guardsmen a withering stare, before turning to walk down the corridor, not acknowledging the strange man again.

But I watched him, and I saw his amused smile fade, and a more calculated look of concern take over his face. Then he caught me glancing at him and a mask of indifference slipped over his features once more, and he turned on his heel and walked away.

* * *

Harald did not speak until we reached Zoe's quarters and were ushered in by yet more guards.

Zoe's attendant Hypatia was waiting for us, thin-lipped as always, and ignored the friendly smile I gave her. She directed us to another room, a shaded interior oasis with a fountain in the wall and a large, comfortable-looking couch beside it where the empress lounged in a decorated linen dress, her hair, usually covered, curled and tied and hanging down the back of her neck and shoulders.

She turned and gave Harald a warm smile and beckoned him over, directing him to the floor in front of her. There were no seats; we were clearly expected to stand for this.

'Basilissa,' Harald said, bowing, a motion I copied. 'I thank you for accepting my request for an audience.' His tone was warm but deferential. This was a meeting with an empress again, despite the informal setting. In fact, we had never met her in a formal setting. They were strange times.

'My dear Araltes, I am so pleased you have returned from the war, and with such glory too.' She gave him such a sweet smile, regal yet friendly.

Harald smiled like a child being praised. 'Your words are too generous, Basilissa. I merely did my duty and I thank you for your recognition, and for your letter of support to the commander.'

She inclined her head with a broad smile. 'I was merely rewarding loyalty and good service, as is my duty. It is important that I have men I can trust in positions of power. Now, come, Araltes, we are friends are we not? You may forgo the formalities.' Then she leaned forwards a fraction. 'To an extent.'

'I am honoured.'

'Now, what brings you to my quarters in such a hurry that I could not even dress and prepare properly?'

It was a preposterous statement, for she looked glorious as she always did, dressed in finery and carefully made up. But Harald squirmed.

'I apologise, it could not wait. I heard of trouble in the palace, and I wanted...' He struggled to find a way of telling the empress of the Romans that he just needed to question her over palace politics so he could prepare to meet her rival. Finally he found his course. 'I wanted to know how I could best serve you and the throne in this difficult time.'

Zoe raised an eyebrow but let the obvious lie pass. 'Your devotion is admirable. Yes, these are difficult times. The city and the palace are in upheaval, and all of us must be careful to navigate its storms.'

'And what are the nature of these storms?'

Zoe said nothing, but her eyes were searching Harald's. Harald inhaled sharply and looked up at the fountain.

'My lady, I cannot help if I do not know what is happening.'

'And how much can I tell a man who goes to meet my enemy tomorrow?' she asked, her tone completely changing in an instant.

'I am ordered to an audience, and I obey. There is no other way,' Harald said firmly.

'And he could order you to tell him what we spoke of, could he not? Would you not be bound to obey that also?'

Harald looked desperately stiff and uncomfortable, because it was a good question. 'I would consider anything you told me in confidence to be above such an order. But otherwise, yes, I will do as my emperor commands.' Then his stance softened. 'But I made sure to speak to you first.'

It was as close to an admission of taking sides that he could go, and Zoe saw it and her defensive expression softened. 'So, what do you wish to know, exactly?'

'I wish to know about the struggle for control of the palace, and the danger to you that we spoke of before I left last year.'

Zoe sighed. 'I have not been idle while you were away, Araltes. While you fought in the east I fought here, and I still have those loyal to me, although their number dwindles as fast as those who oppose me,' she said, bitterly.

'I have heard of members of the court and government disappearing, coerced, banished... murdered. Is it true?'

'Yes. The war for the palace has casualties too, on both sides.' She shrugged. 'Is that not the nature of war?'

'And who is winning?'

Zoe paused for a moment, and then her resolution crumbled. 'I do not know.'

'I see,' said Harald grimly. 'I am sorry, I...'

Zoe waved his platitude away. 'I know – you cannot take sides in this war, it is not your place.'

Harald nodded glumly. 'But I can at least watch the fighting does not endanger you. But I need to know more.' Harald smiled and nodded firmly. 'I am your servant, Basilissa. I thank you for the... enlightenment you have given me. It will help my service to you greatly.'

'Good,' she said, with a golden smile. 'Now, what is it truly that you came to ask for?'

Harald smile nervously. 'My meeting with the emperor tomorrow... I wish to be well-prepared.'

'Well, that is wise.' There was an awkward pause as Zoe watched Harald's struggles with amusement. 'You wish to know what he will want from you?'

'Yes, Basilissa.'

'Well, that is simple – he will wish to secure your loyalty, put you on his side, and turn you against me.' Zoe gave him a patient smile and everyone politely ignored the obvious way she had done exactly the same thing.

'It is what I suspect, but so quicky and openly?'

'Of course. Neither of us have time for much subtlety.'

'So what should I do?'

'What your oaths and your honour dictate, young Harald. I am sure you will have no trouble keeping to them, but it is something you must face alone. I cannot help you with him any more than you can help me. If there is anything else I can enlighten you about?'

He turned to look back at the way we had come in and his brows furrowed. 'Who is the strange man in the outer hall, who I thought was a boy until I saw his greying hair and the lines around his mouth? The way he spoke to me... it was extraordinary.'

Zoe smiled sadly. 'Ah, you have met John the Parakoimomenos, and if you have met John, you have met the true emperor.'

'The true emperor? I don't understand. What is a parakoimomenos?' Harald said, the word unfamiliar to us both.

Zoe's gaze drifted away. 'It means the one who sleeps outside his bedchamber. It is a position of utmost trust. Once he was just a senior palace administrator, but now he has become the chief courtier and assistant to the emperor since my husband Romanos sat on the throne. Romanos scorned the advice and counsel of the great men of the court and the army, who he suspected were still more loyal to my family and the prosperity of the empire. So John became his mouth and ears, and now Romanos is dead and Michael is the emperor, and he seeks only those who are loyal to him so John is still the parakoimomenos, for who could be more loyal than his own brother?'

Harald's eyes narrowed and he leaned back, trying to take it all in. 'That strange little man, John, is Michael's brother?'

Zoe inclined her chin subtly in confirmation.

'And you say in meeting him I have met the true emperor, so John has usurped his brother? How?' Harald was outraged that the rude, sly man we had met could possibly have done such a thing.

Zoe shook her head, giving Harald the sort of sympathetic look you might give a child who could not understand the unfairness of one of life's early challenges. 'He took nothing from Michael that was not given willingly. Michael has no interest in the governance of the empire, so he allows John to do it. Michael is only interested in the wealth and the power and the ability to do as he pleases. He is still drunk on the image of authority and worship that he imagines the throne to give him. And while he drowns himself in all the finest things of the world, John rules in the quiet parts of the palace, and he has the silent power of life and death over all.'

'But I thought *you* chose Michael to be emperor?'

Zoe laughed softly, a beautiful, forlorn patter whose joy never reached her eyes. 'My dear Harald, so did I. But I was manipulated.' She shrugged, a defeated, reluctant gesture and so unregal.

Harald straightened, understanding. 'John manoeuvred Michael into your favour, hoping you would love him, choose him, and make him emperor.'

Zoe said nothing, but her silence and the look of pain in her eyes was confirmation enough.

Harald blew out a great breath and his eyes widened. 'It is worse than I had heard.' His mouth pressed together as he looked at the suddenly sad figure of the empress, surely feeling as I did a great sympathy for her, who had been so completely and devastatingly manipulated. The woman had raised her husband's murderer to the throne, and been instantly betrayed. I saw the flash of anger at the injustice of it run through him.

'He is just one man, even as the emperor's brother.'

Zoe shook her head. 'I have told you before, he is not really a man at all.' Harald looked at her quizzically. 'And I do not mean that as an insult. It makes him far more dangerous; a man with no legacy has only his own lifetime to consider.'

'I don't understand,' said Harald, shaking his head.

Zoe smiled mirthlessly. 'You truly don't know?'

'Know what?'

'Well, you have spent no time in the inner palace and the court so why would you... John is a eunuch. You must have seen them before? Tall, youthful men with no beards.' Now that she said it, I had indeed seen well-dressed servants in the palace that met that description, but I had thought nothing of it. I just assumed they were men who rarely went outside or exerted themselves.

Harald and I still looked at her blankly, the word unfamiliar to us. Zoe rolled her eyes in exasperation. 'A palace eunuch has all the parts that make him a man removed when he is a child.'

Well, let me tell you I felt the horror of that in my stomach.

'What? Why?' said Harald in shock.

'Because it makes them docile, trustworthy – harder to corrupt and impossible to seduce, and fit to work in the women's quarters without fear of scandal. They can have no children so can be trusted not to usurp power.' She laughed. 'Well, that is the normal way of things, but John is different. He has all the ambition of intact men, and more. He can have no children, so in place of them he foists his thirst for power on his brothers and cousins and nephews, setting them up as his legacy.'

Harald recovered before I did from the knowledge that the man we had met had nothing between his legs, and considered the problem. 'I see. And if John were to die, your problems would die with him?' he asked.

Zoe blanched at the words, eyes flicking around in fear, searching the room as if others could be present.

'Do not speak like that, even here,' she whispered. 'John is the most dangerous person in the city.'

Harald smiled his nasty, predatory smile. 'If you believe that, then you do not know me well enough.'

Zoe met his gaze, and I saw a little hope flicker across her features. 'Then I should wish to know you a little better. But regardless, do not speak of that. I give you knowledge, not licence for bloodshed.'

Zoe reached up her hand, smiling with a new fondness, and Harald bowed down and gently took it. Harald gracefully bent his head and kissed the back of her hand, his lips lingering a little more than they probably should, but I could see a sparkle in Zoe's eyes as she watched him. He slowly released her hand and she hid her expression in a moment, before flashing me a guilty look as she realised I could see what she had been hiding from Harald.

She liked him.

Ha! The empress of the Greeks, the most powerful woman in Christendom, perhaps in all the world, and she was falling for Harald.

'If you are truly my servant, Harald, you will not do anything hasty or rash. I know you are a brave man, an honourable man, but you do not understand everything at play. You cannot simply murder John, for he is well-guarded, and even if you succeed it will mean your death. I do not wish for your service to mean the end of your line, young prince. What a waste that would be.' She gave him the most enchanting smile, and Harald grinned back like a child, and I saw that her affection was not in vain.

'I will be patient then, my lady,' he said, with a small bow.

'Good. Watch him, learn, guard against any plots he might make, for surely now he knows you are with me, and that puts you in grave danger.'

'Do not worry, empress, for I am also well-guarded.' He cast me a look, the first time he had looked at me during the entire conversation, and winked.

Ah, that filled me with joy, that simple gesture. He had just praised me in front of the empress of the Greeks! Zoe cast her enchanting gaze on me and nodded in thanks. 'Keep him well, Varangian, for I have great and important tasks for his future.'

'Basilissa,' I said, bowing deeply.

'Thank you for attending me. You may leave,' she said, and without even being signalled, her stern guardian came to her side and helped her gracefully to her feet as we bowed and backed away before turning to leave.

When we reached the outside, passing the four guards and were out of earshot of anyone, I turned to Harald. 'How can a man live with... well, without...' I waved my hands at my groin. 'I would rather die.'

Harald gave me an awkward look. 'I have heard of it before, injuries in battle and such.'

'Yes, but not losing everything? And since childhood? How could you live with the shame,' I muttered.

'Perhaps here it is not shameful. Perhaps it is almost a position of honour and privilege. And anyway, if this happened when they were a child, perhaps they do not truly know of what they are missing.'

We fell into silence as we walked back towards the barracks, Harald no doubt analysing how he would use this information, and me trying to think of a way to improve my armour to ensure I did not share John the Eunuch's fearful loss.

17

'You didn't know about the cockless men?' said Afra, looking at us with genuine confusion.

'No. Why would I know? Do you think I go around the palace checking servants?' I said, annoyed that Afra thought we were fools for being surprised. Afra had a bad habit of assuming people knew as much as he did.

We were in the barracks preparing for our audience with the emperor, dressing in fine new clothes that we had bought just for the occasion in the street of tailors near the palace, the good one that catered to the Roman nobility. Good enough that they had been very reluctant to serve us mere soldiers at all, until Harald had shown them the gold from his purse.

'It doesn't matter. We know now, and we knew about John before Afra and Thorir did,' Harald said, with a satisfied smile.

Afra tried not to look aggravated about that. 'I knew about him. I just didn't know he was the one in power. And how did you find out?' he said in a sharp tone.

Harald winked at me. 'I simply asked my source.'

Afra looked at me, barely suppressing a derisive snort, and then back to Harald. 'No, tell me you were not that stupid.'

'Stupid? We found out what we needed to find out.'

'And no doubt signalled to everyone in the palace, including John, what you were doing.'

Harald gave Afra a stubborn glare and breathed heavily. 'I got what I needed.'

'Shit, and now you are in the game, before you are ready.'

'Nonsense.'

'Exactly – you do not even realise you are in the game, so how can you be ready? Even now John will probably be finding out what you were doing there.'

I gave Harald a guilty look, wondering if he would admit what had happened. Well, he was too proud not to.

'He met us on the way in,' he said, as if it was nothing.

'On the way in? He met you on the way in to the empress's quarters?' Afra looked exasperated. 'Well, then he is already plotting against you. You have revealed yourself as a threat, and are not even trying to prepare to combat that.'

'Combat what?' said Harald. 'This eunuch? What can he do? What threat is he to a komes of the guard? Pray he is stupid enough to attack me, and I can kill him in response.'

Afra gave him a horrified expression. 'He will not attack you himself. This is not Bardas or some battlefield foe. You will never see his hand behind the blows and they will not be spears in the daylight, it will be knives in dark corners.'

'Nonsense, they cannot get to me here. Enough of that cowardly talk,' Harald blustered, but his tone did not have the confidence of his words.

Afra gathered himself and heaved in a few calming breaths. 'Who are you meeting today?'

'The emperor.'

'And who advises the emperor?'

Harald pointed his finger at Afra. 'I am not a child, do not lecture me. So he can whisper lies and denouncements in the emperor's ear. I know that.'

'And have you prepared for it? The emperor is insecure and newly enthroned, at war with his wife. If he is convinced you are against him you will never see daylight again! Do you understand the stakes of the game you have entered, Harald? You are used to dealing with death that comes at you with a sword and a shield, that you can fight with bravery and skill. What defence do you have against a political move to have you branded a traitor, by the man the emperor trusts the most? You cannot fight your way out of this with strength and speed, only cunning and preparation.'

That shook Harald, I could see it. And bless him, for he was stubborn but sometimes he knew when to admit he was wrong, and how to immediately change course without shame.

He took it all in and then nodded. 'You are right. I had not considered he might persuade the emperor himself to move against me.'

'It might even be today, at this very meeting.'

Harald chewed his lip. 'I will take the chance. This late my only choices are to risk it, or flee with nothing.'

Afra's mouth pursed. 'Be humble, wear your loyalty like a cloak, try flattering and—'

'Enough!' Harald held out his hand like he was stopping a column of men. 'I have dealt with great men before.'

Afra mumbled in protest but relented.

'I want you and Thorir to work up a plan of defence while we are at the audience. You lecture me on this style of war; well, be my general, give information on the enemy and their likely attacks, and a strategy to deal with it.'

Afra nodded firmly. 'We will.' He paused and looked at me with concern. 'Good luck.' And then he turned and left.

Harald adjusted his fine, colourful tunic, and then looked at me with a hint of fear in his eyes. 'Do you think he will move against us so fast? I was assuming this meeting would be the emperor flattering and courting us for our support. I may have misjudged.'

I shrugged. It was well outside of my understanding of things.

'Can we smuggle weapons in, anything at all?'

I shook my head. Harald knew we could not, he was just seeking confirmation of his fears. Being without steel made us feel naked, but no weapon was allowed into the emperor's presence other than those carried by the very inner circle of guardsmen and his personal retinue of trusted imperial officers.

'We should go, and whatever fate befalls you, it will befall me too.'

Harald put his hand on my shoulder and pressed his forehead to mine. 'As my brother requested.'

'As my king commanded,' I answered.

* * *

We were searched at the entrance to the main palace and then escorted to the hall of nineteen by some first bandon men. It was a normal process, but I could not help feeling nervous at being surrounded by armed, armoured men, even if they were our comrades in name.

As we went through the shaded courtyard and approached the grand doors to the hall, a figure in a simple but very fine tunic was waiting for us, a small gaggle of official looking attendants with him, and a full dozen guards around the doors in formation.

'John,' muttered Harald.

'Nothing will happen here, too many watching.'

'Hmm. Eric, there is something I must confess,' Harald said quietly.

'What?' I hissed without looking at him.

'You were not, strictly speaking, invited.'

'What?' I said louder, and looked at him that time.

'Uh, the letter, it was not completely clear, but...' Harald fell silent because we were getting too close, and John was watching us with an amused smile.

'Komes Nordbrikt, you do seem to get some wonderful invitations.'

'Being a prince has its blessings,' Harald said evenly.

'Away with the pretence, then?'

'Everyone already knows.'

'Yes, but it is impolite to wave it about.'

'Said like a man with nothing to wave about.'

There was not even a flicker of annoyance on John's face and he laughed heartily, the mirth clear on his face. 'My word, you Northerners are so crude. Even the royal ones.' He stepped closer and smiled at Harald. 'You really think it is a weakness, don't you?'

Harald glared at the thin man, who was nearly as tall as he, but there was no sign of intimidation in the eunuch's posture as he got as close as a lover. 'How can it be anything else you think? Who can respect a man who is not a man?'

John's smile broadened. 'Oh, my dear man. How I hope you live to see the full extent of it. Such interesting creatures, you Varangians.' He reached up a hand to gently cup Harald's cheek, not sensually, but like a man might check a horse. Harald's outrage bubbled and surged, and then, before I could do anything, it burst forth.

Harald raised his right arm and snatched the hand away, aiming to rip it from the eunuch's body, but before he even stressed the joint, four big arms grabbed him and another snaked around his neck as the first bandon guardsmen, who had been watching closely, pinned him in place.

I only then noticed that the mean end of a sword was at my throat, daring me to intervene.

Harald huffed and puffed, but three men were holding him, and he could do nothing except stand there and take the humiliation, or drop to the floor and start a grapple he would lose.

John, as unperturbed by the violence as he had been by any other intimidation, stood there smiling broadly as Harald's fingers were peeled from his wrist. I knew that iron grip must be hurting him, but he showed nothing of it. Then he stepped aside and regarded Harald with amusement before waving the guards away. He was still within striking distance, daring Harald to strike. Fortunately, despite his rage, Harald was not so foolish again.

'Is it a weakness, Araltes? I do not think so. I have seen the weakness you "proper" men are driven to.' He tutted and rolled his eyes. 'One flash of a woman's thigh, a deep flutter of her lashes or a coy smile promising the hint of intimacy and you will do anything! I have no such failings. I cannot be seduced, neither by a woman's wiles or by the charm of a beautiful young man. My children cannot be held and threatened, nor my wife insulted and have me driven to foolish acts of bruised honour or pride.' He looked around the beautiful courtyard, the only one there who was not tense and ready for action, entirely at ease.

'Ah, what do you have? Your strength and violence?' He gestured to the guards who had restrained Harald. 'What use is that when I can do more with a whispered word than you can do with your mighty arms or your little band of foreign bandits?'

He paused and then approached Harald again, standing toe to toe, and leered at him. 'I know what you should fear, Araltes, above all else.' He rapped his knuckles on Harald's groin, hard enough to get a wince. 'That someone takes a little blade and makes you like me.' He chuckled to himself. 'I have seen it done so many times as punishment for treachery. Romanos was fond of ordering it, fascinated by it. So many proud men, sons of great fathers, brothers of generals or rebels, crying and mewling over the ruins of their previous lives after the knife's work was done. Do you know, we have a servant in the palace whose only job is to make those cuts?'

He leaned right in, close enough to whisper in Harald's ear. 'I hope you live long enough, Araltes, for me to see that day. I look forward to it... I might hold the knife myself just to savour it all the more.' He lingered there, next to Harald's paralysed ear, and then he turned and walked away, summoning his attendants with a simple swirl of his finger, leaving Harald, panting and shaking, in the small half-circle of guardsmen.

I couldn't meet his eye. The hot shame of his fear radiated from him, and I wanted to pretend I hadn't seen it, that I hadn't felt it myself.

We waited there, in humiliated silence, for quite some time. We did not speak to each other, and the guards did not speak to us. Then the doors opened and a finely dressed royal attendant appeared with his own small retinue. He, of course, had no idea what had transpired in the courtyard outside, but he immediately saw the tense atmosphere and looked perplexed, looking to the senior guard for reassurance. The Varangian gave him a simple nod.

'Komes Nordbrikt, the reception room is ready for you to attend.'

Harald grunted his acknowledgement, and then visibly tried to compose himself as the attendant ran through the protocol and titles, which I won't tire you with, for it was long and I don't remember all of it.

Finally, Harald had been prepared, and the attendant ushered him through, looking confused when I started to follow. 'Ah, is there some misunderstanding?' he said, putting himself in my path and looking at Harald.

'I doubt it.'

'Then who is this man and why does he think he is entering?'

It was Harald's turn to look confused. 'This is my flag-bearer, my attendant and sworn guardian. He goes everywhere I go.'

'But he was not invited.'

Harald nodded thoughtfully. 'I see your confusion. But he does not need an invite.'

'Excuse me?'

'When a foreign prince is invited to a réception, do his servants and attendants receive invites?' Harald asked politely.

The official was taken aback. 'Well, of course not, but...'

'But they still enter with their master?'

'Yes, of course.'

Harald spread his hands. 'Then what is the problem? Am I not allowed an attendant?'

'He is a guardsman of the scholai Varangian, not a servant,' spluttered the official, who was now clearly in two minds.

'He is not going to speak, or sit, or eat. He is my attendant. I do not wish to appear before the emperor without one, it will humiliate us both for me to be so dishonoured.'

'Well...' The official looked around but no answer miraculously condensed in the air. 'I see your reasoning, Komes, and I suppose it is acceptable.'

Harald smiled magnanimously and winked at me to soften the blow of being called his servant. 'Good. Then I am ready to be presented.'

We were led through the grand doors and into the hall. It was one of the finest rooms in the palace, and I only went inside a handful of times – once in the middle of a serious fight, but that is another story. Rich tapestries hung from every available space. Flags lined the rafters in purple and red and cloth of gold. Trophies lines the upper walls, dripping with gilt and silver.

Each enclave in the wall contained a fine pair of couches, upholstered in rich, patterned fabric, and a table with a top of solid marble edged in sculpted gold and silverwork sat by each pair.

But none of that competed with the magnificence of the Emperor's dais. The steps leading up to it were of rare purple coloured marble, polished to a sheen. The couch was larger, with a tremendous, gilded framework and canopy above, and tied curtains all in gold and purple that could be unleashed to give the emperor privacy hung from its top. His table appeared made of solid gold, and although I am sure it was merely plated it was still the wealth of a rich man on its own.

All this magnificence was lit by high windows, arrayed along the length of the hall, more glass than one of our cities would contain. Truly, it was a glorious hall. And all of it designed exactly to enact the feeling that coursed through my veins every time I saw it: awe. I never felt so small and simple and poor as I did in that hall. I have seen the emperor's bedchambers, and let me tell you, they are not half so rich.

The emperor was not there, of course, for it would not be proper for him to wait for us. So the crowd of attendants ushered us to one of the couches, where we stood and waited. It was only then that I realised we were to be alone. None of the other couches were occupied.

Nor did the emperor make us wait long. It was all theatre anyway, for surely he had merely been waiting the other side of the doors behind the throne, and to make us wait would merely be inconveniencing himself. So, with the sonorous tones of his attendant announcing him with his full titles, the emperor swept into the room with a gracious smile at all around and moved to his couch, where he paused for a moment, before sitting with a flourish.

The attendant gestured for Harald to sit, and then clapped his hands and shooed the majority of the others out of the hall, leaving only a small team of servants and a dozen guards who lined the dais and surrounded our enclave at a polite but proximate distance.

Michael IV was young, perhaps little more than my age. He was very handsome, and I could see immediately why Zoe had fallen for his looks. His smile was warm, and his hair dark brown and neat, with a close-cropped beard curled in the fashion of the very wealthy. His clothes were beyond magnificent, like a statue draped in rainbows and gold, quite dazzling to the eyes. I must be honest, I was rather taken in by it.

The emperor did not immediately speak, as Harald had been warned he would not. First the servants produced refreshments: iced, fruit-scented water, and stuffed dates, which I watched Harald sip and nibble with great jealousy. Then, when the emperor had drunk of his water and carefully eaten a date, he finally set his gaze on Harald and spoke.

'Komes Nordbrikt, I have heard great reports of your service in the east, and am pleased.'

Harald inclined his head. 'Basileus, I am honoured to be so praised, and to have given good service.'

Emperor Michael laughed, an oddly high-pitched laugh, but it seemed genuine. And then he stood suddenly, Harald rushing to his feet to match him, and Michael looked around the room and shook his head. 'I am so bored of this.' He flicked his fingers at the crowd of servants. 'The rest of you disappear so we can be alone.' He practically kicked at one of his overdressed attendants, sending the man scurrying. 'If you aren't holding a sword or a jug of wine, get out!' he said, with a twinkle of mischief in his eye.

I could not have been more surprised, and Harald's eyes bulged, but the few remaining officials scurried to obey, rushing to file out of the side door, leaving us alone with the emperor, the guards, and a handful of servants carrying food and drinks.

Then he came down the steps in a thoroughly unregal manner and simply planted himself on the empty couch across from Harald's, leaving my shocked prince unsure what to do.

'Sit down, Komes. Let us just be men together. By the saints, I am bored of the strictures of being emperor. I am dying to be in the company of those who won't be outraged if I ignore the protocols.' He waved his empty wine goblet at a servant and was immediately poured a drink. Another servant went to get Harald a replacement, which was also filled with wine.

My startled eyes rose to meet another of the guardsmen in bemusement, who broke his statue-like stance to give me the tiniest of shrugs and knowing looks.

Michael looked at Harald, who looked bemused but had managed to sit down with his drink. 'You are not outraged are you, Prince Araltes?'

Harald quickly shook his head. 'Not at all, Basileus, merely surprised.'

Michael laughed. 'Good!' He leaned forwards and gestured towards the door. 'You know I was one of these attendants just two years ago, don't you?'

Harald nodded carefully.

'Well, I used to be in charge of all these rules and procedures. Memorised them, enacted them, watched them. When it was my job I considered it a dull honour, but I knew how ridiculous it all was. I saw Romanos sigh and slump the moment no one was looking, casting his heavy cloak to the ground for a servant to collect. I saw Emperor Basil swear like a stable hand when he tripped and thought he was in private. I saw all this for the farce it was.' He smiled again, and his smile was indeed charming. 'And then I became emperor, and I realised how important it all was, that it wasn't done to make the emperor feel powerful or respected – quite the opposite. It was a tedious duty done to enforce upon those visiting the emperor how powerful and respected he was.' He grinned slightly manically. 'I am a performer, nothing more. That is the great secret.'

Harald smiled then too. 'I have seen a little of it before.'

'Of course you have, you are a prince – which is why I can forgo all the pretences in your presence and sit and drink like a man instead of posing like a living statue.' He took a deep draught of his wine. 'God, I hate it all.'

'You hate being the emperor?'

Michael's face contorted. 'What? No. Being the emperor is glorious, in private. It is the public face I am forced to wear, the ceremonies and speeches I must give and listen to, that are beyond tedium.'

'And none of your own people could see you like this,' stated Harald, nodding his head.

'No, no... They would strip me and drag me through the streets. They dislike me enough already, the rich Romans, for being a nobody. But they think Zoe controls me, a woman of proper heritage, and that keeps them quiet enough.'

Harald nodded. 'Basileus, why are you telling me this? Why did you summon me to meet?'

Michael did not answer directly. 'You are a problem or a solution for me, Araltes of Norway. Báulfr is dead, a man I could trust to do whatever he was asked, without question or complaint, even if it meant his death.' The emperor summoned a refill to his cup, which he was drinking at an alarming rate. 'Which, unfortunately, it did,' he said with a grim chuckle, and I realised he was already a little drunk.

'My wife hoped to use me as a puppet, and while – with the help of my brother – I was able to break free of her at first, most of the wealthy and powerful favour her because she was born in the purple, and I was born in the western districts of the city as the son of a money changer. I am a Roman, you see, but not a proper one in their eyes. I cannot trace my family back to Rome itself.'

He shook his head sadly. 'So, I cannot trust anyone in the palace outside of my brother and my family. I also cannot trust my wealthy Roman subjects, and no one can trust our poor Greek subjects, let alone the rest of the foreigners who live in our lands.' He smiled sadly and stared at Harald. 'And then there is you, and the threat you pose.' And suddenly his tone was not so friendly, and the guards around us were so awfully close.

'You have nothing to fear from me, Basileus. Have I not proved my loyalty to the empire?'

'No. No, you have not. You have proved you are brave and capable, but your actions serve yourself as much as they serve me, do they not?' Michael asked, and all the previous friendliness drained from the room, and his buffoonish good cheer was cast away.

Harald sat up a little straighter. 'I am a man of honour, and you know my oaths. I would not break them.'

'Ah, yes, the famous oathkeeping of the Northmen. A strange habit. You know, not even the most honourable Roman can be trusted entirely to keep his word. You see, we are the children of emperors and politicians going back a thousand years. A thousand years of fine words and then daggers in the dark!' He made a stabbing motion with his empty hand. 'Do you know what typically kills a Roman emperor?'

Harald was expressionless.

Michael swirled his cup and smiled voraciously. 'The *next* emperor.'

'So I hear,' said Harald, with a little more reproach than he should have added. Michael's face tensed a little.

'Yes. And how many of the Porphyrogenita sisters have invited you to hold that position?' he asked, and the guards around us closed in. 'Theodora did, so I am told. And you met Zoe yesterday. Did she offer you my seat?'

Michael glared at us, and I did not dare move. Harald did not show fear, only a fierce intensity. He could only defend his life with words in that room; they were all that separated us from death.

'The empress did not make any such offer.'

Michael stared at him, then nodded. 'But Theodora's faction did?'

Harald squirmed. 'One of her people.'

'It amounts to the same. And if Zoe offers it to you, why should I believe you will not take it?'

'Because of my oath,' said Harald, almost with a snarl, pressing his hands into his knees.

'Your oath is to the throne,' said Michael softly. 'Would it truly break that oath for you to become the one who sits on it? Many of my people regard me as illegitimate, a threat to the throne itself and all it stands for. Could Zoe not convince you of that?'

Harald's eye twitched, and my heart stopped in my chest, because Zoe had been working hard to convince Harald of that very thing.

'I am also sworn to defend the life of the one who sits on it.'

Michael waved that away. 'Someone else could do the killing, and you the sitting.' He pressed his mouth into a grave line and tapped a finger on his knee. I could see we were losing. It was just like a battle, except I could do nothing to help Harald.

'You must give me something better, Prince Araltes, some reason to believe you will not side with one of those damned sisters or some other pretender against me, or your story will end in this hall. So convince me why, Harald. Why would you not take my throne?'

Harald drew himself up, and answered calmly. 'It is the wrong throne.' He stood. Four guards moved to get between him and the emperor, blades outreached, but Michael saw Harald was not threatening with his posture, and he raised a hand to hold them back.

'Explain.'

The guards nervously stepped back a half pace, and Harald eyed them fearlessly and then dropped down slowly, putting one knee on the red-veined marble at the emperor's feet. 'Here is my promise to you: my word. If you sat upon the throne of Norway, I would claw my way over your corpse to replace you. I would shred my oaths, I would burn your cities, kill your family, massacre your men and tear your lifeless corpse from the seat.' Michael swallowed, leaning back from the ferocity of Harald's words.

'But this is *not* Norway, and you do not sit upon its throne,' Harald said, and fast as a snake, he swiped a hand at one of the swords that were levelled at his face, so fast the owner could not react other than to exclaim in alarm. But all Harald had done was cut the side of his palm. Without taking his eyes off the emperor he clenched his fingers into a fist, letting the blood seep between them and drip down onto the red-veined marble, the drops spattering across the rich surface and leeching into the already blood-red cracks.

'You do not know what this means,' Harald said, opening his hand and pressing three fingers to the side of his face, smearing three lines of blood across his cheek. 'But it means death to my enemies, an oath beyond words, so deep it can only be shown with blood. And *you* are not my enemy, Michael of the Romans, and your throne is not *my* throne. So I will guard your life for as long as I am in your service, and none can turn me against you.'

There was silence. Michael was frozen in place by the sheer force of Harald's gaze, and the ghastly spectre of the blood streaked across his face. Harald remained motionless on the marble, staring at the emperor, waiting for his fate to be decided.

Michael swallowed, the dry gulp of a man who has snapped out of a nervous trance, and then he nodded swiftly, reaching for his wine and trying to compose himself. 'Good. You may rise, Araltes.' He waved Harald back to his couch, if only to get the man away from him without being seen to retreat.

Harald rose slowly and sat back down, the guards around relaxing and sheathing their weapons. Behind me, I heard the hiss of steel on wool as the man who had been preparing to kill me put his sword in its scabbard.

'I told John that you were not a threat,' said Michael with false confidence. 'He tried to convince me otherwise, but I know you Varangians better than him,' he said, gesturing to the guards who still ringed us, 'and I know how important your oaths and their honour are. You are strange people, strange indeed.' He stared in mild horror at the blood that still ran from Harald's hand, forming rivulets on his knee and then dropping down to the floor. 'But your fearlessness and your honour are your unique qualities. He either doesn't understand that, or he just doesn't like you.'

'I am sure your brother only seeks what is best for you,' grated Harald, ignoring the blood running over his leg.

'Of course, of course... I assume this means that equally you cannot be persuaded to move against the empress?' said Michael with mild annoyance.

'I cannot.'

'Very well. So, if you cannot be corrupted, and you do not want my throne, why are you here, so far from home?'

'To earn wealth, reputation and experience, all of which I will need to regain my brother's legacy.'

Michael nodded in agreement. 'I believe you. Well, let us eat and drink.' He glanced again at Harald's leg and looked over his shoulder. 'And for God's sake, will someone bring him something for his hand?'

PART III

PEACEMAKER

18

SPRING 1037 AD

Well, having told both the emperor and empress that he would have no part in their schemes, it was no surprise that we had no further invitations from them afterwards. We left them to continue their silent war, and we went about our duties. Bodies washed up in the harbours of the Golden Horn throughout the rest of that summer and winter of 1036, and Afra and Thorir did their best to keep us abreast of the situation, but frankly it was beyond even their skills.

The rest of the banda arrived back from the east a month after we did; with peace secure and no further threats to the empire's rule on that frontier their duty was in the capital again.

The emperor, seeking no doubt to secure our loyalty, bathed the guard in gold from the riches the caliph had paid him for peace. On top of the loot we had gained in the campaign at Antioch, we paid off our debt to the empire in a single payment.

It was during this time, with little to do beyond guard duty and training, that Harald's old warband started to coalesce around him once more. The survivors were still officially spread amongst two banda: his own Storm Ravens and Styrbjorn's Warborn. Styrbjorn was already so devoted to Harald that the banda were practically one, and firmly under Harald's control.

The blood-marked and the others who had joined us in the Rus were together again, but stronger now, with new friends and comrades who had stood and fought and bled alongside us, and seen Harald's leadership and courage.

Báulfr was entombed in the scholai chapel in a marble sarcophagus donated by Zoe with almost the whole of the guard present. Emperor and Empress vied to outdo each other in their generosity, and it was a good time to be a guardsman.

The emperor announced a whole month of victory celebrations in the spring of 1037, when the gold from the caliphate had arrived and the weather was fine again. Michael wanted to make the most of the successful campaign against the empire's most tenacious and frequent enemy, and spent an entire year's income on the series of events and festivals, or so we heard. I believe it, having seen the results.

For us in the guard it was not so much a time of celebration as a time of continuous duties. Our part in the great victory near Edessa had been repeated, exaggerated and lionised to the eager public, so the emperor took every opportunity to show us off, and we had to guard the imperial family at every event they participated in.

The first event was a great parade from outside the city to the west, through the golden gate in the city wall, and then all the way up the great street through the heart of the city, through the line of forums and public spaces and up to the great square of the Augustaion outside the Hagia Sophia, where we paraded past the imperial family and all the great people of the city, seated in a lavishly built royal viewing platform against the buildings on the southern edge.

We were wearing our finest maille and cloaks, carrying polished great axes and bearing all manner of spoils of war supposedly from the campaign in the east, although I believe almost none of them truly were from that campaign. Perhaps there is some great storeroom in the warren beneath the hippodrome where such things are kept for those occasions.

Finally, the entire guard lined up in our massed ranks in the shadow of the cathedral, with thousands of citizens watching, and we shouted our salute to the emperor and empress, who presented a united front to the crowd that belied their intense struggle for power.

That march through the city made us extremely popular. For the entire three-day festival that followed, every guardsman not on duty went out into the city to drink and eat and be treated like heroes. All the main streets were festooned with flowers, banners and signs. It was exciting and beautiful and seducing. I doubt a guardsman had to pay silver for a single drink that entire time, so inundated were we with offers from a grateful and roused populace.

And let me tell you, food and drinks were not the only things on offer. I swear to you, it was noticeable how many unusually pale-skinned or fair-haired babies were born in the city nine months later, often to daughters of good families. Who could blame us for taking the opportunities presented? Bored and usually secluded young women wanted the opportunity to lie with a war hero, and we simply wanted what we always did.

Even Harald. Yes, I know how often I speak of his self-discipline and seeming lack of interest in women. But it was only that he usually had other, more important things on his mind, consumed as he was with his burning ambitions and his plans to recover his throne. But from time to time, when nothing could be done to advance his position, he would remember his other desires. There were many daughters of the great men of the city who wanted to seduce a prince of the North and a hero of the empire. On two occasions I sat guard outside wealthy houses and waited while he... accepted their advances. Well, it was more interesting than most of my more formal guard duties.

* * *

With the deaths in the Arab war and those who turned in their cloaks, the guard was reduced to around two thousand men, so we needed all the recruits we could get. Messages were sent to the Rus and as far as Sweden and Norway, reporting of the great riches and glory the guard had earned, and seeking new recruits. Varangians who chose to retire after the battle, through age or through injury, were gifted fine eastern swords in gold-chased scabbards. It was a cunning ploy. When they returned home with such fabulous riches others would be inspired to follow their example to sail south and east.

Aki Freysson took over Báulfr's duties while we waited for a new commander to be officially installed. It was difficult for us, because Aki still neither trusted nor liked Harald, and the fact that so many in the guard believed Harald had proven himself at the battle on the riverbank while Aki fought unseen on a flank only made things worse. I have said before, we Norsemen were subject to the ranks and rules of the Greeks, but truly, we still believed in the old ways, where leadership was earned through actions, character, and success in battle.

So Aki sat in the office and wore the marks, but Harald was now held in the greatest regard by the men of the Varangian tagma.

Well, we recruited and we trained and we did our guard duties. We attended elaborate church services for feast days to protect the emperor's representatives and control the crowds. We went to several races at the great hippodrome. That was when the first significant event of that year took place, at the victory races given by the emperor towards the end of his great month of celebrations.

* * *

Aki sent for us in the barracks one fine morning, which was unusual in itself as he usually avoided speaking to Harald. We went up to Báulfr's old office and found him there, buried in reports and parchment.

He made us wait while he finished noting something down, then looked up at Harald, tossing a written order across the table. 'The akolouthos has requested you to guard the royal box at the games tomorrow,' he said, with obvious disapproval.

Harald peered at the document in surprise. 'Why us and not the first?'

'The first will have men there too, but they are overstretched and exhausted by this month's events, and need the numbers.' Then Aki looked troubled. 'Apparently your bandon was requested specifically.'

'By who?'

'The akolouthos did not say, but I assume by the emperor or empress, for no one else has the authority.'

Harald's attention was grabbed by that. Despite the danger of his conflict with John he loved any interaction with the imperial family. To him, it was all a series of opportunities and an intrigue he could not resist.

'Regardless, these are your orders: you and twenty of your men will report to the palace gate of the hippodrome at dawn and be briefed on your duties. It is strange, but I do not care why. The guard obeys.'

'As you say, Aki, we will do as commanded.'

* * *

Harald chose twenty of our men and we paraded at the ornate gateway to the hippodrome near the inner palace at the first light of dawn the next day. Explaining the hippodrome to you will be difficult, for nothing like it exists anywhere in the North, but it was a building of supreme importance to the Roman way of life and to the imperial institution. It is a horse racing track about four hundred paces long, with a turn at each end. But it is no course marked out in the earth with sticks; it is an enormous stone edifice with rising rows of seats and standing areas that can accommodate tens of thousands of people, perhaps as many as one hundred thousand.

Yes! In a single building of stone and marble, one in five of the citizens of the great city could gather. The purpose of this building seems trivial, to race horses drawing wheeled chariots, but its purpose is so much more grand.

The hippodrome is the ultimate expression of the Roman ideals of confidence, culture and imperial grandeur. Simply by being wealthy enough to build a structure so vast, and to allow a hundred thousand of your citizens to be gathered within it for days at a time for no other purpose than to be entertained, expresses the sheer wealth of their empire.

It is also the best place where the people could see the emperor and his family, for they had a raised, sheltered platform on one side, positioned to be visible from all parts of the enormous space. There he could give charity to the crowd, make popular announcements, and through positioning of high officials inside the imperial lodge show who was in favour, who was rising and falling in the public affairs of the empire.

It is a grand theatre of politics and wealth, there to help control the population. And it is magnificent.

None of these things, however, were what I was considering on that morning. I was tired, I was bored of the festivals and marches, and I was annoyed that I had to spend all day standing in armour with the certainty that nothing would happen, because nothing ever happened.

Finally, the komes of the first bandon, a dour and relentlessly humourless little Swede whose name escapes me, came down to brief Harald.

'Good morning, Komes.' He cast a disapproving eye over our ranks. 'This is the best you can present yourselves?'

'We are combat soldiers, not palace guards,' replied Harald. 'Our weapons and armour have seen battle many times.'

'Then perhaps they could have seen the armourer and a polishing stone more often. You will be guarding the emperor himself, and you will embarrass us with this ragged collection.'

I was furious. Firstly, because it was my duty to make sure the men were well turned out and this felt like a personal attack on me, and secondly because it was nonsense – our weapons were polished to a shine, our tunics washed and our cloaks freshly dyed and brilliant. Of course, some of the axes and helmets we carried showed the marks of battle, and some pitting and scarring of rust. But these weapons had travelled to the east and back in the belly of a ship, fought battles, been on long marches. Of course they were not perfect! I was fuming silently, trying to keep myself in check.

Harald was not affected. 'If we had more warning that your own men were incapable of fulfilling your duties, we would have prepared better,' he said with a bored expression.

The komes' face reddened a little, but then he grimaced and curtly waved at us to follow. 'Next time, be prepared *before* you are needed, like proper guardsmen. Come, I will show you to your stations.'

We were led through the gate and into the bowels of the building underneath the stands. That gate is solely for the use of the imperial family, staff and guards. The network of tunnels and storerooms inside the stands are only accessible from the palace side, and the imperial lodge built into the stands – while appearing to be proximate to the people – is not reachable from inside the public areas. You see, while the imperial family wishes to maintain an aura of accessibility, fear of revolt or assassination means they are cleverly, and completely, separated.

A series of grand stairways took us to the lodge. The komes left some of our men guarding the lower gate, the stairs and the guardhouse.

The last dozen of us went to the lodge itself. The lodge has two levels. One, inside, contains a room for relaxation, shade and refreshment and a place the imperial family can be away from public view at any point during the long day of games. Behind the imperial room are a series of servants' quarters where food is prepared, and a guardhouse. The upper level is open to the public in the form of a large, marble-trimmed platform with a gilded railing surrounding it, and seating for the emperor and empress in the centre on a raised dais, and a dozen or so guests and family on each side.

The open platform is sheltered by a fabulously decorated wooden roof, suspended over the platform by iron brackets, pillars, and ropes tied to the walls above. The roof has great purple curtains that can be drawn and lowered to cover the front and sides of the platform to hide the occupants and allow a grand reveal to popular acclaim when they arrive.

'Station one man at each corner and two at the door. You and your deputy stand at the back of the platform by the wall, and the rest in the guardhouse downstairs. Swap the guards on the platform out four times a day with those in the guardhouse. I will also be here most of the day, attending the emperor. But if he leaves for any reason I will go with him and you are in command. Questions?'

'What if there is an attack?' Harald asked.

'In six hundred years there has never been an attack on the royal family in this lodge.'

'But what if there is? Why are we here, if not to defend against it?'

The komes gave Harald a glare, but then relented with a sigh. 'We take the emperor and empress back down the stairs and into the palace where we can fortify in their quarters until the situation is resolved.'

Harald nodded. 'Seems simple enough.'

'So simple even a battlefield soldier can manage,' said the komes with a sour drawl, and then turned towards the door. 'My men and I will escort the emperor and empress to the lodge after the crowd arrives.' Then he was gone.

Well, it was quite some time before the stadium filled. The people of the city came into the stadium as the sun was already well-risen. The rich filled the stands near the royal lodge, where they could feel close to the rulers and where there was proper seating, and around the curved end of the track where there was the most action in the races. Most of the rest filled benches or standing areas in the upper levels or on the far side of the track.

Finally, a guardsman came up the stairs and called orders up to the hidden men who operated the curtains from the walkway above the lodge, and the curtains were lowered, cutting the platform off from the view of the public.

I could hear the excitement outside rise as they saw this, and knew it meant the imperial couple were coming.

'Stand tall, men, and don't move unless I order it,' snapped Harald, and the eight of us on the platform went to our assigned positions and assumed the tiresome statue-like poses we were so used to.

We heard footsteps and the rustling of maille coming up the stairs and then four men of the first bandon appeared and following them their komes, the imperial standard bearer, and then Emperor Michael himself.

He smiled at the komes of the first and ignored us all entirely as he made his way to his seat, fussing over his purple cloak and the golden circlet on his head, allowing a servant to rearrange the drape of his clothes for best effect.

Then Empress Zoe appeared up the stairs with more servants and guards, and the large platform was suddenly quite crowded. She noticed Harald and I could see the surprise on her face, quickly replaced with a quick and charming smile. Then she was also escorted to her throne and took position beside her husband. I noted that the emperor studiously ignored her, keeping his eyes on the closed curtain.

Zoe looked at her husband inquiringly, but when she got no reaction, set her eyes on the curtain with a small shake of the head.

Finally, the rest of the royal guests had filed into position in front of their assigned seats, and the men of the first bandon mostly saluted and left, leaving their komes and two men behind. I noticed with shock that Maria was one of the guests. Then Maria's eyes moved to us, and I saw the flash of recognition even with us in our helmets and armour. There was a moment of paralysis on her face, and then a broad smile and a little nod before she turned away to go to her seat near the railing.

'Did you see that?' whispered Harald.

'Yes.'

'What is she doing here?'

'I don't know. I heard Theodora was in the emperor's favour again, but for Maria to be his guest?'

'We will worry about it later.'

Finally, with an audible breath and a straightening of his spine and squaring of his shoulders, the emperor raised a hand and clicked his fingers. Orders were relayed at the back of the platform, and a moment later hidden trumpeters and drummers sounded, calling the stadium to an expectant hush.

The pounding of the drums and the blare of the trumpets rose to a deafening crescendo and then the purple curtains rose upwards and to the sides, revealing the platform to the stadium.

Michael jutted one shoulder forwards as the crowd burst into cheers and applause and raised one hand high to acknowledge them, smiling broadly and swivelling to face all parts of the arena. Then he turned to Zoe and dramatically seized her hand, raising it up with his and giving her a beaming smile and even a slight nod of his head, almost a bow, which drove the crowd into even higher excitement. Zoe bowed graciously to her husband and then surveyed the crowd for a moment.

Two servants brought forwards a wrapped bundle and, at a gesture from Michael, tied cords at both ends to the railing and then unfurled the bundle, which turned out to be a broad blue banner. I did not understand the significance, but it was clearly important because part of the crowd cheered voraciously.

Finally, with a sweep of his cloak, Michael gestured to his wife to take her seat, and then the imperial couple sat down on their thrones, followed by the guests.

I looked at Harald in bemusement at the whole performance, and saw he was enthralled and did not even notice my wry glance.

* * *

Well, with the emperor seated and his favour declared, the competition was free to commence. The significance of the blue banner became apparent when four chariots lined up for the first race. Each one was bedecked in a single colour: green, red, white or blue. Then I noted that there were four huge banners over the enclosed stables at the far end where the chariots had emerged from.

Each colour represented a team, and the emperor had declared his support for the blues. By mid-morning, the blue team was doing well, as far as I could see, and the emperor stood and cheered, waving at the blue chariot to urge the driver on to glory as they secured their first win.

* * *

It was a long morning, but in between the races guests would come and go from the platform, going down to the lower level for refreshments.

At the same time, Michael went to the railing at the side of the box and received petitions and votives of support from the carefully corralled citizens chosen to be able to come and present themselves. This was a huge part of the festivities, and an opportunity to seek the emperor's ruling or favour when he was in a good mood, and outside of the strictures of the formal courts.

It was traditional for the emperor to be both merciful and generous at these events, so being allowed to come forward and petition was highly sought after. I'm sure much silver changed hands to gain such access, because everything in that city was corrupt under the surface.

In one of those breaks, while Michael was attending the crowd, Maria came over to us looking amused. 'Do you rough Northerners understand the races?'

'What are you doing here, Maria?' said Harald gruffly.

'Now now, that is no way to speak to a guest of the emperor,' Maria chided him with an amused look. 'I am *Lady* Maria, and I was invited.'

'Why were you invited?'

'Because my lady Theodora is a member of the imperial family and I am here as her representative. She can't come herself, you understand. It wouldn't be appropriate for a sister of the holy orders.'

'So you are getting close to the emperor so that you can betray him.'

Maria's face twisted into anger and she spoke softly. 'You should be more careful making accusations like that. Words like that can kill, sometimes their wielder.'

'You have never hidden your ambitions; I doubt they have changed.'

'Some of us grow and change with circumstances, Harald. Those with the wit and intelligence to do so. Have a good day at the races, Harald. Perhaps I will see you again afterwards.' She walked off without a backwards glance.

'You shouldn't let her bait you,' I grumbled.

Harald was staring at Maria's back with a concerned expression. 'She is up to something; she was too defensive about it.'

'You are imagining things.'

Harald ruminated on it for a few moments. 'No, something is off.'

Well, there was nothing I could do about that, so I just turned away and resumed watching the emperor talking to his subjects.

* * *

In the mid-afternoon there was a break from the racing while music and dancers entertained the crowd down on the track. The emperor took the opportunity to go into the lower level, but the empress stayed on the platform, rising to her feet and walking to the railing to look over the crowd.

Then she signalled to one of the servants to lower the side curtain, so she could have privacy, and came over towards me and Harald.

We bowed. 'How may I serve you, Basilissa?' Harald asked.

Zoe smiled and shook her head. 'I don't need anything,' she replied quietly. There was no one left on the platform other than our men and her servants. 'Except a husband who acknowledges me,' she added with a tired sigh.

Harald shuffled uncomfortably and Zoe looked slightly embarrassed and shook her head. 'I'm sorry, that is not appropriate for this venue.' Then her charming smile instantly returned. 'Do you like the races?'

'I was not watching them, Basilissa.'

She cocked a perfectly shaped eyebrow. 'Really? Then what *were* you watching?'

'The crowd.'

'Ah, yes, of course. Ever watchful,' she said, in a softly mocking tone.

'It is my duty.'

'It is, and I am glad you are good at it. Well, I am going to refresh myself. Keep my seat safe for a while, will you?'

'Eric, escort the empress,' Harald said, looking at me.

Zoe chuckled. 'Oh, he can't come where I am going. When a lady says she is leaving for refreshment, it is not *quite* what we mean.' She winked at Harald, who looked deeply embarrassed as Zoe walked off with her servants in tow.

The empress and some of the other dignitaries eventually returned, but Michael and some of his guests did not. Zoe looked increasingly annoyed at the glaringly empty chair beside her. Eventually she indicated to Harald, who stepped over to her side. 'Why has my husband not returned? Is there a problem?'

'Not that I am aware of, Basilissa. Perhaps he is… refreshing himself.'

Harald was trying to be light, but Zoe was not amused. 'It looks bad for him to miss the start of a race.'

'Shall I go and inquire?'

She drummed her fingers on the gilded armrest for a moment. 'No, not you – too confrontational. Send your man here to find out where he is, subtly. Are you capable of subtlety, Varangian? If you seem to chide him it will not go well.'

'I am, Basilissa,' I replied.

I headed down the stairs again and went into the large room where the emperor and his guests were supposed to be. The room was empty but for a single servant.

'Where is the emperor?' I asked in shock.

The servant looked at me nervously, unsure if he should answer. My darkening look said that he should.

'The emperor was called away on urgent matter of state,' the hapless servant said.

'What matter?'

'I do not know. They did not leave long ago.'

I returned upstairs and went to Zoe's side. 'Basilissa, Emperor Michael has returned to the palace, some urgent matter of state.'

Zoe looked shocked. 'What matter of state?'

'I do not know, I did not hear.'

'Do you wish me to escort you back to the palace?' asked Harald.

Zoe shook her head firmly. 'No, it would ruin the event if we were both seen to abandon it. The cost in wasted gold and the trust of the people would be enormous. It would cause rumours and possibly panic. Our attendance is essential.' She raised a finger to her lip and chewed on it. 'I will send one of my people to the palace to find out what is going on.'

The empress called over one of the well-dressed ladies who was seated nearby and gave her hurried orders.

Harald looked at where Maria had been. She was gone.

'Something is wrong,' he said again, with more force. 'We should take the empress away.'

I felt it too. 'But the empress will not leave.'

He cursed under his breath, and then shoved the big timber pillar that held up the back of the canopy in annoyance.

It moved.

Harald stood back in surprise and looked up and down the structure. It looked massive and solid, but it had moved under his hand with ease. 'What is...?' I looked at the base of the pillar where it had moved, and saw the bracket that held it in place had completely separated. I bent down and picked a nail out of the bracket, a nail that should have gone through the base. It was cut off near the head. The cut was shiny, rough – new.

A dread feeling crept up over me, and then I looked up at the top of the pillar, where the huge, heavy wooden roof was attached to the wall with large iron brackets, and saw that there were scratch marks around the huge iron nails, and damage to the masonry that supported the bracket was just barely visible.

Harald turned to the platform and beckoned to one of the people responsible for opening the curtains. He pointed at the broken bracket and the damage at the top of the pillar. 'What has happened here?'

The man looked at the base and then the top, and his face fell. 'I… I don't know.'

'Who is in charge of your people?'

The servant turned to point at the back of the space. 'He is.' We looked and saw a glimpse of a simply dressed man hurriedly leaving the platform, giving us a single look of fear. 'Where is he going?' the servant said dumbly.

Then we heard a voice call something out urgently above us, and then the sound of scraping metal on wood. There was a trickle of dust from the gap between the wall and the awning, and then the gap widened.

Harald's eyes met mine for an instant, wide with recognition, and he turned to look at the empress in horror.

19

'Everybody out!' shouted Harald, running towards the empress. I was rooted in shock for a moment longer, staring up at the top of the pillar as the roof separated from the awning and the damaged bracket parted company from the wall.

Then I too turned towards the empress, the full horror of what was about to happen flooding into my mind. Harald grabbed the shocked Zoe around the chest with both arms and started carrying her from the platform as fast as he could go, ignoring her shouts of outrage.

I grabbed at one of the other guests, shoving them towards the back of the platform, but they were all moving too slowly, too shocked and afraid.

'Go!' I roared. 'It's coming down!'

There was a screech of iron to punctuate my outburst, and then the roof shuddered, momentarily balancing on the damaged pillar and then starting to sway.

That motivated the guests in a way my words could not, and they made a panicked rush for the exit of the platform even as I turned to run. I sprinted the ten paces to the sheltered alcove at the rear of the space as Harald reached the entrance with Zoe and shoved her ungracefully through.

There was a creak and snap of protesting wood above me and I skidded into shelter even as the huge, wooded awning finally collapsed with a sickening crunch just a few paces behind me. I heard the muffled sound of a woman who had moved too slowly wailing from beneath the wreckage. One of our men guarding the corner of the platform had jumped off the side of the platform and was lying dazed in the benches below. The other was not visible in the dust and the wreckage.

There was a cascade of panic and screams of horror from down in the stadium, but I could not worry about that or my missing man. I shoved through the terrified guests towards the door and found Harald had backed Zoe into a corner and was covering her, sword drawn. More of our men were coming up the stairs, and he didn't trust anyone we didn't know.

'Get the empress to the palace!' shouted Harald, moving towards our men and kicking aside one of the guests we had just saved from being crushed.

He half pushed and half carried Zoe down the stairs, who had stopped protesting and was open-mouthed in shock and outrage, as the guards formed up behind and in front of us. We ignored everyone else as we made our way down into the bowels of the building and out of the gate into the inner palace.

'What happened, who did this?' she hissed, wriggling again to be let go.

'An assassination attempt. We must get you to safety, it may not be over.'

Finally lowering the empress to the ground and letting Zoe move on her own feet, Harald took us straight to the inner palace where confused guardsmen from the first bandon greeted us and let us inside.

We sent for the rest of the Storm Ravens, and then the komes of the first came running from the emperor's quarters with a dozen armed men, his face red with rage.

'What are you doing?' he thundered at Harald, before turning to apologise to Zoe.

'No, he is right. There was an incident,' said Zoe, trying to compose herself.

'What incident?'

'The roof of the lodge collapsed,' Harald said. 'It was deliberate, an attempt on the empress's life.'

'No, it was not,' said Zoe, and Harald opened his mouth to argue. 'No, listen to me, Araltes, and listen truly. It was an accident, do you understand me? The roof failed, and we saw it in time for me to avoid being harmed. There was no attack, no plot, no attempt on my life.' She stepped over to him and stared into his eyes intensely. 'Do you hear me, Komes? If rumours go out that someone just tried to assassinate the imperial family, in the palace, it will be a disaster. It was an accident – that is what you will say.' She turned to look around. 'That is what you will all say, or God help you.'

Harald calmed himself and nodded. 'As you order, Basilissa.'

'Good.' Zoe turned to the komes of the first. 'Take me to my husband, now!'

* * *

For two days the palace was on high alert. Almost no one was allowed to move around and the imperial family were secluded.

Harald met with Zoe again, alone, and when he came back he was glum. 'We are ordered to do nothing about the attack. Zoe and the emperor are treating it as an accidental tragedy. It cannot be admitted that there was an assassination attempt; it makes them look weak and could provoke more dissent.'

'But don't you think the emperor was behind it?'

'Quite possibly, and Zoe agrees. But something about it doesn't quite make sense. The emperor was summoned to the palace on a false pretence, by a servant who has gone missing. Someone worked to keep Michael out of the way. If he knew about it, why make his exit so elaborate?'

'Perhaps deliberately elaborate to render him above suspicion. And what of the man we saw running from the platform? The one in charge of the servants there. Surely he can be made to say who ordered it?'

'Unlikely – his body was pulled from the Golden Horn this morning.'

'Then Maria? What of Maria?'

Harald looked conflicted. 'We didn't discuss Maria.'

'What? But she was there, and left just before it collapsed!'

'We don't know that has anything to do with it,' said Harald defensively. 'Many guests of the emperor left with him.'

'Why are you defending her?'

'I am not defending her,' snapped Harald. 'I am just not going to condemn her to torture merely for being present. We have no evidence she was involved.' He calmed himself. 'But have Afra and Thorir watch her. I want to know what she is doing, and who she is meeting. I don't know if she was involved in this plot, but am sure she is involved in something, and I want to know what.'

* * *

Well, the failed plot against Zoe, publicly acknowledged or not, only deepened the silent war between the factions. There were rumours of uprisings and mutinies in the provinces, of struggles between the emperor and empress to secure the loyalty of governors and generals. The threat of civil war hung in the air.

It began to be called the lover's war, in the city. As if it was merely a heated argument between husband and wife, just like any other, that had been magnified because of the power each wielded. If only most of the people knew how bad things truly were in the palace, of the murders and the plots, the empire might have fallen into panic and economic collapse. I began to understand clearly why Zoe had wanted to pretend the attack in the hippodrome had been merely an accident.

Afra and Thorir did their best to keep track of Maria and Theodora's actions. Maria was an infrequent visitor to the palace, but we did not know who she was meeting or why. The inner realms of the palace were even more tightly secured than usual, and nothing Afra or Thorir could do would pry them open for inspection.

* * *

As the conflict over the palace was reaching its height we were called to meet the emperor again, Harald and I. By which I mean Harald was invited, and I simply followed. This was no formal event. We were called to the heart of the empire's power, the hall of war, deep within the palace. It was here, with an enormous map of the empire painted on one wall, updated monthly to show any changes in territory, position of armies and fleets, and names of settlements owned or lost, that the emperor would meet his highest-ranking officers and decide the conduct of wars.

The emperor was not standing by the map – he was sitting at the head of a long table, strewn messily with parchments and scrolls, and he looked reduced, fragile. A year of the lover's war had clearly worn at his body and mind. The domestikos of the scholai of the east was there, an upright, greying man who was responsible for all imperial forces east of Constantinople.

There were other officers that I did not know. All looked up as we entered and approached, and the emperor flicked his gaze up at Harald and smiled thinly. 'Komes Araltes,' he said, waving Harald over as we performed our elaborate bows.

'Basileus, I am here to serve,' Harald said crisply. I noted he was much more formal and neutral in the presence of the other officers, who all far outranked him and were uniformly regarding him with an air of distaste. This was not a room accustomed to the presence of a mere komes of the guard.

'Araltes, the empire is going through a period of high tension, despite our recent victory over the Arabs. We need something to lift the people's spirits, and the empress and I have determined that the ideal solution is to reinvigorate the religious heart of our empire by rebuilding and reopening the Church of the Holy Sepulchre in Jerusalem for pilgrims to visit.'

Harald and I looked at each other in surprise, for even we knew of that most famous and holy church, and that it had been sacked and denuded by the Moslems many years ago and lay abandoned, inaccessible to the followers of Christ.

'It is a fine endeavour. How will we serve it?' asked Harald.

'As part of the peace arrangements with the caliph he has granted free access for pilgrims to Jerusalem and the holy sites, and promised materials and funding to rebuild the church – although of course we must do the actual building ourselves. It would not do to have the godless heathen desecrate what remains with their touch any further.' Harald nodded in silent agreement.

'We cannot send builders without an escort, so the caliph has agreed to our demands to allow a small force to escort a party of builders and clergy to the church, and to allow them to guard it and visit other local sites in the Holy Land as the party members see fit.'

'How small a force?' said Harald nervously. Several of the senior officers glared at him in outrage; questioning the emperor, in any way, was clearly not acceptable. Michael tiredly tutted at them and continued.

'Five hundred men, that is what was agreed.'

Harald nodded grimly. Five hundred men was a very small force to send such a large distance, especially through very recently hostile land.

'It is too small an expedition for a general to lead, and too specialist for thematic levies. Only a unit from one of the tagma will suffice, and we need a leader familiar with such expeditions, and with the guarding of important people.'

Harald and I saw where this was going, and I felt him tense with excitement.

'Your name was brought forward, Araltes, as I believe you earned your fame in an expedition against the Pechenegs with a similar force.'

The look on the faces of several of the officers made it clear they heartily disagreed, but they too were not going to argue with the emperor.

'I have commanded such a force on several occasions, Basileus,' said Harald with a bow of his head.

'Yes, so I hear. So I charge you to take five hundred men of the guard and escort a party to the Church of the Holy Sepulchre and to whichever sites they deem fit and necessary, and ensure their safe return to the city.'

'The caliph's forces, will they threaten us?'

'Be quiet,' snapped the domestikos, unable to contain his anger.

'No, let him speak,' said the emperor, and the domestikos bowed his greying head submissively and held his tongue.

The emperor turned to Harald again, and his face was drawn, his eyes hooded. 'No, the caliphate dare not, they cannot afford another war. However, the land is plagued with bandits, and with rebels against the caliph, so it will be a perilous journey, all the more so because of who will be in the party.'

Harald looked at Michael with intense curiosity, but gave the emperor time to elaborate. 'My lady Theodora Porphyrogenita will be accompanying you on the pilgrimage,' he said, and Harald sharply drew in breath.

'Basileus, the risks of that...'

'I am aware of the risks, Komes!' snapped Michael, rising. 'It is a message, a message to our enemies of our confidence, that we would send the sister of the empress into such danger, so confidently, and if she returns unharmed it will be a symbol of our power over our rivals that none will ignore. The people will whisper of the boldness of it in the streets and our soldiers will celebrate the glory of it in their barracks. Do you lack the courage or conviction to conduct this duty?'

Harald dropped his head like a spanked dog and shook it vehemently. 'I do not, Basileus. I apologise.'

Michael let him hang there, temples pulsing as he looked at my prince, and then he nodded. 'Good. You will prepare five hundred men and you must leave in five days, for you will not wish to be travelling when the high summer arrives, I assure you.' He gestured to the grey haired domestikos. 'Your orders and passes will be organised. I must attend other matters. God bless you, Komes Araltes.' He gave Harald a bitter and fearful look. 'And if you fail to protect Lady Theodora, ensure that you do not return.' And then he left the room, stranding us alone with the disapproving domestikos and his officers.

* * *

Aki was deeply displeased, but he accepted the written orders with barely a grunt as he had no say in the matter.

'And who will you take, the seventh and the fourteenth? Who else?'

'The second,' said Harald, after a deep intake of breath.

Aki's face flushed. 'You think you will steal my own men? You fucking cur, you will not.'

Harald did his best to remain calm. 'I have orders to take whoever I wish apart from the first banda, and I need the best men, the most cohesive unit I can make, with no time to train them together. The second has fought with us, bled with us, and you have trained them to be among the best in the guard. It is the best choice. In any case, you are busy here, tied to this office. This will be their only chance for a campaign this year. Would they not appreciate it?'

It was not flattery, and not presented as such. Aki may have been hateful, but none could question his value as an officer, and his Wolfhounds bandon were among the very best.

Aki swore and hammered his hand onto Báulfr the Broad's old desk. 'You would take my banner, Nordbrikt. Do not dress it up with pretty words. You do it to spite me.'

'No, I do it to succeed. And should you have a banner any more? Is not the whole guard yours now?'

Aki shook his head irritably. 'Not yet. The akolouthos still refuses to name me permanently to the post. I am here by acclaim only, and do not have the power to stop this horseshit.' He pointed angrily at the papers. Then he sighed deeply again and sat down. 'Well, it does not seem like you need my blessing, Nordbrikt, so take the men and be gone. For the empire's sake, I hope you succeed. What is your plan of transport?'

'The admiral advises we head to Jaffa, and take the old pilgrim's road down to Jerusalem, and wherever else from there Theodora wishes to go. The emperor intends to make a statement of confidence, and also to clear the road of bandits if we can, stamp our authority on the area.'

Aki shook his head in disbelief. 'With only five hundred men, and guarding a civilian caravan?'

'Indeed.'

'You have someone with you who knows the road? None of us have travelled it. Báulfr did when he was young, but there are few enough men of that time left in the guard.'

'We have been provided guides, and promised more when we reach Jaffa.'

'And supplies?'

'The optimatoi are sending a ship with us, with wagon drivers and store masters. The imperial retinue has cooks and servants. Whatever else we need, we will buy in Jaffa and Jerusalem.'

'Well, you seem well-prepared at least.'

'The domestikos was very supportive,' said Harald blandly, and I barely contained my amusement when I remembered how Harald had practically had to threaten the man to get what he needed.

'Then I wish you good luck. The lady Theodora, and hundreds of priests, builders, cooks and servants, in a journey across the Holy Land?' Aki shook his head in despair. 'I would not wish that command on myself.'

Harald nodded wryly. 'I am somewhat looking forward to it, but I wish it was with fewer additional useless mouths.'

'Looking forward to it?' said Aki, dumbfounded.

Harald's eyes glowed. 'To see Jerusalem myself? To restore the place that our saviour died for us? Yes, I would fight every bandit in all the land to have this chance.'

Aki nodded slowly. 'This is the madness that drives you, Nordbrikt. This ambition and search for endless, unquenchable glory. This is why I dislike you so. One day, this madness will get everyone who follows you killed. I hope it is not this time, with my men.' His words were practically a whisper, and he looked at me not Harald while he spoke them.

Harald's smile only slipped a fraction at the attack, but he straightened and took the letters from the desk again. 'I will remember your warning, Aki, and I thank you for giving it.'

Did Harald remember those words? Perhaps. But let me tell you, they wrote a mark on my soul that never faded. You all know how Harald died, and it was Aki's words that came back and tortured me after that fateful day, a quarter of a century later.

20

'Dear God, there are so many of them,' I gasped.

'Everyone who is anyone wants to be part of this great pilgrimage, a great glory of the empire,' replied Harald without emotion, as we watched half a dozen fat transport ships loading the imperial party and its supplies. With the builders, their workmen, the lady Theodora's attendants, the servants, cooks, horse handlers, mule drivers, supply workers and finally the delegation of the patriarch of Constantinople and their attendants, the civilians on the voyage threatened to outnumber the guardsmen.

The mission to Jerusalem was already a sensation in the city, and crowds were thronging the public part of the harbour, and even clambering along the sea wall, to watch the great expedition depart.

We were watching from the walls of the palace, out of the reach of the crowd, above the sea gate through which the men of the guard filed down ready to board our ships on the other side of the harbour wall.

Not that we were ourselves without attendants. Even we were bringing civilians to help carry, drive mules, cook and help around camp, although not nearly so many as the imperial party.

'We don't have enough men,' I said, dejected.

'We have what we have, and thus it is exactly the right amount,' said Harald in an icy tone that bade no debate. 'Come, it is time.'

We went down the steps from the wall, twenty of our men following, and out onto the narrow strip of land above the harbour where the last of the civilians were boarding. We set up ten guards each side of the boarding ramp with the ease of men used to parade duty, and Harald stood in front of the crowds and waited, with me behind his shoulder, our banner flying over my head with the polished bronze butt of the pole on the stone.

Then, with a stamp of marching feet, the men of the first bandon escorted Theodora's small procession down onto the dock, followed by the lady herself in a litter.

To my surprise, a greater procession of guards and attendants followed, and the gilded litter of the empress herself appeared.

'Zoe is here,' said Harald, intrigued.

That had not been part of the planning.

There was no time to talk about it. Theodora's attendants had gracefully helped her out of her litter and then the waiting crowd erupted into enthusiastic cheers as the lady was revealed.

I was surprised, both by the scale of the crowd's excitement, and by the lady herself. While Zoe was elegant and graceful and beautiful, magnificently dressed in public at all times, Theodora was restrained, her hair tied back carefully but without ostentation, her face rounder and flatter, with none of Zoe's make-up. She looked like a nun, and that is because for most of her life she was. Theodora had spent almost her entire adult life in monasteries while Zoe had spent hers in palaces, and the separation of their paths was evident for all to see.

When Zoe alighted from her litter and strode over the stones the crowd's rapture only swelled, coming to a crescendo when Zoe walked over to her sister with a beaming smile and shared a polite but exaggerated kiss on the cheek.

I could not hear what they were saying over the noise of the crowd, but Zoe held her sister's hand and smiled and said something in her ear, clasping one of Theodora's hands between both of hers as Theodora nodded and smiled back.

'I thought they were enemies?' I whispered.

'Shush!' hissed Harald, and I murmured and returned to my statue stance.

The imperial sisters finally came over towards the dock and I saw Zoe startle as she saw Harald, but she regained her composure and walked past us as the guard all saluted, going with Theodora as far as the boarding ramp, where they embraced again and Zoe wished her sister a good voyage and Theodora blessed her in return.

It was all fodder for the crowd, for whom seeing such intimate moments of the imperial family, even if they were a little theatrical, were extremely rare and prized.

Theodora went down the ramp with her party, and Zoe and her attendants stood aside. The empress edged over towards us and her smile was thin. She got to within a couple of paces and her eyes shot sideways at Harald.

'I was not informed that you were on this expedition, Araltes.'

'I have the honour of commanding your sister's guard, Basilissa,' said Harald, seeing Zoe was trying to be discreet about the conversation and not bowing or turning to her. There was some cover for a short time as the procession of Theodora's entourage boarded in front of us.

Zoe spared Harald a glance. 'Well, I am certain you will see to my sister's safety.'

'I will give my life to ensure hers, if it comes to it. My orders from the emperor were clear. No harm will come to your sister while I live, and I am extraordinarily hard to kill,' he said in a reassuring tone, and with a faint line of a smile.

But Zoe looked unsure, even nervous. I was surprised. She and Theodora were rivals, and it was entirely possible Theodora's faction had been behind the attempted assassination in the hippodrome. If the journey claimed Theodora's life, it would be to Zoe's benefit. But, then again, they were still sisters, and if Zoe had wanted Theodora dead she had had decades to make it happen.

Zoe stared at the ship. The last of Theodora's people were boarding and we were about to be alone on the dock, her entourage and our guards at respectful distances.

'God's blessings upon you, Araltes of Norway. The hopes of our empire go with you.' Zoe gave us one last uneasy glance, and then she turned and swept away with her people as Harald bowed. Then he ordered us to march to our own ship.

* * *

If there were any pirates left after the end of the war, they did not trouble us and our fleet of twelve imperial ships. We sailed from port to port at a leisurely pace over two weeks until we reached Jaffa.

When we finally disembarked in Jaffa, which is a small, fortified harbour city on the coast of the Holy Land, we expected to set out for Jerusalem as soon as appropriate pack animals and carts had been acquired. But after two days, we still had not moved.

We did not meet with Theodora. The whole of the imperial party, and in theory the whole expedition, was led by her chamberlain, a pompous little noble called Mercurius Lecapenas. You see, while the emperor had very much put Harald in charge of protecting the expedition, Mercurius made it immediately and painfully clear that the imperial party would move at its own pace, and decide its own schedule and plans, and that Harald was merely to guard it.

It was only after an extraordinary amount of painful debate that it was conceded that Harald would determine the campsite each night, a concession he won by successfully arguing the way we camped was a military matter. He gave up arguing any other points for fear we would never leave Jaffa.

Well, during those four days of infuriating arguments we were kept well separate from the imperial party's inner circle around Theodora, and we had no wish to meet with her anyway.

On the fifth day, Mercurius finally announced that we were ready to move, but he had made no preparations to actually do so, and by the time that message was properly disseminated it was too late to leave the city and another day was lost.

I do not think Mercurius had ever been on any form of campaign in hostile territory before, and he had no understanding of what it entailed.

I wasn't present for most of his tedious and argumentative meetings with Harald, and I am glad of it.

On the sixth day we finally set off from the ancient city and headed inland on the road towards Jerusalem. We were quite a novelty, a thousand imperial citizens and soldiers in the Arab lands, although we were treated more with curiosity than with hostility. Harald fretted that six days in the city had given anyone who wished us harm far too much warning of our passage, and far too much information of our composition, but there was nothing we could do about it.

We set out as if on campaign, using the lessons we had learned from the army, and from Harald's books. The imperial party were treated as the baggage train and followed the road in the centre. One bandon would march out in front in a solid column straddling the road, and one at the rear. The third bandon was strung out along either side of the baggage train, forming a screen of men between the lady Theodora and the outside world in every direction.

What we lacked, however, from the army's way of marching, was a full vanguard or scouts. We had a few horses, but our men were not well-trained in scouting and there were far too few of them to do the job effectively. We sent a few men to ride the road ahead, whose job was as much to move other travellers out of the way as it was to seek danger, and a few men ranged occasionally towards possible ambush locations, but that was it. We were marching blind through the arid valleys and hills inland of the coast.

The journey from Jaffa to Jerusalem would take a normal force on foot three days. But Theodora's party was painfully slow, required frequent rest and refused to move at all during the middle of the day. There were not enough horses and the soft palace-born servants and attendants were in no condition to march for more than about seven miles a day in the desert heat, and even that came with endless complaints and protests about the pace.

So by the third day we were not even halfway, and Rurik came to us from the scouts with bad news. 'We are being shadowed.'

Harald barely looked surprised. 'By who?'

'I would guess several hundred men, soldiers, all mounted. No civilians.'

'A warband, then. How close did you get?'

'Not close. They have mounted men out, and they were not hostile but very clear in their intent not to let us go near them.'

'Damn. Caliph's men?'

'They are dressed like Arabs, that is all I can say.'

That didn't mean much; we were all dressed much like the locals in the late spring heat. Harald had initially intended to make us march in full armour, but that had proved to be an impossible burden as the days dragged on. In any case, we were not supposed to look like an invading force. So we simply wore maille hauberks under long tunics, and wrapped our heads in the manner of the locals to keep off the worst of the sun.

'Keep track of them as best you can, and I want a report if they change their behaviour or make any indication of moving towards us.'

'Yes, Komes,' said Rurik, and he turned his horse and kicked the unfamiliar beast into a slow trot to return to the scouts.

'Why would the Arabs be shadowing us?'

'I would too,' said Harald. 'Five hundred armed men in their lands? I expect they have men shadowing us on all sides and these are just the ones we have seen.'

'But it was agreed with them that we could come. We are no threat.'

'It was forced upon them, and armed men are always a threat. Our mere presence makes the caliphate look weak, and hemming us in with his forces improves that image.'

'Or risks provoking a war? One misunderstanding, one small fight turned large, and they could bring the empire down on themselves again.'

Harald tilted his head in acknowledgement. 'Such is the way of rulers, constantly throwing the die and assuming the symbols will be good.'

We marched in silence for a time while we both sulked, and then Harald swore and stopped.

'Whether they are likely to attack or not, I will not be stuck here in the open in this plain to be picked apart like those Pechenegs did to us,' he announced. The memory of the last time a mounted force had caught us in the open was too raw and too wounding to ever be far away. It was Harald's one great military failure.

'What do you intend?'

'Come, it's time I met Theodora anyway, and I need to impress upon our charges the new need for urgency.'

'Do you need me for that?' I said, hoping to avoid that particular conversation.

'Yes, I want to look as authoritative as possible. Bring my banner and half a dozen of the men.'

* * *

Well, we marched back down the line of the vanguard, calling a halt as we went, and approached the imperial party where it was strung out in an untidy trail along the road.

The senior members rode at the front, to avoid breathing in the dust of the wagons and mules or treading in their dung, and Mercurius turned his horse to meet us. 'What is the delay?' said the official, which was a monstrously ignorant thing for a man who caused us nothing but delays to ask.

'I need to speak to you and the lady Theodora immediately.'

'Absolutely not, she is not to be disturbed,' he said.

Harald stared at the mounted man for a moment, thinking it over. 'Let me say that another way. I am going to speak to the lady Theodora now.' And then he simply walked past, headed towards the converted wagon where Theodora and a pair of handmaids rode under a purple-and-gold-trimmed canopy.

'You impudent soldier, I shall have you whipped!' shouted Mercurius, turning his horse with consummate skill and urging it past us into our path.

'By who?' said Harald casually, stopping and looking around.

Mercurius stammered to a halt and abandoned the threat, for the only armed men for five miles in any direction were ours. He changed his tactics to adjust to that reality.

'The lady Theodora is on pilgrimage, and in quiet contemplation. She is not to be disturbed! Anything you wish to say to her can be relayed through me at the appropriate time.'

'I don't need to relay a statement, I need an immediate decision.'

'I am empowered to make any decisions required!' Mercurius said firmly, leaning down in his saddle with a hand on his thigh.

'Good. We need to double the pace as we are being shadowed by a warband whose purpose is unknown but is possibly hostile. They may attack at any time and we are defenceless here in this open valley. We need to get into those hills today,' Harald said, jerking a thumb at the hazy peaks in the distance, which were the range of hills before Jerusalem.

Mercurius did not look panicked at the revelation, but he did quieten his voice. 'An enemy force? They intend to attack?'

'I don't know.'

'Well then we will do nothing until you do know. There, you have your decision.'

'Not the correct one, so I will ask your lady,' said Harald, before raising his hand and slapping the horse sharply on its rump, sending the surprised beast springing away, Mercurius barely keeping his seat.

Harald strode the last dozen paces towards the wagon as the men behind me suppressed their laughter.

As we reached the wagon a pair of veiled women walked out to block our path, and Harald was not about to slap this obstruction out of the way.

'I need to see your lady. It is of the utmost urgency,' he said politely, with a small bow.

'My lady is at rest and contemplation,' replied a familiar voice, and Harald's face froze as one of the women unwrapped her veil.

'Maria,' he stammered, then his mouth curled with displeasure, just as Mercurius arrived, having dismounted his horse.

'This is an outrage. The emperor will hear of this!' he said, trying to physically move Harald back.

That was an error. Harald rounded on the noble, face red and teeth bared. 'You will be silent or I will *silence you*.' It was not shouted. The last part was almost a whisper, and the man physically shrivelled like a cut flower on a hot day. I have been the subject of Harald's real anger on several occasions, and it is not an easy thing to face.

Mercurius cut short a whimper of protest and Harald glared at him for a few moments longer and then turned back to Maria. 'The lady Theodora and I will speak, now.'

Maria, on the other hand, was not easily cowed, and showed no sign of fear or compliance, creating an ugly standoff, saved only by a thin voice coming from the wagon. 'You may introduce our guardian, Maria.'

'Yes, lady,' said Maria, stepping neatly to one side without losing her smile. 'It is my honour to introduce you to my lady Theodora Porphyrogenita, daughter of the emperor Constantine the Eighth, sibling to the empress Zoe Porphyrogenita and devout sister of the most holy cloister of Petrion.'

One of the handmaids in the wagon pulled the drape aside with a flourish, which was completely absurd in the circumstances, but the Byzantine nobles do love their ceremonies.

Maria bowed to Theodora, and Harald and I followed suit.

'My lady, I present Araltes Nordbrikt, a junior officer of the Varangians,' said Maria.

Harald ignored the calculated denigration. Everyone present knew who he was.

Theodora looked Harald up and down, and did not look impressed. 'What is it that is so important as to quarrel with my representatives, Komes?'

Harald cleared his throat. 'My lady, we are being approached by a warband of unknown origin, who are observing us and matching our path. I do not know their intention, but if it is hostile, we are in great danger in this valley.'

Theodora tried to retain her composure, but I could see she was alarmed. 'Why can you not defend us? Is that not your task?'

'It is our task, my lady, but there are too few of us to safely defend you out here, in the open ground, against a warband of mounted men.'

'Forgive me, I am not familiar with military matters, but I am sure you are correct. However, my dear Mercurius is of noble family and fine stature and it is quite wrong to menace him in the way that you have, even for this purpose.'

Harald put a hand to his mouth and coughed gently. 'I apologise for my brusqueness, my lady,' he said, before turning to the outraged chamberlain. 'I apologise, sir, I am but a simple soldier and I hope I shall earn your forgiveness.'

Mercurius was disarmed by the sudden and extensive apology, and merely nodded and looked away in embarrassment. Theodora, on the other hand, looked intrigued. 'I am pleased that is settled. Araltes, tell me what we must do.'

'We must make it to the hills as soon as possible. It is about ten miles.'

'Ten miles? In this heat? Araltes, my people are not soldiers, they cannot march so quickly as you.'

'I assure you we must, and that they will manage. We will give them every horse, let them ride wagons and mules, carry them if we have to. They will be capable of more than they believe.' He smiled. 'Especially if you would be so kind as to request it of them directly. I am sure, coming from you, they will be all the more determined.'

Theodora nodded gently. 'I accept your advice, Komes Araltes, and we shall do as you ask. Next time we need to discuss a matter of urgency, ask in a manner more befitting a man of breeding and godliness. God bless you.' She signalled to the handmaiden and the curtain was replaced.

Harald nodded to himself and then turned to me. 'Go and relay the orders to the men. I will stay here and help move the imperial party along.' He nodded his head to Mercurius. 'With your permission, sir?'

'Ah, yes... Of course, as you need,' said the perplexed noble, who was now completely disarmed by the change in Harald's tone.

You see, Harald had learned some diplomacy – the art of applying threats and flattery and submission, all at the appropriate times. It was more powerful than all his skill at arms. Words can achieve far more than blades, sometimes.

* * *

I shall not tell you of the wailings and protests and collapsing that occurred in the imperial party that day other than to confirm that it was great in all aspects. I admit, it was a hard day's marching in the heat. A march of ten miles is nothing on a good road here in the North when the weather is fine. In the Holy Land, in the arid, dusty terrain, going uphill and in terrific heat, it saps your energy like the fiercest fighting. Fortunately, it was not nearly so hot as it had been in the summer campaign near Edessa the year before, which would have killed half of those soft and lazy followers.

The warband following us made no move to attack, which in some ways only worried us more because knowing their intent would have been better than guessing. After a tense night in a cramped, hastily fortified camp in a series of low stone walls, where we destroyed a farmer's field and paid him in good silver for the trouble, we were ready for the final march to Jerusalem.

Jerusalem! Ah, it thrills me even to say it. I walked to Jerusalem, through the land of our lord and saviour, and saw it all with my own eyes. The hills were undulating and full of narrow, steep-sided valleys with rocky, inaccessible slopes – hopeless country for a mounted force to operate. We marched at ease, our formation closed up on the road, and the gentler slopes were thick with olive trees and goat herders and the types of small, scrubby trees that thrive all over the Holy Land.

And then we crossed the final saddle between two mounts and we saw Jerusalem, just a mile or so away from its walls, for although it is called the city on a hill, it actually nestles in between several of those small hills, moulds to them, is spread across their peaks and gullies like a blanket.

The walls and buildings are such a bright and light yellow as to be almost white, and the golden domes of its heathen temples shine in the sun. It is wondrous, and we stopped on the hillside, not by command, but by mutual assent, as we took in the joyous view. The priests alternated between crying with joy and praying together. Theodora broke her solitude to leave her wagon and take in the view and pray.

I think many of the party would have been glad to stay there, but evening was setting in and Harald insisted we pass through the gates before they closed at nightfall. So, with a firm hand, he persuaded the column to move once more.

We entered the city through the western Jaffa gate and along the main street which runs along the base of the great citadel. The Church of the Holy Sepulchre is not far into the city from the Jaffa gate, perhaps three hundred paces. The streets are narrow and the buildings around crowd them; nothing like our cities here, but similar in feel to Constantinople. We were pressed into a long, thin column so that as the head reached the church, the tail was still not passing through the city wall, and Harald was nervous because he could see almost nothing, and any attack then would be chaos.

Most of the local people shrank from us, scurrying into side streets to avoid the march of our Varangians, who must have seemed like an invading army. But not all. I saw more than a few subtly crossing themselves, or simply watching us with joy, and that is when I first learned that the expulsions of the Christian population had not been as thorough as previously believed. Some of them still hid among the Arabs and other Moslems.

Well, all the wonder and joy we had experienced in our arrival and entrance to the city turned to dust as we came upon the ruins of the church that contains Christ's tomb and Calvary.

At the insistence of our guide we stopped in a square in front of a low, ruined wall, behind which some goats were penned in a poorly constructed lean-to. It was some moments before he managed to relay to us that we had arrived. The sad, abandoned ruins behind us were the outer courtyard of the church, and the low wall that now sheltered goats was also the last vestige of the great shrine that had once sheltered the tomb of Christ.

Harald was shattered, almost desolate. He stared at the ruins in shock and shoved the apologetic Arab guide aside as he strode into the mess, looking for and seeking a doorway that led into the inner courtyard. Finding one, he cut through some weeds and pushed through with me following, and we emerged into a completely enclosed space, with the remains of the building sheltering Christ's tomb on our left, and on the right, the shattered remnants of a great Roman hall, much like those in the palace at Constantinople. We could see the remains of arched windows, pillars and columns that once held up a roof that lay burned, twisted and broken on the cracked flagstones below. It was clear from the weeds and the wizened, bleached timbers that the remains of the burned roof had been there for far longer than I had been alive.

The great ruined hall covered Calvary, the site of the crucifixion, the site of Jesus' martyrdom. Harald sank to his heels and struggled for breath as he tried to take it all in. It felt like the site of the end of the world.

21

Eric stared around, the sadness and tiredness in his eyes clear for all in the hall to see, but everyone was enraptured.

'You have been to the very place where Jesus died and was buried, and found it in ruins?' said Jarl Halfdan grimly. 'What terrible joy, and a terrible curse.'

'Did you feel the presence of God?' asked Ingvarr, wide-eyed.

Eric looked at him intensely. 'I have never felt his absence so clearly. We, the followers of Christ, had left that place, abandoned it to his enemies, failed to hold dear to the memory of his son and preserve his final earthly resting place. And the lord too had abandoned that place in shame of us, of that I am certain. It was a dead place, filled with nothing but the misery of the long since lost.'

'But it is not now? It was rebuilt?'

Eric nodded slowly. 'It was, although what was lost can never be recovered. Holy relics and remains, and the structure of the tomb itself.'

'The tomb itself?' said the boy with a gasp of outrage.

'Yes. When Harald and I finally entered the ruins of the shrine, we found the very rock from which the tomb was carved had been smashed away with hammers, the shrine burned from within and without. By miracle or the intervention of our lord himself, the rock-cut bench upon which Christ's body lay was still there, buried in the rubble.' Eric crossed himself as he said it, and Ingvarr's eyes lit with wonder.

'This crime requires vengeance!' said Jarl Halfdan, and there was a chorus of assent around the gathering.

Eric stared at Halfdan intently. 'Upon whom? The caliph who ordered it was long dead, even by that time. The men that wielded fire and hammer were also dead, or old and spread to the winds. But even as we speak the great crusade has made its way through Anatolia, across the hills where we once conquered and even now, so I hear, lays siege to Antioch.' He nodded greedily. 'Perhaps, sparked no doubt by the same thirst for justice I see in you all here today, they will march all the way to the Holy City itself and free it from its heathen masters, if God wills it.'

'Do you think they can?' asked Hakon. 'Do you think they can achieve that?'

Eric tapped his finger on the table in thought. 'Their enemy around Antioch, the ones that are called the Seljuk, are not the Arab armies of my youth. They are more akin to the Pechenegs, I believe. Horse warriors from the deep east.'

I have told you many times – Harald believed the Pechenegs to be the finest force we ever encountered, perhaps even better than us.

'You claim they were better than us?'

'Yes. In the open, anyway, and it is no shame to say so.'

Ingvarr settled back down with a sour expression and Eric smiled at him then turned back to Hakon. 'As I say, if these Seljuk Turkmen are like the Pechenegs, then even the crusader army of the Franks and Normans will have a very difficult time.

'But it is possible. I have a very high opinion of the Normans. They are the best of Christianity's soldiers, as good even as we Varangians were. They have already defeated the Seljuks once last summer in the hill country of Anatolia, and can do so again. We must hope their leaders are wise, and use castles and rivers and the ground as their allies. For if they fight the horse lords in the open, the only path leads to defeat.'

'So Jerusalem could be a Christian city again?'

'I believe it is possible, but only God and the passage of time can know,' said Eric.

'Come, enough of this fortune telling,' said Jarl Halfdan from the dais. 'We will not treat our friend like a cheap teller of futures. He has a story to tell, let him continue.'

The mild reprimand was phrased as a rebuke to those asking questions, but it was clear that Eric was the target; the Jarl wanted an end to the speculation and to continue the story.

'As you wish, Jarl Halfdan,' Eric said, with a glitter of mischief in his eye.

* * *

Well, Harald wandered around the desperate ruins for some time, disconsolate and furious in equal measure, before the delegation of the patriarch arrived at the ruined courtyard to see the scene for themselves.

Some of their party fell immediately to their knees and wailed, somewhat performatively I thought, and others wandered around like Harald, as if in a daze, staring limply at one thing or another, trying to make sense of it all.

But their leader, a dignified old man, a bishop of one of the major churches in Constantinople and much more in control of himself than the other clergy, approached me with a stern look, pausing only to glance towards the ruined tomb of Christ.

Harald, seeing this, returned over and gave the bishop a gracious nod of acknowledgement.

'Excellency.'

'Komes. What a sad sight.'

'It is... beyond words,' Harald said.

'Well, it is not beyond our skills to overcome, nor to repair,' said the bishop sternly.

Harald looked around, gesturing with a hand. 'How? How can we even know what it was like before?'

The bishop smiled sadly. 'I saw it once, as a boy. It was here, in this very spot, after visiting the tomb of our saviour, that I began my journey in his service.'

That caught Harald's attention. 'So you will rebuild it the same?'

The bishop shook his head. 'No, not the same. We will build it anew. The splendour of the old church is beyond us, and the foundations it stood upon crumbled. I see your disappointment, my son, but save the glorious edifices for the empire. Our lord and saviour was a simple and humble man, and we will honour him in that manner.'

Harald smiled, and he nodded at the wisdom in that. 'Whatever you suggest, Bishop, we will support you.'

The bishop laughed in a kindly tone. 'My son, this will take years. You are young and ambitious, and will be gone within months, but I appreciate your words.'

Harald looked insulted but he could not argue, for it was true; we were not going to spend years of our youth guarding a shrine while it was rebuilt, even the shrine over Christ's tomb.

'What you can do to help is find my people somewhere safe to stay, and see them set up there so they can commence their work. That would be a fine service to our cause.'

Harald's spine stiffened, and he nodded. 'It will be done. We will buy every house on this street, and every one that touches the walls all around the church, so that you will have no disruption.'

The bishop nodded and touched his hand lightly to his breast. 'That is a fine idea. I will leave you to your work.' He made the sign of the cross over Harald's chest and turned to gather his weeping, kneeling followers like a housewife might collect a litter of kittens, shooing them all up and gently guiding them back out of that sad place.

* * *

Harald did exactly what he had suggested, sending men with bags of silver, some of it his own silver, to buy every house around the church for as far as a stone's throw. Half of them were abandoned anyway, and others were glad to leave for the silver, which was far more than the structures in the dilapidated old Christian part of the city were worth.

The finest buildings, a series of two-storey houses near the main street, were cleared for the lady, the bishop and their personal entourages, and we set about the business of getting the whole party, including our men, settled for what might be a few weeks or months.

As we were doing so, the sentries we posted at every road and alley leading to the church reported a large group of armed men had arrived, but with no hostile intent. Their leader said he was a representative of the caliph's garrison, and Harald sent instructions to let him and a few of his men through the cordon, where we met them at the entrance to the ruined church.

'Salamun alaykum,' the man said, bowing his head slightly. We stood there, perplexed, and our Arab guide rushed over to join us.

'He greets you in peace, Komes,' said the flustered Arab.

'And you greet me the same, I am sure,' said the soldier with a smile, in perfect Greek, earning a look of surprise from Harald. 'What?' said the soldier with a broad grin. 'Should I not know the language of my enemy? Does it surprise you?'

Harald shook his head slowly. 'No, but you could have chosen not to reveal that fact and gained an advantage.'

The soldier grinned and raised his hands to the sides, palms up in supplication. 'I have no need for advantage. The caliph wishes peace, and I am his servant.'

'Then I greet you in peace too, friend,' said Harald.

'Wa alaikum salaam,' replied the man with a sly smile.

'Sorry?'

'Wa alaikum salaam – it is what you mean when you return my greeting of peace, but in our tongue. If you are living here, you will need to know it, to avoid offending anyone.'

'Walakum salam,' said Harald, trying to get his lips around the unfamiliar sounds.

The soldier smiled broadly. 'Good enough.' He stepped forwards and clasped Harald's hand, not arm to arm like we do, but both hands placed atop one of Harald's, something I have learned is a sign of good faith and trust, since Harald's right hand was free to pluck a weapon and kill, while the soldier was defenceless.

'My name is Abdul-Najm Nassir Al-Quasim, although you may know me as Nassir. I am the commander of the city garrison. On behalf of the governor and the caliph, I welcome you and your party to the most blessed city of Jerusalem, and place myself at your service while you are here, if there is anything you require.'

'Thank you, Nassir, that is most generous. Shall we meet the governor?'

Nassir shook his head sadly. 'Alas, the governor is in Egypt, visiting the caliph's court, and will not return for several weeks.'

'The governor is visiting the caliph's court, for such a long time?'

The soldier tried to maintain his smile. 'The caliph is but a boy. His blessed mother advises him, and many powerful men in the caliphate seek to... advise her.'

'Ah, I see. The governor is securing his position,' said Harald, now that it was clear.

'Or expanding it, Allah willing,' said the soldier with a wink. 'Now, I see you are well-established, and I understand your need to feel safe, but please, keep the peace, do not menace the people, and you will continue to be welcome.' The threat was very softly veiled, but the message was clear.

'We will be careful not to cause trouble. We have been paying for what we need.'

'So I saw. There are many rich beggars who were lucky enough to be living in abandoned houses around here today!'

Harald stared at him in shock. 'None of these houses are owned?'

'Not a single one!' said the commander with a laugh. 'This whole area was abandoned before the latest war, and all this property, legally, belongs to the caliph.'

Harald cursed and looked at me. 'No wonder everyone was so happy to take the silver and leave their homes.'

Then he turned back to the commander. 'And what must we pay to the governor for these houses?'

The commander flourished a hand. 'Nothing. They once belonged to Greeks and Christians, and we are happy to return them to you, as a gesture of reconciliation. Anywhere in this district you have already chosen and occupied by sundown, it is yours.'

Harald's eyebrow raised at that, and he turned to Styrbjorn. 'Tell the men to spread out a bit more; I want this entire section around the church as our garrison.'

Styrbjorn nodded and turned to leave in a hurry, for it was already nearing sunset.

Harald inclined his head to Nassir in thanks. 'Relay our thanks to the governor when he returns. We were not expecting such a friendly reception from former enemies.'

'I will do, and he will be pleased to hear it. Now, may I return tomorrow to meet with the delegation rebuilding the church? I have access to materials and merchants they may wish to use.'

'You certainly may; I will inform the guards to expect you.'

'Good evening then, Varangian. I am pleased this time to meet your ilk in peace. We were at Edessa, and I prefer you as guests than as enemies.' He bowed and left with his men.

Harald looked at the street where the Arabs had disappeared for a while, deep in thought, before turning to me. 'He seems genuine. Perhaps we are safe here.'

'He doesn't know about Theodora,' I said, grasping at a feeling that had been eluding me all through the conversation.

'What?'

'He didn't mention her, didn't even allude to her, didn't offer to greet her or pay homage to her. The sister of the emperor is in his city, he would not simply ignore that.'

'Damn, you are right. That is why she has been hidden the entire way; it's not modesty, it's politics. But why?' He looked at me with a worried expression. 'Why would they not tell our hosts who was coming with us?'

'To reduce the risk of an attack? She would be a rich prize for some bandit lord, or rebel. Or as a hostage for the caliph.'

'Perhaps.'

He put a finger between his teeth as he often did when he was thinking over a difficult decision. 'For now, we will maintain this secrecy, but they should have told me it was a secret!' Then he stalked away, muttering under his breath.

22

A few days later we were summoned to Theodora, who was lodged in the best rooms we could find, an old Greek house with a small courtyard and a non-functional fountain that the builders were trying to repair.

We went through the formal greetings with Mercurius, and then were brought to the lady herself.

'We wish to visit the Jordan, and the place of our saviour's baptism. We can see the Mount of Olives and Gethsemane on the route,' she announced, and it was not phrased as a question.

Harald coughed politely. 'That might not be safe, my lady.'

'Nevertheless,' she replied without emotion.

There was silence while Harald waited for what would come after that, but nothing did. 'I don't know if...'

'Your instructions are to take us safely to Jerusalem, and the sites of pilgrimage,' said Mercurius. 'So, that is what we shall do, and you shall keep us safe.' His statement had an air of finality, and Harald was in a corner, for it was, indeed, his instruction. I think also that the idea of visiting the sacred Jordan thrilled him personally.

He looked at Theodora and saw no hint of weakness in her expression. 'Very well, I shall make arrangements. Please, give me a couple of days to prepare.'

'Very well, we shall leave in two days,' said Mercurius, with a nod of clear relief, and then he turned to Theodora with a beaming smile which she did not return.

'Thank you, Komes. We must pray now and make our own preparations for this journey.'

* * *

'How far is it to the Jordan?'

'A two-day walk, one day with a horse,' said our Arab guide, making an uncertain side to side motion with his head that did not fill me with confidence.

'That means three days with our group,' I said morosely.

'No, we will manage in two. We will not be taking the entire party, only the priests and Theodora and her attendants, and we will take every horse we have, and buy some more if we have to. We will have every one of them on horseback or in a cart. We will manage it with only one night camped on the road,' Harald replied.

'We should plan for two,' I said, giving him a stern expression.

'That means two on the return, and an entire week on the road. Which means a week's worth of supplies, which means more carts and horses and...' He tailed off. 'But you are right, we can't risk running out of supplies.'

'How many men will we take?'

'Just the seventh bandon, one hundred and fifty or so. The second and fourteenth can stay here and guard the church and the majority of the party that remains.'

'Why so few men to come with us?'

'With fewer we will travel faster, and need fewer carts and horses. Now that I have seen the commitment of the governor's men to our safety, I do not feel the need to travel as an army.'

'And the warband who were shadowing us?'

'I do not know who they were and if they are still in the area, but they had the chance to attack and they did not. I assume they are the caliph's men.'

'They could simply have been deterred by our numbers!' I protested. 'And now we leave the city with less than half.'

'It is too many for bandits to take us on, and that is all I expect to face. Enough,' said Harald with finality. 'This is what we are doing.'

'As you command, Komes,' I said, with a grumble of dissent that was all I could summon.

* * *

Two days later and we left Jerusalem early in the morning, a hundred and fifty guardsmen and a small pilgrim party of around twenty, centred on Theodora. Another thirty or so men managed the handful of wagons and the horses. We carried enough food for a week and water for three days, and we were confident we could make it to the Jordan comfortably.

We marched the mile or so to the place called Gethsemane, which I can tell you is a very unremarkable place, a few scraggly olive trees within a poorly maintained low wall, and Theodora sat in the shade of one of them and chatted gleefully with her attendants. They were sitting there for some time before their servants started bringing refreshments from the carts.

It was approaching midday before they were finally finished, and willing to move up the hill the short distance to the pinnacle of the mount, where Jesus once lectured the apostles.

Now, the Mount of Olives is a sobering place, for it might once have been merely one of the many small hills outside Jerusalem, but now it is a city of the dead. The people there, for a thousand years or more, have buried their dead in stone tombs, or little caves cut into the hillside. These are the tombs of the Jews, who still live among the Moslems and have done since before the time of Christ, and it is a haunting place to walk through, despite the beauty of the valley, and the view of the city and the temple mount below and behind us.

At the summit of the mount is the Chapel of the Ascension, and I am afraid it had suffered most terribly under Moslem rule, as had so many other places of veneration. But in the ruins of the circular chapel someone had carefully cleared and laid bare the stone of the ascension itself, the very rock from which Christ ascended to join the lord his father. The rock was cleaned and polished, and the faint marks said to be made by the feet of our saviour were visible, worn smooth by the touch and kiss of a thousand thousand pilgrims over the centuries.

Well, we might have objected to the visit and the delay, but every Christian man in our party wanted to take a moment by the rock, kneeling in that shattered ruin to spend a moment in thought and prayer. It had a power you could feel in your bones, unlike Gethsemane, which had exerted no hold over me at all. We were walking in the footsteps of Christ himself.

Lady Theodora and her attendants, Maria included, knelt in a little circle on the hard stones around the rock and prayed, and the lady quietly wept. This went on for some time, and even Harald did not have the heart to complain as the sun made its way across the sky, and the women made their devotions.

It was well after midday before the group finally appeared from the ruins, and Theodora came over to Harald with a euphoric smile and inclined her head to him. 'My thanks, Komes, for accommodating my needs. It has revitalised my faith, to be able to come to this most holy place. For though the place of our saviour's crucifixion and burial filled me with sorrow, to visit the place he attained heaven and the grace of our father has flooded my heart with joy and hope. Let us continue to Bethany, perhaps we can stay there for the night. It would be a wonderful place to take the midnight prayers.'

And then she went off to her covered wagon, with Maria giving Harald a smile and a wink as she passed.

Harald looked around uncertainly, and then turned to our Arab guide. 'How far away is Bethany?'

'Three miles, perhaps?'

Harald growled and put his head in his hands. 'Three miles. We could have done this whole journey and back to the city in a day, at any time. These nobles and rulers, they have no understanding of how such expeditions are managed!'

'Well, of course they don't,' I said unhelpfully, and Harald glared at me.

'Send ten men back to the city; we are going to need more water. They can meet us at Bethany tonight. It won't take them long to get there will it.' And then he stalked off, barking orders at the men, who were lounging around in whatever shade they could find, to get ready to move again.

* * *

Well, we visited Bethany and the tomb there, which was just a hole in the rock I didn't understand the importance of, and we did indeed spent the night. In the morning, with still twenty miles to go until the Jordan, Theodora surprised us all by announcing that there were no more sites she wished to visit before the river, and that we could proceed uninterrupted.

We marched east, and the reason for there being no more sites to visit was quite apparent. After we passed the ridgeline east of Bethany, the land slowly sloped down towards the Jordan valley, and the olive groves and scraggy forests withered rapidly away, until all that was left was dry grasses, and then not even that, just a valley of dust and sand and rock: the Jordan desert.

It is strange, and I do not understand it, why the land became a desert as we approached the river. But down and down we went into the vast valley, and there was barely a living thing within sight in the dust and haze. It is quite the most unpleasant place I have ever visited, but impressive in its stark beauty.

We spent a night camped on the parched plain, and gave the horses and ourselves most of the rest of the water we carried. That was a worrying moment. If we did not reach the Jordan, or could not find water, we would be thirsty in a barren desert, two days' march from home in the heat.

On the final day of our journey we struggled to get our party going. Theodora was suffering in the heat, as were many of her attendants.

I do not pretend that us guardsmen were immune; it was a terrible place to march, and the thirst and heat affected us all. None of us wore our armour, piling it on the part of the wagons among the empty water barrels and marching wearing only the local robes which we had all acquired in the city.

Finally, as the heat of the day threatened to slow our progress to a crawl, we reached the small cluster of buildings that sit on the western bank of the river Jordan. It was an odd collection: dusty, unkempt, and many clearly ruined or abandoned. But among them were two recognisable chapels and a number of earth-built houses from which a number of nervous inhabitants appeared to greet us.

They were a mixture of Christian holy men of various bizarre kinds, so far distanced from the Church in Constantinople and Rome as to be unrecognisable, and their followers and families.

Some were dressed in little more than rags, and did not speak – hermits dedicated to a life of silence and poverty, inhabiting the ruins of ancient temples and shrines and living off charity that was scarce in those days.

There was a well, and Harald paid silver to water our entire column, silver that the holy men promptly fell into bitter argument over the division of. It was probably more than they had seen in a decade or more. It was undignified and embarrassing, and Harald ended the argument by simply handing out more until they went away.

Disturbed by the terrible condition of the little community, and the people that lived there cut off from the rest of the world, we left the men to set up camp on the outskirts and Harald led Theodora, her attendants, and the delegation of priests down the dirt path towards the river itself.

On the bank, beside the crumbling walls of a small chapel, were steps that led down into a ford that crossed the river. Confused, we stood there.

'Is this the place?' Harald asked, looking to the priests for guidance, but they looked as confused as he.

Then one of the hermits, dressed in nothing but a threadbare woollen tunic-like robe, hobbled over and shook his head, then pointed a sun-wizened finger across the ford, and beckoned us to follow.

Harald looked around uncertainly, but then shrugged and headed off after the surprisingly agile little holy man, down the gentle bank and to the shallow water, where long sticks had been driven into the riverbed and rope strung between them, to allow pilgrims an easy crossing.

We shepherded the party across, the women holding up their long dresses to avoid being dragged away in the flow, and ascended the far bank. Even more confused, we followed the strange little man through a grove of trees that clung to the fertile banks and into a glade beyond, circled by a low earthen bank, where we found a long staircase of marble headed down into a cross-shaped pool fed from the waters of the river by hidden pipes.

'Yes, this is it. This is how it was described to me,' said one of the priests in amazement, before he went over to the steps to look down.

The whole site was half ruined, as all those places were. There had once been a building on four pillars built over the pool, to shelter pilgrims, but three of the four pillars had partially collapsed, and on the remaining one a small shrine, a chapel so small only two people could enter at a time, had been built from the recovered stone.

The marble steps were cracked and discoloured, some of them falling away or missing, but that this was a Roman construction was beyond doubt. This was the site where the early Christian emperors had had a shrine to the baptism built around the very place John had baptised Jesus, so long ago the river itself had moved a hundred paces to the west in the centuries since.

Harald was motionless, staring at it for so long that I went over to see what was wrong.

'Can you believe it?' Harald said, his voice cracking. He turned to face me and I saw that tears were flowing down his face. 'Eric, what my brother would have given to be here, to see this place.' He could not continue, wiping his hands across his eyes and heading down towards the marble steps. I stood there and fought with the lump in my throat. I had never seen Harald like that before, all the hardships and loss we had faced, all the moments of horror and glory – nothing affected him like visiting the Jordan, and the place our saviour was baptised.

* * *

It was not long before the most senior of the priests was disrobing and preparing to enter the waters while his fellows were giving thanks and rejoicing in a small gaggle.

The first priest baptised the others, and then Harald shook off everything except his tunic and went down the steps, kneeling in the shallows and letting the priest say his blessings over the much bigger man, before being immersed beneath the silted water and re-emerging to a chorus of prayers from the rest of the sodden party.

He came up the stairs, his face creased side to side with a smile of pure joy and he put his hand on my shoulder. 'This is the greatest moment of my life, Eric. Look at us! Men from the far North, come to the edge of the world to bathe in the waters where our lord was baptised. Most men where we live would not even believe this place was real.'

'It is... wondrous. Your brother would be proud of us.'

'I know that he is. Come, take your turn in the water. The ladies are waiting, and we must be gone before they come down.'

And so I was baptised again, in the very spot where John lowered Jesus under the same brown waters, and as they closed over my face, and the coolness of it washed over my body, I felt a great weight lifted from my soul.

Whatever else I did or didn't do in my life, I would reach the end of it knowing those waters had washed me clean, even if just for a moment. In all my long years of travelling, that was the furthest from home I ever went. That pool beyond the Jordan the watershed of my great adventures. Yet the purity of peace I experienced under that water was unique, and I have never felt closer to God.

23

That night in the camp was a strange one. We were all recovering from the sheer power of the visit to the baptismal waters. Harald and I sat down by our fire after we had eaten, for it is surprisingly cool in that desert at night, and we shared a complete silence, each lost in the magnitude of our thoughts.

After quite some time, someone approached our fire and curled up their legs to sit near the komes, leaning over and giving Harald a sweet smile.

'Maria,' Harald said, with about as much welcome in his voice as a dog growling at a shadow.

'Come now, Harald, in this place of all places, shall we not make peace? The past is the past, and even if you have forgotten, we enjoyed much of ours together.'

'I have not forgotten, Maria. And that is the problem. You can preach forgiveness, but you left your dog Bardas to kill me, and I will neither forgive nor forget.'

'But he did not kill you! Truthfully, I would have been disappointed if he had. The world is more interesting with you in it, and all I needed to do was let him see that I gave him the opportunity, even if I did not wish him to succeed.'

Harald glared at her for a moment more, and then shook his head. 'You will not capture me with your lies again. I cared for you, and you care nothing for anyone but yourself.'

'Oh, you know that is not true. I cared for you, truly.' Her sarcastic smile went and she looked earnestly at Harald, almost pleadingly. It made me feel ill. Forgiveness was not in my heart either.

'You wished only to exploit me, a useful name to attach to your mistress.' Harald leaned in. 'Or was it for you, not Theodora, that you wished the imperial throne? I seem to remember you planned to betray her and take it, and I, for yourself. A confession you made when you thought I was about to die, or at least never come to the empire. Inconvenient for you, isn't it, that I am here now, just thirty paces away from the mistress you sought to betray.' Harald leered in satisfaction as he finished, the threat of him telling what he knew sure to cow his tormentor.

Maria stared at him for a moment and then laughed, an easy, natural laugh, moving her hand to her mouth to curb it. 'Oh Harald, you are still so new to this. It is wonderful to watch, like a child learning to walk.'

Harald's expression went to fury; I could see his jaw tensing in the firelight. 'I could go and tell her right now, and what would happen to you?'

'Don't repeat a failed threat, my dear, it makes you look silly.' She shuffled over and leaned in, almost giggling. 'I made sure long ago that Theodora had heard rumours that I was seeking the throne, so that I could disprove them and make sure that if she ever heard them again, she would dismiss them. In any case, it was not my plan, only one possibility. I care for Theodora, I truly do. You can choose to believe I thought nothing of you, but for my lady my love is undeniable.'

'Then how could you think to betray her?'

'What if she was murdered? What if she choked on an olive stone and died? What if she did not even want the throne? For I am not sure she does. Harald, you see everything in a single light, that you seek your throne and nothing else. We in the empire see power as a flowing, flexible force. I position myself for many outcomes, carefully collecting power, and whatever the outcome I will be able to take advantage. It is not one position I seek, but merely any position from which to exert the power I collect. That is the politics of the empire, and if you begin to understand that, you will begin to understand our ways.' She brushed some hair lightly off his ear, a casual, intimate gesture, and he swatted her hand away.

'Perhaps you are right, and I could not be rid of you by telling your mistress of your perfidy. But there are other ways of being rid of a troublesome enemy in the desert, out here, surrounded by nothing but me and my men.'

'Ah, there are indeed other ways. But you are too noble to kill me. All your big, scary men, all your nasty, pointy weapons – they hold no fear for me.' She smiled lovingly at him, and curled a stray strand of her own hair with her finger. 'You and your misplaced Northern honour. I am sure you think the emperor is weak, but he would have me killed in a moment if he thought I was a threat, cut limb from limb without a second thought.' She leaned in, putting her mouth almost to his ear. 'And despite your professed hatred of me, you would die on that blade to stop him, because your love and your honour make you weak.'

Harald put a hand onto her chest and pushed her away, his eyes sparkling with anger in the dancing flames. 'Be careful, woman,' he growled.

Maria clasped both her hands around Harald's, pulling them into an embrace and sighing contentedly. 'If you ever wish to attain the greatness you seek, you must learn the art of making threats, and you must know only to make those you can follow through on. You have become a great leader of men, but as a leader of nations, you still lack the ruthlessness required to succeed.' She smiled again and brought her lips down to kiss his fingers, and he did not resist. 'But it's charming watching you learn, my love.'

Then she rose gracefully to her feet and walked away.

Harald sat fuming in silence while I repressed my laughter. 'I fucking hate that woman,' he muttered.

'No you don't,' I said, laughing and shaking my head.

'And what do you know of my thoughts?' he snapped.

'You admire her. I know, because I do too. Her confidence and the ease with which she controls people, it is admirable. She was not born with your strength, or the fear you put into men, yet she has power you do not, perhaps cannot have. Do not pretend you hate it.'

He glared at me for a while and then shook his head. 'Both things can be true. I can admire the thing that I hate. And I can hate the thing that I love.' And then he stood without another word and stalked off to his tent.

* * *

We started the march back the next day without incident, camping in the same place we had stayed on the way down. It was only the next morning that Rolf Hammerbeard, who was out with a few men scouting, came back to us with the news we had feared.

'Trouble ahead on the road,' he said, jerking his thumb towards the low desert hills that lay between us and Jerusalem.

'Is it that warband again?' Harald asked.

'No, bandits. Afra is sure of it. A ragtag group of men with horses, spears and bows. They are waiting for us in ambush on the road.'

'How many?'

'More than a hundred.'

Harald nodded and then looked down the column. 'We can't push through them, they will bog us down in moments with these wagons and civilians, showered by arrows on all sides. I need you to find a way around them, another road to Jerusalem.'

'Afra is already doing it. He is following a local track which may lead to a village. We might have to abandon most of the carts, but we should be able to follow it.'

'Good. Start leading us that way.'

'Eric, go and clear the wagons. Get everything and everyone out of them except the water. Tents, food, blankets, spare equipment – everything.'

'Food?'

'Yes. We either reach the city before we starve, or we die anyway. The men can shove some into pouches or hang it off their belts if they are quick. But the only thing I want hauled up that slope is water, in as few wagons as possible. Go!'

We rushed to obey, ignoring the outrage of the imperial party as we dumped everything out of the two lightest wagons and moved all the water into them.

Then came the most difficult part: we couldn't haul Theodora's wagon. It was the largest, and for bandits its richness made it an obvious target. Harald and I went to Maria, who was standing by the side. 'Maria, I'm afraid Lady Theodora must come down. We are going to be attacked if we continue on the road, and we must leave the wagon and go around, through the hills. Can she ride?'

'Of course I can ride,' came a voice from the wagon, and the draping was pulled aside to reveal Theodora's hard-set face. 'You are sure we are going to be attacked?'

'My lady, there is no need to listen to this nonsense!' said Mercurius, arriving at a breathless jog. 'We shall burst through this ragtag band. I will give the order to cancel this stupidity and continue along the road. Please, remain in the comfort of your wagon.'

Theodora looked at Harald, ignoring the nobleman. 'I asked you a question, Komes.'

'Yes, my lady. It appears there are bandits blocking the road, ready to ambush us.'

'They will fight a force this large?'

'Nonsense! They could not possibly defeat a force of guardsmen this large. This is cowardice!' spluttered Mercurius.

'They will not intend to defeat us, merely to trap us and force our submission. It is our wealth they want, not our lives.'

Theodora frowned. 'Perhaps we should pay them?'

'We cannot risk it. If they know who you are, they might wish to take you for ransom and we will not have enough with us. It is possible someone in the city has told them you are here.'

'We took great pains to keep her presence here a secret, Komes,' said Mercurius hotly.

'I know, but word always gets out. My lady, we cannot risk it,' Harald pleaded.

The thought of being taken hostage visibly terrified Theodora, and she nodded. 'We will do as you say, Komes. Our lives are in your hands.'

'Thank you, my lady.'

Theodora was helped down out of the wagon, and a horse was provided. She looked absurd on horseback in her fine clothes, and her close-fitting dress, not split or made for riding in the slightest, rose up, exposing a scandalous amount of her legs, almost to her hips, but she did not appear to care, and we all pretended not to see.

Then we set off after Rolf, following the road for a time before breaking off up a ravine, following what looked to be little more than a goat track. We marched hard. Only the guardsmen were on foot, some helping the two wagons along the difficult route by pushing them and lifting their wheels around obstacles.

The wagons slowed us down, but we did not dare abandon our water – it would mean death in that parched land.

Afra rode in with two of the scouts. 'They are coming!' he shouted, and he reined in near us in a clatter of hooves and splayed legs. He was not a good horseman, bless him. 'They have seen us leave the road and are moving to intercept us. We do not have long; they are all mounted.'

Harald looked fraught. He scanned the low ridges that surrounded us. 'We would be slaughtered in here. We must get to high ground.' He looked up the path, seeing it wound past a low barren knoll at the head of the valley, which had a steep rocky slope on the other side.

'There! Get everyone onto that point. Send fifty men with Rolf to claim and hold it now.'

'Do we abandon the wagons?' I asked, desperate. 'We will move much faster.'

Harald shook his head. 'No. If we make it to that hill without water they will simply besiege us, and we will surrender within a day.'

We redoubled our efforts, twenty men with each wagon, pushing and shoving and cursing and sweating as we drove them up the hill.

'They're here!' shouted a voice when we were about halfway to our destination. I looked up and saw figures on the crest to our right, figures who shouted back behind them, and then more appeared, dozens.

'Hold it, HOLD IT!' I heard a voice shout, and then I turned my head and saw a wagon that was being manhandled over a rock tipping over as men tried to control it. Then there was a rending crash as a wheel collapsed, and the whole wagon rolled, men falling and diving out of the way as barrels split and water gushed out into the thirsty soil.

'Leave it!' I shouted, waving at the men to abandon the lost cause with a grim expression. 'Get your shields ready!'

We formed up into a loose group and rushed on up the hill in the wake of the sole remaining wagon. Arrows started to fall around us now, just a few at first and scattered, but in greater numbers and with more accuracy as time went on. We saw Rolf and the vanguard scatter a few of the enemy as they pushed through and claimed the summit just a couple of hundred paces ahead, and I roared at the men to keep going.

Arrows thudded into shields and stuck into the earth. Somewhere ahead a horse was hit and threw its rider, a terrified servant girl, who fell and broke her back on a rock with a sickening crunch.

'Keep moving!' I shouted, and the fear was rising in my throat. An arrow had stuck into a water barrel, and the wagon was leaving a thin rivulet of darkness in the light soil as the precious fluid leaked.

Then I passed the servant girl, and saw that someone had ended her misery, her shocked eyes and slashed throat open to the heavens as she lay shattered across the rock.

We huddled together around the last wagon and the people on horseback but they were exposed, and after a priest fell with an arrow in his ribs, we forced everyone to dismount where we could cover them with our shields. At that time, the bandits were still only on our right side, although we could see them moving across the ravine floor behind us, tying to work their way onto our left. If they managed that before we reached the summit, we knew we would be in dire trouble. We could not effectively shield from both sides.

We urged the men helping the second wagon onwards, driving the horses as hard as we could, and herding the terrified civilians along in the shelter of our shields.

The first guardsman went down, dying with an arrow in his throat, and we had to leave him on the ground, with nothing to hurl back at the bandits but curses and promises of revenge.

Finally, we reached the foot of the little knoll and moved off the track, a block of guardsmen covering us as we wrestled the wagon up the difficult slope with nearly fifty men pushing it and pulling on the harnesses that we had disconnected from all but one of the horses.

I do not know how we made it to the top, but we did, and our overheated, exhausted men got the wagon to the flat ground at the summit and then collapsed around it, exposed in the vicious sun.

'What now?' I said, leaning on a wheel and panting as Harald came over.

'We wait.'

'For what?'

He looked around. 'I don't know. They cannot attack us here, and there is no vantage point to shoot arrows at us other than to annoy us from the bottom of the slope. We wait until they leave, or we are relieved.'

'Did we send word to the city?'

'I tried,' said Harald, pointing grimly down the path, where I could see two horses and two dead guardsmen, riddled with arrows, and twenty or so bandits blocking the way. 'They were ready for it.'

'Fuck.'

'Indeed.'

* * *

We gave everyone a portion of our limited water and then we settled in, using our shields for shade, leaving fifty men in a solid wall along the slope leading to the summit. The bandits wasted their arrows on the shield wall for a while, doing nothing but wounding one man in the leg, and then gave up and withdrew to a distance to watch us.

'I wonder who will run out of water first?' I asked Harald, as we examined the situation.

'We will. We have enough for two days, if we use it carefully. They can ride off and bring back as much as they want. There must be a well in a village nearby.'

'Surely Styrbjorn will send men to look for us?'

'Eventually, yes, but I told him we might be delayed. It might be several days before he sends anyone.' Harald looked glum. 'I might have sealed our fate with that.'

'They will not kill us, surely. It is just our wealth they want. You said it yourself.'

'I said that to keep the civilians calm,' he said quietly. 'This is no ordinary band of bandits. I suspect they are here for Theodora, or maybe all of us. No ordinary thieves would take on a small army like us, not fifteen miles from Jerusalem.'

My heart sank. 'So what do we do?'

Harald looked grim. 'I have a plan, but I don't like it, and we need to wait for them to come and negotiate. I am sure it will be soon; they would prefer this be done easily.' He turned to me. 'Find out how many horses we have left, and then who our best horsemen are.'

I looked at him. 'You would ride away and leave most of our men behind?'

He looked at me with cold determination in his face. 'Our duty is to save Theodora, even at the cost of our lives. Go, find out what I need to know.'

* * *

As he had expected, the enemy sent a party up the hill, weapons in hand, but clearly not threatening attack, as the sun was at its height. Harald told the Arab guide to ask them to wait a moment and we approached Theodora. Her attendants were sheltering her under a cloak. She looked up at us and I could see she was exhausted, sweating and pale.

'My lady, the enemy have come to negotiate.'

'Oh, good. Can you secure our safe passage to Jerusalem?'

'I hope so, but if I cannot, we have an alternative plan. I need you ready to mount. I will take you and thirty of our men and break out and ride for the city.'

'Thirty? What about the rest of my people?'

'We only have thirty-four horses.'

'I only have seven people, so take seven fewer guardsmen!' she said, aghast.

'Can your ladies fight on horseback?'

'Well, no.'

'Then we take the guardsmen. There will be a hard fight to break through.'

'And leave my ladies to die? How could you!'

'No, we will leave them here guarded by the men who remain. We will return for them from the city tomorrow. They will have enough water, and nothing will take this hill while a hundred of my men defend it.'

That mollified her a little, and she nodded in defeat. 'As you say, then.'

'Thank you.'

Harald and I left and went down past our men and walked out to meet the enemy, being careful not to let them far enough up the slope to see our people preparing at the summit.

The bandit in the centre, a tall man with a fine curved sword that looked far too expensive for him to own, waited for us with a satisfied smile.

'Salamun alaykum,' the bandit said, with a flash of white teeth that no deprived outlaw would boast.

'He wishes peace upon us?' whispered Harald in outrage. He turned to our Arab guide. 'Tell him I wish death upon him.'

'Wa alaikum salaam,' replied our interpreter, and Harald gave him a filthy look.

'You wished him peace! What did I tell you?'

The man shrugged nervously. 'It is the way things are done here.'

Harald grumbled, but listened in silence as the bandit leader spoke to our interpreter.

'Our opponent wishes to let us know that if we surrender, and hand over our weapons and our wealth, we will be allowed to leave with our lives,' the interpreter said, with some degree of relief.

'What is his name, and why is he doing this?'

'He did not say.'

'Then tell him we will not hand over our weapons. He does not know us, but we would rather die.'

The guide relayed this to the bandit, who smiled slightly and nodded before replying.

'He says you are indeed welcome to die. He will collect your wealth and weapons from your bodies in three days' time, when the heat and thirst has killed you.'

'Then tell him my men will have come from Jerusalem before then, and we are happy to wait.'

There was another brief exchange. 'He does not believe anyone is coming, and you cannot see this hill from the main road. He thanks you for conducting this affair away from prying eyes.'

The bandit smiled at Harald smugly, and those bright white teeth were on display again. So perfect, such a complete set. Harald saw it too, and looked at me. 'A very comfortable life this bandit has lived.'

'I thought so too,' I muttered.

'Tell him I am willing to take my chances, but if he will leave now, I will pay him well in silver.'

There was a brief discussion between our Arab and the bandit, and then our guide spoke to us again. 'He asks how much silver you have?'

Harald looked around. Almost every man in our unit was wearing silver and gold – arm rings and necklaces and broaches. The bandit's eye followed Harald's and he nodded appreciatively.

'He says he will consider it, but he does not think it is enough. You will need more.'

'We do not have more.'

'You can return to the city and leave hostages behind with him.'

'I will leave ten unarmed men,' Harald answered. The bandit laughed and shook his head.

'He says you do not care for your soldiers, but he will accept the woman from the purple wagon. He knows we must be guarding her and cannot abandon her. If she is made his guest, he will allow the rest of us to go to the city and return with more silver.'

Harald turned away and swore under his breath.

'He knows who she is. This is what it has been about, all along.'

'Ransoming the sister of the empress? That is beyond a bandit.'

'But he is clearly not some common bandit. Perhaps one of the caliph's lords, perhaps a mercenary. I don't know.'

'Will he know what Theodora looks like?' I said, suddenly having an idea.

Harald worked out what I was saying immediately and nodded grimly. 'No, he will not.' He motioned to Rolf. 'Rolf, go to Theodora, get her and one of her attendants to swap clothes immediately, and bring the one dressed as Theodora back when I call. We may have to trade her but do not tell her that. Say it is just for show.'

Rolf nodded and left the line to go back over the summit.

'He wants to know what you are doing,' said our guide, and we saw the bandit nervously trying to peer over the line of men.

'Tell him we agree to his terms, and will give him the hostage.'

'What are we doing here Harald? They might kill her, even if we return with the ransom,' I said.

'They might kill her, but what choice do we have? We will hope a ransom is enough.'

'Are you going to be telling her that?'

'No.'

I was shocked by the ease with which he considered it. Perhaps Maria's goading had affected him. I was used to him sacrificing his men when needed, but soldiers knew that death might be what awaited them in his service. This was different. I had never seen him do the same with an innocent woman.

Finally, there was a commotion behind us, and my heart sank as I saw who was wearing Theodora's finery: Maria.

Harald saw it too, and I saw his jaw freeze, but he swallowed hard and waved Maria forwards and took her arm. 'Be calm and do as I ask. You will be safe.'

'Swear to me,' hissed Maria.

'I swear it,' answered Harald, and his face was almost ashen.

We went down the slope and the bandits came up, and our Arab told them Maria was the lady from the wagon, and he looked her up and down as Maria did her best to look serene, and he nodded his acceptance.

'He says it is agreed. We may go to the city and return in two days with fifty thousand dirhams, then she will be returned to you.'

Maria's eyes went wide and she turned to stare at Harald in horror. 'You are giving me to them.'

'Yes,' said Harald, who could not meet her eye.

'Harald! You can't, they will kill me!'

'They will not, we will ransom you.'

Then the bandit leader approached the terrified Maria and firmly took her by the arm. She resisted but it was no use, and with a last pleading glance back over her shoulder, she was led away.

'Harald, they will not ransom me! They will kill me! They are not here for silver!' She wriggled against the bandit's grasp as she wailed.

Harald watched them go a short distance, and then his brows furrowed. 'Ask him about the silver we have; he said he would take our silver now.'

The guide shouted after the bandit, who stopped and smiled nervously, and then waved the concern away, before taking Maria down the slope again, increasing his pace. 'He says you can deliver it later.'

Harald shuffled on the spot for a moment. 'Curse her, she is right. He doesn't care about the silver. This isn't a hostage taking, this is an assassination.' He looked at me in despair and indecision.

'Harald, we have Theodora – we can make it to the city with her.'

'And Maria dies.'

'And Maria dies,' I said, pleading.

Harald looked at the bandit, who was already halfway down the slope. 'Rolf, get your men and Theodora mounted. The rest of you, on me, now!'

He looked at me with a grim shrug of apology, and then he drew his sword and started running down the slope. Fifty of the guard went with him.

I swore and started off down the slope behind Harald. The startled Arab bandit and his men were too slow to react to the sudden attack, and we were within ten paces of them before he tried to goad Maria into a run, and then changed his mind and drew his sword to cut her down on the spot.

But Maria was not unprepared, and pulled a little dagger from her borrowed dress and jammed it into the false bandit's face with a wild scream, stabbing again and again as the bandit recoiled in agony and panic.

Another of the bandits tried to intervene, bringing his sword back to strike Maria down, but Harald jumped into him, shield first, hitting him so hard the man bounced down the slope and didn't stop until the bottom, rolling and skidding in a mess of broken bones.

Other men killed the only other bandit too stupid or stubborn not to flee, and I put my sword through the maimed bandit leader and kicked him away.

Then we were alone on the slope, but the enemy some fifty or so paces away had started to react, and the air was suddenly full of arrows. 'Shields!' I called, as they started hammering down around us and on us.

'Back up the slope!' Harald shouted, and then there was the sound of horses, and I assumed we were under attack, but I looked out from under my shield and saw Rolf approaching, leading a riderless horse in his off hand. Mercurius was with Theodora, riding doubled up on his horse. She looked fraught but Mercurius looked surprisingly calm.

'Get up!' Rolf shouted to Harald. 'We ride now or they block us!'

Even as he shouted that, one mounted guardsman was hit in the arm and lost control of his horse, being thrown onto the rocky ground with a thud. Harald pushed Maria up onto the horse Rolf had brought for him, and grabbed at the other riderless horse as Rolf swore at him for being an idiot for not leaving the girl.

I thought I was being abandoned, but Afra saw me looking forlorn and dismounted, shoving his horse's reins into my hand. 'Go with him!' he shouted at me, thumping me on the shoulder. 'I'm a fucking terrible rider anyway.'

I thanked Afra as I mounted. 'Hold this hill, Afra. We will come for you.'

'I know you will, brother. Go!' He slapped my horse's arse so hard I nearly fell off, and then I was slithering down the slope, trying to remember the little I knew about horse riding, for I was an even worse rider than Afra.

Well, despite the arrows and the chaos, and the two fallen horses with broken legs that I passed on the way down, most of us made it to the flat ground at the bottom, and I chased after the pack as we charged at the thin line of dismounted bandits that blocked our path.

They had been caught unprepared for the attack. Their horses were hobbled down the slope, and they could do little except fire a few arrows and throw a couple of spears as we passed, scattering them, and then we were through, headed along the path as it followed the ridgeline west, towards the city.

* * *

It had all happened too quickly for the enemy to respond, or perhaps, without their leader, they waited too long to decide, but by the time they gave chase we were several miles ahead, and we could see them behind us under a small cloud of dust, too far behind to stop us. We were going to easily make it to the city by nightfall.

We slowed our exhausted horses to a fast walk after a few miles, saving them in case we needed to run again, when we saw another, much larger, group of horsemen angling in from the north-east.

'Who are they?' asked Mercurius nervously. He had managed to stay in the saddle on the treacherous ride, even with Theodora riding with him. It was a testament to his skill, if nothing else; I doubt any of us could have ridden down that hill with Theodora.

Harald stared at them for a few moments. 'It's the warband from before we reached the city.'

'There are far too many to fight, and they are coming for us,' I replied. 'We'll kill the horses if we run again now.'

'We will leave it as late as we can, let them tire pursuing us. But it's going to be close. Find whoever is on the best horse, send them ahead and warn the city garrison we are coming and we are being pursued. Come, let's go.'

24

We got to within sight of Jerusalem before the two pursuing bands merged behind us. We dipped into the final valley and the dust cloud of our pursuers kept coming behind us so we pushed our ruined horses around the base of the Mount of Olives as fast as the poor creatures would go.

When we arrived at the north-eastern gate, Nassir was waiting outside for us with a hundred of his men on foot, and he ushered us through the gate with a furious expression. We explained to him what had happened as we rode into the space behind the gate and dismounted. One of the horses simply collapsed and wouldn't move. The rest stood around with heads drooping, sweat foaming from their flanks, as boys were sent to fetch buckets of water from the great pool that sat along the south side of the square.

'A thousand apologies that this could happen. I will have these scum cleared from the land tomorrow, and we will go with you and rescue the rest of your men.'

'You swear to me that you are not party to this attack?' Harald said, glaring at the commander.

'By Allah's grace, I swear it. These men were not under my orders.'

Harald nodded his acceptance.

'But you brought the emperor's sister to my city without telling me?' he said, and another of his senior men crowded in to hear the response.

Harald chewed his lip. 'I apologise for the secrecy, but we were trying to prevent this very incident.'

'And the lady Theodora survived, the bandits did not kill her?' asked one of the garrison soldiers, standing next to Nassir.

'Be quiet,' Nassir said indignantly, but the man was not cowed.

'Yes,' said Harald, 'she is safe.' And he looked at Theodora, who was standing with Mercurius.

'I told you to be quiet,' said Nassir, gesturing to the soldier. The soldier looked back at him with disgust, drew a dagger, and in one movement plunged it into Nassir's throat.

I stared in shock as the garrison commander choked and gasped, wide-eyed and panicking, and then chaos broke out in the square as most of the soldiers turned on the ones around Nassir and started slaughtering them. Several of our guardsmen who had been over by the pool fetching water were cut down before they even had time to react, as the Arab militiamen around them pulled their weapons without warning.

The Arab who had stabbed Nassir left his knife in the commander's throat and drew his sword, pointing it at Theodora and shouting something in Arabic. Its intent was clear from his face; she was their target.

'To me!' roared Harald, recovering more quickly than me from the sheer outrage of what was happening, and leaping to Theodora's side to cover her as she quailed from the violence. Mercurius drew his own slim, eastern-style sword and shouted in panic and outrage.

Varangians, jolted from their stupor, and given precious seconds to prepare by the Arab guard turning on itself, desperately scrambled into a group around us, drawing weapons and putting up their shields.

A guardsman near me went down with a sigh, and I saw a pair of shafts protruding high in his back near his spine.

'Archers!' I cried, and more shafts whistled into the group. Harald and several others shoved the two women down and protected them from the hail as a dozen or so archers appeared on the roofs nearby.

The Arab traitors were finished slaughtering those loyal to Nassir, and they turned their attention to us.

There was a shrill shout and more armed men, in a variety of garb, poured out of side streets, completing the ambush and outnumbering us terribly.

'We have to go!' I shouted at Harald, and he nodded. He stuck his head up for long enough to look around, and then pointed west, into the city, where the street narrowed to the width of two carts. There were a dozen enemy blocking our path.

'Varangians, into the street. Move!'

There was a roar of agreement, and the whole mass started running, shields up as best we could, simply hammering through the lightly armed enemy in our path as the rest charged and tried to close us down and trap us. Harald kept hold of Theodora, pushing her along in the centre of the formation, his shield over her head and Mercurius struggling to keep alongside. Maria scampered along behind them with Rolf covering her.

In moments we were fighting for our lives, cutting through at the front, defending ourselves as best we could at the rear, only our big shields and good maille and the sheer violence of our actions keeping us alive.

I nearly tripped over a body, and saw that it was one of our attackers. I stabbed down at it just to be sure it was truly dead.

Then we reached the entrance to the street, and we funnelled into it, forming a column four men wide at the front and rear, the two women herded along in the centre.

'Which way?' shouted someone from the front.

'West!' shouted Harald, because none of us knew any better.

The enemy poured down the streets parallel to us, attacking us at every junction and alleyway. Nimble archers ran along the rooftops, lancing occasional arrows down onto us that we could not protect against.

I stepped over another body, and it was a Varangian. Our ranks were thinning, and there had been so few of us to start with.

We fought our way across a bigger crossroad, hacking and slashing at the attempted resistance in front, big axes working over the heads of the men in the lead rank, hewing the desperate assassins even as we were pummelled from the flanks, rear, and above.

The slaughter in the crossroads was terrible. Two Arabs shoved their way through our group in the chaos and lunged at Theodora. Harald put his sword through one of them, but the weapon was trapped by the body, and the second jabbed a spear at Theodora.

With a bellow of outrage, Mercurius stepped into the gap and tried to parry the spear away. His swipe was wild and mistimed, and his light sword clattered off the spear as it buried itself in his chest.

Theodora screamed in horror as Mercurius gasped and fell to his knees. Harald finally got his sword free and cut down the second man, clearing the space around the two women.

'Move!' he roared, and he urged the front ranks into the next narrow street while the rest of us fought to keep our little formation intact. I was supporting a man on my left, and suddenly he was gone, pulled into the enemy mob by his shield arm to be butchered, and then I was alone in the face of them.

And my sword sang. I put my shield up high and I thrust my blade again and again into flesh, no space for skill or swings or cleverness. I thrust and twisted on the withdraw – thrust and twisted. The screams were all around me, and then someone was pulling on the back of my maille and shouting in my ear.

'We are going!' I chanced a look around and saw Rolf dragging me, and that we were now at the back of the column. I saw a pair of guardsmen down in the carnage in the crossroads as we retreated, saw Mercurius's open, outraged eyes staring at the blood gushing from his chest as he knelt in the carnage, abandoned. And then he was overtaken by the tide of the mob that followed us, and I shouted pointless curses at them as they tramped the Roman nobleman down.

The archers on the rooftops couldn't get across that broad cross-street, and we were mercifully spared their harassing as we continued through the city, blindly heading westwards, hoping to find somewhere we recognised.

We came to another small square, an opening in the city, and we sprinted across it, seeing a broad set of stairs heading up the side of the northern wall of the temple mount where it met the corner with its western wall. The stairs led to an old archway that led deeper into the city to the south.

The enemy flooded into the square behind us, and threw themselves at us once again. 'Stairs!' shouted Harald, and we surged towards the stone steps, the enemy clawing at us to drag us down.

We got Theodora and Maria up the steps, arrows chasing us like angry hornets, and our men formed a solid wall behind, retreating one step at a time as the enemy surged after us.

'We can hold here,' Rolf shouted, and we stopped halfway up the steps and formed a shield wall, five men wide, holding back the voracious tide of our far more numerous attackers.

Harald looked around and nodded, ducking as he caught an arrow in his shield. Then I looked out over the rooftops and saw the great pool and the city gate, and saw that it was standing open, forgotten in the chaos.

Outside the gate, not more than half a mile away, was the warband that had been chasing us, riding hard.

'Christ save us,' muttered Harald in horror. 'We can't hold against them, even here.'

'They are not our enemies!' shouted Maria, and Harald turned on her angrily.

'I do not want your opinion! Be quiet!' He looked away again.

'We need to get to the sepulchre, to the rest of the men. Maybe we can reach the citadel on the western wall,' Rolf said.

'If the men of the citadel have not turned on us,' I added.

The enemy were throwing themselves against our line on the steps. Their bravery was almost suicidal, and with their numbers and our growing exhaustion, it was threatening to overcome us.

I looked to my left and saw dozens of men running along a side street northwards, going the long way around the obstacle we were making.

'Look!' I said, pointing with my sword. 'They are going around us.'

'We will be surrounded if we have to retreat while fighting. We cannot let them through this archway,' said Harald. He cursed and looked around once more. We were running out of time.

'Go!' shouted Rolf, turning and shoving Harald. 'Take her to the church!'

We all knew what that meant. Harald nodded grimly and pulled Rolf into a quick embrace, even as the enemy pushed our men another step up the stairs.

'Hold them as long as you can, brother,' said Harald.

'The guard obeys,' Rolf said through gritted teeth, turning back to the desperate fight on the steps.

There wasn't time to say more.

'Let's go!' shouted Harald, taking everyone who wasn't in the first two ranks on the stairs and shoving them through the archway.

I saw Rolf jam his helmet back into place and take up his great axe, leaning back and howling his defiance at the oncoming mass. Then the first rank was falling back again, and Rolf swung his axe up and down over their heads, shouting curses and reaping the lives of the poorly armoured men who dared to climb to meet him.

Arrows were skittering around us and I realised Harald was screaming at me. I turned to look at him and he waved me through the archway, an arrow bouncing off the stone near his head. 'Not you, Eric! I need you!' His eyes were desperate.

I stood there, torn, turning one last time to see the Hammerbeard's red-slicked axe rise and fall again before running up the last stairs, joining Harald and the few men still with us in a desperate flight through the city, a race to the sanctuary of the church.

We took the first major street turning west that we found, quite lost now, running through unfamiliar streets where the locals were scattering, hiding from the sound and warnings of fighting that was preceding us through the normally bustling thoroughfares. Doors were slammed and barred and we were channelled westwards, blindly groping around for the Church of the Holy Sepulchre, where Styrbjorn and over three hundred guardsmen would surely provide safety.

We took a bad turn and came to a dead end, having to retrace our steps, wasting precious time. We went back and tried the next street, finding we could catch a glimpse of the big tower of the western citadel at the end of it, knowing if we followed that, we would reach the church nearby.

We were halfway down that street when the sound of shouting and conflict reached our ears from ahead. Harald waved at us to slow down, and we peered around a corner to find, two streets down, a group of the traitor militia moving parallel to us, headed towards the church.

'Damn, they are ahead of us.'

'We have to go around them, get to the church another way.'

As we stood there assessing the situation, huddled against a wall, there was a shout behind us, and we turned to see a half dozen of the Arabs on the street behind, fifty paces away, shouting and pointing in our direction.

'No time for that, run!'

We set off down the street, hearing the calls of our hunters to our rear being echoed by those to our right and then ahead of us. We could hear fighting off to the right too, but could not tell who it was. Perhaps Styrbjorn was moving out into the city, trying to quell the violence, although he could not have known we were being hunted or where we were.

As we pounded down that street, no more than a hundred paces away from the district around the church, a group of the enemy appeared in the street in front of us and turned, running towards us. I looked back and another group of enemy was close behind, and down an alleyway to our right was the sound of pounding feet.

'We are trapped,' said a guardsman, aghast.

'In here!' shouted Harald, kicking at a half-rotten door. 'We'll find a way through.' It was common, in the buildings in that city, for them to interconnect via doors, balconies and courtyards.

We all shoved through the big door, and I pushed the pathetic thing shut behind us. We were in a dilapidated courtyard, perhaps twenty paces across, with a single exit at the back leading into a fine, dressed stone building. I grabbed two of the men. 'Hold this door,' I growled, gesturing at a third to join them.

'Aye,' said one of them, and thumped his nervous fellow on the shoulder.

I had no time to inspire them. I headed off into the stone building after Harald, who I could hear shouting in front of me. I went through into a dilapidated antechamber of some sort, lit by high, thin slit windows near the ceiling. At the back of the antechamber was a dark passage, which I followed through several corners until I reached an archway.

Harald was through the archway in front, and I could hear him cursing amid the sound of breaking wood.

'Find a way through!' I heard him shout desperately, and went into the room to find it was an abandoned chapel, strewn with goat droppings and broken furniture. The room was long, with flat sides and a half-circle at the end where a shrine sat forgotten and unattended. I could not see a door, and Harald and the last three guardsmen were tearing at the wall hangings, furniture and the plaster itself trying to find an exit.

'We are trapped,' said Maria with a sob, holding her hand to her face and looking around in despair.

'Now, now, my child,' said Theodora, maintaining her composure. She took Maria and pulled her into an embrace as the chaos swirled around them.

'Back out into the street?' I said hopelessly, but I could already hear the fighting by the door behind us as our pursuers tried to force their way in.

'There has to be something,' said Harald, looking around and then up to eye the slit windows that lined the tops of the walls on both sides, but were as unreachable as the heavens themselves.

'Look, the mother Mary herself! This is shrine to her,' said Theodora, a smile creasing her exhausted, dust-covered features. She went to the curved end of the room, Maria in tow, and brushed some debris away for a large carved icon of a woman with a wrapped baby.

'That doesn't help,' protested Harald with an exasperated glance.

'Of all places, we were brought here.'

'She won't save us.'

'Not our bodies, no, but our souls, maybe.'

Theodora knelt in front of the shrine, and the distraught Maria knelt with her, and Theodora started to pray, her voice loud and calm in the noise of the chapel as the guardsmen gave up the search for an exit that did not exist, or at attacking walls that were backed with stone that would not give way.

'We are about to die and she is praying for deliverance,' said one guardsman with a scowl.

'What else can she do?'

'I won't stay here to die on my knees,' he replied, picking up his sword. 'Not while my brothers fight.' He headed back out into the passage, towards the courtyard, from which I heard a faint but blood-curdling scream.

'We were so close to safety,' muttered Harald. 'So close we could touch it. How can this be it?' He looked around, his eyes dull. 'Rolf on the stairs, Afra and the others on the hill... Have I condemned them all to death and yet failed?' He looked at me aghast, bowed and miserable with the cost of his decisions.

'They are doing their duty,' I said with a ragged stutter, my parched throat barely letting the words through.

Harald looked at Maria, who looked back with tears running down her cheeks. 'You were right. I should have been more ruthless. If only I had the strength to let them take you. But I love you still, and I'm sorry I failed to protect you.' He turned away from her in shame. 'Don't let them take Theodora alive. I know you have a blade. If we fall, I trust you will have the strength to use it.' He turned to me and the others. 'Come, let us join our brothers. We are not dead yet.'

We filed through the passage into the antechamber and saw our men retreating into it, fighting with the enemy, having been forced back from the courtyard.

We charged into the room, arriving just as the defenders were about to be split up and overwhelmed, and launched into the enemy with a new vigour and desperation. The fight spread out across the antechamber of the chapel as more of the enemy tried to shove through the entrance. We desperately held them back, but their numbers were overwhelming.

I lost my shield in the press and held one of the attackers by the front of his tunic as I killed him, then when he fell another enemy stepped over his body and plunged his dagger into my chest with a yell. The pain blossomed across my ribs, but my knees did not buckle, and I thought the maille must have held. I grabbed at his wrist with my free hand and worked my sword between us with the other, wriggling the point up under his armpit and then driving it into his chest with a grunt as he squirmed and wailed.

He would have killed me, that young man, if he had been wearing maille, and I had not. But he wore nothing but a tunic and I had good Northern iron link, so I am here telling you stories and he is dust. That is why we wear maille.

Well, as that stupid boy fell limply from my sword, I suddenly had space and saw that a dozen of our attackers were being butchered by another group of white-robed men who had burst in and were attacking our enemy from behind. They were wearing armour under their robes and looked like proper soldiers. I could not decipher their intent, but I recognised their attire.

'Those men are from the warband that followed us into the city,' Harald said from beside me, as the fighting died away and we stared at the newcomers warily.

The last of our attackers was cut down, and the robed men looked at us, no hint of hostility in their attitude. 'Varangians?' one of them asked in Greek.

'Yes,' I answered, suddenly certain they meant us no harm.

'You are safe. The city is being cleared of the assassins as we speak. Return to your master, if he lives.'

Harald shoved me aside and stepped out in front. 'I am their master. Tell me, who are you?'

'Ah, Harald it is you!' the man said, with his eyes betraying the smile that was hidden underneath his wrapped face.

'Yes.'

'And the lady Theodora, is she alive?'

Harald paused, uncertain if he should answer, but then nodded. 'She is.'

The man looked happy and bowed. 'I am relieved to hear it. We have sent word to your men at the church, they will be looking for you. I shall tell them you live and where to find you. It is best you stay here until then. Some of the enemy may yet roam the streets.' He waved at his men to leave.

'Come back here! Who are you?' shouted Harald angrily, but the man ignored him and turned to follow his men out of the broken doors.

Harald ran across the space and snatched the man back, provoking a cry of surprise from him, and alarm and outrage from his men, who turned to come back after their leader.

'Back!' shouted Harald, and the robed men looked at each other in confusion.

'We saved you!' protested the wriggling man in Harald's grasp.

'And you will answer me why.'

Harald pointed at the men with his free hand. 'Stay in the courtyard, or saviours or not, you become my enemy.'

'Don't do this, Harald. Let me go!'

I recognised that voice, now that I had time to focus on it. It was the way he said *Harald*, it brought back memories.

Harald clearly had the same feeling, because he shoved the smaller man against a wall and reached up to rip away the cloth that covered his face. He let go a breath with a hiss and stepped back.

'Bardas.'

The Greek mercenary stumbled as he regained his balance, and tried to regain some dignity with an outraged glare. 'Yes, you fool. Now let me leave!'

'What... Why are you here? Explain to me before I take the chance to make good my promise to you that the next time we met, you would die,' Harald growled, advancing with his sword.

'My men outside will not let you go if you kill me!' Bardas protested, looking nervous.

'I don't need their permission to leave – my own men will be here soon enough. Speak!'

Harald put his sword into Bardas's armoured chest, and the Greek looked at it nervously.

'What are you doing here? Protecting Theodora?' Harald demanded.

Bardas sneered. 'That much is obvious.'

'By whose orders?'

'I am commanded to keep my duties a secret.'

'I am here on behalf of the emperor and I don't care who else commands you!'

'You should, for we have the same master!' he spat, and Harald pulled back a touch.

'The emperor sent you?'

'Yes, now let me go!'

'Why would he send you, when he also sent me?'

'For surety. I was to travel anonymously and make sure no harm came to lady Theodora.'

'A task you so nearly failed at.'

'I would have succeeded far more easily if you were not so bone-headed, leaving the road and then leaving your men to run with so few! My force arrived and cleared those bandits away from the hill not long after you abandoned them. Your men are fine if you even care, and on their way to the city now.'

That hit home and Harald straightened, dropping the sword a fraction. 'My men are safe?'

'Yes.'

I could see the relief wash over him.

'Those were no simple bandits that trapped us on that hill, did you know that?'

'They were hired to kill the lady Theodora, which is what I was here to prevent.'

'By the emperor?'

'Again, yes,' said the exasperated Greek.

'If he knew this journey would be so dangerous, why would he send her?'

'His hand was forced.'

My mind raced back to the meeting with the emperor, how sour he had seemed, how angry, even. If this expedition had not been his idea then who, who could have forced him? The answer hit me before it hit Harald.

'Who? Who forced him to send Theodora on this pilgrimage, who ordered her to be killed?'

Bardas gave Harald that look, the one he had always given Harald in the Rus when Harald was being naive.

Then Harald's sword fell, the tip bouncing off the ground. 'Zoe,' he said, sounding deflated.

Bardas spread his hands like it was childishly obvious.

'Zoe engineered this expedition to have her sister killed,' Harald said, dumbstruck. 'Why?'

'Because she was worried Michael would eventually use Theodora to replace her,' I suggested.

'But wasn't Maria working to find someone to take the throne with Theodora?' Harald asked.

'Maria found someone to take the throne with Theodora. His name is Michael,' said a voice behind us, and I turned and saw Maria standing in the doorway.

'Maria,' said Harald with a gasp. 'You knew about this? That means...' He squinted and shook his head. 'You have allied yourself with Michael?'

'Maria, don't say another word!' said Bardas desperately.

Maria held up a hand to still him. 'Trust me, Bardas, it is time he knew. He will make the right decision.' She looked at Harald again. 'Yes. When we heard there was a new emperor, we returned to the city and found new alliances. I told you, power merely waits for an opportunity.'

'How? How could you even arrange that?'

Maria shook her head at our ignorance. 'John approached me with the offer, and we were only too glad to accept. He wanted to be rid of Zoe, but he needed Theodora to replace her. We agreed.'

The pieces all fell into place for Harald, finally. 'John planned the attack on Zoe in the hippodrome, not you.'

'Yes. I didn't know, nor did Michael. Once Zoe was dead, we would have put Theodora on the throne and everything would have been under our control.'

'You and John, controlling the empire through your puppets.'

'Yes,' she said, without boast.

'And why didn't you warn me Theodora was in danger here? How many of my men would that have saved?'

She shrugged. 'I could not, I did not trust your reaction. I needed you to see, I needed you to see that Zoe was willing to sacrifice you.'

Harald muttered something and turned back to Bardas.

'So maybe Zoe is behind all of this, not you two traitors, but how did she do this? These men that attacked us were Arabs, soldiers of the local leaders.'

'Not all in the caliphate agree with the peace. There are some who wish the war had continued. Zoe must have made a deal with one of those factions to betray their caliph, who is only a child, and restart the war. Perhaps they hope to become caliph themselves in the chaos,' said Bardas.

'The governor… he is in Cairo, far from the blame and suspicion, but his men are here,' I said.

The scale of it was astonishing.

'Zoe would have restarted the war, just to secure her position. And she was willing to sacrifice us to do it,' Harald said in wonder and disgust.

'Finally, you two foreign fools understand the most basic parts of our politics. Now, release me! It is the emperor's command that this remain a secret. If what happened here becomes known, it could lead to war with the caliphate, or civil war with Zoe. None of this can become known, do you understand! I speak with the emperor's voice in this matter!'

Harald looked around, thinking, furious with himself. 'I understand, except one thing. Why did he send me? Why not some Roman lord?'

'Because he knew Zoe hadn't corrupted you, that you had refused her and you would not help her kill Theodora. He also knew you have an absurd habit of surviving when you should not. He valued both things. There are few in the empire he trusts; the empress's claws are everywhere,' Maria said.

Harald shook his head and looked at me. 'When we left the docks and Zoe saw us, she was surprised and concerned. I thought she was worried I would die, but she was not.'

'No,' I said, with a blush of anger. 'She was worried we would live.'

'And you did, so now you are her enemy, and we are your allies.' Maria stepped over to Harald, looking into his eyes earnestly. 'Join us, Harald. I do not lie, I care for you also, and to Zoe you are nothing but a tool. With all of us together there is no limit to what we and the empire could achieve!' She was pleading with him, her eyes flicking back and forth between his. 'I have risked everything to tell you what I have told you, so please, join me.'

Harald looked deeply conflicted, but before he could answer we heard footsteps in the passage, and Theodora's voice calling out nervously. Bardas looked at Harald pleadingly. 'She does not know about Zoe's plot; ensure it remains that way! Too many questions will be asked.'

Harald grimaced and nodded his head towards the door, and Bardas pulled his wrap back up around his face and headed quickly out of the door with a final glare of disgust in our direction.

'Maria?' Theodora said, stepping timidly into the doorway to the charnel house that was the antechamber.

'We are in here, my lady.'

'And the assassins?' she said, looking around in horror.

'They are dead or gone. They were chased off by some of the local garrison, returned to restore order,' Harald replied.

'Oh, lord be praised. I will go and give thanks to the blessed Virgin,' she said, retreating from the sight as fast as she could with Maria in tow.

'Theodora will claim we were delivered by her prayers,' I muttered.

'Let her believe that and say it, it is better than her learning the truth that her sister tried to have her murdered.' He shook his head. 'Come, let's clear a path through these scum and get the women out of here.'

'Shouldn't we wait for Styrbjorn?'

'No. I am not going to be rescued twice in one day. We will go out and find them.'

He turned again to Maria, his features twisted, but no longer full of spite. 'We will speak later.' She nodded meekly in response.

* * *

We met a party of guardsmen searching the streets outside, who were elated to find us alive, and they escorted us back to the church, where a desperately apologetic Styrbjorn was waiting.

'Komes, I did not know! There was fighting in the streets, and skirmishing with some of the men I sent out, but I did not know you were involved until a local came and warned us.'

'It was not your fault, Styrbjorn. I will explain everything. Have your men found Rolf?'

Styrbjorn shook his head in confusion. 'He is not with the rest of your party outside the city?'

'He is not.' Harald grimaced and looked at me with a heavy air. 'Come, let's go to them.'

* * *

We retraced our steps through the deserted streets until we came to the arch, and there we found Rolf Hammerbeard, resting as if sleeping with his back against a pillar of the archway. His bloodied axe lay at his side, a spear was embedded in his chest, and a tight knot of our men lay scattered around him.

The bodies of the enemy's dead and wounded were strewn around our comrades on both sides of the arch, and littered the stairs in heaps where a pair of guardsmen were also crumpled on the stones.

The tale of the battle was clear. Rolf and his men had held the stairs until the enemy had circled around behind them, and then the survivors had retreated to the archway to make their stand, back-to-back, until the end.

We mournfully checked each one of them but the traitor militia, in their fury, had torn into the bodies of our fallen comrades with blades a dozen times or more, and not a single one of them were still alive.

'Oh Rolf, how much better you deserved than to die in this place,' I said, putting my hand on his shoulder and failing to hold back my tears.

'If they had not won us time, we would have been overcome,' said Harald, and his bottom jaw was set in stone.

I looked up at him, because he was still a heartless bastard some of the time, and he had the decency to look a little ashamed.

'They did their duty well, and will be remembered for it, and the world will know that unto death, the guard obeys,' he said.

Then he turned to two of the men with us. 'Go and bring the men of the fourteenth banda with shields to bear their bodies.'

'How many of the fourteenth, Komes?'

'All of them,' said Harald. 'These men died as heroes, and we will give them whatever honour we can.'

25

CONSTANTINOPLE, LATE SUMMER 1037

'Basileus, I am honoured to be received.' Harald executed a crisp bow, and the emperor acknowledged it from his chair.

We were in the private rooms of the emperor, several months after the desperate fight in Jerusalem. We had returned to the capital with no fanfare, not to be feted as heroes. The story the emperor wished to portray was of a successful, and peaceful, imperial pilgrimage to the Holy Land, where some minor skirmishes with bandits and thieves explained the rumours of fighting by the expedition.

A new governor of Jerusalem had been appointed by the caliphate, new men brought in, and guarantees given that the builders and priests would be safe as they continued their work. Harald had been given a small fortune in Moslem silver by way of apology, and to buy his silence. He had given half of it to the men, and by the apostles did they love him for it.

Few knew the truth of what had happened in that small, abandoned chapel near the Holy Sepulchre, and they were all sworn to secrecy.

'I wanted to thank you, Komes, for all that you have done for us, and for the empire – that which our subjects are aware of, and that which they are not. You have proven your loyalty beyond reproach, and you have my personal thanks.'

With that, he gestured to the side, and a train of servants brought in three heavy wooden boxes, each the size of a man's chest, ornate and finely carved, and laid them in front of us. With a flick of his fingers, the servants opened the boxes to reveal their contents. They were each filled with leather sacks, and I could see each sack was bulging. Silver and gold coins spilled from a few of them.

Harald's eyebrows rose and he looked at the emperor. 'Your generosity is remarkable, Basileus. My deepest thanks.'

Michael smiled as if it was nothing, and that he had not just laid enough money to buy a small fleet in front of us.

'It is a reward you and your men deeply deserve, but it is not the total. I have been considering the replacement of Báulfr as field commander of the guard, and, along with the head of the scholai, have made my decision.'

Harald straightened and his eyes lit up with far more intensity than the silver had inspired.

'Harald Nordbrikt, I bestow upon you the title of protospatharios, the first among my bodyguard: the axe of the emperor. Upon your battle-tested shoulders will the safety of the throne and those who sit upon it be laid, and on your fire-tested honour will the trustworthiness of the Varangian tagma be placed.' He stood and advanced down the few steps that separated us, the scant attendants and officials present turning solemnly to stare at Harald.

He reached my friend and offered his hand, knuckles up, and Harald knelt and put his hand under the emperor's.

'Do you accept this honour?' Michael said, with all solemnity.

'I do. The emperor commands, and I obey.'

'This is not a command, Araltes, this is an invitation.'

'Then I accept it without hesitation,' Harald replied, and he bent forwards to gently kiss the emperor's hand.

'Then it will be done. You will be taken to the chapel of the Varangians, and with your hand upon your predecessor's tomb you will swear your oaths in the presence of your own men and be bound to your own words. While you have my ear, is there anything you would wish to ask of me?'

Michael's brow raised and he looked at Harald expectantly. Harald's temple pulsed as he considered it. I wondered what favour he might ask, or what information he might seek. There were so many options, but the silence became embarrassing and Harald shook his head.

'Not yet, Basileus.'

'Not yet? Intriguing. Well, you may go about your new duties with my thanks.'

And with that, we were dismissed.

* * *

We returned to the barracks, with the emperor's appointment written and sealed on fine parchment, and we went up to Báulfr's office where Aki was berating two guardsmen who had failed to show up on time for guard duty.

When they were done, Aki waved us in with a scowl. 'What is it, Komes?'

Harald cleared his throat gently and tapped the parchment in one hand with the other. 'I have a command, from the emperor's hand.'

'What?' Aki looked at the gilded scroll, with the emperor's massive seal affixed to it, and he leaned back in his chair. 'Is that for you, or for me?'

Harald carefully put the parchment on the desk, and Aki picked it up and started reading, his eyes narrowing and his mouth curling.

'I want you to know I respect you, Aki, and there is no spite in this,' Harald said.

'You? He gives this to you, after the work that I have been doing? You, some jumped up newcomer fresh off the boats?'

'Be careful, Aki,' said Harald, tapping one finger on the desk. 'I will give you that one outburst, but you are talking to your commander now, and you will not do it again.'

Aki's temple pulsed and his teeth ground, but his discipline won out and he nodded curtly. 'So I see. Well, you will find it to be a curse. I will actually be glad to be rid of all this work; it is suitable for scribes, not fighting men.' He waved his hand at all the papers that lined the room.

Harald smiled. 'I will do things a little differently. I have someone who will take care of some administration for me, someone far better at it than me, who has proven themselves dedicated and competent. A true second in command. I find it strange that the position does not formally exist, and I believe I have the authority to create it.'

'Ha! You have been commander for one moment and you wish to upturn fifty years of knowledge? What, you will make Eric here your second? He is not even a komes.'

'No, Eric is not suited for the task.' He gave me a look and a shrug. 'I mean no offence; it is not your skill.'

I smiled. 'I know it.'

'Who then? If it even matters to me,' said Aki, standing from the desk in disgust.

'You,' said Harald simply.

Aki's eyes narrowed and he stared at Harald. 'Me? You know my feelings about you, so why would you make me your second? Is this a sick joke, a punishment?'

'No, it is no joke or punishment. I know you disagree with me on most things, but I know you are loyal and disciplined and will do what is best for the guard. A second who questions me and shows me if I am wrong can be a great asset, if I know he will follow my commands, nonetheless. Tell me, Aki, can you put aside your enmity towards me to uphold your oaths and the discipline of the guard?'

Aki's back straightened. 'Of course.'

'I believe you. So I name you second sword of the Tagma Varangian. In battle you will bear the emperor's standard, and take command if I fall. In peace you will be responsible for discipline and order in the guard, and in ensuring my orders are carried out.'

Aki's expression softened a little. 'It is a brave and wise move, Harald, especially since I know that mostly, you simply wish me to do all this bureaucracy for you,' he said with a hint of a smile, looking around the office.

Harald beamed at him. 'You see, you understand me already. This will work well.'

'And what of my Wolfhounds?'

'Who would you want to take over?'

Aki thought about it for a moment. 'Sveinn.'

Harald nodded. 'Good, then it shall be so. That would be my choice, too.'

'Not one of your men? Rurik, perhaps?' said Aki suspiciously.

'No. It is best the men are led by one they know well, and Sveinn has proven himself for longer.'

'Are you not afraid Sveinn will be my man, not yours?'

Harald smiled and half turned to leave. 'No, Aki, I am not. Because he will be your man, and you will be mine. We will swear an oath on it.'

* * *

I cannot tell you of the ceremony Harald and Aki took with the other komes of the guard, partly because I was not there, and mostly because it is a deep secret, the oaths of the Varangians. In fact, I have told you more than I should by even saying where and how it was done. But the shades of my old friends will forgive me that weakness.

It was a wise appointment, making Aki the second of the guard. He was a popular and respected figure, and it smoothed over the transition to Harald, who had the respect of a great many of the men, but who was not universally popular. Aki, much though he enjoyed snide remarks and complaining about the paperwork, was good at his work and loyal.

Harald made changes, of course. Firstly he put Afra, who had taken a leg wound in the Holy Land that would not fully heal and was not fit to go on campaign again, into the first banda with his brother, Thorir. Of course the real reason for their new position was to give Afra and Thorir full access to the palace, and thus be able to better keep Harald informed of goings on inside the secretive household.

It did not take long before that access paid off.

Harald and I were practising in the yard with about fifty other men one cool evening in the early winter of 1037 when Afra came into the yard and beckoned to us. It was not uncommon, as Afra had a lot to report these days, but he looked more urgent than normal.

We went over to him, curious, leaving our practice weapons against a wall. 'Come, down to the cellar. I have something that needs your attention.'

We followed him down the stairs to the warren of storerooms under the barracks, carrying an oil lamp to guide the way. We approached a room where light was coming from around the door, and Afra knocked.

The door was unbarred from inside and we saw Thorir when it opened.

'Spatharios,' he said, with a nod.

We went inside, and then I noticed a cowering figure in the corner.

'Who is that?' asked Harald.

'That is the problem,' said Afra.

'Explain?'

'It is complex, Harald, and I am concerned we have done the wrong thing, but we did not feel we had a choice. I hope—'

'Just explain, Afra,' said Harald, holding up a hand to forestall the nervous man.

Afra closed his mouth and nodded. 'Well, simply put, this is the eunuch Sgouritzes, one of Empress Zoe's household staff.'

Harald closed his eyes and pinched his nose between his thumb and forefinger. 'And why, why is this eunuch huddled on the floor of my cellar?'

'We caught him with a vial of poison in the palace.'

Harald's eyes snapped open. 'An assassination attempt? By God, have you sounded the alarm, brought out the whole of the first bandon?'

Afra raised his hand to forestall Harald's panic. 'Apologies, the emperor was not the target.'

'Are you sure?'

'Quite sure, Commander. The emperor was not in the palace, and this wretch was heading for John's quarters.'

Harald looked at him. 'And you know this how?'

'We questioned him. We are very persuasive.'

Harald chewed his lip. 'So Zoe has sent him to kill John.'

'Yes.'

'And how did you catch him?'

'Well, Thorir has made certain acquaintances, and paid them to give him information if anyone seeks poisons or easily hidden weapons or seeks to hire thugs or assassins, that kind of thing.'

I smiled at Thorir, who kept his expression blank.

'Well, one of them informed us that a vial of poison had been smuggled into the palace. We followed the man who had brought it in until we believed it had been handed to this eunuch, at which point we seized him.'

'Excellent. That is excellent. This is why I pay you so well, Afra.'

'You could pay me better,' said Afra with a sly smile.

'And after this, I shall.'

'What do we do with him?'

'Well, that is a difficult question. Technically, it is not our business if the empress kills John.'

'I might encourage it,' I added.

Harald laughed. 'Maybe. But nor can the guard allow people to wander about the palace with vials of poison.'

'So what do we do, release him?'

'And have the empress find out we ruined her plans and tortured one of her staff? That is also difficult.'

'We have done the wrong thing?' asked Afra, visibly nervous.

'No... No, you did the right thing.'

Harald went and knelt down, examining the terrified eunuch. 'Do you have some way of passing messages to the empress, a way that she will know is from you?'

The eunuch looked pained, but then with a single meaningful glare from Thorir, who I had never until that point considered to be intimidating, he nodded quickly.

'Good. You will write a message to her, tell her I have intercepted you and I have a better way of dealing with John, and that she needs to meet me in the hall of war after the change of guard at midnight. I will make sure the right men are on duty, and they ignore her passing. Understood?'

The eunuch looked relieved, and nodded. 'Yes, Protospatharios.'

'Good. Afra, make sure he writes that message, and then have Thorir deliver it immediately.'

'As you say, Commander.'

Harald stood up and gestured to me and we left. Once we were alone he stopped and leaned in towards me. 'Eric, I have another message to write, and I want you to deliver it to John.'

'Harald, you are going to join Michael's side, as Maria asked? They will ask you to help murder Zoe!' I said, horrified.

'I will put an end to this. Zoe wishes John dead, and it is not my responsibility to stop her, but I cannot do my duties with John and Zoe and others plotting and murdering in the palace... I will explain later. For now, I will write orders for the first bandon. I need you to take them and then wait for me in the war room.'

I gave him a very reluctant look, but he was not relenting. 'Just trust me, or if you don't trust me, simply do as I ask.'

I nodded. 'As you command, Protospatharios.' I left, but I was wracked by doubts. Harald had spoken to Maria in Jerusalem after the battle, alone, and had refused to tell me about what was said. I had not seen them together since we arrived back in the city, but I was fairly certain they had met several more times.

To make my suspicions worse, Michael had obviously trusted him to be raised to the head of the guard. I started to wonder if he had made a secret deal with the emperor that even I was not privy to. I knew the power Maria held over him and my head was full of the deepest concerns.

But there was nothing I could do except follow his orders, until he gave me an order I could not follow.

* * *

From the hall of war, I watched the guard change in the palace at midnight, and saw that the presence was doubled. The whole thing, and Harald's secrecy, made me nervous.

Finally, Harald arrived, alone, and joined me. 'What is happening, Harald?'

'All will be clear, very soon.'

'Why will you not just tell me?'

'Because you will argue with me about it, and we don't have time.'

'They are here, Commander,' said one of the guardsmen on the southern doors to the great room.

The doors opened wider, and two women and two guardsmen came in. I recognised Zoe and her ever-present handmaid Hypatia. Zoe looked around the room in confusion for a moment, her look turning fearful, and then she turned to leave.

As she did, the guardsman firmly closed the door behind her.

'What is the meaning of this?' she said in a hushed voice. 'Is this some trap? Guardsman, release me!'

'You are here for your safety, Basilissa,' said the guardsman. 'No harm will come to you. The commander has discovered a plot.'

'Thank you, Lendir, you may guard the outer door,' said Harald from the shadows.

The two guardsmen turned and left, leaving us alone with the two women in the room.

Zoe looked around her, still concerned, but then moved over towards us, trying to hide it.

'What is this about? What plot is this, Araltes?'

'I will explain in a moment – we are waiting for one more party.'

'One more party?'

'I will explain in a moment,' said Harald firmly. Zoe stopped and fidgeted with her gown.

'You have not come to see me, since you returned from Jerusalem,' she said, sounding a little hurt.

'I have been busy.'

'But you are my sworn protector, the commander of my guard. I would have thought you saw it part of your duties to see me.'

'You could have summoned me at any time, Basilissa, and I would have come.'

'I did not wish to summon you, Araltes. Can we not be beyond such formality?' She moved over and stood near him, looking up into his eyes with a pleading expression. 'It is just us here.' She placed a hand on his arm. She looked so vulnerable.

'Stop,' said Harald, brushing her hand away.

Zoe looked shocked, hurt even. 'Excuse me?'

'Stop these theatrics, this play as a poor, helpless woman. I am tired of it. You are neither poor nor helpless.'

Zoe's face contorted slightly, but she shook it slowly. 'I don't understand. You know my position, how I am abused and restricted. Surrounded by my enemies.'

'Oh, I know, Zoe.' Harald leaned down slightly to meet her eye to eye. 'I *know*.'

Then he drew himself up to his full height. 'I know you are surrounded by enemies, but you chose them, placed them. I know you pretend to be a prisoner in the palace, sneaking out to see me, to earn my sympathy with your vulnerability and pretend you care for me, but you are free to go as you like, and it is those who oppose you who end up floating in the waters of the Golden Horn.' He shook his head. 'And I know something that you don't.'

Zoe's eyes blazed in the lamplight. 'What is that?'

'I know what happened to those assassins you sent to kill us.'

Zoe's face went tight like a drumskin, and I saw the first trace of real fear in her eyes. Not the feigned, womanly fear she had so often portrayed, but the feral, wild fear of a lion backed into the corner of its cage.

She stepped back, and her hands were no longer nervously toying at her waist, her face was no longer fraught and demure, her posture was no longer slight and refined. She expanded, her presence blossomed and grew in her fear. It was like another person had been hatched from the quiet, reserved woman, shedding her old self like a cocoon, and I saw a small blade was glittering in her palm.

'So the plotter is you this time,' she spat, and her voice was powerful and clear. 'Revenge, is it?'

'Ah, there you are, Empress Zoe. It is so good to meet you, at last. And no, you are in no danger here. My oaths hold true, and you will come to no harm.'

'Then what is this? Do you seek to admonish me? You think that I will care? Yes, I sent men to kill my sister, because she is a threat. Would you not have done the same? And I was willing to let them kill you too, if necessary. Have you not sacrificed your men for your own ambitions?

Bah, you foolish boy. What is the purpose of this? I am not ashamed of my actions.' She stared at Harald and her eyes glittered in the firelight.

'You didn't need to play the helpless woman, not with me. I respect strength, not lies.'

'I do what I have to! I was cursed to be born a woman with no brothers. The heir to a throne only a man can sit. All my life men have needed to see me as helpless in order to help me.'

'You are right. I know why you did what you did, and I might have done the same. But you tried to kill me and failed, and there is no greater mistake on this earth.' Harald glared, and Zoe glared right back.

Zoe relaxed a fraction. 'I apologise. Not for letting you go to your death, but for not including you in my plans. I clearly misunderstood you.'

'You treated me like a soft boy, looking to save a beautiful woman in trouble. Instead, you should have dealt with me as a prince, a man of power and honour.'

'And would you have killed Theodora for me?' she asked, raising an eyebrow.

Harald shook his head firmly. 'No, but I would have removed her as a threat. As I am going to do now.'

Zoe's expression softened. 'You are going to help me? After all this?'

'You are the empress and I am sworn to protect you. Theodora, John, even Emperor Michael are a threat, and I will end that here, tonight.'

The words took my breath away. He was talking about a coup, about putting Zoe into power. I had worried so much about him siding with Michael I had not even considered that he might be planning to turn on the emperor.

'Oh my, Araltes, how I have misjudged you,' said Zoe in a breathless whisper, and she quietly tucked the small blade back into a fold in her robes. Her face lit up with excitement and barely concealed lust. Lust for power, lust for Harald? It was hard to say.

'Harald!' I hissed, desperately worried about his intentions.

'Be quiet or leave, Eric. Now is the time to prove your commitment to me.'

'I have oaths, Harald. More than just to you.'

'I know it, now be quiet... or leave,' he said, glaring at me, and I recoiled from it. This was not the man I knew. Something had awakened in him, something dark and terrible. I saw the monster uncoiling in him, finally rising to its full stature.

I was just considering leaving when the doors at the northern end of the room opened, and three men walked in with a pair of guards escorting them.

The three men caught sight of Harald and Zoe and came to a dead stop. 'What is this?' the central man said in outrage, and as he stepped forwards into the light I saw it was the emperor, dressed in simple robes but unmistakable.

'It is a coup, we must go!' hissed John next to him, dragging at the emperor's sleeve.

'Thank you, Afra,' Harald said, waving to the two guards. Afra and his companion nodded and left, closing the doors behind them even as John, the emperor, and his attendant turned to leave. The doors slammed shut in their faces.

John turned to glare at Harald, pointing at him with a shaking, furious finger. 'I told you he would do this! I told you that if we trusted him he would seize power for himself and that bitch whore!' John said.

'You are perfectly safe, Basileus, no harm will come to you here. But none of you may leave the room until you have heard me speak. Please, come and join us.' Harald indicated the other side of the table from where Zoe stood in shock and confusion.

'What madness makes you think you can do this?' Zoe said, staring at Harald.

'You accept no limits on your power, Zoe, so you understand precisely. I do this because I can, and because I must. Now, *sit*.'

He pointed to the chairs on our side of the table, and Zoe, looking around and seeing no alternative, sat down.

Seeing that, Michael waved away John's hand and strode over, his brows knotted, still glancing side to side to see if there truly was a threat. But it was just us in the room, and Harald was not even armed.

Reluctantly, he sat, while John stood behind him and glared.

Harald leaned forwards, and carefully placed the vial of poison on the table between the two parties.

'What is that?' Michael asked.

'It is poison, meant for John, intercepted by my men,' said Harald.

John stared at the poison and then at Zoe, who laughed. 'This? This is the reason for this outrage? Some poison I ordered given to a eunuch? My dear boy, this is none of your business.'

'No, it is not about this one vial, it is merely a symptom of a greater threat. My oath is to the throne, and to the people who sit upon it. However, the two people who sit upon it are both plotting to kill each other. This poison was for John, and frankly, I don't care. If he had died it would mean nothing to me personally.'

That comment got a gape of outrage from the normally composed John. The surprise of this whole situation had thrown him terribly from the confident, arrogant man we had met before.

'But if John died, Michael would be exposed and afraid. Michael would lash out, seeking revenge, escalating and killing more of your people. Eventually you might decide to kill him and replace him, as you did with your previous husband.'

'That is outra—' Zoe protested, cut short by Harald.

'Your denial is pointless, Basilissa. Everyone in this room apart from me was involved in that plot. Was it not John who held his head underwater?' My eyes flicked to John, and the eunuch did his best to look impassive, which more than confirmed it was true.

'And Michael knew it would happen in advance,' Harald said, turning his fearsome gaze on the emperor.

Michael also failed to deny it.

'So, you see my concern?'

'Do not frame me as the assassin here!' Zoe hissed. 'They would do the same to me.'

'Oh, I know it. They plotted to replace you with Theodora, and failed in at least one attempt.' Harald gave Zoe an almost affectionate smile. 'You are far too dangerous for them to allow to live.'

'This lecture of the obvious, does it have a purpose?' asked John, recovering his poise.

Harald nodded to him. 'Yes. It is my sworn duty to protect both of their lives, and none of you understand how seriously I take that oath. It has become clear that the only way for me to do this, is to protect you from each other.'

'So it is still a coup,' said John slowly, his face falling into a grimace. 'You will take power, under the excuse that it is for their safety.'

Harald tilted his head to the side. 'I will take some power, yes, but not over affairs of state. No, this is solely about peace and order in the palace. I will broker an agreement between the two of you. I will end the cycle of killings and plotting within the palace, enforced by my guard.'

'*My* guard,' said Michael, leaning forwards.

'They will be my guard now,' said Harald coldly. 'And I will ensure both of you live long, unhappy lives, free to run the empire in whatever way you see fit.'

John snorted in derision. 'Your guard? You have forgotten our past meeting, Araltes? I could shout for the guards and we would find out who their real master is. Your title doesn't make them yours.'

'Oh, I have not forgotten,' said Harald with a smile. 'You told me half the men in the first bandon were loyal to you, and that they would kill me if you ordered it. I thank you for that warning. I spent a great deal of effort finding out who those men were, and I ensured none of them are on duty at this moment. Go on, try shouting for them! But I promise you, if you do, one of us will die, and it won't be poison that causes it.' Harald smiled his wolfish smile, and John looked uncertain, nervous. The eunuch swallowed and glanced at the door, but did nothing.

'I thought not.'

Harald leaned back and looked at the two rulers of the Empire. 'But John makes a good point. He admits openly, in front of you both, that he corrupted half of the palace guard, the last line of defence against treachery. This must end. I will have all of those men reassigned to other banda and have them replaced with men I trust.'

'Men you know you can control instead, you mean,' hissed John.

Harald nodded. 'Yes. I am the commander of the guard, I need to control every single one of them.' He looked at the two rulers. 'The reason your predecessors created the Varangian tagma was to guard against the corruption and degradation of the old guard regiments. Where are the Excubitors, or the Hikanatoi? The guardians of the emperors of the past are all banished, shadows of their former selves – so corrupted they are not even trusted to set foot in the palace. I will not allow the Varangians to go down that same path, to be worn away by cronyism and corruption until they are discarded. And this—' he pointed at John '—this is how it happens.'

Harald looked at the emperor. 'You promised me a favour, and I said I would name it later. Do you remember?'

Michael nodded reluctantly.

'Well, this is it. You will let me reform the guard, you will remove the akolouthos and make me the sole commander. I will make a new law, that anyone found trying to corrupt even a single member of the guard will be put to death by the guard itself. I will hang them from the palace walls.'

'You can't do that!' said Michael. 'There are laws here, ways of doing things!'

'Yes, but any assault on the integrity of the guard is an assault on the throne itself. And if I am the commander of the guard, the real commander, I will be allowed to deal with such threats, with absolute finality. You think it does not matter that John corrupted your guard, maybe you even approved because it was in your interest. But what about the day when it was not John, but some other plotter who did it? What if they are your enemy? What if it was Zoe's people who secretly owned their allegiance?'

That gave Michael a pause for thought, and he finally nodded. 'Your words make sense.'

'Good, we are agreed. I will keep my oaths to you, and you will do me that favour that you promised.'

Harald stood up straight and moved around the table towards the nervous-looking eunuch.

'Now that John has confessed to this crime, my only question is, do I have permission to apply the law to him?' Harald stared at John, who gulped, and looked from Michael to Zoe.

'You – you can't, it was not the law at the time!'

'But you knew it was wrong,' said Harald coldly.

'I... Basileus, I was looking after your interests!' he said, desperately looking at his brother.

'I approve this application of the law,' said Zoe with a smile. 'Make an example so that all know it will be punished.'

John stammered, staring in disbelief at Michael, pleading. Michael looked deeply unsure, and finally leaned over to Harald. 'I think, in this case, you can be merciful, can you not?'

Harald pretended to consider it while he withered John with his stare. John stared back at Harald with fear and loathing, genuinely shaken, and stepped back, holding onto the post of Michael's chair for support. Harald stepped forwards, pushing John towards the wall with his presence.

'Do you remember what you said to me, in the courtyard outside the hall of nineteen?' Harald asked softly.

John babbled a bit, backing up further.

'You said that you could kill me with a word.'

'I... I meant...'

Harald reached out and seized John by the throat, lifting the slight man clean off his feet with one hand and pushing him into the map wall as his eyes bulged and his feet drummed.

'So here is something for you to remember, eunuch.' Harald leaned in so that his mouth was next to the gasping, gargling eunuch's ear. 'I won't even need a word.'

Harald gave him one last stare and then dropped him to the floor, as Michael looked on with a queasy expression. Harald turned away from the gasping, wheezing eunuch and spoke as if nothing had happened.

'In this one case, in respect and at your request, Basileus, I will have mercy. But never again. This will be the new law of the guard, and the palace. You trust me, and so I must trust my men. And when I die or retire, you must agree on a new commander you believe is incorruptible. This is the only way the guard's integrity can survive, and the only way the two halves of the throne can know peace.'

The sheer breathtaking arrogance of it appalled even me. Here he was, a palace guardsman, dictating terms to the rulers of the Greek Empire, the most powerful people on earth. And the worst or greatest thing about it? It was working. They were both accepting this new power structure, visibly, in front of my eyes. Such was his presence and authority that they could barely see fit to challenge him. Truly, you could never understand it unless you had seen him.

'And what will the terms of this peace be?' Zoe said, fuming that John had survived the moment. 'I'm sure you have plans for that too,' she snapped.

'I do not,' said Harald. 'I mean what I say – only the safety of your persons and the integrity of the throne matter to me. How you rule the empire is up to you, but you *will* rule it together. I will ensure peace in this palace and guarantee the safety of each against the other.'

He stretched and walked over towards the wall, staring at the shaded map painted there, ignoring John as he scrabbled to his feet and backed away with one hand to his neck. Harald swept his hand over the whole extent of the empire, laid out in paint and charcoal. 'I have seen some of the far reaches of this empire and the damage this silent war is causing, and it must stop. If either of you care about your people or your legacy in the slightest, you will come to terms. And you will not leave this room until you do.'

'We will not leave this room?' said Michael, aghast.

'No.'

'Under what authority?'

'My guardsmen have cleared the palace and no one will be allowed in. We will bring refreshments if required, we will bring bedding if it is needed, but you will come to terms, so for all our sakes, be quick about it.'

And then he slowly drew up his own chair, the legs grating excruciatingly across the marble. Finally he sat down, leaning back and waiting for them to speak as the emperor and empress gazed at each other in shock.

26

Well, I will not bore you with the negotiations. They dragged on long into the next morning. Harald was bluffing, and his ability to keep them prisoner in that room was severely limited. But an accord was indeed made and the truth is I think both of them were relieved to do so, or they would not have agreed it.

Everyone in a hard fight pretends they are strong and ready to continue, until it is over. That is when you see the survivors slump to the ground in relief, smiling and happy that it is done, suddenly showing their aches and pains.

By the end of that great accord, which was kept utterly a secret, the emperor and empress of the Greeks had made their uneasy peace. They split the responsibilities of state, with Michael taking rule over the military and foreign relations, Zoe over the Church and commerce, sharing the control over the finances so neither could ruin or control the empire alone.

They agreed to split the palace in half and would live entirely separately, communicating via envoy like foreign rulers, taking whatever lovers they saw fit and only maintaining a facade of marriage in public for ceremonial events. There was no hope of the marriage producing a child anyway, with Zoe's age.

John's sprawling power was severely cut, so that he could no longer lord over the entire bureaucracy, something that caused him to fall into a silent rage for the rest of the meeting. In return, Zoe agreed to let him appoint various of his other brothers and family to important, lucrative, but not particularly powerful positions throughout the empire. One brother, also a eunuch, and with no experience of governance whatsoever, was made the Dux of Aleppo. Such is empire politics.

The highest compromise was that Zoe was allowed to choose the imperial successor, because she would not tolerate John turning the empire into his family business. The house of Macedon and the heirs of Basil would decide the future of the empire and the male line that sat upon its throne.

Harald had only had one more condition for his involvement, and a week after the accord was agreed, he took me down to the royal docks to see it was carried through. We stood on the sea wall, watching as a ship was loaded, and as two figures were escorted onboard by members of the first bandon.

'I still don't understand why you insisted on her exile,' I said, shaking my head. 'Bardas? Yes. But Maria...' I turned to him and gave him a sympathetic look. 'I thought that...'

'That I love her, despite everything? Yes.' He stared at the sea, looking morose. 'I started meeting with her again.'

'I know,' I said, although truthfully I had only suspected it.

Harald nodded. 'It was like the old times again, for a moment.'

I looked away awkwardly. 'Yet you insisted on her exile?'

'Yes. She is dangerous and she will still seek the throne. But it is more that she is dangerous to me personally. I am weak around her. I make poor decisions and men die. And worst of all, she knows it. She knows she can use it against me and I nearly surrendered to it, I nearly betrayed my oaths and joined her plotters, just for the chance to be with her. I laid in bed with her in the city and we spoke of treason, and I was almost convinced, such was my anger at Zoe.' I was horrified at the admission, that what I had feared and suspected had been true.

'So, she has to go. I would have asked for her death, but she was right – I cannot kill her, even with words.'

I stared down at the ship, and saw Maria turn and look up at us, shielding her eyes from the sun. Then she kissed her hand, slowly, and gave us a wave.

'So how long do you think you can keep the peace between Zoe and Michael?'

Harald laughed. 'Hopefully until we leave.'

'And when will that be? When will we return home to claim what is yours?'

'What is *ours* Eric, what is ours. And when we have the gold, the men and the opportunity to do so.' He looked at me and saw my doubt. 'You fear that I will forget who I am and stay here?'

'I am worried this empire is too interesting for you to ever truly leave it.'

Harald gave me a wry smile. 'Come, Eric. Leave your worries aside. We have never been in a better position than we are now. This is our time and we have so much more to achieve before we are done.' He thumped me on the back and turned to walk away.

I nodded and looked back down to the ship, seeing Bardas escorting Maria into the stern cabin of the vessel, and then, pushing my concerns aside, I turned to follow my prince. I didn't know what the future would hold for us. The empire was finally at peace and Harald was a man of war, not suited to this palace life of separating a squabbling married couple, even if they were the most powerful couple in all the circle of the earth.

I should not have worried. Ha! This is the Roman Empire we speak of, and peace is merely the breath caught between wars. Even as we strode along the city wall on that cool winter's day, a thousand miles away in Italy, the thin tendrils of the storm of war were gathering, growing, darkening, readying to break into Harald's beloved maelstrom of flesh and fear and steel.

War was brewing on the empire's fringes. But that is a story for another day.

* * *

Eric laughed to himself as he looked around the hall. 'I thought I could tell this tale in one day, but already it is late. I feel my bones yearning for rest and I know my mind must soon follow. Perhaps the tale will not even be complete tomorrow, for the greatest of Harald's adventures are still ahead of us.'

His bleary eyes scanned around the packed hall with a hint of nervousness, the old man's body incongruous with the tales of youthful vigour he had just been describing. 'Perhaps some of you will return to hear its end?' Men around the room called out their agreement, and Eric was delighted to see the nodding heads and smiles.

'Wonderful. I must say, I am enjoying the telling of it. But I do not wish to interrupt your meeting and politicking any longer. I will go to my bed now, and leave the night of drinking and celebration to younger, more vigorous men.' Then he pointed vaguely at Ingvarr. 'And boys too, of course.'

Ingvarr went bright red and there was a roar of laughter around the room as he tried not to look insulted. Eric stood and gave the young man an exaggerated wink.

'It's just a joke, boy. You must learn to defend yourself from the tongue as well as the blade,' whispered Jarl Hakon as he felt his son tense at his side.

Ingvarr nodded gruffly and forced a smile onto his face, which delighted Eric, and then the old warrior made his way through the crowd, progress slowed by the number of men who wanted to clasp arms or say a few words as he passed.

Finally Eric had escaped the throng, and the room settled back down into the loud burble of conversation and drinking.

Up on the dais, Jarl Halfdan leaned over to his brother-in-law, Jarl Bjorn of the Fjordlands. 'I think we may have a problem.'

Bjorn looked down at him, surprised. 'What do you mean?'

'I don't believe Eric is here telling his story by chance, or to fill the time. He is too wise and too canny a man.'

'I don't understand. What do you think he is doing?'

'I think he is preparing the ground for the Frostating, seeking some specific outcome, winning the audience over to his side.'

'What outcome?' whispered Bjorn, eyes wide.

Halfdan tapped his fingers on the arms of his chair. 'I don't know, but send word to the king first thing in the morning. He should complete his journey here with all haste, else I am worried his plans will be ruined before the assembly has even begun.'

Bjorn's eyes widened further, and he nodded. 'I will see to it, brother.'

'Thank you.' Halfdan's brows knotted together in concern as he looked around the room, seeing the excitement on the faces of those speaking with wonder of what they had heard. His fingers tapped on the arm of his chair again, his mouth twitched, and he felt the tiny, stomach-churning buzz of fear.

AFTERWORD AND HISTORICAL NOTE

The Eastern Roman Empire, or the Byzantine Empire as it is now often known, is one of the most intriguing and perplexing political and military entities in the history of Europe.

It seemed on the verge of collapse for the majority of its existence, yet endured for a thousand years, far longer than the more famous Western empire. It was initially formed and ruled by the Romans, but for most of its history the bulk of its ruling class, citizens and 'middle classes' were Greek-speakers of various ethnicities, not Latins. And Greek as a descriptor at that time did not mean what we now know as the peninsular nation of Greece and its people. It was not a single ethnicity or culture. The Greeks at that time were a connected web of peoples who lived throughout modern Greece and most of what is now Turkey, as well as all the eastern islands and initially, in Egypt and the Holy Land too.

The empire also ruled over vast and constantly changing provincial lands that incorporated dozens of different nationalities and languages and creeds on its borders in the Balkans, Italy, eastern Anatolia (Turkey/Caucus), and the Middle East.

It was beset on all sides by powerful and relentless enemies. To the east and south the great Arab caliphates and then later the Seljuk and other Turkic empires, culminating with the Ottomans who would eventually overrun it. To the north and east the Rus and Pechenegs, and to the north and west the various confederations and nations of the Bulgars, Italians, Normans and even, on several occasions, hostile crusades.

Internally it was constantly riven by infighting, corruption, stagnation and frequent near economic collapse.

Yet it endured for a thousand years. The sheer tenacity of the splinter of the Roman Empire based in Constantinople is a wonder, historically speaking. It left a fascinating historical record and an enduring artistic and architectural legacy. The empire was a fanatical writer and keeper of records, including, rather uniquely for the time, the personal accounts of many of its imperial family. We have multiple complete or near-complete books written by the emperors and their families on military, ceremonial, political and even architectural subjects.

It was also controversial, even in its own time. There were two Roman empires after the division of 286 AD: the Western empire, based in Rome, which would last only another two hundred years, and the Eastern, in Constantinople, which would last another 1,200. When the Western Roman Empire fell, the Germanic peoples eventually claimed its legacy, in the form of the Holy Roman Empire. The papacy in Rome endured, more or less constantly (with a few periods of exile or entrapment), and set itself up as the 'Roman' Church and the seat of Christianity.

So there were now two empires that called themselves the Romans, neither of which truly were, and two centres of power for the Church, in Constantinople and Rome. Eventually, that would lead to the great schism where the Church in Constantinople arose as the head of the Eastern 'Orthodox' Church, and the Western Catholic Church followed the papacy in Rome.

So, the way the rulers and people of the Eastern empire thought of themselves, and the way outsiders thought of them, was often very different. The 'Byzantines' as we now call them (which is not a contemporary name from the time), called themselves the Roman Empire and at least in the ruling and upper class in the core cities (the ones who wrote their literary works) referred to themselves as Roman. Most of the rest of Europe referred to them as the Greek Empire, or just the Greeks. So the narrator in this book mostly refers to them collectively in that way, as most Scandinavians would have. But he also, when referring to the structure of the state, or its institutions and rulers, and especially its army, often refers to them as Romans, because those are the things that were left over from the Roman Empire, and often followed much the same rules and customs.

Harald Sigurdsson arrived in 1034 at a time of intense dynastic and military conflict. The empire had just reached one of its several peaks of power. The Macedonian dynasty, of which Zoe and Theodora were the last members, had taken over the empire when it was a degraded rump state, clinging to the lands around Constantinople and parts of Anatolia, Greece, and various islands. Through wise politics, military reform, and aggressive campaigning, the Macedonians recaptured much of the empire's old lands and wealth.

But the male line ended, and the throne was handed over to the weak and ineffective Romanos III Argyros, who was then murdered and replaced as you have read in this book. It could not have been a more interesting and opportune moment for someone like Harald to appear on the empire's stage.

Harald's time in the Kyivan Rus is extremely poorly documented, but that is not the case for his time in the empire. We have multiple sources, including the Icelandic sagas, but also some Byzantine works, for what he did while he was there, in broad terms. It is specifically mentioned that he fought with the Arab pirates during the Byzantine-Arab conflict of 1035-6, and helped in their complete defeat. In fact, the defeat was so complete the Byzantine navy would enjoy a period of almost unchecked power for the next hundred years in the eastern Mediterranean.

It is also specifically related that he took part in the campaign around Antioch and Edessa, and that he captured 'eighty forts and settlements, and did much plundering'. While eighty may of course be an exaggeration, it seems he did indeed have some sort of independent command and a mission of conquest and pacification.

It is also fairly well-attested that he went on pilgrimage to Jerusalem, and it is absolutely clear that in 1038 the Byzantines began the process of rebuilding the Church of the Holy Sepulchre, a process that would take another thirty years.

At least one source says he went as far as the Jordan, the zenith of his travels, that he fought with the bandits that used to prey on pilgrims, and that on his return he was raised to being the commander of the Varangian guard, something also recorded in the empire's records.

Dealing with a story set in Jerusalem is a sensitive subject. The popular culture image of relations between the Christian and Muslim world in the Middle Ages is largely framed by the crusades, of a religious war driven by fanatics. However, for most of their multi-century conflict, the Arab caliphates and Byzantine Empire were rivals for power and territory in the fairly typical way that great powers of the time were often at war with their neighbours. There was no obvious or particular hatred for the Arabs, or Muslims in general. Nor did the Arab caliphates have some special hatred for the Byzantines; their territorial wars with other Muslim factions – for example, the Seljuks and various Mongol successor states – were just as bad, if not worse.

So the pre-crusades conflict between Byzantium and the Caliphates was not a war of religion, and atrocities like the destruction of the Christian holy sites committed by caliph al-Hakim bi-Amr Allah in 1009, where he had the Church of the Holy Sepulchre and dozens of other Christian and Jewish sites razed, was not only rare at the time, but an outrage even to some of his own people. For the majority of the Muslim rule over the Holy Land in the time preceding the crusades, Christian and Jewish holy sites and their clergy and guardians were rigorously protected by the caliphs, and those protections were enshrined in law, even during times of open war with the empire.

This is what makes the destruction of the Church of the Holy Sepulchre such a seismic event, and its rebuilding such an important mission for the Byzantines. In fact, it is often argued that the destruction of 1009 was one primary factor in the launching of the crusades nearly a century later.

Harald's involvement in the mission to Jerusalem was thus historic in its own right, even without all his later adventures. Unlike so much else that he did it was not overtly a quest of conquest or war, but of peace and rebuilding – even if, Harald being Harald, it inevitably ended up including a good deal of fighting and self-enrichment.

* * *

I tried to use as many figures from the Sagas and the Empire's historical records as possible. Some of the named men in Harald's warband are real historical figures. Ulf and Halldor are well-attested followers of Harald, and it was they who helped bring his story back to Iceland, for Halldor Snorrasson was an ancestor of Snorri, the most famous and perhaps most important of the Icelandic saga writers, who really was just a collator of older stories.

I would go as far as saying Snorri was a historical fiction author, one of the greatest, because he gathered together the previous stories and fragments of what was known and wove them into a single great lineage of tales. He did not pretend to be historically precise; he was a storyteller, and I love weaving his work into mine for that reason. We tread in the footsteps of giants.

One of the most fascinating figures of the period was the empress Zoe, a formidable and slightly tragic figure, the last of her family line, who spent her entire adult life trying to gain absolute power over an empire that did not tolerate the idea of a sole female ruler. She murdered 'at least' one co-emperor husband, possibly two, and was involved in a lifelong rivalry with her sister, Theodora.

John the Eunuch was also a very real person, and at one point, arguably the most powerful man in Europe. The empire had a great number of eunuchs, and they were often very important people, not the palace slaves people think of, which is more of an Ottoman phenomenon. In fact, to be appointed to certain important imperial positions you *had* to be a eunuch. Eunuchs were regarded as less corruptible, less prone to familial ambitions, and generally more trustworthy. Many men of semi-rich birth would be made into eunuchs at a young age merely as a career path decision, a stomach-churning idea to a modern audience but quite accepted at the time. Next time you have to make a sacrifice to apply for a job, spare a thought for them!

John broke out of that pattern by trying, with a great deal of success, to establish a familial, dynastical control over the empire. He came from nowhere, from nothing, to being the power behind the throne, taking advantage of the chaotic end of the Macedonian dynasty and establishing his own power through manipulation, murder, and creating a reign of terror among the palace denizens where anyone not loyal was blackmailed, threatened, beaten, tortured or even murdered.

Even the eunuch Sgouritzes and his attempt to poison John on Zoe's orders is attested in contemporary records written by the Byzantine historian John Skylitzes. Skylitzes, being both alive at the time of these events and writing a detailed record of them, is one of the primary and most reliable sources of 11th century Byzantine history, and of the events around the course of this novel.

The historical basis for the intrigue and remarkable events of Harald's time in the empire is thus extraordinary. By chance or fate, he arrived at a seismic moment in the empire's history and of course, being the man that he was, he could not help but become a key player in that time.

His time in the empire was so long and so full of excitement and well-documented events that it simply couldn't be told in one volume. So the tale of his time in the legendary Varangian guard will continue in book three, where Harald's newfound power and position will be put to the ultimate test, and the royal house of Macedon will continue in its internal conflict for absolute control of the Empire.

Harald's blood-marked warband will march again, and the fate of empires and kingdoms will be decided at the edge of his sword.

ABOUT THE AUTHOR

JC Duncan is a well-reviewed historical fiction author and amateur bladesmith, with a passion for Vikings.

Sign up to JC Duncan's mailing list here for news, competitions and updates on future books.

Visit JC's website: www.jcduncan.co.uk

Follow JC on social media:

x.com/jcduncanauthor
instagram.com/j.c.duncan
facebook.com/JCDuncanAuthor

ALSO BY JC DUNCAN

The Last Viking Series

Warrior Prince

Raven Lord

Milton Keynes UK
Ingram Content Group UK Ltd.
UKHW041326290324
440174UK00002B/11

9 781805 498179